AN ACCOMPLISHED WOMAN

As a young woman, clever, self-reliant Lydia Templeton scandalised society by rejecting Lewis Durrant, the county's most eligible bachelor. Ten years later, Lydia has no regrets and, having concluded that matters of the heart need no longer trouble her, she is quite happy to remain unwed.

But others still seek Lydia's advice on their love lives, and when her godmother implores her to take her young ward Phoebe's search for a suitor in hand, it's hard to refuse. In truth, the prospect fills Lydia with horror (especially as she must go to Bath of all places to do it), but poor Phoebe, having managed to promise herself to two men at once, rather needs her help.

However, finding a solution to Phoebe's dilemma proves far trickier than anyone imagined. As affairs become increasingly tangled, Phoebe more muddled and Lydia's exasperation grows, the confirmed spinster finds that her own heart is not quite the closed book she thought it was...

AN
ACCOMPLISHED
WOMAN

Jude Morgan

WINDSOR
PARAGON

First published 2007
by Headline Review
This Large Print edition published 2008
by BBC Audiobooks Ltd
by arrangement with
Headline Publishing Group

Hardcover ISBN: 978 1 405 64937 7
Softcover   ISBN: 978 1 405 64938 4

British Library Cataloguing in Publication Data available

Printed and bound in Great Britain by
CPI Antony Rowe, Chippenham, Wiltshire

For Tanya, Jason and James

CHAPTER ONE

Not enough naked flesh, Lydia concluded, and too many horses.

'Oh! I do beg your pardon.'

The pain of having your foot trodden on is always surprisingly intense. Luckily the young woman who had accidentally backed into Lydia, and who now turned in startled apology, was a slip of a thing. Still, Lydia's smile was really an adapted grimace.

'Not—not at all.'

The young woman—girl, in truth—blinked her large, pale, distracted eyes.

Lydia had a moment of peculiar recognition. 'Do I . . . ?' she began; but the moment flitted away along with the girl. No, she didn't know her. A mistake.

Lydia tried to return her attention to the paintings. But here was the dissatisfaction.

Oh, there was some fine work: she had locked eyes with some spirited portraits, and stood long in undecided fascination before a turbulent new landscape of Mr Turner's. But really no Royal Academy Exhibition was complete, she felt, without the proper portion of decorous and classical nudity. Actaeon, say, peeping through fronds at a rumpy dimply Diana; Orpheus, disconsolately strumming whilst wearing nothing but sandals and a curiously adhesive towel round his loins. That was what was wanted, and it was sadly lacking this year.

Instead (surely she had seen that girl somewhere

1

before?) they had overdone the horses.

These were mandatory too, and Lydia would have been disappointed if she had entered the exhibition-room at Somerset House to find there were *no* long-necked, impossibly smooth quadrupeds standing sideways on billiard-table pastures. But this was excessive. There was even, she saw now, a cow. She drew the line at cows.

Yet an old gentleman paused before it and, pouting with admiration, pronounced: 'Magnificent. Magnificent animal, hey, my dear?'

'I must remember to order a chine of beef before next Saturday,' replied his wife, perhaps from association of ideas.

Next to the cow, a grandly framed general was winning the smoky battle behind him by pointing disdainfully at a map. 'Can't be one of ours,' growled a young man in naval blue and braid. The lady on his arm fanned herself with the catalogue and gave a distressed laugh, as if something were starting. A shadow touched Lydia's mood. She suddenly wished for fresh air, began the tortuous wending and shuffle through the crowd towards the doors. As for that girl . . .

The mystery lay in the certainty that she *didn't* know her—because Lydia's memory for faces was depressingly retentive. During this two-month stay in London she had endured countless introductions. A dull evening could be like a parade-ground inspection: Miss This, Mr That: carry on, at ease. But the bobbing faces always remained with her. There was nothing she could do about it. She would remember the old gentleman admiring the cow, with his look of owlish complacency, and the old lady's nutcracker

2

jaws.

But the known, unknown girl . . . Something persisted mildly, like the throb in Lydia's toes. Difficult, though, to think in here, with the crush and the noise, top-boots scrunching and gowns crackling and swishing and the endless London-season-company babbling, thrown back by the domed ceiling as a churchy rumble.

It was something about those eyes, something almost painful about their unshaded blue largeness—and suddenly, there they were again. A momentary parting in the crowd revealed the girl sitting alone, a full-length sketch of melancholy, on one of the low benches. A shaft of light from the glass dome struck a gleam from those eyes—a wet gleam.

Compassion completed what curiosity had begun.

'I do beg your pardon if I intrude,' Lydia said, sitting down beside her, 'but may I ask if you are quite well?'

Clutching her handkerchief like a weapon, the girl turned on Lydia a boiling, swimming stare, and a violent silence.

'Or—whether there is anything I can do?' Lydia went limply on, already concluding that she had intruded terribly. The question now was how to apologise and go. How did rejected Samaritans walk away? With smooth unconcern? That suggested you didn't much care in the first place. Or stalk off faintly offended?

Lydia had just decided on a sort of regretful glide when the girl abruptly responded.

'I am not at all well, thank you, that is if feeling wretched, absolutely miserable and wretched

3

beyond anything and everything is not being well, which I cannot help but think it is.' She unfolded the handkerchief and cracked it out like a whip. 'And there isn't, thank you, anything you can do. Unless you can bring my brother back to me.'

'Oh. Oh, I am indeed sorry. How very . . . Was it a recent loss?'

The girl shrugged. 'Half an hour. Perhaps more—perhaps even an hour—I can't tell, there's no clock in this horrid place that I can see, and don't you think there ought to be? It's not as if there is an insufficiency of *pictures*.'

Lydia rearranged her skirts, and herself. 'Ah. Your brother was here, and now he is not.' I sound like a French grammar-book, she thought.

'I only came because he said he wanted to see the exhibition, which as soon as he walked in he plainly didn't—but then he is in such a shocking state of spirits lately that one hardly knows what he's saying or what he means, and neither does he . . . My great fear is what he may do, or what he's already done.'

'My dear Miss—I'm sorry, I don't know your name, and I don't *think* we have met, unless—but please, you alarm me, tell me what you mean—'

'James has slipped out and gone somewhere to drown his sorrows.' The girl confronted Lydia with a face of pale, tragic finality. 'Oh, yes. I know it. I was looking at a picture of a ship, or it might have been a mountain, and he pressed my arm and said he was going out to get some air and—it is prodigious hot in here, though, is it not? Why, do you suppose? Is it because of the paintings, something like keeping butter except the other way around?'

4

'I dare say.' Lydia glared away a hovering young buck, strenuously pantalooned and about to simper at them. 'And so your brother left you—and he was your only companion here?'

Lip-biting, the girl nodded. 'I see how it will be. He'll drink brandy, or something else he simply hasn't the head for, and then he'll forget about me, and I shall have to go home alone in a chair or something.'

'Well. I cannot help but think this remiss of him, though I don't know the circumstances—that is, these sorrows you spoke of—'

'Oh, I don't blame him for anything. I blame *her*.' The girl could do a lot with a handkerchief: now it was having its neck slowly wrung. 'That woman—that *jilt*. James, you know, has always possessed the most amiable, the steadiest of tempers. He would never have left me like this before. But he has been so abominably treated by this—I don't know what to call her—that he is quite overset. Oh!' She leaped up from the bench and sat down again all in one movement. 'Oh, I thought for a moment that was him. But it's someone quite different, except for the coat.'

'Have you far to go home? I might accompany you if—'

'Oh, I don't care about *that*.' The girl's face loomed with fierce confidentiality. 'I've tried to tell him, you know, that she simply isn't worth it. More than that—he has had a lucky escape. I said to him, "The next unfortunate to be ensnared by your precious Miss Templeton may be caught fast. A blessing she has revealed herself now and not later." One wants to be kind, of course, but one must put the sensible view.'

5

'Oh, certainly. There was, then, I collect, nothing like an engagement between your brother and this—you said a Miss Templeton?'

'That is her name, and I am heartily sick of hearing it. We have had nothing but Miss Templeton this past fortnight. Oh, not that I ever saw the creature, but she was all James would talk of. No, there was no undertaking, but I feel sure James had it in mind to ask . . . Well, never mind. He is too susceptible, that is his trouble—too impulsive. But it is her loss, make no doubt of it. James is seven-and-twenty, and *she* is all of thirty, it seems. Thirty, if you please! Really, at such an age she is lucky to receive any such attention, never mind playing the coquette over it. Nor is there any great fortune or connections in the case—simply a respectable family in Lincolnshire. One would suppose them very ready to get her off their hands—'

'A moment. I believe—I do believe I know the lady you refer to. Lincolnshire is my country. Is not the Templeton place south of Grantham, off the Great North Road?'

'I think that's what James said. Mind, when she has played him so false, she may have lied about that too—'

'No, no. I am convinced that is the very place—and that I know your Miss Templeton.'

'Do you? Then you'll surely agree that she is the most . . . Dear me. I hope not a near friend? Forgive me if . . .'

Lydia shook her head and patted the girl's hand. 'Oh, no. I *know* her pretty well—let us say no more than that.'

The girl nodded solemnly, leaning closer. 'Then

6

perhaps you can tell me—is she generally known as a jilt? I only ask for the sake of information, and so I can reassure James he is not the first. Though for myself I find it hard to credit as she sounds from his account like the most monstrous bluestocking. Horribly clever and bookish and superior about her accomplishments—'

'This assuredly *is* the same Miss Templeton. You have described her exactly. In our part of Lincolnshire she is well known for it, and I have even heard it remarked that—well, the *mot* is rather cruel, but they say she has Latin in her veins instead of blood.'

'Latin in her . . . ! What delicious funning! I must tell James—only, you know, to reassure him.'

'Of course: and I may add that your brother has indeed had a fortunate escape. Miss Templeton has a name as a proud, ill-natured woman, disdainful of society and civility, and—to speak candidly—quite the dowd besides.'

'Exactly as I thought! Though no doubt,' the girl added reluctantly, 'she must have *some* superficial attractions, to have made such a conquest of James—'

'Superficial, as you say; and she knows well how to dissemble, I suspect, when she takes it in her head to torment a man. I am afraid your Miss Templeton is that species of woman—cold to the male sex, yet still seeking to demonstrate their power over them: lifting them up for the pleasure of seeing them fall.'

'How very shocking!' the girl said excitedly, dropping her handkerchief.

'I grieve to report it, indeed; but her true nature, as you said, must show itself sooner or later. And

7

where her temperament does not betray her, liquor surely will.'

Stooping to retrieve the handkerchief, the girl froze. 'You don't mean to tell me she is a toper?'

'It is not a thing evident,' said Lydia, 'though I don't positively say she isn't: but it is certain to come. When books and music pall—as they surely must—and there is nothing more to be got from this parade of cleverness, and when she has so stubbornly chosen to reject society, what resources remain? What solace but the decanter? This is a harsh reflection I know—but I fear nothing is more probable. And *then* she will be glad to catch at her father's steward, or even an attorney's clerk, to avoid being an old maid at last. Mind, I don't doubt she will make a parade of that too, for it is well known she has no proper sense of distinction.'

'A clerk . . . ! Good heavens! And yet, you know, on reflection one can only conclude that these are her just deserts.'

'Quite so; and one must pity the poor clerk, for a woman of such inconstant temper will surely be false to him within a twelvemonth.' Lydia picked up the girl's handkerchief and gave it to her. 'Probably with a footman.'

The girl's mouth opened, but only a vague, shrill noise came out.

'Believe me, I don't intend to shock,' Lydia went on soothingly. 'But it is an unhappy truth about women like Miss Templeton that under the cloak of superiority they are concealing the grossest of appetites.'

'Grossest . . . I never thought I . . . And yet I believe you are absolutely in the right of it, for such an unnatural woman must be unnatural in

8

everything. Really it could hardly be plainer, when one thinks of it.' Very bright and brisk now, the girl began to gather up her mantle. 'Well, now poor dear James can hardly fail to listen. I shall take a chair at once, and when he comes home I shall have a vast deal to tell him—'

Lydia rose with her. 'May I help you to find a chair, or—?'

'Oh, I shall manage very well, I thank you. Before—before, you know, I felt unequal to anything: but now my spirits are quite restored. But I am greatly obliged to you for your concern, and for the information also, Miss—dear me!' the girl faltered, with a shy smile. 'I'm sorry, I haven't your name.'

'Templeton.' Returning the smile, Lydia extended her hand. As the girl seemed seized by a temporary paralysis, Lydia reached over, got hold of her hand, and shook it as one would a dog's paw. 'Lydia Templeton. Are you sure I can't call you a chair?'

CHAPTER TWO

Being a guest in someone else's house, even that of your brother, inhibited certain physical expressions of emotion. When Lydia got back to Queen Anne Street she found George, Susannah and the children were all out; but still she felt it inappropriate—lacking decorum—to slam doors or throw things.

So the impulse must be mastered. Seating herself in the long drawing-room, which was full of

9

afternoon light and quiet, she contrived to relax her shoulders, open a book, turn the pages.

But the same unmeaning sentence was still dancing before her eyes when she heard George come in.

'Poor Lyddie, all alone and neglected.' George's big presence immediately shrank the room. Floorboards groaned at his hearty tread. 'Where's Susannah? Oh, airing the children, I should think.' He greeted his reflection in the pier-glass, grimacing as if trying to make himself less handsome. 'We'll have dinner as soon as they come in. Have any luck with the British Museum fellow?'

'Hm? Oh, that. No.' This morning seemed an age ago. 'No, he insisted that every gentleman must duly apply for a ticket of admission. When I asked if it was the same for ladies he gave a sort of sickly smile, which terminated the conversation.'

'Great dunderheads. I hear the collection's in a shocking state. Stuffed monkeys rotting away and so on,' he said, through a yawn, disposing himself comfortably on the sofa, stretching long booted legs with a cat's supple satisfaction. 'Well, I hope at least the Royal Academy didn't disappoint.'

'It did not disappoint, indeed: I came away thoroughly . . . enlightened. And with a new acquaintance—that is, new to me, though it is highly possible you know her. A Miss Sissons.' The girl had stammered the name out before mortification had sent her scurrying flame-faced away.

'Ah? Oh, that would be Kitty Sissons, I should think. James Sissons's younger sister.' George cradled his leg and studied the sole of his boot, coughing, or making a noise as if he wanted to.

10

'James Sissons you know, of course.'

'I do; though even when I heard the name it took me a moment fully to recollect the gentleman. He has only called here a few times, after all, and our acquaintance has been but slight. Yet Miss Sissons seemed to think it was of a much more developed character.'

'Did she? Curious thing. Of course, you know, people will take up these wrong ideas . . .'

'George, tell me—do I sleepwalk?'

'Eh?' After a dubious moment, her brother's scalp lifted in relief at the change of subject. 'Sleepwalk, Lyddie, no. Never. At least, never at home as I remember, and I'm sure you haven't done it here. I remember I did once, though, at Oxford. A bad mutton-pie disagreeing with me, I think. Proctor found me in the quad in my nightshirt. Put the worst construction on it. Rather unfair, I thought. Cold, too. Feet and so on.' He offered her a hopeful smile. 'Curious things you fret about. I must say I'm ready for dinner, I wonder when Susannah—'

'I ask this question,' Lydia said, 'because it is the only explanation I can see for what Miss Sissons told me today. According to her, I have encouraged her brother to believe that I entertained for him the strongest attachment— that a love-match was all but made—and now, I have jilted him in the most heartless manner. This was a great surprise to me, because although I do remember the gentleman—in particular the very pale blue eyes, which his sister also possesses, and which made me think I recognised her—still I cannot recollect showing him anything but common civility. So I can only suppose I did these

11

dreadful things while in a state of unconsciousness, which gives me some unease as to other things I may have done likewise. When next a robbery is reported in the *Morning Chronicle*, I quite expect to reach under my bed and hear the clink of stolen candlesticks.'

'Oh, Lyddie,' her brother said. The words seemed to exhaust him. He sagged like a shorn Samson.

'Oh, George.' She joined him on the sofa, half seriously slapping the back of his large golden-haired hand. 'What *have* you been saying about me?'

'Now, look here, Lyddie, in the first place I never—well, I never supposed old Cribs would take on so. I ran into him yesterday at Gunter's, and I saw he was in the dismals, and I took him to task pretty stiffly. "Cribs," I said, "these things happen—"'

'George. Go back, please. What is—who . . . *Cribs*?'

'Cribs Sissons. Well, James Sissons, that is, but at Oxford we always called him Cribs. It was a, you know, a name. In fact there's a story behind it . . .' George's eyes met hers. The story died. 'He is an excessively good fellow, Lyddie, taken all in all. And I did warn him not to let his notions run away with him, which has always been his failing. From what you say, I'm afraid he has been pouring out his woes to his sister, who is rather a romantic little creature. The fact is, though, my dear, he *is* disappointed, and I can't help feeling for him a little—though I'm sure you meant no harm in what you did.'

'Oh, George, I did nothing!' she burst out,

12

leaping up and pacing. 'During my stay here you have had numerous friends calling, and I hope I was civil to them all, including Mr Cri— Mr Sissons. With whom I estimate I have exchanged perhaps two hundred words in our whole acquaintance. Many of which were "yes", "no", "indeed", and "quite".' She reflected. 'Also, I think, "dromedary", though I can't imagine how that came up. George, I am sorry for your friend, because he has been grievously misled, but if anything I found him something of a bore.'

George watched her with mild unhappiness. 'Poor old Cribs. Never has expressed himself very easily. But he was very taken with you, Lyddie. He said as much, or hinted as much, to me, and I never saw a man more in earnest. Oh, not that he spoke with anything but the greatest delicacy; and he is much too honourable to venture upon such a subject unless he were sure of its being welcomed.'

Ah. 'Ah. By you.'

'Well, yes. By me, possibly. The fact is, when I heard from Cribs what was in the wind, I was altogether gratified. Cribs Sissons, one of my oldest friends, and my dear and only sister—why, nothing could have pleased me better. Susannah and I talked of it—just incidentally, you know— and we agreed that it would be an excellent match. And as there were indications that the regard was mutual—'

'Indications? My dear George, what could they be? If I had been caught carving Mr Sissons's initials on a tree, or addressing him in rhyming couplets—"Behold, the tears of passion clog my nibs, Whene'er I seek to pen the name of Cribs"— stop it—then I would have to confess. But I am

13

convinced that the greatest mark of regard I ever showed him was to stifle my yawns in his presence.'

George was shifting about and trying not to quail.

'I think, George, that the only indications Mr Sissons received came from you. I think you encouraged him to believe his affections were returned—which was unfair to both of us. I only hope he has not been made very unhappy by it, because I do not wish him ill in the slightest; and I would apologise to him, if I felt the fault lay with me, and not with my incorrigible brother having a fling at matchmaking—an occupation usually reserved, George, for elderly ladies with too much time on their hands: so if you intend taking up carpet-making next, or appliqué-work, please give me warning.'

'Now I know you're not *very* angry with me, because you're talking in long sentences,' he said, with a satisfied look. 'But look here, Lyddie, I did think it a promising development—no more—that should be given time, and perhaps the odd nudge. On my honour, I didn't suspicion old Cribs was so very deep in. But fair now, at the end you did lift him up and then drop him—think on it.'

Queasy echo of her own words in the exhibition-room. Surely not? 'I am thinking on it, George, but truly I—'

'It was quite a blow for a man like Cribs, you know.' George sighed, gusty and pensive. 'All in all I think he took it rather well. And I was there for the first part of it, so I can testify to—'

'George. I'm talking in short sentences. Beware.'

'My dear sis, the drive. The drive! It was after dinner on Tuesday—remember now?' George unwisely adopted a solicitous sickroom tone. 'Cribs was talking of his curricle-and-pair, and what capital drives the park affords, now the weather improves? And you remarked how delightful those drives must be? In an open carriage?'

'George, one more question-mark and your head goes in the fire.'

He laughed, then looked at her, and at the fire; weighed up the odds, and grew grave.

'Well, the very next day he called. Quite a declaration in itself, you know; and he asked you, in my hearing, whether you would not like to be driven about the park on such a fine morning.' George's voice was husky with transferred shame. 'Lydia, you refused.'

On a side table there was a decanter of canary wine. For some time it had been winking at her, blowing kisses and generally carrying on. Lydia gave in. She walked over to the roguish saucebox and let it have its way with her.

'I politely declined the offer,' she said, with a refreshed gasp. 'I wasn't at all inclined, though it was civil of him to ask. Yes, I remember thus far. So, what next?'

George was all pained, eggshell reproach. 'There was no next, Lyddie. That is the point. You declined—whereas the night before, you know, you had expressed an interest in his equipage.'

Sometimes there were simply too many replies. Lydia made herself think of sad things, and at last was in command of herself sufficiently to take a seat and look her brother in the face.

'Was that it?' she asked. 'The trifling and jilting? Mr Sissons told me about his carriage, and then I didn't go for a drive in the park in it?'

'Ah, it's not driving, it's being driven, Lyddie, that's the difference.'

'But I don't want to be driven round the park, George. It has a thoroughly cattleish sound, for one, not that there's such a word as "cattleish". For another, it is mere circular, pointless, jiggling motion.'

'Oh, you'd be in no danger with Cribs, you know,' said George, grasping the wrong end of the stick with both hands. 'Don't be afraid of that. His curricle has a pretty high perch, to be sure, but he understands the balance perfectly. Never had an upset. There's not a better hand at the ribbons in the country.'

'Oh, Lord,' Lydia heard herself wail. The decanter made eyes at her again.

'What's the matter?'

'Nothing, nothing, George . . . Won't you have a glass?'

'Is that a way of saying you're having another?'

'I do love it when you're moral.' She poured for two. 'George, it's the ribbons.'

'My dear Lyddie,' he said, with the practised promptness of a five-years-married man, glancing over her dress, 'they look very pretty.'

'Not that. Those. For heaven's sake, I'm not wearing any. It's that ridiculous slang. It means, I suppose, he can drive a horse well—or two horses—something to do with the reins, at any rate—'

'Good hand at the ribbons, yes,' said George, perseveringly. 'I don't think, in truth, that I've ever seen a better.'

'But why should it matter? Why should anyone care about the—the ribbons, and the hands, and all

16

of that?'

George came over and took his glass of wine, studying her judiciously, dubiously. 'Plenty of girls do.'

'I'm not plenty of girls. I'm not even one girl. I'm a woman, a rational human creature with a thinking mind . . .' She saw, without wanting to see, her brother's look of mild boredom. Off she goes again. 'And as for this good ribbons—with the hands—thing—'

'Hand,' said George, encouragingly. 'Good hand at the ribbons.'

'Yes. That.' Lydia hesitated, caught up by a sort of despondent warmth. She liked him very much, and also—a different thing, or different in its effects—loved him. 'You know, George, I cannot fall in love to order with a man you approve of, no matter what qualities you think he—no matter what qualities he possesses. I hope Mr Sissons very soon forgets this nonsense, and lives happily. And I'm flattered you should take this trouble over me. But please, no more of it. Else I shall begin to suspect you of wanting to be rid of me.'

'Bless you, no. I see that I've been a blundering fellow over the whole business.' George swallowed another glass of canary. 'This will sound miserably sanctimonious, I fear, but the fact is I simply want you to have what I have.'

Thinking of Susannah, Lydia said carefully: 'Not everyone is so fortunate in their choice.'

'Oh, yes, I've been very lucky. But that doesn't mean you mightn't be likewise, if you were to . . .'

'To be a little more of the husband-hunter?' She smiled. 'I'm quite happy as a single woman, George. I fancy that the urge to matrimony

17

manifests itself as a feeling of vacancy—that there appears something missing or lacking; but I am conscious of no such lack in myself, and do not feel the need to be completed by a husband, like the third volume of a novel.'

'Now that's very like you, to compare yourself to a book,' he said, smiling too. 'Well, you know best. I've no head for philosophy myself. But what I *can* see, and it is monstrous unjust but true nonetheless, is how women are prized for their youth in a way that is never applied to we men. As far as eligibility goes, there is little distinction made between a man of five-and-twenty and a man of forty, so long as he has sense and teeth. But for a woman, alas, it is no such matter.'

'My dear brother, you are very delicately alluding to the fact that just before I came here in March I passed my thirtieth birthday; an event that the world views less as a matter for celebration than condolence. At least for women, as you justly remark.'

'I'll tell you this,' George said, with sudden hot gallantry, 'you could pass for three-and-twenty anywhere.'

'Thank you: I doubt it is true, but I am not displeased to hear it. There, I am not so very unnatural after all. But I assure you I have no consciousness of time running out—and no feeling of discontent. Reading, and writing, and music, and drawing, and helping Papa in his studies—all these make an ample sum for a woman of my tastes and inclinations. A woman, by the by, who knows her own good fortune. With ten thousand pounds I need not fear governessing or seamstressing, and I am equally safe from fortune-

18

hunters. My portion will secure me a modest independence, at least. So you see there is no need—'

'Oh, Lord, Lyddie, you must know that when Father dies—perish the thought—you will always be assured of a place at Heystead. I should be miserable if you could ever suppose anything else; and so would Susannah.'

Lydia had her own ideas about what would make Susannah miserable, but she kept them in. 'Well, in whatever way, I need not fear poverty or dependence—and it is the fear of those which often stampedes a woman into marriage, so that she hardly knows she is in before the gate swings shut behind her.'

'Loneliness, though,' George suggested quietly. 'What about loneliness?' A sound from the street made him cross to the window. 'Is that—? Oh. Thought it might be Susannah.' The spring-afternoon light, turning cool and meagre, stamped his strong blond head and hearty profile with a sad, exposed look. He could not be long without his wife. Consciousness of this, and of her own difference, made Lydia grope for something—some sort of amends.

'I have never been lonely, or understood loneliness, but then I have never really been tested,' she said, 'so I should perhaps not make a boast of it. And I do not declare that I have no intention of marrying on any general principle. If I were to see the right man, no doubt I should eat my words with a ready appetite. The simple fact is, I have never seen him yet, and at the age of thirty, reason inclines me rather to conclude that he does not exist, than to persist in the belief that he is still

19

somewhere to be found.'

George turned and shook himself genially. 'Well, I shall never understand women,' he said, meaning her. 'Oh, I don't doubt you're in earnest. You turned down Lewis Durrant, after all, which no one can understand to this day.'

'If people are still troubling themselves over such an unimportant matter, eight or nine years after the trifling event, they assuredly have little to think of.' Trying to keep her voice light, she detected in it a mosquito's pointed whine.

'Well, that's how people are,' George said, maddeningly amiable. 'I've never understood it myself, but never mind. How does Mr Durrant, by the by? I ask for a particular reason, as I—'

'When Mr Durrant proposed to me,' Lydia said, ignoring this, 'he had taken a good, careful, lofty look about him, and decided I would suit his matrimonial purposes admirably. And when I dared to raise the question of whether *he* would suit *me*, he retreated into mortified pride. That is the whole story, as you well know. I did try my best to blush, giggle, and swoon in bashful rapture at this mark of attention from such an eligible gentleman, but I was unequal to the task. I don't swoon well, George.'

'I know that,' he said, with a jaunty look. 'In fact, thinking on it now, I don't believe it would have answered, for Durrant's a stiff-necked fellow after all, and you . . .' He swallowed what he was about to say. 'What was I—oh, yes. I saw Hugh Hanley the other day. Quite the young buck still. And now it seems he's not content with the militia. He's after purchasing a commission in the Regulars. The Prince of Wales's Own, he said to me.'

'He can't,' said Lydia. 'That would cost . . . the expense—'

'I know,' George said soberly. 'After he told me, I asked some fellows I know, who are well up in these things: and I am assured that a cornetcy in the Tenth Light Dragoons is not to be had for less than seven hundred pounds. Add three hundred to that for the uniform, and then there's the cost of your horse and stabling. But he's raising the money on his expectations, you see. Hanley's his uncle's heir, after all, and he can get any amount of credit on the strength of that. Lewis Durrant's no dotard, of course, but then he can't live for ever either, and he must be seven-and-thirty now—'

'Eight. Eight-and-thirty in January.'

'And no other heir for Culverton. Well, unless Durrant decides to leave it all to the Society for the Reformation of Manners.'

'Unlikely, I think,' Lydia said, with a half-smile.

'Sour as ever, is he?'

'A good deal sourer. Lately he got cross with Lord Brownlow. There was a county meeting, to do with voluntary contributions for the internal defence of the county in case of a French invasion—*or* riots and disturbances. Mr Durrant, it seems, stood up and opposed the resolution because of the latter part. Treating our fellow-countrymen as if they were enemies, he said, was precisely the way to turn them into Jacobins, and small wonder if they ended up setting a guillotine in Lincoln market. Apparently Lord Brownlow, who was in the chair, took it very ill.'

'Dear, dear, that was unwise. Wasn't there some rumour once of Durrant being made deputy lieutenant of the county?'

'If it was ever a possibility, it is not now.'

'Mind, you would agree, of course, with his radical notions,' George said playfully.

'I concur with the sentiment,' Lydia said, refusing to rise. 'But in this case I think it rather a pose on Mr Durrant's part. He has many qualities; but the fact is, he cannot drink a dish of tea without making it appear a gesture of stubborn independence.'

'Well, he'll be sourer still when he hears his nephew is already spending his inheritance. Ah . . . !' Below, the sound of the front door. Halfway across the room George paused, sheepish. 'Oh—excuse me, Lyddie—'

'Go, go.' She laughed. His absence would give her a little space to fortify herself against Susannah with another glass of wine.

The children were the first upstairs. Lydia submitted contentedly enough to the flinging, shouting and knee-scrambling. She was very fond of her nephew and niece, little George and Lucy, and they of her: she did not pretend to understand them in the least, which they seemed to like. Next came Susannah, singing under her breath. A very blooming young woman, Susannah Templeton; and if the bloom was of a sort to make Lydia wish for a sharp frost, then the fault surely lay with Lydia.

'Where did you go on your walk then, my dears?' George asked, swinging his son up to the ceiling.

'What a question!' gurgled Susannah. 'I do believe we went to a fairy kingdom at last, quite without meaning to! Oh, we intended at *first* to go to Cavendish Square, but it is so very dull to follow intentions, and so we took another way entirely—simply because the sky was so blue!'

Susannah did not so much sit down as demonstrate sitting-down's beautiful possibilities. From the sofa, all full breasts and flowing muslin, she beamed at her children and her life. Her face was that of an exceptionally pretty and well-made doll transmuted into blissful flesh. It was always difficult for Lydia to remember quite how much she hated all this, sum and parts: it was like a megrim headache—only getting one reminded you of how horrible it was.

'George, you look tired,' Susannah fluted. 'Was it very hard at Craven Street today?'

'Oh! not excessively. Just a little fagging.' George was a sort of partner in a banking firm off the Strand, set up by a friend from Oxford. The friend did most of the work as a banker, because he liked it and it suited him; George meanwhile went conscientiously to Craven Street for a few hours each day and sat reading the newspaper. Yet he liked to have Susannah make a great cherishing fuss of him before dinner. Though an intelligent man, he hankered after the easy comfort of the stupid, which Susannah, a great puller-off of boots and stroker of brows, was very ready to supply.

Just then little Lucy, trying to imitate her brother, launched herself off Lydia's knee and fell on her face. Lydia jumped up, prepared to soothe, but Susannah was there before her. Splendidly regardless of her gown she scooted along the floor to seize and embrace, leaving Lydia to stand redundantly over them.

'There—never mind—the fairies will come and take the horrid hurt away,' Susannah crooned.

23

Then, turning her lovely guileless face round at Lydia: 'Lord, look at you up there. Aunt Lydia's like a giant, isn't she? Right up to the sky!'

Lydia was—yes—quite tall. Susannah was, inevitably, of medium height, meaning just the right height for gazing up with trustful adoration into a man's face. On the mantelshelf, easily within Lydia's Amazonian reach, was a statuette of a horseman in bronze, as invitingly grippable as a hammer. But just then George saved his wife's life by announcing: 'Well, I'm ready for dinner.'

Dressing in her room, Lydia examined her own excessive irritation with her sister-in-law—and found underneath it the figure of Mr Cribs-Sissons. Yes: Susannah brushing her lustrous hair at the dressing-table before bed and remarking to George what a very good thing it would be for Lydia to marry his friend—she is after all thirty now . . . Wretched presumption! Was it so very tiresome entertaining her here for a couple of months of every year? It had been George's insistence, when he first married and took a house in town, that Lydia come and spend a part of every winter season with them. So she had, and relished it—her delicious annual infusions of theatre, concerts, opera, exhibitions, reading-rooms, bookshops. But now, looking back, she saw her visits in a different light. Had there been, each time, a hopeful humming in the air of Queen Anne Street—that this time they would get her married off—and each time an equivalent disappointment?

Of course, Susannah had a practical aim in view. When Lydia and George's father died—and Dr Templeton, though in fair health, was nearly seventy—George would become the master and

Susannah the mistress of Heystead Priory. She would not want an unmarried sister-in-law prowling the galleries of the old house like a family ghost. Well, let her fly away in a high wind on a broomstick. Lydia had no intention of marrying to *oblige*—any more than she had nine years ago, when she had turned down the most eligible man in the district.

And perhaps that had been productive of a little irritation too—the mention of Lewis Durrant. But George, being George, could not forbear bringing up the subject again at dinner.

'Oh! yes,' he said, interrupting his manly flourishings of the carving-knife. 'I was telling Lydia, my dear, that I ran into an acquaintance of ours. I'm not sure you ever met Hugh Hanley—but you remember, I think, meeting Mr Lewis Durrant at Heystead last summer?'

'Oh! to be sure,' Susannah said, turning her smiling sweetness on Lydia. 'Your old beau!'

Old beau. It suggested a powdered wig, ruffles, and face-patches. 'An old friend,' Lydia said temperately.

'Well, young Hanley's his nephew—and his heir, as Durrant never married—'

'Lord, another one,' Susannah murmured.

(And a sword and a silver snuff-box.)

'Last time I saw the young rip he was fashionable enough. But now he's setting up as the greatest swell you ever saw.' George sniffed the mutton appreciatively. 'Made me wonder, you know, seeing him all fligged up, how I would feel if young Georgie started living high on his expectations like that. Dice and horses and so on.'

'Oh, but that's quite a different case,' Susannah

25

said. 'Georgie is your *son*, and filial feeling must always prevail. Mr Durrant is only the young man's uncle—and uncles and aunts, you know, can never be very important to the feelings. Only between parent and child does one find the true sacred bond. After all,' she accused Lydia, 'look how uncommonly attached you are to *your* father.'

('Pon my soul—sink me!' cried the beau, lifting his quizzing-glass.) 'Papa and I are very good friends, certainly,' Lydia said. 'I am fortunate in my home life, where there is no disparity of mind or taste: no malice to be encountered, or dullness to be endured.'

Susannah laughed her silvery laugh. 'Yes—I do like to think of you two pottering about amongst your books. Oh, I should love to see dear Heystead again. Does my tree still flourish as beautifully as ever?'

'That's the great oak, on the rise before you strike the path to the fish-ponds,' George put in. 'Susannah is so very fond of it—she calls it her tree.'

'It is so noble—it seems to spread out its great arms in welcome,' Susannah said. 'Do, Lydia, remember me to my tree.'

'Certainly,' Lydia said reaching for her wine. 'It is always asking after you.'

'That won't be long now,' George said, with a gentle plunge into melancholy: Lydia was to leave for home the day after next. 'Can't believe it. Only seems a moment since you arrived . . . Well—tomorrow night we must give you a proper farewell,' he went on decisively. 'I say we go to Vauxhall. Music and supper and rack-punch and so on. Then I shall get a sore head and not be able to

26

do what I want to do, which is make you stay with us longer.'

'Oh! dear George,' cried Susannah, slinking round the back of his chair, and fastening her arms around his neck like a lovely noose. 'The things you do say!'

CHAPTER THREE

'For *you*, Miss Templeton,' the maid said the next morning, coming upon Lydia reading alone in the drawing-room, 'Lady Eastmond.'

'Yes, it's me, my dear, and too late for you to hide in the escritoire, not that you could as it's too small altogether, and why must we call a writing-desk by a French name, I ask you? It's not as if one *writes* in French, though *you* could to be sure, and Italian no doubt. German too perhaps? You must tell me. If you run to Swedish, mind, I shall doubt you. One only presumes or supposes that there *is* such a language as Swedish. There are, assuredly, Swedes, but beyond that I cannot go. Come: kiss me: old women are allowed to demand this— indeed how else are they to get kisses at all? Contrast young women, who must be begged for them, a matter of name your price in fact. *You* might name any price, I'll venture. And so where then *is* George, though don't tell me, he is toiling in the vaults—which is what I conceive men do in banks, or do they do something else entirely?—and charming Mrs Templeton, whither she? Not that I mind in the least, because I wanted thoroughly to *have* you to myself, and here you are.'

'And here you are, and now sit down, you're making me giddy, besides wearing out the carpet. Yes, George is at Craven Street, and Susannah I think has taken the children for an airing—'

'Makes them sound almost like bed-linen, does it not? Or at least as bed-linen should be, though I went to stay *many* years ago at Burghley, which is made such a great thing of, and there was not only dampness but *residue*. If I mention hairs that resemble the tiny springs inside watches I need say no more. For myself I recommend country washing and no bleaching—of course, with poor Henry these things are more a matter of necessity than choice.'

'Sir Henry's health does not improve?'

'It does not *degenerate*, but it does not improve—it's delightfully like you, by the by, to enquire, you dear thing—and the doctor is inclined to suggest that Henry does not sufficiently *rouse* himself. I have answers for the doctor in *that* regard, but never mind.' Lady Eastmond at last seated herself. 'My dear Lydia, I needed to see you. First, to refresh my old eyes with the sight. They are refreshed. Second, to ask how you do. I know we have run into one another while you have been in town, but still not *often*—you have too much sense to move in the sort of circles in which *this* old body rattles her perennial bag of bones.'

'My dear Lady Eastmond, I do very well, and so, I collect, do you, as you show already more energy than I can command in a twelvemonth. And I am waiting for the *third*. Which in fairy-tales is always rather important and alarming.'

Lady Eastmond, uncharacteristically, even uniquely, was silent.

'Dear me. I hope not bad news.' Fear rapped at Lydia's chest. 'You have heard nothing untoward from my father?'

'Bless you, nothing of the shape. Your father is good enough to write me often, and the last I heard he was very much himself, excited about the discovery of a manuscript fragment at Boston. Medieval, I fancy. The very word puts me flat in the dismals but then I've no more brain than a butterfly. No, the third, my dear, is a sort of request, but nothing of great consequence. Now my memory is going with my teeth but I *think* the last time we met—wasn't it at the Hanover Square concert-rooms, where there was that frightful Italian singer?'

'Madame Bartolini. Her voice is not what it was five years ago, though I think she makes better faces now.'

'And there, I believe, you told me you would be leaving town before the end of April.'

'Just so: I depart for Heystead tomorrow.'

'Ah, a pity, we might have travelled up to Lincolnshire together, but I cannot think of leaving before next week—I have been donkey enough to promise *two* friends my attendance at their receptions, sad dull squeezes you would find them and doubtless so shall I, but then as Henry often reproaches me I have never learned to say no. And here's an example for you,' Lady Eastmond said, with her liquid laugh, gripping her bonnet with both hands. 'You're too well-bred to stare as you want to, my dear, but trust me I am thoroughly aware that no scarecrow ever looked more hideous—only my milliner was so *very* persuasive and before I knew it the disastrous purchase was

29

made. Thirty years younger, and handsomer than *I* ever was, and one might carry it off.'

The hat was a crimson crownless straw with very little brim, fastening under the chin, and topped with black plumes. Not a hat to flatter large features or a sallow complexion; and Lady Eastmond, never of delicate looks, was at nearly sixty as brown as a root with a face little smaller than a horse's. Yet it was a face in its way splendid, and easy to live with. The great Roman nose alone was like a declaration of unaffected honesty. She was Lydia's godmother: much loved by her: much liked by her vast circle of acquaintance. She possessed both warmth and sense, but not so much of the first as to make people sneer at her, nor so much of the second as to make them fear her.

'I like the hat very well,' Lydia said. 'It has a— decided air. Will you have a glass of ratafia?'

'Bless you for a charming fibster, my dear, and thank you, the only cordial I need is the sight of you, and now where were we? At the concert-rooms to be sure—and *there*, I don't need to remind you with your prodigious memory, I introduced you to my ward, Miss Rae. The work of a moment, alas, as I recollect the little gadfly was off the moment she'd made her curtsey, but more of *that* anon.'

'Auburn hair—the true red-gold one never sees—very pretty, and slight. I do remember.'

'Pretty, as you say, my dear, and too pretty for the peace of anyone entrusted with her care, when you add to her looks her prospective fortune. I could hardly talk of it when she was by, and presently that singer started her noise, but now we are tête-à-tête I may give you the history. She came

30

to us before Christmas. I say *my* ward, but she is from Henry's side of the family—her mother was his cousin. The Raes of Edinburgh. Not at all a fashionable family, but highly respectable and *very* rich. The father died when she was a girl, and then, an only child, she was brought up by the mother in a way that was quiet but—dare I say indulgent? Well, Mrs Rae died last year, and then the poor girl was shuffled about various relatives until the courts decreed that Henry be appointed her guardian until her coming of age. Henry was content enough—that is, one supposes so: it is often difficult to tell what Henry feels, though there are certain physical manifestations . . . However, I was delighted. Lacking children of our own, I thought it quite a blessing—oh, I still do, don't mistake me—and when I first set eyes on her, I knew I should love her. Now when she came to us, I was about to set out for town for the season as I always do—and though staying at Osterby for the winter suits Henry very well, I thought it the dullest prospect for a girl of scarce twenty—and when I proposed that she come to London with me, she was all eagerness.'

Lady Eastmond made a sort of apologetic pause. Her kindly nature had, like everyone's, its pockets of selfishness: one was her refusal to give up her London season for anything. The pause gave room for recognition of this fact, and for Lydia's fond allowance for it.

'I am sure nothing could have pleased her better,' Lydia said, 'especially if her life has been so retired. You suggested her father was wealthy?'

'Partly, I think, from being a monstrous nip-cheese,' Lady Eastmond whispered, 'but no

31

matter. The fact is, Phoebe is heiress on her majority to fifty thousand pounds.'

'A sizeable sum,' Lydia said, suppressing the urge to whistle. 'Also, I fancy, a sizeable responsibility for you.'

'I knew you would understand, my dear. Not that I don't shoulder the responsibility gladly—she is an absolutely charming creature, and it's well for an idle old rattle like me to have something to occupy her. And it has been a delight introducing her to town: will you believe she has never been in London in her life before, except once as a child?—and *then* her father kept to their lodgings the whole time and allowed her to see nothing. She really has lived quite out of the world and is absolutely artless and unspoiled—and yet there is not the least awkwardness or timidity. That is why . . .' Lady Eastmond's smile was again apologetic. 'Well, at first I intended taking her about in society only a *very* little, but as she relished it so I saw no reason why I should not bring her out in the proper fashion. And she has acquitted herself more than tolerably, you know: there has been a good deal of attention.'

'Attention? A charming young girl with fifty thousand pounds? I only wonder you have not had to put a guard upon the door.'

Lady Eastmond's spluttering laughter grew suddenly rueful. She reached out for Lydia's hand. 'Lord, my dear, how you remind me of your mother sometimes.'

'And other times, Bonaparte.'

'Go along with you. *She*, God rest her, had something of Phoebe's look when she first came out—how it all struck her, I mean: great eyes drinking everything in. All open like an ox-eye daisy.'

Lydia gently disengaged her hand. 'That,' she said carefully, 'must be a resemblance both tender and troubling for you.'

'Well. Certainly it adds to my sense of responsibility.' Lady Eastmond rose and began to roam again. The sunlight that had been filling the tall windows was suddenly gone, with that plunge into darkness peculiar to fitful spring. The edges of the furniture seemed to leap out in the gloom, bristling and inimical. 'Mind, when your mother and I first came out together I was a little envious of her, for all we were good friends: she was so very handsome and graceful and as for me—well, "*durable*" is the word Henry applied to me once, and he meant it in compliment, bless him. But at least my eyes were not so inclined to be dazzled, and so I wish I might have been a better friend to her then—oh, I did my best *after*, but you take my meaning. What she needed was a good, strong, level head at her side. And that is what my ward needs also.'

'And she is all the more fortunate in her guardians, say I, and you know I do not run to flattery. You have been the staunchest friend to George and me. I cannot conceive a better protectress for such a girl as you describe—not that I know her, of course—'

'But you shall,' Lady Eastmond said eagerly, 'for that I must absolutely engage you, my dear. It is my greatest wish, when we are all back in Lincolnshire, to present Phoebe Rae to you. That I cannot do *now*, because I packed her off to Osterby just the other day. I thought it best, as last week she was quite low with a fever—nothing alarming, the town air I think—but once she was recovered, I decided the country it must be, for the complete restoration of her health. I shall follow, of course, once these *wretched* receptions are over. And then . . .'

Lydia looked at her godmother's restlessly tapping, large, kid-shod foot. 'Lady Eastmond, I think you are not telling me the *entire* truth.'

'My dear, you are quite the lawyer, and I declare if I had to stand at the bar, or the bench or the dock or whatever it is, and you were to rise from what I think is called the *well* of the court—and where *do* these terms come from, one wonders, they seem to belong to the farmyard—I know I should be overpowered in a moment and begin confessing to everything. Very well. Phoebe's indisposition came fortuitously, for I had been considering, at that very moment, how to get her out of a scrape.' Lady Eastmond breathed deep and smilingly, her eyes on a miniature painting above the mantel depicting three fat underclad children embracing a lamb and each other all at once. 'A *sort* of scrape. What a pretty picture that is!'

'Yes,' Lydia said, glancing, 'in a hideous, ghastly, repulsive way. What sort of scrape, Lady Eastmond?'

'Oh, bless you, nothing of the serious sort, heaven forbid. Call it a tangle. To be plain, Phoebe has received such particular attentions that she fancies herself at least half in love.'

'Well, if I know you, she has attended every ball and rout and *soirée* going, and ridden in the Park, and worshipped at the Chapel Royal, and gone to

34

the theatre and the opera and the Pantheon—and if she were *not* at least half in love with someone at the end of it, I should think there was something wrong with her.'

'Spoken with your customary good sense,' Lady Eastmond said, dashing back to her seat as if she were playing at musical-chairs. 'And I was certainly not unprepared . . . But I had supposed so inexperienced a girl would only, as it were, dip in a toe—perhaps wade—but not absolutely dive in. What a regrettable metaphor that was. The fact is, my dear, Phoebe finds herself with two admirers, and says she is in love with them both.'

'Only two? Not a creditable showing. Where have all the fortune-hunters gone, that a girl with fifty thousand pounds is limited to two admirers?'

'You dry thing. "Admirers" is not perhaps the word—oh, there have been plenty of *that* sort, and doubtless there will be more to come, but I have a very good eye at a fortune-hunter, and they may expect short shrift from me. No, these are two gentlemen she has met in society quite respectably: both, I believe, very much taken with her—and not with her fortune. Though of course that must *weigh*, in any match. Such a ticklish question! I would rather she simply be giddy and thoughtless and not even consider such things, at least until she is of age, and even beyond then. But there is something a little intense about Phoebe, for all she is the most good-natured girl in the world. She could talk of nothing but these two gentlemen, before I sent her to the country—before I took fright, to be frank. She inclines to both of them, it seems; and most earnestly desires to know what she should do; and I hardly know how to answer her.'

'If she inclines to both of them, then this is as much to say she inclines to neither of them,' Lydia said. 'They must be very watered-down affections that can be offered about so liberally. I'm sure you do right to remove her: a good dose of absence is the best cure for the condition.'

'Partly my thought . . . but she *is* very serious, my dear, and that's why I wanted to speak of it with you. Phoebe, I fear, is not about to forget either of these gentlemen—unless she is afforded some means of comparison, and given besides an example of female sense and judgement. I have done my best, but I am an old woman, or soon will be: and I have the greatest distaste for old people who pretend to a sympathy with the feelings of the young. And so I wish—Lydia, I wish that you would take my ward under your wing.' Lady Eastmond slapped her own knees, as if in self-congratulation: done it. 'Now, take a little time before you answer, my dear.'

'I . . . Lady Eastmond, I am flattered you should ask me,' Lydia said: the usual reply one makes to an unwelcome request. 'But really I don't think I have a wing, of the sort that a young girl such as you describe would care to shelter under. In town, my amusements are of the kind to make her yawn: at Heystead, even more so. And thrusting enforced dullness upon Miss Rae would be the surest way to drive her to the other extreme.'

'My dear Lydia,' Lady Eastmond said, with a surprised look, 'I have never heard you describe yourself as dull. You, with all your taste, elegance and accomplishments—'

'Dull for others,' Lydia said, faintly nettled, as

36

she was probably meant to be. 'I would never apologise for the things that interest me, nor for the fact that I prefer to talk of books rather than sprig-muslins. I mean that Miss Rae, as you have described her, and just entering the world—'

'Ah, but you don't know her, you see. There is something rather sweetly serious about Phoebe, in spite of everything. I fancy she would welcome rather than reject guidance. She has the most endearing way of asking me what she ought to do, in all ways—and sometimes I am at a loss for an answer. Which is why I thought of you.'

It was Lydia's turn to roam now: she was alarmed. A noise just outside the street-door gave her the pretext to go and look out of the window, though she knew what it was: the coal-seller heaving a sack down to the basement. The familiar sounds of her London stay: not unpleasantly familiar, but not loved either: not home. She was always glad to leave, as she was always glad to arrive, and her mind before Lady Eastmond's entrance had been comfortably dwelling on her packing. So, selfish then: you want just what you want and no more, as your response to this perfectly civil request of Lady Eastmond's shows. But . . .

'But, Lady Eastmond, I—forgive me, this is surely a heavy responsibility. If Miss Rae is to ask *me* what she should do—that is, which of her two gentlemen she should choose, then . . .'

'Trust me, my dear, I do not mean anything so bald and plain as that. My concern—my feeling is that Phoebe thinks that after a London season she has now seen everything.'

'"O brave new world, that has such people

in't." '

'I knew you'd have a quotation for it, my dear—Shakespeare I would venture, for time was when Henry was mightily fond of reading Shakespeare aloud to me in the evenings, but he *would* do all the voices, and when we got to the Three Witches I could hardly keep my countenance. I seem to remember him at last throwing the book across the room with exceptional force, for him . . .'

'Who are these two gentlemen?' Lydia asked, with reluctant curiosity.

'Well: one is certainly quite eligible. Allardyce is the name. No *vast* fortune, but a good family, and it seems he is quite the coming man—he is in the diplomatic service, and has lately been at Vienna about the war-alliance, and has connections in the government. I fancy, so well-travelled and cultivated as he is, that Phoebe's open, unspoilt quality is refreshing to him. There was great decorum in his attentions, but they were together a good deal at several balls, and afterwards he made his morning call in person each time, rather than sending his servant. A very sensible, gentlemanlike man, I thought.'

'Very well: Lady Eastmond, you know I trust your judgement, and so I think Miss Rae cannot do better than to marry Mr Allardyce directly.'

'I fear I have put the case rather too simply,' Lady Eastmond said, with a meek smile. 'If Phoebe does have a preference—not that the margin is wide, for whenever she speaks of one he is the most estimable man in existence, and whenever she speaks of the other he is likewise—but my guess is that the other gentleman, this Mr Beck, has the advantage.'

'*This* Mr Beck,' Lydia said sitting down. 'I detect a twang of disapproval.'

'He is, perhaps, an oddity. It is not that he is awkward in society, but he seems to care little for it. Indeed his tastes seem to run rather more in your . . . That is, he is of a literary bent. A little of a Radical too, though not to any shocking degree. Really he would never have come in Phoebe's way if it were not for Mrs Mansfield. You will have heard of her, no doubt. Just lately, after years of living at the very centre of fashion—and, between ourselves, on the very edge of scandal—she has taken into her head to set herself up as a bluestocking hostess. Terribly *vieux jeu* nowadays, of course, but there it is: she surrounds herself with pet poets and dresses in drab stuffs and talks learning. Which, really, my dear, would make *you* laugh, for even I can see the sham. The latest *on-dit* is that she has been raving about Homer, and now that she has read *The Odyssey* and *The Iliad* she can hardly wait, says she, to read the rest of his works. But there, I have known her for years, and she still lays on an exceedingly elegant reception, and so Phoebe and I went, and the introduction was made.'

'This Mr Beck is one of her pet poets?'

'He has written verses, I think, and other things: and he has started some species of review or periodical, and Mrs Mansfield likes to play the patroness to him. Not that he is poor: I find, from asking about, that his father is a Bristol merchant with a West India fortune, and I believe he may do much as he likes, and so she is not above his touch. Not such a distinguished connection, perhaps: but Mr Beck never struck me as ill-bred. Only rather odd and melancholy.'

'I see. You have pictured me an affected young poetaster fribbling away his slave-got money; but again, if Miss Rae likes him, I do not think it should lie in anyone's power to dissuade her. There, now you see how unfitted I am for your task, Lady Eastmond: I am choke-full of prejudices, and I deliver them without care for the sensibilities of the hearer.'

'Exactly as I hoped! It is precisely that kind of downright and unimpressible character that Phoebe needs to have about her. I am, as you well know, much too inclined to like everybody.'

'That, certainly, is one failing I shall never own; but I must own to so many others that you will surely be convinced at last that I am the least likely person ever to put Miss Rae upon the right road. I believe, for instance, that love is an infection best contracted and got over when one is young, like the smallpox; and then one may rest secure from it and get on with life.'

'*Do* you, Lydia?' Lady Eastmond said, fixing her with her great grey eyes. Lydia was a little discomfited: she had to remind herself that Lady Eastmond fastened the same eager look on you when she was asking if you thought it might rain later.

'What is today—Wednesday? Well, I believe it on Wednesdays and Fridays. The rest of the week I am an ardent romantic. And on Sundays I believe neither, I am then a mere soulless, mindless vacancy, like one of the royal dukes. Really, Lady Eastmond, I shall be very happy to meet Miss Rae when we are back in Lincolnshire: no one to whom you are attached could ever be less than an object

40

of friendly regard to me, and I am already disposed to like her because you do. And when we walk about the shrubberies of Heystead, or the lawns of Osterby, I shall try to dispense wise saws as we go, but—'

'Bless you, Lydia, those aren't the places I'm thinking of. Bath, my dear.' Lady Eastmond slapped her knees even harder: done it again. 'I want to ask you if you will accompany Phoebe to Bath.'

'Oh.' Not much of a reply: but the sound she wanted to make would have brought the maid running in alarm.

'Now let me explain. I had it vaguely in mind that Phoebe, after London, should spend some time at a watering-place—some other resort of society, where the too-hasty impressions of town might be corrected, and her views enlarged. Indeed I had fixed on Bath as the likeliest—at Brighton there is rather a *set*, and Weymouth I find quite the deadliest place in the kingdom. But now Phoebe is in any case all agog for Bath. For one, Mr Allardyce and his sister always repair there for the summer, because that is where their mother has retired—and once he had told her this, and asked if she knew Bath, Phoebe assured him she meant to go there as soon as she could. It was not exactly an assignation—but for Phoebe it is now impossible that she should *not* go to Bath. Which she was quick to tell Mr Beck: and he being from Bristol, very near at hand, has expressed a hope of seeing her at Bath—and she hopes so too; and so you see the difficulty. But also, the *opportunity*.'

All Lydia could do was repeat, flatly: 'Bath.' For some reason the old beau had popped up in her

41

mind again. He was holding up his lily hands in delight.

'Quite so, my dear, and on reflection I do feel that Bath would be the very place for her. There she will find as much society as in London, but with more decorum, and less temptation. And if she does encounter her two suitors there, so much the better. For as you are surely about to remark, you clever thing, to *banish* them from her presence would be to turn her romantic and defiant immediately. Whereas what we want is for her to adopt a measured and sensible view of her situation and prospects—do we not?'

'Certainly,' Lydia answered mechanically, 'that is the attitude one would wish every young person to take, though it is a wish very unlikely to be fulfilled . . .' She hardly knew what she was saying: the old beau was simpering in her ear. *Bath, m'dear! Beau Nash, and the Pump Room, and all that! Overpoweringly elegant!*

'I knew you'd agree,' Lady Eastmond cried, 'and I am so glad you are falling in with my scheme. Of course, I *would* be happy to go to Bath with her: but in all conscience, I cannot desert poor Henry any longer. And besides, my presence would be very much *in loco parentis*, and that, so coddled as she has been, is the very last thing she needs. Phoebe should have a young companion—she will feel a greater sense of liberty, and more inclination to confidence—but a young companion with some experience of the world, some wisdom, some independence of mind and coolness of judgement. Now, my dear Lydia—have I not described you to a hair?'

'You have flattered me most shamelessly,' Lydia

42

said, struggling to recover herself. (*The Master of Ceremonies! The Assembly Rooms!* trilled the beau, sticking patches on his face.) 'Which is like your kindness, Lady Eastmond; and I am sensible of the very great honour you do me, in placing such trust in my character and abilities. And because I honour you so much in return, I would not for the world see that trust abused. I would have to be strongly convinced of my fitness for such a responsibility before I could even consider taking it up. Anything less would be a betrayal of your faith in me. And I am so very far from convinced that even to say I will think on it seems an unworthy prevarication. If I have any of the cool judgement with which you so generously credit me, that judgement declares at once that your task is beyond my powers. I am sure I would show myself a most awkward, unsuitable, and generally unsatisfactory companion for Miss Rae—and that my vanity could not endure. You have given me such a character of perfection that I would not see it put to the proof. Let me rest for the moment on my unearned laurels. You will very soon find someone else who truly deserves them.'

Lydia was thoroughly uneasy: perhaps that was why she seemed to see in Lady Eastmond's face, usually so broad-brushed in its expressions, a faint scribble of disappointment. Not so much at Lydia's answer as what lay behind it: what it revealed. While Lady Eastmond hesitated, the old beau appeared again out of a cloud of powder and pomade, enthusing. *The Royal Crescent! The Circus! The North Parade!* Yes, Lydia retorted—by now hating him—and old prosing tabbies carried about in sedan-chairs, and pretended invalids

43

sipping lukewarm water and pretending to feel the benefit, and card-parties . . . dear God, card-parties . . .

'I have *surprised* you with this,' Lady Eastmond said at last, with her warmest, most equine smile, 'and I am quite a fool not to anticipate that it would knock you back a little. Lord knows I have never been a friend to surprises—Henry sprang one or two upon me in our younger years that were, at the very least, in doubtful taste, though that era is *long* past—and so I quite understand. This is sudden. You have your preparations to make for returning home tomorrow. Very well. I am content to leave the seed germinating—is that the word? it sounds unpleasant somehow—growing, rather, in your mind, until we meet again. That is, when we are both back in Lincolnshire, and I may have the pleasure of introducing you to Phoebe at last. I have greater hopes of *that* than of my poor persuasions. For I know you will love her.'

Probably no purer incitement to hatred existed, Lydia had found, than being told of anyone or anything: *you will love him, her, or it*. The spirit immediately rose up like a fanged cobra.

'Lady Eastmond, I had better say at once that I cannot undertake to go to Bath with your ward. I know nothing of her, but I know pretty well the world we must enter, and . . .' *Card-parties!* 'And if, for example, we are invited to a card-party, I cannot promise to bear it as she has a right to expect. That rational creatures should spend the limited time we have on earth in sitting about a table and exchanging pieces of greasy cardboard to no worthwhile result seems to me a folly without equal—'

'Oh! trust me, I fancy Phoebe has no great taste for cards, and no more do I—a sad spoiling of conversation I always think. No, you will have to do better than that to convince me, my dear: and as I say, I wish only to leave the notion with you and let it take its chance. All I *absolutely* ask is that when we are all settled back in the country, I may bring Phoebe over to Heystead. I would dearly like her to meet your excellent father, besides—well, besides the rest.' Lady Eastmond rose: she looked quietly triumphant, as if retiring from a greasy-cardboard game with a clear profit. Wagging a gloved finger in playful admonition, she added: 'Now *that* at least you cannot refuse me, Lydia, and if you do I shall positively dislike you—and there's a piece of nonsense to end on, as I could never do anything but love you to excess—which is why the old gargoyle demands another kiss—there. And now my compliments to dear George and his pretty wife and the children too—and I wish you a safe journey tomorrow . . .'

Lady Eastmond was halfway down the stairs before the maid could be summoned, or Lydia could follow her. She was always fast, but not that fast. She had discerned, perhaps, that her proposal had been unwelcome.

Discerned? brayed the old beau. *Damme, ma'am, 'twas as plain as the pox on the face of a strumpet—*

'Fop—off,' she told him, and fetched her cloak.

45

CHAPTER FOUR

Vauxhall Gardens: newly reopened for the season, the gravel walks freshly raked, the trees pruned, the thousands of lamps restrung, the Grecian columns repainted, the temples dusted, the grottoes regilded—and the admission price up again, as George contentedly grumbled that evening. 'I thought it was steep at two shillings. Someone's making a pretty thing out of it.'

'Hush, George, you shocking monster,' said Susannah, who was in good spirits, being fond of a lot of company: in fact she had once said, in her shining way, that she would like to meet everyone in the world. At Vauxhall you could encounter a fair cross-section of it: old-fashioned tradesmen, defiantly wigged, on the spree with their nervous wives: packs of young bloods already shouting-drunk, and daring each other to climb up and smash the lamps: prostitutes patrolling the Dark Walks: young girls newly out, amazed by everything, look Mamma, oh Papa, do look. Lydia was touched, and then she wondered if Miss Phoebe Rae was like that, and grew uncomfortable.

She had said nothing to George of Lady Eastmond's request, for the simple reason that she expected him to say she ought to comply: there is enough unwelcome advice in the world without going searching for it. And the interim had been spent in trying to put it from her mind, not with entire success. She was glad of the crowds, which precluded much conversation, for she was afraid her preoccupied mood would betray itself.

Up in the gallery of the music-pavilion the celebrated Mrs Fuller from Covent Garden sang a florid air while the liveried fiddlers below tried to keep up with her. The air was called 'Why Won't You Go To Bath, Miss Templeton?' and had as its refrain the words: 'Is it because you are selfish, selfish?' That was how it sounded to Lydia, at any rate.

Why not Bath? Anyone would think you had been invited to spend the summer down a coal-mine, or in Newgate. But no: Bath, the most genteel and respectable watering-place in the kingdom.

Exactly, she moaned to herself, exactly.

'They'll be ringing the bell soon,' George said. 'Let's get nearer to the boxes. There's always such a crush.'

They were passing a cluster of young gentlemen, and at the sound of George's voice something detached itself from the compound of Hessian boots, hard laughter, lounging, staring and starch, and became a handsome young blade greeting them. For a moment Lydia feared another Cribs, before recognition chimed. 'Mr Hanley. Forgive me—I did not know you for a moment.'

Hugh Hanley bowed, making a very elegant business of it. 'I am intensely relieved to hear you say so, Miss Templeton. We last met, I think, at Heystead more than a year ago—when, in other words, I was a mere mewling boy scarcely out of leading-strings and crying for tart. If there had been no alteration from that distressing spectacle, I should be mortified.'

'Quite so—but such a rate of growth, sir: does

47

this mean that by next year you will be a toothless old man with a stick?'

'As I shall then be in my twenty-fourth year, I may as well be.' He sighed. 'What a *horror* growing old is.'

'Now this is extraordinary,' George cried, pumping his hand, 'this—allow me to introduce Mrs Templeton—Hugh Hanley, my love, you recall me saying—for I ran into him, you, the other day, and I was telling Lydia about it— extraordinary coincidence!'

It was, if anything, a very ordinary coincidence; but it made George happy to go on exclaiming over it until the supper-bell rang, whereupon he asked Hugh Hanley to join them in their box.

'I can only accept if I can be assured I shall not be *de trop*: for this is surely a family party.'

'Oh, not in any special sense, sir.' Susannah dimpled.

'No, no, you must sup with us,' cried George, who believed that every addition to a party was an improvement. 'You're of the old Heystead set after all: and Lydia can perhaps give you news of your uncle—you still see Durrant a good deal, eh, Lyddie?'

'Yes, I dare say: though I can't think of any news I can give you, Mr Hanley, other than that your uncle is very well.'

'Which, of course, is the very news I am not supposed to like, as everyone knows I am desperately waiting for his decease so that I may begin wasting his fortune.'

'Oh, come now, my dear fellow, no one thinks that,' said George: long exposure to Susannah was making him immune to irony.

48

'It is a miserably ticklish situation, though, Miss Templeton, when you think of it,' Hanley said, as they were seated and the cloth laid. 'If I do ask after my uncle, I am a designing hypocrite: if I do not, I am a cold-hearted rogue. Put yourself in my position.'

'The sorrows of an heir. You have my sympathy, Mr Hanley. Or, pardon me, should I be addressing you by a military title?'

'I hope you would never do so in any event: it smacks of the parade-ground. But no, the officer in the Regulars is yet to be, and the lieutenant in the Militia is no more. It has been a thoroughly diverting occupation. One gets about the country, meets a good deal of company, and is admired without the inconvenience of being sent abroad to fight the enemy. Still, a man can only rise so far in the Militia; and I am not such a hypocrite as to pretend I don't want to rise.'

'But the Tenth Light Dragoons, now,' George said, 'this is aiming high at a stroke. The cost . . . What shall we have?' The oldest waiter in the world was hovering outside their box. 'Chicken and ham, of course. And salad. Shall we have wine, or cider? I always say there is nothing like Vauxhall cider.'

'The cost is excessive,' Hugh Hanley said readily, 'as it is for most things out of the common. The regiment is, without doubt, the most fashionable of all; and that is why I want to join it. I could oblige you with pious cant about duty and service instead if you like, but I had rather be frank. *There* are connections to be cultivated, influence to be gained, interest to be exerted, as they are not in a common line regiment. The cost

49

is really an investment.'

'And is not the regiment sometimes called the China Tenth?' asked Lydia. 'As it is too fragile to bear rough handling, and chiefly devotes itself to guarding the Prince at Brighton?'

'Another excellent reason for choosing it,' Hanley said, smiling, and not at all put out. 'I certainly did not join the army with the vulgar intention of seeing bloodshed. But you may be assured that if Boney lands at Brighton, I shall be there with my sword drawn ready to defend my prince. Or a bit of him. I do dislike these references to His Royal Highness's girth, but in truth it would take half a brigade just to surround him.'

The cider appeared with the ancient waiter—so ancient and shrivelled that when he turned away from the box his livery-coat stood still and he had to tug it round after him. Outside the box a frisky wind had sprung up, setting the lamps in the trees dancing, fooling with epaulettes and ribbons, and flourishing on an invisible tray the smells of boiled fowl, bruised turf and night-time.

Lydia, seated beside Hugh Hanley, employed the moment to take the measure of him, knowing he was doing the same of her.

At home in Lincolnshire she knew him as the nephew of her father's friend and neighbour—and yes, very well, her former suitor—Mr Lewis Durrant of Culverton. After one of his infrequent visits to his uncle, the gossip of the country would invariably run on two themes—which young girl was pining for love of him, and how violent the quarrels had been at Culverton House. What she had seen of him hitherto had fixed him in Lydia's

50

mind as a pert fellow with a degree of self-regard exceptional even for youth; but now she found herself at least prepared to revise the opinion. He had turned, as George had said, into the complete dandy—but it suited him: the languor, the artfully dishevelled hair, the garotting cravat. It was as if in affectation he had found his natural self. The heavy-lidded eyes seemed designed for quizzing a suspect hat from the bay window of Brooks's: the rather too red and full lips made for dropping choice *on-dits*, probably not kind ones. And it was a relief to find a man of his age simply at ease with her. Usually they became chucklesome.

'And how much longer do you stay in town, Miss Templeton? Shall you be here for the King's birthday?'

'His Majesty must celebrate without me: I leave for Heystead tomorrow.'

'Ah, then you will be able to report to my uncle at once, and tell him you have seen me, and assure him that I am absolutely as delinquent as he could hope.'

'Oh, I will certainly, for there is nothing more important to me than talking about *you*; though you might consider the possibility that not all the world feels the same.'

'I shall not rest until it does.' He smiled, brushing an imaginary speck from his pantalooned leg. 'There is only one thing worse than being talked about, and that is *not* being talked about.'

'And why do you think Mr Durrant should *hope* to find you delinquent?'

'Oh, my dear Miss Templeton, being disappointed in me is his life's work. It's what keeps him going. If I were to start behaving

51

sensibly, my uncle would be lost: Othello's occupation's gone, and whatnot. After all, what else is there for him in his autumnal years?'

'Mr Durrant has never struck me as a man lacking occupation. He is constantly at work improving Culverton.'

'Exactly! Culverton! I dare say he has every last tree and shrub counted and measured by now—every slate and gate repaired—every needy widow supplied with enough firewood to warm her for a lifetime. This is a man sadly in need of diversion; and if I can in my small way supply it, by vexing, astonishing and infuriating him, then I am at least doing a little good in the world.'

'Oh Culverton, yes,' cried George, who rowed in and out of conversations with a cheerful disregard for their drift, 'the handsomest place—the finest park. Next time we are at Heystead, my love, I shall have Durrant invite us over there—or we may have to invite ourselves, Durrant being the unsociable sort.'

'If it is anything like my dear Heystead,' Susannah said, 'I know I shall love it.'

'Indeed, you had better see it, ma'am, before I ruin it with my extravagance.' As supper arrived, and George and Susannah busied themselves with it, Hanley turned in his lithe, coiled way to Lydia. 'Well—is that not what my uncle believes?'

'You credit me with an oracular comprehension of Mr Durrant's thoughts. I know he is greatly proud of Culverton, and concerned for its future: but so much is common knowledge.'

'Ah, as to that, who knows? I may turn out to be the perfect squire after all, handling estate-maps like old love-letters, and waxing lyrical over crop-

52

rotation. But surely, Miss Templeton, you must hold the key to some aspect of my uncle's character. As there is no polite way of putting it, I shall ask with maximum impertinence: why *did* you turn him down all those years ago? I was a mere schoolboy at Winchester at the time, being educated in bad habits, and only heard the bare facts.'

'Your education was certainly imperfect, if you suppose that a lady would answer such a question. But if you are in possession of the bare facts, then really you have the whole matter. Mr Durrant proposed marriage: I considered: but, as I told him, I was not contemplating matrimony, with him or anyone else. I wish I could garnish the tale with romantic consequences and twists of fate; but there aren't any.'

'Yet he has never paid addresses to any woman since.'

'Oh, Mr Hanley, now you are embroidering upon those facts most shamelessly. You wholly misjudge Mr Durrant, if you suppose him nursing the broken heart of the disappointed lover these nine years. In order to propose at all, Mr Durrant had to overcome a strong dislike of humankind, and womankind in particular; and my refusing him only confirmed, I imagine, his prevailing notions, reinforced his pride, and allowed him to pursue his solitary and self-sufficing way without ever being troubled by such nonsense again. In that respect I fancy it was even a relief to him; and so, you see, you are not your uncle's only benefactor, Mr Hanley.'

'Indeed—and you are mine also, Miss Templeton; for if you had not refused him, there would surely be a brood of little Durrants now, to bar me from the inheritance; and I would have had to *apply* myself to something. And no doubt would have turned out a much more creditable fellow. So you see, there is nothing like a rich, childless uncle to ruin a man: really, with such disadvantages, what chance did I stand?'

'A sad history: but a man may rise above his disadvantages, Mr Hanley.'

'Oh, no, not in dear old England, ma'am: why else are we fighting France, but to keep that sort of idea down?'

'Come, none of your Radical talk here,' put in George. 'Lyddie, take some chicken—and some ham, if you can see it.'

The sparrow-like chickens and tissuey ham of Vauxhall had long been a joke, and there was perhaps more meat to be found in the slugs adorning the salad. Yet Lydia experienced a moment of peculiar well-being, looking out at the lamplit avenue, observing the flicker of grins and grimaces, struts and slouches, content to be where she was. No quarrels with time or place: perhaps that was felicity.

Or perhaps it was because she had not thought of Bath lately.

'Shall you remain in the country until next season?' Hugh Hanley asked: a mere civil enquiry that went through her like a jolt.

'Why—why do you ask?'

'Because it is the sort of tedious question one asks over supper,' he said, with a sidelong amused look. 'I asked you a much more impertinent one a moment ago, so I supposed I was safe.'

'Yes, of course, I was just . . .' Curiously, she felt

better able at least to touch upon her reasons with Hugh Hanley than with someone close to her like George. 'I do have an invitation to Bath in the summer, but I am not at all inclined to take it up.'

'Eminently sensible: I should think you would be bored half to death. I was there for part of a summer two years ago, and found it a devilish glaring, baking sort of place in hot weather. And then the chief amusements of the spring season are over: being Bath, there is always *something*—some little genteel assemblage as tepid as those ridiculous waters—but one must be very easily pleased to find much entertainment in it. I am sure you, of all people, would find it monstrous dull.'

'Me? Why me of all people?'

'My dear Miss Templeton, this is like conversing with a terrier. Not that I mind it, there is a sort of interesting suspense in wondering when the next *snap* will come. I say *you*, because you are a woman of intelligence and learning, as is well known: a genuinely accomplished woman. I have heard my uncle remark that you are the cleverest woman in the county: though, to be sure, he adds "and she knows it". For my part, I am a great blockhead at learning, unless it be the *very* important things like how to tie a cravat, but even I can tell that the Pump Room in June is not the place for a lively mind.'

'I confess I found it somewhat insipid when last I went. My father decided to try the waters one year, and we spent an intolerably long month there. Then, at least, I had my father's company; but otherwise, it was all so prosy—so bonnety—so whisty and teacuppy—you see, the adjectives for it do not even exist, and I must invent them.'

'Well, here's a real one: dowdy. Brighton, now: that's the place for fashion.'

Not quite her point: still there was relief in even beginning to make it.

'Rack-punch!' cried George, suddenly. 'Lyddie, it's your last night with us, and we are at Vauxhall, and so we must mark it with rack-punch. Hanley, call that waiter, if you will be so good. Now, now, none of your faces. It must be rack-punch.'

Rack-punch was another Vauxhall tradition, but not as harmless as the rest. Plentiful sugar and lemon could not mask the leer of potent spirits. The ancient waiter brought them the bowl leaning backwards, as if hefting a full bath. George's big-jawed face beamed through the steam as he stirred.

Lydia had a strong head for liquor, and took a cup. Even as it went sulphurously down she knew it must be her last. But it did ignite a final, definitive thought about Bath and Lady Eastmond's request. She resisted, she saw now, because she did not wish to be recruited into a silly and sentimental novel, in which, while sweeping disdainfully about Bath and advising her innocent young charge against all entanglements, she was all unconsciously ready to be swept off her feet by imperious Lord Wideacres who, not put off by her advancing years, was set upon curing her of her bluestocking ways. Last chapter, double wedding of young charge and mature bluestocking, both Brought To Self-knowledge by respective spouses. Bluestocking softened, and reconciled to a lifetime of annual visits to, and blissful mindless saunterings in, the Pump Room.

Meanwhile George, affectionate even when

sober, drank several cups of the punch, and was soon heartily shaking Hugh Hanley's hand and embracing Susannah: an excellent fellow, never more pleased than running into him tonight: the best of wives, any man who found even half her equal could count himself the luckiest in creation, and so on. Lydia's turn must come. There was music about to begin in the Rotunda, and she started to mention it, but George's warm unsteady hand seized hers.

'Never mind that, Lyddie: I know you don't like to receive compliments, but I am in the chair, and you must suffer it: you must let me say what I mean, and that is, you are the best sister a man ever had: and look here, the kindest and warmest likewise. All head and no heart, some might say— but if they do, they'll have me to deal with first, for I know better. All head and no heart? Not Lyddie. Anyone who says that is only revealing their ignorance. Besides the fact that I'll fight them to the death. No, they don't know Lyddie, if they say she's all head and no heart. You have to look beneath.' Visibly, George entertained a fleeting idea that he had dropped something, and began perseveringly to look under the table for it. 'Never mind what happened to poor old Cribs. I'm sorry for him, but he wasn't the right one. Ow. No, there is a right one, and we simply haven't found him yet. And he will be a lucky man, because it isn't true what they say—all head and no heart. It isn't.' George suddenly rose with a severe, judicial look, and grabbed hold of the table to stop the world spinning. 'I think, by the by, I shall go for a walk along the Walks.'

Wanderingly, he went. Susannah followed, all

57

tolerant fondness of male exuberance. Lydia sat on, rather more rigid than she wanted to be, reflecting on the way the people closest to us are able so effortlessly to thrust us to the farthest distance.

'All head and no heart,' Lydia repeated. 'What would you say to that, Mr Hanley?'

'Oh, lots of things: because, of course, as you reminded me this evening, there is nothing more important in the world than talking about *you*—except that at the time *you* was *me*. Or were. This is becoming dismally grammatical.' He called for the bill. 'Shall we go and hear the music?'

He was, perhaps, slightly bored with her, as she was with him. The result of understanding without sympathy. They squeezed into the Rotunda, where to her intense gratitude a string orchestra was playing: no singers. She had had enough of the human voice. The *Allegro* was in B flat major, with a subsidiary theme in the relative dominant. Because I know this, does it mean I don't enjoy it? Head not heart. Listening to those shimmering complex sounds, it seemed to her that both were present. Surely that was the ideal. Surely one should not have to sacrifice one for the other.

And surely she could escape going to Bath. One simply said no—just as she had said no to Lewis Durrant all those years ago: and then one lifted free, buoyed on the cool current of decision, untrammelled by the cords of regret.

CHAPTER FIVE

'Heystead.' Lydia sighed; and settled herself back against the biscuit-thin upholstery of the post-chaise as it skimmed out of the yard of the White Bear in Piccadilly. Which jarred her spine and rattled her teeth: it was better to sit forward until you were off the cobbles. No matter, though, because it was really Heystead that she was leaning back against. Heystead, her cushion.

'Heystead,' said Mary Darber. The way she uttered it suggested the dropping of a heavy stone into a deep brackish well.

Mary was Lydia's maid—meaning she was a servant at Heystead, who always accompanied Lydia on her annual visit to London because no respectable woman, not even one as independent-minded as Lydia, could do such a thing quite alone. As Lydia required very little fussing about hair or dress, there was not much for Mary to do during the two-month sojourn at Queen Anne Street: so she passed the time by falling in love. Being young and startlingly handsome, she had no difficulty in accomplishing this each year. The tender victim this time was, Lydia understood, a bookbinder's apprentice from nearby Bentinck Street.

'You're sorry to be going home, Mary?'

Listlessly Mary examined her fingernails. 'Oh, I shall get used to it.'

These loves were intense, difficult, stirring. Too stirring, Lydia had feared at first, and kept an eye on Mary's waistline: but the girl seemed to know what she was about. And hints that the family might help her to a job in London, rather than break her romance, had been indifferently received. The parting, Lydia began to see, was the thing. Two months of the year were consecrated to passion: the rest of the time Mary was rational and comfortable. It seemed to Lydia a sensible solution. There was only the painful transition from one state to another, from town to country, to be got over. London made Mary very smart and quick in her manner. 'Lord, ma'am, only look at that,' she cried, rousing herself to stare out of the window as they waited at the Islington turnpike. 'Did you ever see such a frightful old dowd? Surely no one has worn their hair dressed high like that these fifteen years. Not in town, at least.' She sank back with another sigh, expressive of her reminded doom: return to the rustic world where dowds and frights were in the majority. Lydia patiently commiserated. Usually Mary began to recover by Hatfield: at Baldock or Biggleswade she would eat with a country appetite, and by Eaton she would be remarking with interest on the state of the crops.

Which, Lydia could see, was poor. After the coldest winter in memory 1799 could come up with only a damp, laggard spring. Distress was still hovering over the country and agitating the nerves of propertied gentlemen who feared an English Bastille; though the invasion scare of last year was gone, and the victory of the Nile had raised hopes that the war could be won, or at least not so persistently lost.

Lydia ardently wished it over because it would stop men being killed, because it would put an end to the tiresome military fashions, and because she longed to go abroad again. She had visited Paris with her father just before the Revolution, been entranced, and had hoped for a present return. Ten years was a long time to nurture a hope, but she had done so: knowing, however, that lately she kept the spindly thing alive only by ignoring her father's declining vigour. Doubtless if the Continent opened again he would put his age and lameness to the test of a Channel crossing and a French *diligence*, just for Lydia's sake—if, that is, she were so spoiled and selfish as to allow it.

Spoiled and selfish. The Bath song trilled in her head again. She silenced it by an act of will and an invocation: Heystead. She would only think about that dilemma (what dilemma?—there could be none: she was not going to spend the summer bear-leading a feather-headed chit about Bath, and that was that: problem, then, call it a problem) when she was back at Heystead. There reason and harmony would be restored along with Mary's Lincolnshire vowels.

At post-chaise speed it was just possible to complete the journey up the Great North Road to Heystead in a day. Lydia had done it once: never again: you arrived fractious and exhausted and then had to sleep on your face. Instead they broke the journey overnight at the Wheatsheaf in Alconbury, where the mutton and the fleas were alike tolerable, and came into Lincolnshire fresh the next day, under a noon sun beginning to fight free of marauding cloud. Everywhere looked green. A fallacy, no doubt, but she was too contented to explore it.

And here was the steep lane between ancient beeches with its wickerwork of shadows, the ruined gatehouse, the mossy stone walls, the winding

61

drive; and Heystead Priory itself heaving into sight, a listing ship in a turf sea. Lopsided: heavy: splendid. Behind the neat horizontal line of the parapet jostled the old medieval roofline, all spikes and twisting chimneys: relics in a hatbox. The colour of the walls was somewhere between chestnuts and cider.

'Oh, I shan't be hurrying to goo away from here agin for a proper while,' Mary said cheerfully.

Lydia's heart echoed her. The post-chaise drew up in the courtyard with a last soft gravelly growl, and Dr Templeton emerged from the shady whale's-mouth of the great porch. Very lame now, and leaning heavily on his stick, but determined, he came to let down the step and hand Lydia and Mary out of the carriage.

'That's it. That's well. Ah, here we are. Sound in wind and limb, yes? Capital, capital . . . Daniel, if you will be so good as to see to the luggage—and, Mrs Gilmore, I feel sure the postilion would welcome some of your veal-and-ham pie . . .' At last Dr Templeton took Lydia's arm and smilingly said, as he always did: '"The harvest truly is plenteous."' And then she knew she was home.

An observer, knowing nothing of Dr Templeton and his daughter, and recruited to spy upon their reunion from behind the priory's oak panelling, might have concluded that no very strong attachment existed between them. No fond embraces, no gabbling of news and I-missed-you avowals: instead civil enquiries and measured exchanges, before Lydia presently went upstairs to change out of her travelling-dress.

What the observer would have missed was the steadfast warmth, which needed no raking up into

62

a blaze. Lydia and her father's relation maintained its closeness by a mutual allowance of space.

Unpacking could wait: first, this.

Her bedchamber overlooked the terraced gardens that descended in lazy steps to the river, and one of the two windows contained a window-seat broad and deep enough for a bed. Here she sat, legs drawn up, one of her new books placed by her side, unopened: call it a rehearsal, or appetiser, for the summer to come. She listened. Heystead, never noisy, was never silent. Even a new chair may give off a creak a few moments after someone has got up from it: the old Priory made a constant murmurous reply to its six hundred years of occupancy. She opened the diamond-paned window and admitted a polleny waft of spring: it met but did not mingle with the cool dark scents of beeswaxed wood and secretive stone. Very thinly, like sharp straws stuck into the quiet, came the bleating of sheep from the meadows on the other side of the river; but there was no song except that of a blackbird, which did not demand to be listened to.

*   *   *

Dinner was early. 'Unconscionably early, no doubt, when you are used to town hours,' her father said, as they sat down. 'Which reminds me, is Mary out of love yet?'

'The last sigh was at Stamford, so I think the cure is complete.'

'I have been unable to resist looking into that volume of Cyprian—a magnificent thing, and I'm sure not easily come by. I hope, my dear, you did

63

not waste all your time seeking out presents for me.'

'I wish I could have brought you something more—the notes on the Harleian manuscripts you wanted; but I am afraid the British Museum would not even open its doors to me. Next time I must ask George to lend me coat and breeches, so I can go *en travestie*.'

'You might do no better then: the collection is sadly ill-run. I'm sorry you were put to the trouble, my dear.' Dr Templeton poured the wine while Lydia carved the pork: they chose not to be waited on at table when dining alone. 'But you had better entertainment in town than that, I hope.'

'George and Susannah were all kindness,' Lydia said, feeling a peculiar restraint in talking of London, 'and the children were more or less delightful. You will find them very much grown when they come to us in August.' She accepted her wine gratefully. 'How odd that we always exclaim over children growing, as if in the ordinary run of things they shrink . . . Oh, you remember I wrote you about the patriotic songs that *must* be sung after every theatre performance now? Well, I braved Drury Lane again last week—Mr Kemble's Coriolanus, very fine, he even moved about a little—and for the climax of the evening the tragedienne reappeared dressed as Britannia and led us in a spirited composition called "United and Hearty, Have at Bonapartee". Really I protest— what is left for the satirical mind to invent, when reality so surpasses it?'

Watching her father chuckle with his quiet dry relish, Lydia was caught unawares by a giddy gust of emotion. For the past two months he had eaten alone in this lofty dining-room: no conversation, no company but the sad scraping echoes of knife on solitary plate. Leaving aside every other reason, what sort of daughter would she be if she were to leave him alone again merely to flit about Bath all summer? Righteous indignation filled her. Really it was a shocking proposal. Lydia regarded him with fondness strengthened by her impromptu outrage. A slight, neatly made man: a fine head, plentiful grey hair plainly dressed above a prominent brow: features less handsome than strong and decided: lines, many lines, patient and deep-grooved: intelligence in every one of them.

'We live in strange times,' he said. 'Hard times also, alas. I have given away as much stock and fodder as I can this spring, and Mr Durrant has done likewise, but what we need above all is a kindly summer and a good harvest. The hay and clover promise poorly, but one must hope.'

'How is Mr Durrant? I have some news for him from London—well, not news precisely. Probably a confirmation of what he already knows. I saw Hugh Hanley: very agreeable, very dandified, and very pleased with himself, and seemingly bent on every extravagance that may bring his uncle to grey hairs. A commission in the Prince of Wales's Own is the latest.'

'Ah! Poor Mr Durrant had more than a hint of it, in his latest letter from the young man. He told me about it when he dined here last week.' (Well, anyhow, Lydia thought, dining alone *most* of the time.) 'I fancy his nephew's conduct has become something more than an irritation to Mr Durrant now: it seems to be preying on his mind most vexingly. He has been here often of late, and seeming to wish to talk.' (Very well, alone *some* of the time.) 'And loquacity, as you know, is not his habit.'

'I am sorry for Mr Durrant—and would be more sorry, if I did not suspect he enjoys being miserable. But if the thought of Mr Hanley as his heir is so very detestable, there must surely be some remedy—some legal recourse.'

'I fear not. Culverton is entailed; and though there is some part of Mr Durrant's property that is alienable, I know he is loath to break up what he has worked so hard to consolidate.'

'Then there is only one answer. He must shut up the house, take up residence in London, and become a great swell: apply himself to running up vast tailors' bills, fribbling away a nightly fortune at the gaming-tables, and driving a high-perch curricle through Hyde Park. With a good hand at the ribbons. You see, I am up in all the new slang. Now *that*, I think, would put Hugh Hanley's nose thoroughly out of joint.'

'I'm sure it would,' her father smiled, 'and I might suggest it to Mr Durrant, if I thought he could endure such a life for a moment. But I believe he has *something* in mind to, as he put it, "make the little coxcomb sit up".' He laughed at Lydia's expectant look. 'My dear, I don't know what. He did not say, and I did not ask.'

'To be sure—though you have been friends for years, you are men after all; nothing short of torture will make you give a confidence, or solicit one. Well, I must ask Mr Durrant myself: he takes everything I say as an impertinence, so it won't signify.'

'I do have thoughts of asking him to dine,

perhaps the day after tomorrow. I did not wish to inflict a dinner on you too promptly after your return. But I am thinking of your friend Mrs Paige, who has her sister staying with her, and is, I think, finding her entertainment rather difficult.'

'Not again. Poor Emma. Is Mrs Vawser—is she much as she ever was?'

'Even more so, if you take my meaning,' Dr Templeton said, wincing: to speak ill of someone cost him a physical effort. 'I thought if we held a dinner it might *dilute* Mrs Vawser, at least for an evening, and relieve Mrs Paige a little. And, of course, you will have the opportunity to hear all the news of the neighbourhood.'

'Well, you must tell me it first: you will make it more amusing.'

'Oh, there is very little. Miss Beaumont's brother had one of his turns, but there was not much damage done.'

'Did he keep his breeches on this time?'

'Approximately . . . But come, you must have much more to tell than I. London can be ghastly, but never dull. What are the latest fashions, and the latest scandals—or are they one and the same?'

'At Queen Anne Street,' Lydia said, after an undecided moment, 'there is just now a fashion for marrying people off: but I declined to adopt it.'

'Ah,' said her father, and applied himself to his dinner for a tactful moment. 'Well, I have always believed that one should wear just what is comfortable and suitable; and I think the same holds good for fashions of another kind.'

'Oh, it was no great matter, Papa, and if I made it so then that was my fault and folly. I trust that the candidate—a perfectly blameless, boring

67

man—has forgotten about it as quickly as I should have. But I have brought home a—a disquiet, from quite another source, and that quite unexpected: from Lady Eastmond.'

'Now, indeed, you do surprise me,' he rumbled, in his slow sonorous way: next to Dr Templeton, everyone's voice was a twitter. 'Surely *she* has not been pressing you to marry: she has such good sense. Unless you mean she is ill—?'

'No, no—nothing of either sort. Lady Eastmond is thoroughly herself. I saw her only twice in town, but she . . . Well, you recollect that they have taken in a relation, a ward of Sir Henry's.'

'The Scotch girl, yes. I had a rather mournful letter from Sir Henry lately, lamenting that his wife would be deserting him even longer now that she had her young charge to show about town. So, did you meet her?'

'Only briefly. I thought no more about it, until . . .'

Very soon, it was out. She was scrupulous in the telling: just Lady Eastmond's proposal, and what it would entail, and what her answer had been. And as soon as it was over, there was relief, absurd relief: for there was so little to it, after all! Certainly not enough to warrant her rehearsing this speech in her mind all throughout the journey up from London, as she realised now she had, ridiculously. She felt light, and revived: she took another glass of the wine, which was excellent. She thought, with tolerant amusement, how odd the world was.

'I am only sorry for poor Sir Henry,' she concluded, going to the sideboard for the second course, 'if it means that Lady Eastmond, after all, is the one who takes Miss Rae to Bath; but there, perhaps, I may do some real good, by pleading his cause, and persuading her to choose some other companion for the task. Lady Eastmond has after all such a vast circle of acquaintance: there will surely be someone suitable, who will find the pleasure in the prospect that I cannot.'

'Oh, yes,' her father said after a moment. 'Oh, yes, I'm sure someone will be found.'

'Will you have apple-dumpling, Papa? Or the gooseberry tart?'

'Just a very little of the tart, my dear . . .' He waited until she had sat down again before saying, in his gentlest and most unargumentative way: 'Of course, the person Lady Eastmond would have preferred is you.'

'I know—is it not the most curious misjudgement on her part? As if I could be anything but an ill-tempered hindrance in such a situation. I am glad I was able to give Lady Eastmond a definitive answer there and then, so as to save trouble later.'

Dr Templeton picked at the sliver of tart. Smaller appetite, she noticed. 'You did, then— forgive me, I may have understood imperfectly— you did say, absolutely, no?'

'Well, to be sure: it seemed a very much more reasonable thing than yes, to a proposal that fills one with horror. Oh, Lady Eastmond was—was Lady Eastmond, in short: not at all put out, and declaring that she would persuade me at last. She would bring Miss Rae over to Heystead and improve the acquaintance, and so forth: but still my mind was made up.' Lydia looked down at the apple-dumpling on her plate. She could not

69

imagine wishing to eat it. '*Is* made up.'

Her father nodded thoughtfully. 'You must, of course, do what you believe to be right. Which is a shocking truism, forgive it. I know you have no taste for such a place as Bath—'

'And neither do you, Papa,' she said, seizing what looked like an advantage. 'Confess, you were as bored as I when we went there; and we had each other, at least, for rational conversation.'

'True. You do not consider Miss Rae likely to be rational?'

'She is twenty years old, has seen nothing of the world, and is in love with two men whom she has just met. If there is rationality to be found in such a creature, she must be a wonder: the Royal Society should put her under glass.'

Dr Templeton smiled reluctantly. 'Yet Lady Eastmond, you say, speaks well of her.'

'Yes, simply from the sheer goodness of her heart. And Miss Rae may indeed have, leaving brain aside, the disposition of an angel. This still does not alter my resolution—though I do not, by the by, generally rub along well with the angelic— not to be placed in such a false position. I would hate it, Miss Rae would see that I hated it and start hating it too, and Lady Eastmond would wish she had never thought of it.'

'Oh, I doubt that last: Lady Eastmond tends to find the best in everything; and as I said, she is so very attached to you that I do not think she could find fault in anything you did.'

'Papa, you are quite playing the devil's advocate today,' Lydia said, with a lightness that was somehow thin, like the note of a string about to snap. 'If you are not careful, I shall suspect you of

70

wanting to be rid of me for the summer.'

'I should be sorry to lose your company again, under any circumstances,' Dr Templeton said, in his steady way. 'And I quite understand why this proposal does not appeal. Indeed, if it came from any other quarter, I would not trouble about it. When it comes from Lady Eastmond, who has such a claim upon the family, it is of course more problematical—and requires the serious thought that you have plainly given it, my dear.'

'Yes, I . . . Yes.' Lydia had a stranded, helpless feeling: as if in walking up a familiar staircase she had found the top step missing, empty. 'I hope I would never dismiss anything that was important to Lady Eastmond.'

'I know you would not.'

He smiled his twinkling, faintly melancholic smile; and for a moment Lydia saw that it would be possible to be afraid of him, as one is afraid of the truly good.

And then he gracefully dropped the subject—his peculiar skill: talking with Dr Templeton you could always move smoothly on to other things, with no feeling of something left unsaid, lumpy and protuberant through the conversational surface. Yet Lydia was vigilant against the subject's return through the rest of the evening, and as a result could not be easy: the pianoforte clattered dully at her touch; and at last, pleading tiredness as an excuse for her want of spirits, she declared for an early bed. She took with her a new-lighted candle, and a feeling she could only describe to herself as thwarted.

Which made no sense: unless she had been privately hoping for something from her father—a

71

complete endorsement, even absolution—which it was not in his nature to give, nor hers to require.

And yet, following her up the broad staircase like her own flowing shadow, she felt a reproach. A voice, plaintive and otherworldly, whispered along with the rustling of her skirts, and would not be denied. Admitting defeat, Lydia stopped at the first landing, lifted the candle, and conjured the ghost.

The full-length portrait of her mother was by Gainsborough, painted when he was beginning his fashionable career at—of course—Bath, and she was the fascinating young heiress Rosina Holdsworth. The canvas was an intersection of two kinds of beauty: the luminous young woman looking over her ivory shoulder at the wielder of those brilliant tender brushstrokes, transfigured by them and transfiguring them. And yet the portrait had never given Lydia any strong sense of her mother's presence: instead it placed her among the other painted, fictionalised, absent people— ancestral Templetons mostly—whose framed faces loomed decoratively up the stairs and along the gallery.

There was very little of her mother at Heystead altogether. In the winter parlour her spinning-wheel did still stand in its old place, devotedly dusted and polished by Mrs Gilmore the housekeeper. Lydia also kept a silver locket of her mother's in her jewel-box, and in the library a few books bore her fading signature on the flyleaf. But beyond that, it seemed, Rosina Templeton had scarcely inscribed herself on Heystead in her thirteen years of life here, as bride, wife, mother, woman.

Lydia lowered the candle, and her mother went smiling into the devouring dark. She seemed to know, as Lydia knew, that there was more than one way of survival. She would after all be accompanying her daughter to her bedchamber: sharer of the sleepless hours she had created.

CHAPTER SIX

Undressing, Lydia thought about stories.

Undressing, pushing her gown to the floor, Lydia thought about her body, and thought about the stories written on it. As she stepped out of the ruffled pool of muslin the narrative of flesh began to tell itself. The white arms related her status as a lady, but also the family fairness: the hint of rounding about her shoulders recalled the adolescent consciousness of her height, the urge to stoop and draw in, conquered only in the chapter of adulthood. Unrolling her stockings, she unfolded her habits and tastes: the long slender delicately muscled legs spoke of her pleasure in walking, her dislike of riding. There was even a corroborative detail in the rough little spur just above her right ankle, remnant of the broken bone she had sustained in falling from a pony when she was eleven.

Self-stories, authenticated by memory. How slippery and vague, by comparison, were family stories, which sprang from the void before your birth. Handed down, amended, distorted even for reasons personal and protective, they became dubious heirlooms that would not stand up to

73

objective scrutiny. Yet Lydia believed she had as fair an edition of her mother's story as was possible. Little of it came from her mother, who had never been confidential with her; but the deficiency had been made up by her father and Lady Eastmond, the two people who—perhaps— knew Rosina Templeton best.

She had lived with the story as you live with a favourite book, which changes with you as you change and grow. The version retelling itself in her mind as she sat nightgowned and wakeful on her bed was appropriate to the thirty-year-old Lydia Templeton: who was sceptical, mistrustful of passion as of all imbalances, and inclined to subversive amusement, but not without a strain of fancy. For example, the story had to begin with that of her father, because that narrative seemed— fatefully, yes, romantically—always to be moving towards the moment of meeting with her mother: to be waiting for her.

*   *   *

Edmund Templeton, at sixty-eight the much-respected proprietor of Heystead Priory and its considerable estate, Justice of the Peace for Kesteven, and a private scholar and antiquarian of more than local repute, had never been intended by destiny for any of these things.

He was certainly born at Heystead, which for five generations had been the seat of the Templetons: sturdy Lincolnshire gentry with, on the whole, little pretension and much self-satisfaction. The line, the inheritance, naturally proceeded through the eldest sons. Edmund

Templeton was the youngest of three. Old Mr Templeton was the type of the country squire, only deviating from the model in an absence of geniality, and an excess of harsh self-consequence; and he had been very little affected by the loss of his wife at a young age, except in so far as it deprived him of one more person to dominate. Of his three sons, the eldest and heir, Francis, was turned off the same lathe as himself, and hence enjoyed the greater proportion of his regard: he rode and hunted with his father, studied with him the arts of deep drinking and swearing, and cultivated a proper indifference to the feelings of others. The second son, Charles, was less brutish, but just as energetic; and on reaching his majority acted suitably both to his inclinations and his father's expectations, and took a commission in the army.

This left Edmund: never a favourite with his father, as lacking that boisterous assertion which the old squire considered as manliness, and too bookish for his patience. Still, even this seemed not incompatible with the appropriate destiny of a younger son. It was absolutely expected at Heystead and in the district that Edmund Templeton would enter the church.

But Edmund Templeton refused to be educated for a clergy-man. There were scruples—almost doubts. These in themselves, his baffled father considered, were scarcely enough to warrant the boy's refusal—he did not know one parson in three who believed in the cant he was obliged to produce of a Sunday; and indeed Edmund did not take up his position wholly on a negative. Instead, he had a settled desire for his future profession, which was medicine. And for all that he was less forceful than his brothers, he had a quiet determination all his own.

It was a determination that Squire Templeton regarded as nothing less than a malicious intent to lower the family name. A profession medicine might be, but the lowest, fit for Scotchmen and the sons of merchants. There were many heavy sarcasms about starveling apothecaries, and even more violent expressions of displeasure, before a reluctant consent, hardly to be distinguished from rejection, saw the young Edmund depart Heystead for his medical studies, first at London and then Leyden, on a meagre allowance.

It was while Edmund was studying in Holland for his licentiate that his father died a conventional death of gout and apoplexy, and his eldest brother Francis entered into his inheritance; or, rather, flung himself into it. He commenced a career of hard riding and hard drinking, of high living and high spending, and of the kind of amorous adventure that left his liberty unencumbered and his reputation exalted. Soon afterwards Charles, the middle son, died gloriously of malarial fever on his first posting abroad; and in the meantime Edmund, having qualified as a physician, set up in practice in London. To his natural gifts he added learning and diligence: he began to thrive, and presently counted distinguished families amongst his patients. There was little communication between him and Heystead; but the young squire would sometimes remark, when in his cups, that his curious brother who had gone for a sawbones was doing pretty well for himself after all.

As the proprietor of Heystead was not. Properly

76

managed, the estate should have yielded a comfortable income. But Francis Templeton was more concerned with the well-being of his high-bred hunters than of his low-born tenants; and by his thirty-fifth year, he had mortgaged everything he could, and found himself at the end of his credit. Being still handsome, and being still of *good birth*—a natal distinction that no subsequent amount of vice and folly could cancel out—he formed the easy project of marrying money, and a short foray into the London marriage-market soon settled the business. He contracted an engagement with the young heiress to a City brewing fortune; and returned to Heystead for what he pleasantly referred to as his last hunting-season of freedom.

But a fortnight before what he termed his delivery into matrimonial custody, Francis Templeton drove his mount at a perilously high fence—for the last time. Both horse and rider were carried from the field with broken necks: the widow-to-be mourned, the moralists wagged their heads, and the creditors of the late squire prepared to press their claims on the estate. This now passed to the London physician, Dr Edmund Templeton; and it was confidently expected in the neighbourhood that he would waste no time in selling Heystead, and realising what he could from a property much encumbered and dilapidated, and surely lacking fond associations for him.

Instead the new heir, after a period of reflection, left his London house and practice, and came to take up residence at the Priory. For all that he had seldom been happy there, Dr Templeton loved the old building, cherished its antiquity, and respected what it stood for; and the man who had been the family disappointment applied himself with industry and shrewdness to the repairing of Heystead's fortunes. The estate was set in order, renewed and improved with such success that the debts of the late incumbent were cleared within two years; Dr Templeton continuing in the meantime to practise as a country physician, and securing as high a reputation with his patients as with his tenants.

His own wants and tastes, perhaps as a result of the early habits of economy forced upon him, remained modest. The chief employment of his leisure was in scholarly pursuits, in which his painstaking intelligence had long delighted; the only indulgence of his prosperity, the stocking of an excellent library. If prudence had prevented him marrying young, it was generally assumed, as he turned thirty-five, that choice had now replaced necessity; and in the wide circle of friendly acquaintance that his temper and his talents had procured him, he was confirmed as a bachelor until the very eve of his wedding.

Rosina Holdsworth came into rural Lincolnshire as a gorgeously plumed and exotic bird might stray into a flock of starlings. She was the orphaned daughter of a wealthy and ambitious London lawyer, who had bestowed on her a comfortable fortune, which had seemed likely to be augmented by the much older brother who was her guardian when he brought her out in society in the winter of 1765. The brother, a prominent man in Parliament and aiming high in the ministry, had hoped to extend his influence by the profitable disposing of his sister's hand; and the twenty-year-old Rosina, accomplished, vivacious, and every bit as hauntingly beautiful as her recent portrait by Gainsborough presented her, did not lack for distinguished admirers. A favourite candidate was at length chosen—that is, her brother forcefully pressed the match, and Rosina seemed to acquiesce in it. The man was past thirty, and neither handsome nor sensible; but he had an uncle in the Treasury and an aunt at Court, and there were coronets on his family tree.

The contracts were being drawn up when Rosina made the shocking defection that so outraged respectable opinion. She had fallen secretly and passionately in love with another man. Her brother had known and suspected nothing about it, until the night Rosina ran away with him.

The man was a soldier: young, good-looking, fascinating and, as presently appeared, quite without scruple. Mr Holdsworth's frantic enquiries had not succeeded in tracing the runaways until it was too late. Whether Rosina's soldier had ever proposed or contemplated a Gretna marriage was not to be known: certainly he had tired very soon of the game, and after the satisfaction of those appetites that she had mistaken for devotion, he swiftly deserted her for a fortuitous posting overseas. Rosina had little choice but to throw herself on her brother's mercy. Even now, she might have shrunk from that—but she had two lives to consider, not one.

That Rosina's brother did not absolutely turn her out of doors was due less to compassion than calculation. Society might conclude that Miss Holdsworth's reputation was conclusively lost after such an adventure; but still, not all the facts were known, rumour could cast doubt as well as convict—and in short, if she were not pregnant, something might yet be salvaged.

She was: but presently she was not. Rosina miscarried her soldier's child—and this could not be hidden from the London world's watchful eyes, and Mr Holdsworth was foolish if he supposed it might be. Doctors, callers, servants—the truth might creep out in a dozen places, and did.

There was only one recourse for Mr Holdsworth. As a public man, he must sacrifice his familial feelings on the stern altar of morality. He cut off all communication with his sister, depositing her with a female relative too ancient and obscure to understand what was going on. He made sure the world was aware that poverty would not be added to Miss Holdsworth's disgrace, as she would retain her parental portion (which he could not touch). But beyond that, he would have nothing to do with her.

Meanwhile Rosina accepted her banishment without protest, or any demonstration of feeling except a desolate blankness. Retirement with the bewildered old lady at Chelsea offered a sort of peace; but such wounds as her body and spirit had received could only be healed by a more active treatment. So thought Harriet Eastmond.

Harriet and Rosina had been at school together, and had renewed their friendship in London the previous winter. As the elder by two years, Harriet had always tended to add to the role of confidante that of counsellor. Where Rosina's first season had ended in disaster, her friend's had been happily crowned by marriage to Sir Henry Eastmond, an uneventful baronet of thirty with a good property in Lincolnshire, a stumbling manner, and a very large jaw. The bride, having seen and approved her new home, paid her wedding-visits, and accustomed herself to the embarrassing novelty of being addressed as Lady Eastmond, now descended on her friend at Chelsea.

She remained steadfastly loyal to Rosina; and was the more eager to be of use to her now, from a suspicion that she had neglected their friendship at a crucial time, when her advice might have prevented Miss Holdsworth's worst misjudgements. Lady Eastmond had then been much occupied with the matter of her own engagement, and could surely be forgiven her inattention—but she did not forgive herself, and was determined to repair the omission.

In spite of the several sympathetic letters she had received from Harriet during her reclusive summer at Chelsea, Rosina had scarcely been able to conceive even her best friend's remaining faithful to her. But the arrival of Lady Eastmond herself, all fondness, generosity and encouragement, left no room for doubt. And Lady Eastmond did not come to say cheering things and go away again. She had a plan in view. Rosina must not consider her life at an end. Rosina was going to begin it anew, and her old friend was going to help her.

The issue was not decided at once. Grateful though she was for Lady Eastmond's kindness, Rosina quailed at the idea of re-entering the inimical world. Her late experiences had left her a shrinking, stiff, withdrawn woman. Lady Eastmond, though careful not to reveal it, had been shocked at the change in her; but she would not allow this appearance to weaken her resolve.

The country: there lay Rosina's salvation. Good air and broad prospects would restore her health, while the limited society of a country neighbourhood, far from both the knowing sophistication of London and its painful associations, would gently reintroduce her to company, and assist her to a better opinion of herself. Such was Lady Eastmond's plan of campaign, and Osterby—the Lincolnshire seat of her compliant new husband—was to be the place. Rosina was to stay as long as she liked, to be sociable or be quiet, just as she liked; and she was to consider herself entirely under the protection of her friend, who would shield her against the remotest of slights, and bolster her wounded reputation with her own.

The doubts, the hesitations were not few; but they must have been much greater, to have withstood the persuasions of Lady Eastmond, commencing a long career of benevolent coercion; and at last the Eastmonds' travelling-coach bore the notorious Rosina Holdsworth north, to a destination wholly unfamiliar to her.

Osterby lay in the south-west of Lincolnshire, in a civilised country of flourishing brown soil, green water-meadows and low, wooded hills: the house stood commodious, neat and symmetrical as the drawing of a careful child, in a well-barbered park. Certainly this was a place for ease, for recuperation; and there were sufficient families in the district to permit a gentle immersion in company, without any danger of getting in over her head.

It was in this part of her friend's rehabilitation that Lady Eastmond found the least success at first. A hundred miles was no absolute bar to the spread of gossip and innuendo: if there was no hostility, there was a prurient curiosity of which Rosina, in her state of flayed self-consciousness, could not fail to be aware. Accordingly she shied away from all but the most unavoidable of company: took her walks as far as the next parish, but no further: was perforce present when her hosts gave a dinner, but could not be prevailed upon to dine out; and after six months at Osterby, though her health and to some extent her spirits were improved, she had only the most trifling acquaintance around the neighbourhood, and had exchanged her dubious reputation for the less exciting one of impenetrable reserve.

There was one exception: a ripening friendship scarcely remarked, because of the quietness of the parties, and the casual manner of their meeting. Sir Henry Eastmond was older than his years in many ways, particularly in his cultivating a rich crop of ailments. He had never found a satisfactory physician before the coming into the district of Dr Edmund Templeton, in whom he soon placed an abiding trust. Dr Templeton's house at Heystead being only five miles off, he was often at Osterby, sometimes to consult, sometimes simply to listen as a friend, and placate the baronet's anxious mind. Lady Eastmond soon learned to value and esteem their frequent visitor, in part for his relieving her of some portion of marital tedium, but also for his sound sense, talents, and amiable temper. It actually occurred to her that such a man ought to be married, before she noticed the increasing civility, the marks of mutual sympathy and regard, between Dr Templeton and

Miss Holdsworth; but once the two ideas were put together in Lady Eastmond's mind, there was room for nothing else.

To see her dear friend, after such a wretched passage in her life—and after such a loss of honour as even dauntless Lady Eastmond, in her secret heart, had feared must degrade her for ever—respectably and comfortably settled, with a man whose large views and generosity of mind inclined him to disregard her past, and whose steady, uneffusive character must offer her just the repose she needed: and to see her settled moreover close at hand in Lady Eastmond's own country—there could be nothing better. Lady Eastmond could admit no impediments.

To be sure there was the disparity of age—some fifteen years: but she was far from considering that a drawback. The recklessness of youth had already played such a baleful part in Rosina's life as must throw the discretion of maturity into the best possible light. More seriously, perhaps, there was an imbalance of attachment that even Lady Eastmond's optimism could not deny. It became clear to her that Dr Templeton, for all the grave restraint of his manner, was very much in love with Rosina; and quite as clear that Rosina loved him—that is, warmed to him, admired him, and felt able in his company to talk, laugh, and be herself again—without entirely being *in love*, as the term was generally understood. But this likewise Lady Eastmond refused to see as an insuperable obstacle. As she found an excuse once again to excuse herself from the drawing-room at Osterby where Rosina and Dr Templeton were deep in talk, she firmly believed that the match she was promoting was a good thing: good in itself, and not to be cheapened to the price of second-best. She saw opening a prospect of, at the very least, reasonable contentment for two people who deserved it; and the heartening change in Rosina from the pale, awkward, frosty figure who had first come here was reward in itself.

The interest aroused in the neighbourhood by Miss Holdsworth's arrival, and which had sunk so markedly when she did nothing shocking, was briefly revived by the news of her engagement to Dr Templeton of Heystead. Surprise was the general first reaction; but as no one likes to admit their failure of observation, the event was swiftly transformed into something that had been plain all along. One extreme wing of opinion said that a woman with such a history could only have come here to trap a man by the surest way: others, more moderate, reminded each other that town ladies could manage to put these things behind them, and that she was still after all a pretty young woman with a fair fortune—in that respect, quite a desirable match for Dr Templeton, past his youth and a little dry. The entering of Edmund Templeton and Rosina Holdsworth into blameless matrimony, very quietly at Heystead church, rendered the couple uninteresting once more. Lady Eastmond could congratulate herself on her success; and Heystead Priory, after a long interval, accustomed itself again to the chancy enterprise of a family.

For Lydia, thenceforth, the story became dimly and haltingly her own. The carefully collated historical figures of Edmund Templeton and Rosina Holdsworth became her parents, and

George's, and everything swarmed with the sharp yet scattered detail of memory. And as a child, of course, even a young girl, she had known little or nothing of what came before. She had always felt, perhaps, that there was something different about her mother, and when later her adult mind could receive the truth, by gentle steps, from her father and from Lady Eastmond, she had chiefly felt a sort of unsurprise. Her mother had never, for Lydia, been entirely present. Even at cheerful family occasions—Christmas, George coming home from school—she had seemed to perform her role with a faint constrained bewilderment, like a trusted governess or nurse called down to make up the numbers. Loving her and admiring her, still Lydia had always looked to her father as one looks instinctively at the clock: *that* must be right. That will tell me where I am.

Then when Lydia was ten her mother died: her illness was slow and yet swift: there seemed time only to register the oddness of her busy, frowning, twitching mother becoming the flat, solemnly watching woman in the bed before all was over. George, who was also present, seldom referred to this afterwards: Lydia never. Like her he learned the whole history in adulthood, and he had at last fortified himself with a short, round lesson: 'Sad business: horribly sad: and yet not, you know, because she met Father, and there was a good happy time before she was taken from us.'

Half concurring, Lydia envied him his wholeness of sentiment. She had reflected on the story time and time again—sadly, wryly, with worldly cynicism, with stern morality—but had never been able to reconcile all the things she thought and felt

86

about it. Which was not to say it had not affected her. She was prepared to admit, as she hugged her knees and blinked at the peopled darkness of her room, that it had affected her more than anything in her life.

But it was harder to admit how much she owed Lady Eastmond—because that meant admitting that the debt really ought to be paid.

CHAPTER SEVEN

'Oh, Lydia, I am glad you are come—I am so very concerned about Charlotte, and I know you will be truthful with me. Look.' Emma Paige thrust the shawled milky-smelling bundle into her friend's arms. 'Now look. The whites of her eyes—is there not a faint, a very faint yellowish tinge?'

'It must be very faint indeed. She looks to me the picture of health, and twice the size she was when I went away. And that, I believe,' said Lydia, as the baby gave her finger an experimental suck, 'is another tooth coming.'

'Where . . . So it is. Ah, now that explains a great deal. Dear, I only hope *she* will not begin biting, like Sophie. The other day she bit my sister, quite hard, and in public.'

'That shows sense, if not discretion. And so, where is Mrs Vawser? How long have you had her and, more importantly, when does she leave?'

'She is a—a little indisposed, so she is taking a late breakfast in her room. Oh! that reminds me— I forgot to ask the maid about Mrs Vawser's coddled egg.'

'Her coddled egg.'

'Yes—only I am afraid it was not quite soft enough for her yesterday, for it must be just right . . .' Rising, Emma turned. 'Lydia, what are you doing?'

Lydia had taken her pencil and tablets from her reticule, and was writing it down. 'There. Now, my dearest Emma, let me read it back to you. "Mrs Vawser's coddled egg . . . I am afraid it was not quite soft enough for her yesterday . . ." Shall I go on?'

'No, you tormenting creature. Perhaps I do fuss over her a little. And here *you* are—my dear Lydia, I have asked you nothing—how you are, and your brother in London and the children—'

'Ah, Miss Templeton!' The Reverend Mr Paige burst in like a draught. 'I thought I heard your voice. You must pardon me for intruding upon your tête-à-tête.' He pronounced the French with breezy condescension, as if quoting baby language. 'You must pardon me also for paying my *very* brief respects to you as I am on my way to an urgent parish visit.' He bowed. 'Ma'am, your servant: I hope I find you well, likewise your excellent father: your family in London also. They flourish, I hope?'

'Yes, thank you, Mr Paige: I was very glad to see them, and I am glad to see old friends again. And as I was about to say to Emma, I bear an invitation: my father would be very happy if you were able to dine with us at the Priory tomorrow. Your guest Mrs Vawser also, of course.' Lydia glanced sidelong at Emma, who gave a grimace of thankfulness.

'Tomorrow, ma'am, certainly—we have, my dear, I believe, no engagements; and indeed it would be hard to think of one that could not be willingly put aside to enjoy the hospitality of Dr Templeton. And that of Miss Templeton, of course, our excellent hostess upon such occasions.' He gave another of his crisp bows. Mr Paige was full of these pointless punctilios, which left you floundering for a response. He was a robust, unresting man with a round, sleek head and a perpetual close-lipped smile—not of cheer but a sort of professional assertion, as if defying anyone to be impiously miserable. 'If I may venture to say so, Miss Templeton—in my pastoral capacity, call it—I do not think you in your best looks. I believe I have the reason. London. The air of the modern Babylon is not conducive to health. This is, I suspect,' he added, with a significant nod at his wife, 'the source of poor Mrs Vawser's trouble. Miss Templeton, I have not, I hope, offended: I speak from solicitude: and in the absolute confidence that country air will effect a swift restoration.'

As so often with Mr Paige, there seemed no appropriate reply, beyond diving under the table, or bursting into song: so Lydia made do with thanking him.

'I wonder, Miss Templeton,' he went on, slapping his gloves against his potent thighs before putting them thrustfully on, 'did you observe, during your late stay in the metropolis, much evidence among the populace of continued disaffection—of a rebellious and insubordinate temper?—But of course I cannot stay to give your answer the attention it merits: you must tell me at dinner tomorrow: till that time I am full of anticipation.'

'What am I to say?' Lydia protested, when he had whisked out. 'After all I am disaffected, rebellious and insubordinate myself.'

'Hush,' Emma said, listening for the boom of the front door, 'you know Mr Paige does not care for that sort of jesting.'

Mr Paige did not care for any kind of jesting—alas for him, and still more alas for his wife, Lydia thought.

It was nine years ago that the young vicar of Heystead, as energetic a huntsman as a moral reformer, had gone in quest of a bride, and brought back from his own county of Kent his pretty, kind-eyed, neat-figured quarry; and in the course of their friendship since then, Lydia had seen Emma Paige grow each year more worn—or, rather, more smudged and indeterminate, like one of Lydia's own drawings when she could not leave it alone. Besides being wife to an exhaustingly dutiful clergyman and bearing his over-frequent children Emma had also taken on the burden of Mr Paige's elderly mother, bedridden and, it was reliably reported, mad as Ajax. If questioned on the matter, of course, Emma would have said with painted sincerity that her life was supremely happy. Lydia would have rejoined, silently, that her friend's contentment was that of the prisoner who has forgotten what the world beyond his cell is like.

'Well, now tell me of your sister,' Lydia said, as Mr Paige's unstoppable figure passed the parlour window. 'Is it the London air—or is it the old trouble?'

Her husband being gone, Emma permitted herself a sigh. 'The latter. Good Lord, I have never said "the latter" before—you only read it in books and even then I always have to look back to see which was the former and the latter—and now I can't remember what came first—'

'Never mind: I can tell it is the old story. And suspecting that it is proving somewhat tedious, my father hopes that a dinner at the Priory will help, at least for one evening. I think we can only muster eight: but eight may take the *edge* off Mrs Vawser, I hope.'

'I confess she has been a *little* trying this time. But that, you know, is her grief: poor Penelope has been sorely misused again!'

'Let me see, wasn't it an actress last time?'

'Of a sort. A tightrope-dancer, from Sadler's Wells. Though apparently it seems she was very handsome.'

'Especially in tights.'

'After that, you know, Mr Vawser made the solemnest of promises to my sister—she would not have returned to him otherwise—and that is why she is so very desolated now it has happened again. This time—' Emma lowered her voice '—it is a Frenchwoman who makes papier mâché.'

'Good Lord, does he consult a directory of curious trades whenever he feels his appetite grow jaded? I hardly know which is the greater marvel—his tastes, or his wife's forbearance.'

'This is the fourth time, to my certain knowledge,' said Emma, sadly, 'and still she will go back to him. Of course, my dear Lydia, you understand that I speak in confidence—even excluding parties very near at home, if you understand me.'

'Mr Paige still does not know why your sister periodically descends on you?'

'I maintain the fiction of her health requiring a cure in the country—which Mr Paige, as you saw, is very ready to believe. Normally I would never countenance falsehood—' Emma winced in apology '—but Mr Paige is strict in some of his views.'

'Ah.' Meaning that in such a case Mr Paige would always blame the wife, who must have brought her troubles on herself by lack of that proper submission, domestic competence, and diligent exercise of feminine charm, which must always prevent a man straying.

'I think,' Emma resumed, 'she is a little improved in spirits. She will eat, sometimes, and she does not give that alarming laugh quite so much. The first fornight,' she added, with an inward look and a reminiscent shudder, 'was the worst.'

Lydia could only press her hand in reply. The trouble was that no amount of female solidarity could get over the fact Penelope Vawser was an intolerable woman.

'And now that's about enough of me, I think,' Emma said, with a timid, tender look. 'My dear Lydia, Mr Paige expressed himself rather baldly, perhaps—but I must confess you seem just a little pale. I do hope you are in health.'

'Oh, I slept poorly, that is all—missing the nocturnal sounds of London, no doubt. There is no lullaby like the rattle of the night-soil cart, and three drunken men having a fight beneath your window . . .'

No, Lydia thought, coming away from the vicarage, I have no ordinary indisposition: no ague or fever. Only an inflammation of the conscience—

most wretched of afflictions. Oh to be an Emma Paige, whose conscience was as superbly developed as a coal-heaver's muscles. Instead, Lydia felt, she had a weak, susceptible one, which would not function without careful treatment. The moral equivalent of a liver complaint.

And yet I don't ask for much, she thought—only to do just what I like, and still have people think well of me. But the ghosts of last night were not impressed by this levity, and fixed on her the same stare of reproach.

At the Priory an old, square, heavy, unfashionable carriage, like a great trunk on wheels, stood before the leaded porch. Though its owner seldom used it, she recognised it at once and with an emotional sip of vinegary anticipation. As Mr Lewis Durrant made it a rule to think poorly of her in any case, there would be a kind of paradoxical relief in his needling presence. Besides, she had her encounter with Hugh Hanley to tell him about: and the passing on of unwelcome news is always refreshing.

The summer parlour was stony-cool as a buttery despite the bars of strong sunlight thrown by the great oriel window. Dr Templeton, sitting at ease in his Windsor-chair, appeared small as a benevolent gnome beside his companion. Mr Lewis Durrant, not at all at ease, stood before the fireplace in all his overpowering and somehow unnecessary height: one booted foot tapping restlessly at the fender, arms crossed, one hand gripping his hat—for it was his idiosyncrasy, or, Lydia thought, his affectation, never to look settled but always on the point of leaving.

'Ah, my dear, I hope you found Mrs Paige well.

Here is another old friend to welcome you back, you see.'

Mr Durrant uncoiled himself sufficiently to deliver a short bow. 'Miss Templeton. I trust you had a pleasant stay in town.'

'More than pleasant, thank you, Mr Durrant. The Thames is still gently smoking from my presence.'

'Mr Durrant and I were just talking of the new income-tax, my dear; and I was wondering what George makes of it.'

'He groans over it, but will not hear anyone else do so, because it is Mr Pitt's measure and he venerates Mr Pitt—almost as much as you detest him, Mr Durrant.'

'Violently dislike,' he grunted, 'not detest.'

'Aren't they the same? Oh—is that the new *Universal Review*?'

'The carrier just brought it,' her father said, with a wry smile, 'and you will find, my dear, that your contribution to the debate on the new translation of Horace has produced a lively response.'

Lydia, with her greedy appetite for things of the mind, had long acted as willing amanuensis to her father in his scholarly researches; and with his initial encouragement, and later under her own volition, she had explored other avenues of learning with fascination. She was rare among women in knowing Latin: the headmistress of the Young Ladies' Academy at Fulham, when she discovered that Miss Templeton was learning such a thing from her father, had recoiled as from an impropriety.

Horace was a favourite; and lately an aristocratic gentleman of letters had produced,

94

with much puffing in the periodicals, a new translation of the *Odes*, on which Lydia had seized with interest, and then disbelief. Turning them into rhyming couplets seemed a dubious enterprise from the start: but when the verse had all the smoothness and ease of a higgler's cart traversing cobbles, she could not help but protest. In a critique sent to the last *Universal Review* she had suggested, quite temperately, she thought, that the translator was a pedantic dilettante with a tin ear, signing herself *Canidia*. The unequivocally female pseudonym, she now saw, had sealed her doom. Reading the rebuttal, and knowing that Mr Durrant was watching her, she strove to present a face of calm, detached amusement; but it was difficult.

'Your nostrils are flaring, Miss Templeton,' he observed.

'A spirited response, but full of inaccuracies, I thought,' her father said.

'Please, Miss Templeton, do read it out,' Mr Durrant said.

'Oh, I won't weary you with it, it is very long.'

'A judicious selection, then.'

She glared at him, then back at the journal. 'Well, here is the anonymous gentleman's peroration. "Canidia would do better to confine her attentions to her proper sphere—the domestic: the only regularity of measure that should concern her is the quiet music of the turning spinning-wheel, the only rhymes those lisped by children at the knee of their mother, who will be much more reverenced as the cheerful goddess of home than the shrieking priestess of petticoat learning."'

'Strongly put,' Mr Durrant said, his jaws

95

working. 'Though I should have to hear it again to judge properly.'

'Hey, well, written no doubt by some place-seeker, hoping the honourable poetaster will do something for him,' Lydia said. She meant to toss the journal back on to the table with a light, gay carelessness, but some freakish strength must have got into her arm, and it landed with a broad, even buttocky slap.

'Canidia,' said Mr Durrant, after a moment, stroking his chin. 'Yes, the lover of Horace, I see. But did he not end up by calling her an old witch?'

'Once she had deserted him, yes. It is remarkable how, when a woman refuses a man, the scales at once fall from his eyes, and he sees what a harridan he has been swearing love to,' Lydia said, seating herself on the oak settle.

'And thanks his stars for his escape. Quite.'

'Canidia is alluded to as a sorceress who could bring the moon from the heavens,' Dr Templeton rumbled, 'and there may be a hidden theme of woman going dangerously beyond what were perceived to be the prescribed limits of her nature.'

'Sorceress, or enchantress, when they love us,' Lydia sighed, 'and witch when they do not. Mr Durrant, I saw your carriage outside. This is not like you. Usually you ride from Culverton, or walk, if the weather is sufficiently bad for you to make a virtue of it. Pray, do not begin adopting infirm habits. You will only excite Mr Hanley further.'

'Dr Templeton was just telling me you ran into him in town,' Mr Durrant said, with his most bleak and mordant look. 'Well, and how was the little coxcomb? As arrant a fool as ever?'

'Too well grown to be *little*; but much affected to the dandy, certainly. He was eager that I bring back to you the full report of his delinquency, as he called it—in that delightfully jesting way of his, you know.'

Mr Durrant frowned—though on his face this was not so much a discernible change as a slight intensification of his normal expression. As a young man he had been handsome, if in a rather gaunt, forbidding way: at thirty-eight, the forbidding gauntness stood chiefly to the fore. His figure was still good, his hair, uncropped, was no less black and thick—but the light in his uncomfortably pale eyes was harsh; and the lines of humour about his mouth, which Lydia had once found (perhaps, possibly, potentially) worth loving, appeared set into a saturnine stubbornness.

'Hugh will always be little to me,' he rapped out. 'I suppose he bragged of his latest idiocy—this commission in the Prince of Wales's Own.'

'Shockingly expensive, I know.'

'Hm. But in a way suitable enough: a fool should be guarded by fools, after all.'

'Fie, Mr Durrant, spoken like a Tory. Has infirmity driven out the Radical in you?'

He contemplated her with a sour absence of pleasure. 'I hope I shall never speak like a man of any party. The Prince is a vain fool: his royal father better only in lacking vanity. As for my nephew, he combines both failings with a hundred others.'

'He is very young, my dear sir,' suggested Dr Templeton.

'So he is: and so is John Carr, who has the care of all my vegetable gardens and fruit trees, understands every detail of horticulture, keeps an excellent record-book, and talks ten times more sensibly than Hugh Hanley. Stupidity is not a necessary part of youth: though it does tend to thrive there, like fungus in a cellar.'

'But, Mr Durrant, this, I am afraid, is just the sort of thing Hugh Hanley likes,' Lydia said, straying partway into seriousness. 'I believe half the motive for his extravagances is the relish of knowing how they will infuriate you.'

'Yes—he enjoys it: I know that,' he rejoined, very stiff. 'Well, let him enjoy. This may be the last satisfaction he shall receive from me.'

Dr Templeton cocked his head. 'My dear sir, you have dropped a hint before to this effect, and my curiosity is thoroughly whetted. Do you mean there exists some way of barring him from the inheritance of Culverton?'

'Not as it stands.' Mr Durrant stalked to the window, his profile all bony disquiet. He cleared his throat. 'I have a friend.'

'That in itself is certainly remarkable,' Lydia could not help saying, 'though I am not sure how to respond to the unlikely news: whether to congratulate you, or commiserate with him.'

'I have a friend,' he continued, addressing himself entirely to Dr Templeton, 'lately settled at Clifton. Of my own age—we were at Cambridge together; and of my own sentiments. He has married: and he invites me to visit him and his bride at any time I choose. For all this strange lapse—as I first thought of it—my friend seems by the evidence of his letters still the sensible, rational creature I knew, perhaps because he has fixed upon a woman of like mind; and perhaps also because the fatal contract has been made at a later period than is common. He enjoys, it seems, domestic comfort, and expects to be a father; and in short, I am interested.'

'Ah!' said Dr Templeton, on a long bass note, full of subtle harmonics of understanding.

Lydia could hardly contain herself. 'Mr Durrant, you don't intend to follow your friend's example? Merely out of spite towards your nephew?'

'Not spite: irreconcilable loathing: and they are not the same, Miss Templeton, before you say it. I intend nothing, as yet. But I admire my friend's way of proceeding. Conscious of his solitary state, and wishing to amend it, he made the matter *known*, without a lot of coquetting and nonsense. He went to Bath, and entered what is quite reasonably termed the marriage market; and emerged comfortably accommodated. Knowing my peculiar difficulties, he suggests that I might do the same. Clifton is near enough at hand to Bath so that he might give me introductions to the company there, and so on. I have never liked these trifling resorts of pleasure; but they do appear different, in the light of utility.'

'Papa,' Lydia said, 'I know it is a bright spring day, but let us have a fire built at once—I was never so cold in my life. Though in truth the chill you have given me, Mr Durrant, is rather invigorating. I must have it right: you, of all people—going to Bath, of all places—'

'I have been to a great many places in my life, Miss Templeton, though nowadays I prefer to stay at home: why do you seize on Bath so?'

Lydia disguised, she thought, her hesitation very well. 'Because, sir, it is surely what you call it: a trifling resort of pleasure—the last thing I had supposed you susceptible to. And actually to go there like a—I will not say a prize bull, but pretty well with a sign slung about your neck, advertising your availability: I cannot believe it. Which is not to say I would not like to see it. Indeed, I could almost wish to spend the summer in Bath after all, for such an entertainment.'

'You in Bath? What do you mean?' Mr Durrant said sharply. 'Are you ill? You don't look it, particularly.'

'Oh, your honeyed compliments,' Lydia said: flourishing the flippancy quickly across her grubby discomfort.

'You know, of course, Lydia's godmother, Lady Eastmond of Osterby,' her father explained. 'She has lately a young woman, a ward, come into her care; and there was a suggestion, no more, that Lydia might perhaps be the young lady's companion for a short stay at Bath.'

'I see,' was all Mr Durrant said; but he directed at Lydia his first full look since her arrival.

'I detect in your project, my dear sir,' Dr Templeton said, with considering interest, 'a sort of dual aim, if I may so phrase it. There is on the one hand the actual procurement of a wife, a mistress of Culverton, and in time a direct heir who would cut Mr Hanley out altogether: and on the other hand there is the possibility that you *might* do this—the alarming hint to your nephew that he should not so blatantly depend upon his future fortune, and would do well to mend his ways to prevent it. Do I have you right?'

Lewis Durrant smiled, or rather showed his teeth. 'I knew you would grasp it, sir. The fact is, the boy has traded on his expectations for too long: I am come to the end of my patience: it must be decided. And as I am not quite an old man, *nor* infirm, then I may yet surprise him. But first I am going to see his mother—that poor deluded sister of mine, who thinks she whelped an angel. I doubt I can persuade her to rein him in, so late in the day, but I shall try, one last time; and she shall know that this *is* the last time. If nothing else, besides, she can tell me the sum of all the other debts he has been running up on my account. Hence, Miss Templeton, the carriage. I go from here to Melton Mowbray, to learn the worst.'

'There can be no better place to learn it. But wait, Mr Durrant—' Lydia glanced at her father '—are you not engaged to dine with us tomorrow?'

'I am, and will do so: I shall spend only tonight under my sister's roof, which is as much as any man can tolerate, and return tomorrow early. You do not expect a large company?'

'We do not: but consider, Mr Durrant, this aversion of yours to society will not do in Bath. Imagine thirty or forty people in the Assembly Rooms, or Sydney Gardens: how will you contrive to ignore them all? How will you get by with a single grunt every half an hour?'

'It is a consideration, sir,' Dr Templeton smiled, 'that rather wearisome etiquette of watering-places. Still, I like your plan. You know I am a friend to marriage, where there is sound and solid attachment; and anyone who knows Culverton must wish to see the family of Durrant continue there. My acquaintance with Mr Hanley has not been extensive, but he does seem to think a great deal of what is due to himself, and little of what is due to others. I fear, indeed, that whatever the outcome, such a temper will lead him to unhappiness.'

'You speak like yourself, sir, in taking thought for the fellow's future: I honour you for it. But I am selfish,' Mr Durrant said. 'I don't care about Hugh Hanley, or what becomes of him—except that he will bring Culverton to ruin, and all who depend on it. I don't like this aristocratic conception of debts, as if they were only another fashionable amusement. An unpaid debt does not mean you are a fine fellow: it means the tradesman who sewed your coat, or built your carriage, doesn't get his money for it, and can't feed his family.'

Lydia—as so often with Mr Durrant—was precisely divided between agreement with what he said, and disgust at the arrogance with which he said it: emotionally the effect was like one of those sneezes that do not quite come.

'But what *would* make you relent towards him, Mr Durrant?' she asked. 'Supposing he were to undertake solemnly to mend his ways—what evidence would you require? What would satisfy you? Fasting, hair-shirts . . . ?'

'Perfection,' he snapped, 'only perfection, Miss Templeton, will ever satisfy me.'

'Dear me,' chuckled Dr Templeton, 'is this not, Mr Durrant, deliberately to court disappointment?'

'Quite so: and as disappointment is the inevitable result of life, better to seek it out than wait tamely for it to come to you.' Abruptly Mr Durrant shook Dr Templeton's hand, bowed in Lydia's approximate direction, and was gone.

'Well, well,' Dr Templeton said, 'what do you think, my dear?'

'I think Lady Eastmond's ward should dispense at once with her suitors,' Lydia said, 'as there is coming to Bath a gentleman who is sure to put them in the shade, with his elegance of address, his romantic sentiments, and his cheerful temper.'

'Ah, who knows? You like to be severe on him, but our friend has much to recommend him still. Stranger things have happened.' He smiled mildly on her. 'It is a pity, my dear, that you will not be there to make the introduction.'

'What shall we give our guests tomorrow, Papa? Do we have saddle of mutton?'

CHAPTER EIGHT

Dinner at Heystead: preparations. In the kitchen, hasty contrivances: the mutton good but scanty, requiring the supplement of boiled fowls. Thought to be given on the matter of stable-room—who would come by carriage, who ride—and on who would need to be fetched. Being a hostess was a trivial thing to like, perhaps, but Lydia did like it: she liked to dress well for the occasion, to see the table well ordered and supplied, to minister to the little habits and whims of her guests.

Besides, all this helped to suppress the thought of the letter that had arrived, that day, from London, with the direction in Lady Eastmond's boisterous hand. Helped, a little.

First to arrive were the vicarage party: Mr Paige all aggressive compliment, Emma looking prettily tired, and on her arm the reason for her dark-ringed eyes, her sister Mrs Vawser. Here, at any rate, was a person to drive out niggling thoughts; for no one was ever allowed to forget that Penelope Vawser was present. When she was not in spirits, her muffled mumble, paralytic gait and petrifying stare suggested some ancient prophetess stricken by the certainty of doom. When she was in spirits, her eager laugh rattled the windows, and she overpowered with her vivacity and playfulness. She was a tall, fair, full-figured young woman who, if her face had ever been allowed to relapse into a natural expression, might have been accounted very handsome. Today she was in flourishing form; and her low-bosomed evening-gown of silver gauze, drop-earrings and ostrich-plume headdress announced her intention of bringing a little fashion into the lives of these country mice.

Soon followed Mr Shipley, her father's friend, land-agent and lawyer, from Bourne: a rotund, convivial little man with a mirthful weakness for the absurd: then, not at all inclined to mirth, Miss Beaumont—who had, it was true, very little occasion for it.

Twenty-five years ago she had been the accredited beauty of the district, indulged by a father with an East India fortune, and with eligible gentlemen at her feet. But the fortune was lost in speculation, and the father shot himself: the eligible gentlemen got up from her feet and went away: the tiger-skinned mansion was sold, and Miss Beaumont had retired to a small house on the edge of Heystead, there to take responsibility for a brother whose youthful eccentricity had reached the threshold of outright madness. Now she had few pleasures except the exercise of a sharp tongue and a censorious temper: she had become, in fact, the living caricature of the dry spinster. Lydia made every allowance, but could never be easy with her; partly because she suspected that in Miss Beaumont she herself ought to behold an Awful Lesson.

Mr Lewis Durrant completed the party. He looked very well in the evening clothes he despised; but in Lydia's eyes he scarcely troubled to conceal the fact that he came here only out of respect for Dr Templeton, and otherwise considered the evening as merely something to be got through. Yet these old vexations with his manner were familiar enough to be disregarded, beside her still wonderfully fresh and tart delight in his scheme of wife-hunting. Nothing could mar the amusement it afforded her to think of it—of Lewis Durrant transporting his grim looks, curt speech, and hardened carapace of self-opinion to the ballroom and the circulating-library. (Nothing, that is, except the name of the town where this delirious scene might take place—and Lady Eastmond's letter had reminded her sufficiently of that.) She greatly looked forward to tormenting him a little more about it—and likewise to learning what had happened at Melton Mowbray.

There on a very moderate income lived his elder sister Mrs Hanley, the relic of a clergyman who six years ago had done the only noteworthy thing in his life, by dying; leaving fatherless not only Hugh but three young daughters. That this female household was ruled by only two ideas—that Hugh was a picture of perfection, and that their rich uncle Durrant must always do something handsome for the family—Lydia had gathered only from Mr Durrant's own jaundiced account; but she found it believable, and was much interested to know the result of the momentous meeting.

No chance of that for now, however. Mr Durrant's attention was monopolised as soon as he entered the drawing-room by Mrs Vawser.

Though everyone except the obtuse Mr Paige knew her marriage to be ruinously unhappy, still she made much of her status as a married woman. She exhibited a vast condescension to those unfortunate females—like Lydia—who had reached and passed the age of discretion without acquiring a husband; and she liked to indulge in the sort of arch, showy flirtation with gentlemen that in a single woman would have been reproved as fast, and that gave her the opportunity to be splendid, fascinating, and so forth. Lydia's general attention to the comforts of her guests allowed her to lend only half an ear to Mrs Vawser's efforts to captivate Lewis Durrant; but a screech of 'Oh, sir, I see you are *determined* to play the rogue with me!' and Mr Durrant's look of mingled scorn, amazement, and titanic gloom gave her a fair idea of its progress.

She was glad, as they took their seats at dinner, that her father had congenial company in Mr Shipley on his left, and Emma on his right; but she was less happily accommodated. Mr Durrant was on her right, but he naturally had Mrs Vawser at his other side—no more capable of being ignored, even by him, than a pillar of flame. Lydia's other companion was Mr Paige, all ready to make good his threat of discussing with her the state of the nation.

He had scarcely begun on the poor, however, when he was obliged to turn to Miss Beaumont on his left. She had much to tell, and complain of, in the insolence of servants and labourers, which she put down entirely to the French example and freethinking. Here was Mr Paige's subject: Lydia was free of him throughout the soup, fish and oyster-sauce, and could observe Mrs Vawser's campaign against her neighbour.

'But to be sure, though we are newly *acquainted*, I have always *heard* of you, when I have visited my sister,' she cried. 'Oh, yes: Mr Durrant of Culverton—everyone must know *him*—he is the one who will go a whole week without speaking.'

'You are mistaken, madam: sometimes I go a fortnight.'

'I like your style of joking excessively! I dare say you have picked it up in town: it is not the sort of thing that suits a country neighbourhood— charming though Heystead *is*, and indeed I will not hear a word said against it. As far as the country *goes*, I contend there is no sweeter spot anywhere: I often tell my sister so: no, anyone who would disparage Heystead must first deal with me.' Mrs Vawser gave a laugh—so enormous and purposeful that she might have been demonstrating to some curious denizen of another world, where laughter was unknown, exactly what it was. 'Oh, dear, yes, they would first have to deal with *me*, and that, you know, is no matter for the faint-heart.'

Mr Durrant murmured that he had not a doubt of that; and helped her to the sole with as much discriminating care as if there were poison in certain parts of it.

'But I always maintain that there is country—

and there is town,' she resumed, using her two hands to illustrate this difficult concept. 'There is a distinction, as I need not remind *you*, that is defining—that is essential. Whenever *you* are in town—'

'You must pardon me, I never go to London unless I can help it.'

'Oh, dear me, Mr Durrant, upon my word that I cannot believe. This is more of your joking, but you won't catch me out with it—oho, you must bait a better hook than that to catch me . . .' She embarked on the laugh again: but as Mr Durrant only went on eating, she looked over at Lydia. 'Come, then, let us refer the question to Miss Templeton. *She*, I am sure, will know: she must be *au fait* with all the little gossip of the neighbourhood—when precisely Mr Durrant is at Culverton, and when in town, what day he returned, and what his conveyance—'

'You credit me with a knowledge, and above all an interest, that I do not possess,' Lydia said placidly. 'But I can say, knowing Mr Durrant as an old neighbour and acquaintance, that he seldom goes to London.'

'Ah, but then you are so attached to Culverton—are you not, sir? Is that not it? Everyone knows of Mr Durrant's attachment to Culverton and no one wonders at it—if they were to wonder at anything, it would be his spending any time in town at all—I am sure *I* should wonder at it if he did—and I have never yet been to Culverton myself.' Mrs Vawser having shifted her ground so swiftly and completely, proceeded to dig herself in. 'It is a great matter of wonder to me why a person who is so admirably situated as you are at Culverton, sir,

108

should ever be supposed to wish a removal to London, even for a little time in the year: who *could* wish it? No, no: they would have to deal with *me*, before proposing such a self-evident piece of nonsense.'

The removal of the first course interrupted, though it did not entirely stop, Mrs Vawser's tireless waving of the flag of personality. She could still subject Mr Durrant to glances, glances away, and sharp suppressions of hilarity accompanied by slaps with her handkerchief: to all of which Mr Durrant presented the same look of a man being turned slowly into stone, and welcoming it. Little observant Mr Shipley, primed with wine, was already beginning to quiver under his tight waistcoat, and might soon be emitting his uncontrollable giggle. Sobriety was restored by Miss Beaumont, reverting to her favourite topic of the impudence of servants, and wondering aloud how it was that they lived so long when they were always complaining of their poverty.

'There is a tiresome old creature, who was one of my father's maids, still living at Ingoldsby: I do what I can for her, as one must: but what is offered as kindness is received as if it were obligation. Yet she must be seventy if a day and, believe me, enjoying such health and vigour as I would be glad of. Really I suspect she will outlive me.'

'Our earthly lot is scriptural,' announced Mr Paige, automatically: and then, considering: 'But there is a robustness about that class of people, to be sure, ma'am: perhaps length of years may be a providential recompense, for their lives do not have much to trouble or concern them; they are given in large measure what they could never appreciate in little.'

'They appreciate nothing,' contended Miss Beaumont, with her fiercest face.

'The bestowal of years is indeed a question for the moralist,' said Lydia. 'There are so many people whose early loss is mourned: and yet so many, Miss Beaumont, whose existence seems to persist long after it is wanted or justified.'

'As I have lately had cause to remark,' put in Dr Templeton, peaceably, 'human longevity is a great preoccupation of ours—and yet one that has a finite solution. However long we live—as earthly creatures, that is—' with a bow to Mr Paige, bristling '—the term must end. Indeed it is an engaging philosophical consideration, that in sixty or seventy years—' he smiled '—all of us gathered here will be in the grave.'

'Not all in the same one, I hope,' muttered Mr Durrant: while Mr Shipley made a suppressed noise like a mouse being strangled.

'But is it not the case,' said Emma, looking perturbed, 'that we look to a longer future in the lives of our children? I'm sure when I look at my little ones—'

'Quite true,' Lydia put in quickly, suspecting that her father, in his zealous objectivity, would cheerfully remark that they would eventually die too. 'That is a consideration. And reminds me, Miss Beaumont, that I was lately with my brother and his family; and George especially asked to be remembered to you, and to present his compliments.' George had done no such thing, but he might have if he had thought of it.

'Mr George Templeton is very good,' Miss Beaumont said, with the faintest warming of

110

severity. 'I suppose, sir, they will be coming here at the end of the summer?'

'Such is my happy expectation,' Dr Templeton said, as the mutton and fowls were brought in.

'It must be a great comfort to you, my dear Dr Templeton, having a son married, and respectably settled,' cried Mrs Vawser. 'I may have mentioned to you before Mr Vawser's cousins, the Randals—the Randals of Holme Park, you know, in Hertfordshire: we were there last Christmas: quite the sweetest country spot I ever saw—'

'I thought that was Heystead,' said Mr Durrant to his wine-glass.

'Tut—you see how this beau of mine rallies me! I shall attend to your nonsense in a moment, sir. I was talking of the Randals of Holme Park— excellent people—taste, elegance, yet nothing of affectation, which I detest above all things—I yield to no one in my absolute dislike of affectation. *He* is the most sensible, well-bred man: and *she* is all that is amiable, and one would never guess that she is near fifty. Yet it is their misfortune to have two grown children still about the place—a boy and a girl, I was going to say, but they must both be past twenty-five—great awkward things, showing no inclination to make a proper match, or do anything for themselves! I do pity the Randals excessively, for *they* have spared no effort in seeking an establishment for their children. It seems so very unnatural!'

'Well, now, I have observed from studying estate and parish records at Heystead that a later age of marriage has become more prevalent in the last hundred and fifty years or so,' Dr Templeton said thoughtfully. 'This may reflect various changes: the

111

decline of marriages absolutely arranged by the parents, for example, in favour of free choice.'

'The tendency to late marriages may reflect nothing more than the growth of sense,' Lewis Durrant said. 'At twenty-one, a man seldom knows what he is doing, or where his best interests lie.'

'I am glad you say *a man*, Mr Durrant, and exempt woman from this youthful imbecility,' Lydia said.

'I do: a woman's imbecility is not dependent on youth: it flourishes at all ages.'

'You *are* a provoking creature,' exclaimed Mrs Vawser, returning to the attack, 'trying to tease me so! But you won't win, you know—I shall give as good as I get, I assure you! I have not half done with you! Now, what were we talking of?'

'Death,' said Mr Durrant, with a face suitable to the word.

'Before that, monster. It was Culverton: we were talking of your heavenly place at Culverton, and you were telling me about it, or you were just going to.'

'You were kind enough to suggest, madam, that everyone knew about Culverton: so I will not weary you with repetition.'

'But then *I* have not seen it—and I take nothing, you know, on trust. Dear me no!—I cannot help but laugh, for there are a good many friends of mine who would absolutely stare at the notion of my taking anything on trust. "Not Penelope Vawser," they would say. I assure you I have heard them say it. "I will not believe it," they say, "until I have it from Penelope Vawser's own lips, for she takes nothing on trust." That is the way I am, I'm afraid, Mr Durrant: you will not change me!'

It was plain that Mr Durrant's interest in changing Mrs Vawser, except perhaps into a toad, could not have been less: so he merely helped her to the mutton.

'You, of course, Miss Templeton, will have seen Culverton,' she went on. 'In a country district everything of course is known, and talked over a hundred times, for want of anything else. But you must allow for the curiosity of the visitor. Now I remember my sister saying it is not very far off— but exactly *how* far off, Mr Durrant, is the question that must be settled, before we make a plan.'

Mr Durrant looked so chillingly appalled at the word 'plan' that Lydia felt she had better answer for him. 'Culverton House is about eight miles north of here, by the Sleaford road.'

'Ah! and a very good road, I dare say, if it leads to dear Culverton,' Mrs Vawser said, with a sentimental look. 'And I dare say many pretty views along the way—my sister tells me it is only to the west that the country grows rather flat and dismal.'

'Even the flatter parts hereabouts do not lack beauties,' Mr Durrant said, pricked by local pride into speech. 'But Culverton lies, yes, among the gentle slopes, in a fine country.'

'Then really, you need persuade me no more— nothing could be pleasanter, now that the weather has turned at last, especially as you have such beautiful grounds there—everyone says so. Yes, an expedition to Culverton it must be,' said Mrs Vawser, with satisfaction; and then, loudly to her sister: 'Emma, my dearest, do you hear? We are to make an expedition to Culverton House— Mr Durrant invites us—it is all settled.'

Though no such offer had been made, Mr

113

Durrant could hardly say so, at least without disrespect to Mrs Paige—which, to do him justice, he would never show. To Lydia's silent amusement, he must make the best of it: though hope flickered in his eyes, as Mrs Vawser addressed the practicalities of the scheme.

'But how are we to get there? And who is to be of the party? Here, have I been running on, in the way I do, without stopping to think of these things! Dear me!—my friends would laugh, they assuredly would, for that is always my way. For of course a party there must be. I cannot go anywhere, of course, without Emma—' her voice became low and confiding as she leaned towards Mr Durrant '—not merely because I am a visitor here, but because she would feel dreadfully left out: she does attach herself to me so. You, Miss Templeton, will surely be a third, for your time must be absolutely at your disposal. And then perhaps Dr Templeton—I do think it a great pity that he stirs so little, and if only—'

'Dr Templeton does as he chooses, and requires no one's pity,' Mr Durrant said coolly.

'Oh! very well—you shocking bear, you—then Miss Beaumont perhaps, whose position one must *surely* pity. Here are four already: how are they to be conveyed? For Mr Paige keeps no carriage.'

This was true, though he had lately been talking of setting one up, probably for the pleasure of denying himself the use of it on the sabbath. Dr Templeton kept a gig that seated Lydia and himself comfortably, but no more. Mr Durrant sighed at the inescapable conclusion. 'Of course my own carriage is at your disposal.'

'Oh, Mr Durrant, that is excessively obliging of

114

you. Do you hear, Miss Templeton? This shocking bear is actually going to bring his own carriage for us. What do you drive, Mr Durrant?'

'Drive, madam, I drive nothing. I have a travelling-coach.'

'Oh, but you don't mean a closed carriage— Lord, what is the good of that, when we wish to enjoy the fine weather, and take in the sweet views? You must have something else in your coach-house, something light and open. You are a bachelor after all: every bachelor keeps his tilbury or curricle.'

'Bachelor I may be, but feather-headed coxcomb I am not.'

'Oh, come, I don't mean one of those fragile high-perch affairs: to be sure, that would never do in a rough country. But a barouche, now—that is the very thing. Every woman loves to make an exploration in a barouche: every man shows to advantage driving a barouche. You cannot do better, Mr Durrant, than to set up a barouche: I can recommend a very good coach-builder—in London, to be sure, but—'

'I have no thought of a barouche, or any such contraption. I pay my coachman a good wage for doing what he is good at, which is driving. I see no reason for alteration.'

'Why,' Lydia said, 'if you drove, you could show yourself a good hand at the ribbons.'

He stared at her for a moment as if she had dropped into Hebrew: then burst out laughing, for the first time since his arrival. Laughter made him look very much younger, which was perhaps why he avoided it.

'Good God, yes—and a *famous whip* too, no

115

doubt. Was there ever such idiotic nonsense talked?'

'I take it you don't wish to be thought a great swell, then.'

'Swell. So much for the language of Shakespeare and Milton. At the first sign of my swelling, Miss Templeton, I urge you to shoot me.'

Mrs Vawser looked without favour on this shared amusement: for a moment the shadow of tantrums flickered across her face. But then she blasted the two of them apart with a laugh of her own, declaring: 'Oh! yes, dear me yes, the town slang, it can be a monstrous bore—indeed no one dislikes that fashionable way of talking more than me. Sometimes I am so severe on it my friends are amazed: "Penelope," they say—but still, a barouche, you know, Mr Durrant, is the very thing, the only thing—'

'Ah, if it is the only thing that would make the expedition a pleasure to you, madam, then really we had better give it over altogether,' he said, with grim hopefulness.

But he was not to be let off so easily. Mrs Vawser was determined on a party to Culverton— quite as determined as if she cared anything about the place: the closed carriage was accepted, and it only remained to arrange the day. 'You may leave that to me: we ladies shall discuss it after dinner. I am very well accustomed, you know, to making arrangements: somehow it always falls to me. My friends often remark on it . . .' Having secured her victory, Mrs Vawser stemmed her flow of spirits a little, and Mr Durrant was allowed to finish his dinner distracted by nothing more than the occasional swipe with a handkerchief, stifled

116

shriek, and loud whisper that she never knew a more shocking flirt.

Still, the prospect of Mrs Vawser's vivacity in the drawing-room made Lydia wish, when the time came for the ladies to retire, that she could stay at the table with the gentlemen and drink port. But even before the tea-things were set, something happened to alter Mrs Vawser's mood. Impossible to tell what it was, or who it came from—a word, a look, an omission: perhaps one of these that had happened a week ago, and had been insufficiently brooded on. But something mortally offended, wounded and dejected her, so that she took a seat apart, and donned her veil of dolefulness. Emma timidly asked her whether she did not want to discuss the party to Culverton; but as her only answer was a suffocated mumble that she did not care a hang about it, now or ever, it was plain that Mrs Paige's duty for the rest of the evening must be to sit at her sister's side, sympathising and cajoling. Lydia had to endure nothing worse than Miss Beaumont's strictures on the shortcomings of her neighbours, which required only mechanical assent. Meanwhile her thoughts hovered again about Lady Eastmond's letter.

She was returning to Osterby the day after tomorrow; and as soon as she was settled, she would come over to Heystead, bringing her ward with her.

You need not suppose, my dear, that I have abandoned my scheme of Bath—not I! But I shall say no more till then—indeed not then— Phoebe's sweet and amiable character shall speak for me—and I have no doubt of its swiftly

117

overcoming that unwarranted modesty—you dear thing!—that makes you suppose yourself unfit for the task . . .

Lydia had a sensation of doors closing with an emphatic boom. Spoiled and selfish. Canidia would do better to confine her attentions to her proper sphere . . .

'And yet they continually leave that gate open. The dogs wander at will, and altogether it presents a most slovenly appearance. I have told them . . .' Miss Beaumont frowned. 'My dear Miss Templeton, if you find the subject tedious, have the goodness to say so.'

'Oh! here come the gentlemen,' Lydia cried with relief, making for the tea-table.

Not even the appearance of Mr Durrant could rouse Mrs Vawser from her funereal state; but for this Lydia was selfishly thankful. Having done the duties of the tea-table, she could invite Mr Durrant to a place by her on the sofa, and satisfy her curiosity.

'Am I safe?' he asked, with a suspicious glance at his late persecutor. Wine, rather than making him flushed, turned his bony face paler.

'For now, I think. Mrs Vawser is not in spirits. They will eventually return, mind: the scheme to Culverton will not be forgotten, Mr Durrant.'

'I did not suppose it would be. Hey, well, it must be borne. The day had better be soon fixed, however: I expect to be gone from Culverton within a fortnight.'

'To London, to order a barouche?'

'A different kind of folly—though with, I hope, a useful end. I shall take up my Clifton friend's

118

offer.'

'Then you are really going to do it! You are really going to Bath, to—'

'Yes, the prize bull, all of that. You have already expended sufficient wit on the matter, Miss Templeton. But why so surprised?' He folded his arms. 'I always do what I say I will do.'

'Just as you always make the commonest things sound like some wonderful virtue in you. No, my surprise, Mr Durrant, is only a sort of continuation of my initial astonishment. You found nothing hopeful, then, at Melton Mowbray?'

'I found four silly women, who have even been subsidising Hugh's extravagances out of their own limited income. I found a heap of bills and promissory notes, all drawing on his expectations from me, in the most careless and insolent manner. Curious that we have been talking of carriages: for I found also that my nephew has ordered one of those same high-perch absurdities, for a hundred guineas—the security for the sum being, of course, Mr Durrant of Culverton. I think indeed that was what decided the matter for me. That young imp will *not* be my heir. I have another resource. I shall employ it.'

'Indeed: and when you put it with such bewitching tenderness, who can doubt your success? What young woman would not melt and tremble at being called an employable resource?'

'I do not seek a woman who melts and trembles, as you call it. She sounds like a fool.'

'Still, you know, you may have to converse with her—you may have to overcome your abhorrence, and actually talk—rather than simply setting out your terms like a contract for tenancy.'

119

'The wife I would choose would not be forever talking: quite the reverse.'

'Ah. Then I am afraid in going to Bath, Mr Durrant, you do not go sufficiently far afield. You had better send to the Grand Turk, to see if there is a spare harem-wife going, preferably with her tongue cut out.'

'You women are very odd,' he said, in a neutral, considering tone. 'You fire up at what you consider the least insult to your sex: and yet amongst yourselves you are absolutely merciless to one another. Any woman who walks into a room containing six others may be assured of being hated by most of them at sight.'

'Ah! I see what you are doing. You are giving me a sample of those graceful compliments to the female sex that will be a feature of your courtship.'

'I have always supposed a woman likes to hear herself praised, not other women.'

'Very well: what are these praises to be? What other accomplishments, besides continual silence, do you look for?'

'No, you will not persuade me to answer that: you do not wish to know: you wish only to be satirical. Let me question you instead. Yesterday your father mentioned some scheme of Lady Eastmond's to send you to Bath with her ward. What does this mean?'

'It means only that the girl is young, and untried in society, and so Lady Eastmond seeks a companion for her.'

'Ah, a chaperon. But are they not usually married ladies, or ladies of mature years?'

'I will not answer that, Mr Durrant, as you wish only to be satirical. Though I may as well add that I

120

find nothing to dislike in the idea of being of mature years—quite the reverse.'

'Hm. Well, why you? Why not Lady Eastmond herself?'

Reluctantly, and as briefly as she could, she explained. She half expected some such reproach as her father had made—or rather, as he had so delicately not made, only clearing a space where her own conscience could operate. Mr Durrant's first remark when she had finished seemed to confirm it. 'And so you refused?'

'I—thanked her for the compliment she paid me, in thinking me a fit person for what she proposed; but I strongly doubted my suitability.'

'Indeed! You do well to doubt.'

'Thank you,' she said, eyeing him as he lounged back with folded arms, and an infuriating look of absolute knowledge. 'Thank you, that is, for agreeing with me for once: though I am sure something disobliging will follow.'

'Oh, as to that,' he said, after a moment's abstraction, 'I speak only the plain truth, which you have acknowledged yourself. You would not enjoy it: you would resent it: and you and I have at least this much resemblance, that when we resent something, we cannot hide the fact.'

'True: the sole difference being that you do not even try to hide it.'

He ignored that, or carelessly concurred in it; and went on, with what was for him a kindly look: 'And, of course, as you have admitted, you would not be good at it. You would not be good for any such girl as you describe; and altogether it would be disastrous.'

'I would not go so far as *disastrous*,' she

121

answered. 'It would be tedious for me, and no doubt I would ill conceal my impatience with the vacillations of a silly girl over her suitors, who I imagine are both equally insipid, but—'

'Yes—there you have it, you see. The role of the chaperon must always be secondary: she must cease to think of her own interests and inclinations, and subordinate them to those of her young charge—which may be so different from her own, that the effort of sympathy at last becomes intolerable.'

'The—the effort of sympathy,' she said haltingly, with a perplexed feeling as if she had been offered a hand to shake, and then found it snatched away, 'to be sure: not that it would be beyond my abilities. It is an effort I simply do not wish to make.'

'Exactly,' Mr Durrant said, with a shrug. 'Yes, it was an odd notion of Lady Eastmond's altogether.'

'You are not to suppose, Mr Durrant, that I refused from any selfish attention to my own comfort. I was thinking only of the young woman—Miss Rae—and what would be best for her.'

'Quite so, and I honour you for it. You have referred the question to your self-knowledge, where many a woman would have consulted only her vanity. Your father is opening the pianoforte: you will be wanted, I think.'

'Yes.' She rose, and as he rose with her it was as if he translated his laconic superiority of speech into that aloof, uncompromising height. How he likes being up there, she thought, where everyone must strain a little to look at him and speak to him. 'You will allow me, then, some proficiency in music, despite my other incapacities.'

'You are the most accomplished woman I know,' he said, conducting her to the pianoforte; and then, as he released her arm: 'But even the most accomplished woman must admit that there are some things she is not good at.'

In place of a last word, she struck a *fortissimo* chord as he walked away, and had the satisfaction of seeing Lewis Durrant jump, a little.

CHAPTER NINE

A rule of life: any dreaded event will turn out to be at least three times as bad as you expected it to be.

This rule, ever since she had invented it, had stood Lydia in good stead; but it was powerless against the coming of Lady Eastmond and Miss Rae. In a short but effusive note, like a small firework, her godmother announced her safe arrival at Osterby, and appointed the inevitable morning for her descent on Heystead with her ward in tow. Now the morning was here, a pearly and beautiful one after a night of drumming rain— but to Lydia, a morning that blinked at her, sickly and sinister, like a lizard's eye.

She could not entertain herself. She sat at her harp, trying over a new *canzonetta* she had brought back from London: it would not go. For a few moments she was aware, through the back of her neck, that her father was standing in the parlour doorway—listening, or watching; but he said nothing, and moved on. The harp sounded in her ears like a stick against railings. She went out to walk in the gardens, and was back in three minutes.

At last she resigned herself to sitting stiffly in the parlour with her father, listening out for the dreaded chock of hoofs and mumble of wheels.

The dread, she reflected, was partly of herself: of the feelings she might betray. The poor girl would surely see that her entrance into Lydia's life was an unwelcome one—would sense her unwillingness and resentment. Probably there had been a grain of truth in what Lewis Durrant had said the other night: though Mr Durrant did have a habit of saying excessive things merely to provoke. It was a deplorable failing.

'Ah, here come our visitors,' said Dr Templeton, standing at the window—and then with supernatural swiftness Lady Eastmond was in the room, almost trampling down the maid, and talking at a great rate.

'Here we are, you see—bless you, Mary, you needn't announce *me*, such a drearily familiar old body as I am at Heystead, quite the bad penny or family ghost if you like, wailing and clanking its chains, not that I have ever quite understood *how* a ghost can carry chains about, being one supposes incorporeal and without substance or at best rather *wafery*—you, Dr Templeton, could no doubt explain it perfectly, not that the answer would lodge in my poor noddle for very long—so let me shake your hand instead. Oh, my dear sir, it always does my heart good to see you—not to mention *you*, Lydia—standing there like patience on a whatsname—let me kiss you, my dear—and let me have the pleasure, the very great pleasure of introducing—'

Miss Rae: entering the room shyly, though not with that shyness which seems to offer an apology for existence: she smiled, she looked about her as if ready to be pleased. Tall: nearly as tall as Lydia, who recognised that consciousness of height which made Miss Rae give a precautionary dip of her head as she passed through the ancient low-lintelled doorway. She was very beautiful—and her beauty was more than a simple fact, it demanded a response, whether admiration or envy, or sheer wonderment at what it must be like to carry such beauty around. Her grace of movement was part of it: a particular, tentative, long-limbed grace, which Lydia would have called doe-like if she had allowed such a miserably trite simile into her mind.

'Miss Rae. My poor dear Phoebe, you have heard me talk of these people so much I dare say you are quite sickened of them—but of course you will *not* be once you know them—my very good friend Dr Templeton—my goddaughter Miss Templeton.'

'Miss Rae, you are very welcome, how do you do?' Dr Templeton was prompt with his old-fashioned courtesy. 'I hope you had a fair drive of it from Osterby. It rained rather heavily last night.'

'Oh! the road was tolerable all in all,' cried Lady Eastmond, 'only a little churned up this side of Burton Coggles, and John always has the sense *not* to slow down at such places, but to take them at the lick—one bumps about a little but not in any disagreeable way . . .'

'Miss Rae,' Lydia said, while Lady Eastmond talked on, 'I am so very glad to meet you at last.'

Miss Rae smiled by way of reply. And such a smile truly was a reply, Lydia inwardly admitted, with a fresh apprehension of the young woman's beauty. The hair—well, hair as rich as that was

125

never simply one colour: there was chestnut and gold and everything in between. Pale complexion, creamy not waxen: clear dark brows: long-lashed eyes of the penetrating brilliance that makes you fancy for a moment that either they or yours are slightly squinting. Simply but elegantly dressed— though of course she could have carried off a coal-sack. Yes, the enslavement of her two suitors was amply explained. Now it remained only for her to talk, and to reveal herself as a twittering idiot. Lydia could not help regretting what, with those looks and fifty thousand pounds, was a sad inevitability.

'And how does Sir Henry do?' asked Dr Templeton.

'He does as he does,' said Lady Eastmond, with a significant grimace. 'If I cannot say better, at least I can say no worse. His *temper* is somewhat improved for which I have dear Phoebe to thank— she is quite a favourite with him, and has developed an admirable knack of ignoring those odd things he tends to say after dinner. I'm sure you manage him a good deal better than *I* can, my dear.'

'Oh, Sir Henry has been very kind to me,' Miss Rae said, in a soft voice agreeably lined with Scots. 'I could not have wished for a kinder guardian. I had gained rather an unfortunate impression, from reading novels, that guardians were always villainous and locked you up in a tower.'

'Lord!' cried Lady Eastmond. 'I should like to see poor Henry lock up anything nowadays, short of a tea-caddy.'

'You have read Mrs Radcliffe, I collect,

126

Miss Rae,' Dr Templeton smiled.

'Yes, sir—*Udolpho*, and also *The Italian*, and *A Sicilian Romance*—indeed I have read them all.' She hesitated, glanced around with shy humour. 'Shall I leave now?'

Dr Templeton chuckled, Lady Eastmond hooted, and Lydia was forced, behind her smiles, to such a rapid review of her preconceptions as left her quite stranded in perplexity. Prettiness she had been prepared for: the pleasantness of disingenuous youth also, perhaps; but she had not expected to be charmed. It was delightful—but it made everything more difficult.

'Oh, I was a great novel-reader in my youth,' sighed Lady Eastmond, 'but we had no Gothic horrors in those days. Sentiment was all the fashion—and *Tristram Shandy*, which I could not endure for five pages together—only I dared not say so as everyone was crying it up—what sad sheep we mortals are! Not *all* of us to be sure—thank heaven there are those who will think for themselves, like *you*, my dear Lydia, and not be swayed by every piece of nonsense.'

'Thank you, Lady Eastmond—though I fear some would say that thinking for oneself amounts to being awkward, cross-grained and selfish; especially when the thinker is a woman.'

'Oh, pooh—who would say such a thing about you?'

'*About* me, many I'm sure,' she said, smiling, 'though if they were say it *to* me, no doubt I should fire up and give them a dressing. Whilst admitting to myself, deep down, that I sometimes thought so too.'

'Ah, but that's because you have a brain in your

head, my dear!' said Lady Eastmond, her broad face all shining with admiration. 'And you have *kept* it there, instead of letting the heart drive it out. Now this is what I say to Phoebe. The heart is a very good thing for a person to have—is it not, Dr Templeton?'

'Indispensable, I would say professionally,' he rumbled.

'You dry old thing—I love you for it—the heart, I say, is a very good thing to have, as long as it stays in its place.'

'A balance, I think, is needed,' Dr Templeton said judiciously, 'between head and heart: nothing easier to say: nothing harder to achieve.'

A rattle from the old ghosts—they had never really gone away—gave Lydia a shiver, and jolted her into speech; anything would do. 'Miss Rae, how do you like Lincolnshire?'

'I like it very well—though I have seen so little of England. Except London, of course. And after Mama died I was staying with relatives in Durham for a time, which I did not so much like, though I think that was partly my coming from Scotland and some people there not being able to get over it somehow, and forever saying, "Well, miss, this makes a change from porridge, hey," and so on.'

'Such prejudice,' Lydia said, amused again (but this must stop), 'and you from Edinburgh—surely the most cultivated city in the kingdom . . . You must miss home,' she found herself adding with sympathy (which must stop also).

'I fear I shall sound unfeeling when I say I do not greatly miss the *place*. We lived such a very retired life there that Edinburgh for me has few memorable associations—except those of family,

128

of course, and those one takes everywhere—in the blood, you might say. I do so much enjoy seeing new places—I'm afraid I am quite greedy for them, and I must tire Aunt Harriet's patience.'

'The eagerness of youth for life, my dear—who could reprove it?' Lady Eastmond said. 'She has been all agog to see Heystead, you know—a real priory, all redolent with the past and whatnot.'

'I hope you are not disappointed, Miss Rae, to find that we do not live in a romantic ruin,' said Lydia, trying by asperity to deny the warmth she felt towards the girl.

'Oh, the Priory is all I had hoped,' Miss Rae declared solemnly. 'It is so very solid and genuine. In Durham there was a family who lived in an abbey, and made much of it, but it was only a modern house built where there used to be an abbey, with a bit of crumbled wall attached. Which seemed to me a little like the old broom that has had two new heads and three new handles.'

'Oh, my dear, I know that sort of gingerbread taste,' Lady Eastmond said. 'In my day there was a fashion for grottoes. Henry even talked of setting up a grotto at Osterby. What would he do with it, I wanted to know. "Sit in it", quoth he. Well, my dear, anyone who knows the effect on Henry of even a *draught* would share my amusement at the idea of the poor fellow sitting in a grotto. But he had it fixed in his mind, and I had to go to the very limits of persuasion to prevent him, though that's a tale for another time . . .' She fixed on Lydia her usual look of devouring benevolence: but, Lydia realised to her fleeting shame, Lady Eastmond was also rather nervous. 'Well, Lydia my love, I hope you are fairly settled back at home, and not finding the country dull after town—not that you could ever be dull anywhere, good heavens, with your accomplishments. Such talents and refinements of mind—I wish you could hear Miss Templeton play, Phoebe, you would be in transports—and then her drawing—that admirable half-length figure above the mantelpiece, I believe, is hers—'

'Do you play, Miss Rae?' Lydia asked quickly, anxious to escape commendations that had something of the auctioneer about them.

'Very dismally. I cannot stop thinking about the left hand and the right doing different things, and how strange and awkward that is. I remember my governess, or one of them, saying I approached the pianoforte as if it were the pillory.'

'Phoebe was educated at home,' put in Lady Eastmond, 'and I fear, with all possible respect to her mother, that the governesses were not always well chosen.'

'Mama tended to choose them for their morals,' Miss Rae said, with a faint rueful smile. 'And they were, indeed, very good women.'

'And the good are not always clever, and the clever are not always good—is that a proverb, or a quotation, or have I perhaps just made it up?' Lady Eastmond chuckled. 'What do you say, my dear sir—you who unite *both* qualities?'

'You flatter me so shockingly that I hardly know what to say.' Dr Templeton smiled. 'Virtue may be found in unworldly simplicity, to be sure; but I think it is much better reinforced, and directed, by good sense. See, here is that ticklish question of head and heart again.'

'The advantage of a head, or mind or brain, is that it will be a resource and support to you in life,'

Lydia said crisply, 'while the heart is liable chiefly to cause you pain.'

'I think there is a great deal in what you say,' said Miss Rae, turning on Lydia her full, intense attention—which was very attentive indeed. You felt that she was ready at once to suspend everything, indefinitely and without condition, to hear what you had to tell. 'I was so attached to my old nurse that Mama warned me it was unnatural, that I ought to moderate my feelings, but I couldn't help it—or I thought I couldn't, perhaps. And then when she grew old, and ill, I could hardly bear it; and when she died, I was in an absolutely ungovernable state. I almost wished I had *not* loved her so much: because then I might have remembered her better, in a way; instead all I was thinking of was her being dead, and my grief— which was a sort of selfishness. But can one feel to order, as it were? I wish I knew the answer.'

Lydia hesitated, glancing into and away from the distressing violet eyes. She had forgotten this quality of youth, which could make the very air thicken with significance—while at the same time clearing and freshening it. Yes, she was being won over. Miss Rae had probably a thousand absurdities, but no matter: Lydia was now helplessly interested in her. Interest, no doubt, was one of those cool attributes of the head not the heart—but it was no less powerful for that.

Thank heaven, though, it could never be powerful enough to take her to Bath as Miss Rae's companion. And hadn't she set herself so stiffly against the poor girl because she feared being pushed or betrayed into that quagmire?—whereas she would be quite happy to walk the neat trimmed

131

paths of acquaintance, even friendship. Realising this, Lydia experienced that kindly relief which follows the waking from an uncanny and troublous dream: life, yes, has its difficulties, but it is recognisable, it is not like *that*.

'I wish I knew the answer too, Miss Rae,' she said; and in her new security of feeling, added pointedly: 'I am afraid Lady Eastmond, in her kindness, may have been holding me up to you as a species of oracle, but that I assuredly am not.'

'You must know a great deal more than me,' Miss Rae said seriously, 'for I am shockingly ignorant. But really, from what I have read of those ancient oracles, I think they were monstrous frauds. A king would come along and ask, "Shall I go to war with another king?" and the oracle would make a lot of smoke and say, "If you do a kingdom will fall." Surely, this is the most shameless imposture. They may as well have said, "What will be will be." '

'But just suppose, Phoebe, there was a real, truthful oracle,' Lady Eastmond said, with a sudden swoop of eagerness, 'what would you ask it?'

'Why, I should not ask it anything, in case it gave me an answer I did not like,' said Miss Rae, reasonably.

Lady Eastmond looked dissatisfied; while Dr Templeton, settling himself to rumination, said: 'Ah, which of us would truly wish to foresee the future? The ancient world was devoted to this idea, and it survived in the medieval mind: but if it were really a possibility, who would look? Who would dare to lift the veil?'

'I don't believe it could be possible, sir, because

the future depends on the choices you will make, and you haven't made them yet,' Miss Rae said: then frowned, paused, and silently ran this over again in her head. 'Yes. That.'

'What did I tell you, Phoebe? These dear Templetons will have you talking philosophy in a moment,' chuckled Lady Eastmond: happy, but also a little dismissive; their amiable weakness, you know. 'Choices, aye, what tremendous choices one has to make—especially when young—on the threshold of the world, with tempting fascination on every side! You'll know, of course, my dear sir, that Phoebe has just enjoyed her first London season. Enjoyed—Lord, that's the right word indeed: you will hardly believe what a success she was! I was almost afraid of what I had done in bringing her out so. Many a girl would have her head turned by it. But not Phoebe—or if so, only a very little.'

'A tribute to Miss Rae's good sense, and that of her protectress,' Dr Templeton said smiling.

'Bless you for saying so, my dear sir—and I only hope I may be as useful to Phoebe in the future— but as you so rightly remark, who can foretell the future?'

Who indeed? Lydia thought: but she knew very well where Lady Eastmond's thoughts were tending. It was time to anticipate them—forestall them. For the past week she had had the uncomfortable sensation—supremely uncomfortable for one of her temperament—of her life slipping out of her control. Now she would take command of it again. Show herself a good hand with the ribbons.

'It just occurs to me, Miss Rae,' she said

brightly, 'as you are kind enough to admire Heystead, whether you would like to see the very finest house in the district? Culverton—it is the home of my father's friend Mr Durrant, and justly admired, as the guidebooks would say. The grounds and gardens are indeed beautiful, even I will allow, and usually with me a little vegetation goes a long way. There is a scheme to take a party there soon, and I should be so very happy if you would join us.'

Miss Rae was all pleasure: Lady Eastmond beamed, and gently slapped her own knees. Lydia's satisfaction lay in knowing the limits of her own proposal. Let us walk and talk: let there be friendship, confidences: let there be, God help her, advice; and then—do you hear, ghosts?—let that be the end of it.

CHAPTER TEN

The excursion to Culverton was settled for a week hence. Lewis Durrant accepted his fate with, for him, good grace: he would lay on a luncheon for his guests, he told Lydia in a short note, and the punishment for anyone who trampled his flower-beds would only be a brief whipping. Lydia did not consult Mrs Vawser first: instead she arranged everything, then called at the Vicarage-house, reminded her of the scheme to Culverton, and assured her that all her careful directions for it had been followed to the letter. There was then only the fatigue to be borne of Mrs Vawser's self-congratulation, and loud wondering how people in

134

this dear, pottering place ever got anything done without her.

For Lydia there was real pleasure in the prospect. She was always glad to see Culverton, in spite of the equivocal associations the spot bore for her; but above all, there was pleasure in Phoebe Rae being of the party. In the interim Lady Eastmond brought her over to Heystead again, and she and Lydia had some conversation apart.

Yes: there was much to like in this gentle young woman with the slow-dawning smile and soft clarinet voice. It was not simply a negative matter of expecting a giggling scatterbrain and finding instead someone tolerable. Miss Rae was positively engaging. The real respect she showed for Lydia's father was a point in her favour at once; and the fact that she obviously admired Lydia also had, no doubt, its effect: the stupidest people suddenly become a little cleverer when we learn that they think well of us.

But beyond this there was something pure and unaffected about Phoebe Rae that struck on Lydia's sensibility like a perfectly tuned major chord. Her sheltered upbringing—and from a few hints Lydia had been able to construct the sombre echoing house in Edinburgh, the remote and imposing father, the smothering mother—had not been without its benefits. If her education had been patchy, at least she had been protected from learning the wrong things: how to be arch, smart, vain, trivial and worldly. Nor was her seriousness unsweetened by humour—and Lydia was disposed to like anyone who made her laugh.

Still, Miss Rae was undoubtedly intense: in her curiosity, her tastes, her openness to impression, even her attention (the one alteration that Lydia could have wished in Phoebe's appearance, was that she would blink a little more often). It was plain from her feeling talk of her late parents, of beloved servants and even household pets, that her attachments were intense likewise. In this anyone who took an interest in her welfare—even the carefully measured interest that Lydia intended to take—must perceive a potential danger. Indeed Lydia saw now that her first flippant dismissal of Lady Eastmond's kindly anxieties about her ward's suitors had been wrong. No one could wish to see such a trusting and candid nature exposed to the consequences of a mistake for which only her inexperience, not her character, could be blamed. (There were young girls aplenty, on the other hand, whom one could watch very happily going to blazes.) Phoebe merited every effort of sympathy, understanding and involvement—short of going to Bath with her.

It was agreed that, as the party would be setting off for Culverton early in the morning, Miss Rae should come to Heystead the afternoon before and stay the night. It was a thoroughly pleasant evening: Dr Templeton, who had taken a great liking to his guest, listened with rich enjoyment to her description of the rigours of the Edinburgh sabbath.

'Because the curtains were always closed on a Sunday, I had an idea as a girl that there must be things out there I must not see. So inquisitiveness made me daring, and at last one Sunday when my governess was not by I opened them a little and peeped out. For a long time all I saw was an empty street; but at length a man came along, all red in

136

the face, and walking very unsteadily. When he fell down and lay still I shrieked. My governess came and I cried that there was a dead man out there. She looked, and said that he was not dead but he might as well be. She was a very *good* woman, but a little severe. It was a long time before I understood that walking out on a Sunday did not actually kill you: that the poor man was dreadfully drunk, and had quite sensibly decided, as there is never a carriage to be seen on the sabbath, to lie down there and sleep.'

After dinner Lydia played. Her suggestion that Miss Rae might like to approach the pianoforte was met with the emphatic negative of flaming cheeks, bitten lips and frenetic head-shakings; but Phoebe listened devotedly; and at the end of one piece tears stood in her eyes, and she was wrapped in melancholy for some time afterwards.

'I heard that piece several times in London,' she huskily confided, when Lydia rejoined her on the sofa, 'and it has such tender associations for me. I wonder how it is that music has the power to bring back recollections so forcibly?'

She lapsed again into pensive silence, the mystery of which required very little penetration. Either Mr Allardyce the diplomat or Mr Beck the scribbler is behind these sighs, thought Lydia. Or possibly both, which is where the difficulties begin.

Phoebe's usual cheerful temper was restored, however, the next morning: a warm bright morning combining the best qualities of spring and summer. 'Nothing like a blue sky to lift the spirits,' observed Dr Templeton over breakfast. 'Which cannot, of course, be the case in hot desert countries, which in turn must prove something about the relativity of human pleasures—but I am too content to pursue it.'

He was to accompany them to Culverton, the others of the party being Mrs Vawser and Mr and Mrs Paige. Miss Beaumont had declined Lydia's personal invitation, declaring that she had something better to do than go on idle jaunts about the country. As she plainly had nothing better to do, beyond staring at the faded pattern on her parlour wallpaper, Lydia could only conclude that she refused for the simple pleasure of saying no, and perhaps the more refined pleasure of causing offence and discomfort. (If she was expecting to cause *disappointment*, she was sadly misled.)

'I shall go about the park with you as much as my legs will allow, my dears,' Dr Templeton said, as they took their places in the carriage—Lady Eastmond's chaise, which had brought Phoebe here. 'But I confess my chief temptation is the opportunity of consulting Mr Durrant's excellent library: so if I disappear, you know where I am to be found.'

'Is Mr Durrant a very learned man?' asked Phoebe.

'Not by Papa's standards; but taken all in all he is a pretty well-read man—intelligent and cultivated,' Lydia conceded, 'even if he chooses not to show it.'

'Now you alarm me,' Phoebe said. 'I shall be surrounded by clever people.'

'Ah, but Mr Durrant is not so clever as he thinks he is,' said Lydia. Phoebe looked interested, or more interested even than usual; but the bustle of departure prevented further speech.

They were to drive first to the Vicarage-house, so that the two carriages could proceed together. Mr Durrant's venerable travelling-coach, as promised, stood before the gate, and the Vicarage party were ready to climb in; but Mrs Vawser, if not quite in marble mood, appeared disgruntled.

'Oh, dear,' Dr Templeton said, 'I fear it may be because Mr Durrant has done just what he said he would—send his carriage to fetch them; but he has not come himself.'

'Oh, dear,' echoed Lydia. 'I wonder how she will contrive to punish him for it. Perhaps she will ignore him, and decline to speak a word to him all day. How he will hate that.'

Her father smiled. 'I fancy he will hide away in his study for the whole time in any event.'

The Vicarage party took the lead. There were, as promised, many inviting views on the road to Culverton—pockets of meadow lined with silver streams, expanses of green hills with all the room in the world to roll and shelve and maze their way to the delicate horizon; but though the Heystead carriage was slowed several times so that they could look and admire, the other proceeded at a lick. Doubtless the beauty of the countryside was useless without a barouche.

Culverton House came stealthily into view on its gentle rise above the straggling stone village: a great house without grand airs. Lydia had made extensive tours about the country with her father in his younger years, and had yawned her way through the stateliness of many a mansion: the vast halls that could have no reason for being so large, except to make people feel small, the Blue Rooms and Red Rooms, the fusty riot of gilt and ormolu,

139

the allegorical paintings tumbling with drapery and cupids. Half consciously she had measured them all against Culverton. She had been often here as a girl, during the time of Lewis Durrant's father, a sociable man who liked to gather young people about him; and in spite of certain intervening events, it remained one of those good places under the sun that the mind can visit for comfort and refuge.

It was of much later date than Heystead, built in ruddy brick faced with pale stone, and accordingly more regular—but not too much so: no dull stare of multiplied windows. The compact front, neat as the three panels of a folding screen, was offset by a lower wing on the left side, which gave the pleasing notion of there being two sides to every question. Smooth lawns and topiary flanked the drive up to the house: but behind and beyond it the eye was beguiled by dense woods and the lazy glitter of a lake.

Lewis Durrant was waiting on the steps to receive them, and not hiding in his study—even though he looked as if he wished to, when Mrs Vawser, recovering her spirits, began captivating him the moment she alighted. Such a delightful place—in love with it already—apologies for lateness, but such charming views along the way she could hardly bear to get along—excessively kind in him to indulge her little expedition. 'And you see it has all come off rather well—nothing omitted, everything arranged—but that is my way, I'm afraid—I must have things perfect and to the letter. My friends absolutely laugh about it. "Penelope," they say, "is so thorough—such a stickler"—but you'll acknowledge, Mr Durrant, there can be no pleasure without preparation.'

'I am perturbed, ma'am. I had supposed a pleasure-party, not a military exercise.'

'Oh! heavens above, nothing so precise as that. Dear me no—there is nothing so odious as over-preparation: consequences of this and that, and how and when and so on—it quite takes away all enjoyment. Oh! Lord, you would have to search pretty hard to find someone who deplores that sort of fussing more than me. Spontaneity is the thing—indeed I would lay it down as a rule that there can be no pleasure where there is preparation.'

Adopting two opposite positions within a minute exhausted even Mrs Vawser's energy: for now she was content to pass on into the hall, and point things out instructively to her sister, who was too polite, or tired, to reply that she had been to Culverton before, and knew a great deal more about it than Mrs Vawser did.

'Sir,' barked the Reverend Mr Paige, presenting his dogmatic smile, 'allow me to express my thanks for your receiving us here today. I find you well, I hope. Mrs Paige I know joins with me in appreciation of your cordial welcome. It is always a pleasure to see Culverton. Once again, sir, my thanks: please accept them.'

Reeling a little from the bludgeon of Mr Paige's courtesy, Mr Durrant welcomed the Heystead party, and was introduced to Miss Rae. His manner was merely correct: but Lydia felt him turn momentarily on her his sardonic gaze, like a hot spark from a sulky fire. He was longing—she knew it—to say something about chaperons of mature years.

141

They made the tour of the principal rooms, Mrs Vawser in raptures about everything and taking in nothing. Phoebe meanwhile reinforced Lydia's good opinion of her by her just appreciation of the qualities of Culverton House: the elegant proportion of the rooms, airy but not lofty: the balance between the dark antique of the great carved staircase and the freshness of the white plaster mouldings and niches: the judicious collections. Mr Durrant's father had been a great traveller, but he had resisted the usual urge to load his house with curious lumber, and the paintings, tapestries, and cabinets did not oppress the eye with abundance.

Lydia's own admiration of the place was seasoned with other emotions, the flavour of which it would be hard exactly to describe. For this house might have been her home: she might have dined daily at that great mahogany table, drawn up her evening chair to that marble fireplace, and climbed that staircase so often that every carved flower and festoon would have been as familiar to her as her own fingertips. Perhaps because of the presence of Phoebe, a stranger here, the memories of that time when her destiny was so nearly linked with Culverton were coming strongly upon her. Not powerfully—for they certainly had no power over her now: rather they appeared as scenes in an intriguing and instructive story.

Their tour ended at the breakfast-room, where the housekeeper was supervising the laying of an ample table, and where the French doors stood open to invite them to the gardens.

'Mr Durrant, you monstrous thing, I declare you have gone to a shocking amount of trouble for my little party,' Mrs Vawser cried. 'You make me quite ashamed. Such quantities of food—I must warn you I eat like a bird—absolutely like a bird—I am well known for it. Often my friends beg me to eat. "Penelope—"'

'A pity—but I am sure my other guests have healthy appetites.'

'Oh! to be sure, no doubt—but you must promise me faithfully, Mr Durrant, that next time you will not put yourself out so.'

'You have my solemn promise, ma'am, that I shall not put myself out for you again. Will you see the gardens?'

From the stone terrace a flight of steps led down to the lawns and gravel walks—steps that Mrs Vawser, in her irrepressibility, must scamper down with a squeal, as if they were an exciting novelty. The sun was now strong enough for parasols, though Mrs Vawser kept hers folded, the better to prod and tease Mr Durrant with.

'What a very agreeable man Mr Durrant is!' Phoebe said.

'Do you really think so?' Lydia said, amused. 'Well, I suppose he has at least refrained from taking an axe to Mrs Vawser, but there is still plenty of time.'

'His look, perhaps, is a little dark and severe. His manner also, and his way of talking—'

'My dear Miss Rae, of what then can his agreeability consist? Not that agreeability is a word.'

'You are very good with words. I wish I were. Sir Henry has Johnson's *Dictionary* on his shelves and the other day I was looking into it and I thought how sad it was that I shall never use above half of them in my life. Perhaps one might use all of them, if one really set oneself to it, but it would require a good deal of forethought.'

'One letter at a time, perhaps. This month I am on the letter *b*. It might make one's conversation rather peculiar.'

'No, but I do think he is agreeable, though I can't say precisely how. Just as one can tell whether a strange dog is friendly or vicious.'

Lydia laughed. 'I wonder what Mr Durrant would make of your comparison.'

'Oh, dear, I'm afraid I—I really didn't mean to be rude—especially as . . .' Phoebe blushed. 'Well, especially as he is our host.'

'You have not been rude at all: I would guess that you never are. But you were going to say *especially* something else.'

'This is dreadful—I feel like the worst kind of gossip . . . It is just that Lady Eastmond mentioned to me that you and Mr Durrant—were once engaged.'

'Ah, is that it?' Lydia smiled, pressing her arm. 'My dear Miss Rae, this is no secret: everybody hereabouts knows that, and no one minds it. And above all you should not think it gives me a moment's uneasiness.'

'Oh, I'm glad of that. That is—it is not a thing to be *glad* about, rather . . . Shall I stop talking?'

Lydia laughed. 'Lady Eastmond is perhaps a little liberal in her phrasing, to say *engaged*. Mr Durrant and I were much together, some years ago: our attachment was to a degree an expected thing in the neighbourhood. And there was a proposal, which I civilly declined. There was an interval of inevitable awkwardness, but presently

144

we carried on with our lives—as you must do in a country district where the families are on close terms, and you will often find yourselves in company together. There is nothing in the recollection to embarrass me—or, I would say, Mr Durrant either.'

'I am intensely relieved,' Phoebe said, the blush fading—but leaving a tinge of curiosity.

Lydia's feeling, as they passed into the shady walk of great holly hedges, was as mild and balmy as the day. A fresh and present memory rose before her: strolling with old Mr Durrant along this same path. He is telling her something about the depredations of herons on his fish-ponds, but his humorous keen eye speaks of something else: of the Grantham assembly where she and his son danced last week: of expectation.

'I beg your pardon? Oh, yes—the door in the wall, there, that's our way to the shrubberies . . .'

All this time Mrs Vawser had attached herself perseveringly to Mr Durrant; as assiduous in asking him the name of this plant and the antiquity of that tree as she was in not listening to his answers. But her time was coming to an end. This was his own ground, where Mr Durrant might do as he liked; and Dr Templeton growing tired, Mr Durrant undertook to escort him back to the house, and see him settled in the library. Mrs Vawser might protest all she liked at his desertion: he was gone; and there was nothing for it but to put up her parasol and sulk until they could return to the house.

Phoebe's curiosity was as perceptible as the hovering of a bee. 'When—?' she began, then faltered. 'When were the gardens laid out, I wonder?'

'When did Mr Durrant propose to me, you mean? It was the year 'ninety-one: the autumn. Truly, I don't mind in the least alluding to it.'

'Ninety-one: across the Channel the French King has tried and failed to flee the Revolution, and in Parliament Burke and Fox are quarrelling over it. George Templeton has just moved to London, and old Mr Durrant is planning a ball at Culverton House.

'I was then a little older than you, and very happily settled at Heystead. I had more than happily left behind the young ladies' seminary at Fulham—the stated aim of such places, very appropriately, is to *finish* your education—and I had accompanied my father on a tour of France, and all in all I was conscious of my high degree of comfort and good fortune. At least, I hope I was conscious of it, sufficiently to be grateful. My mother having died when I was a girl, I was mistress of Heystead: mistress of my own time, which I had no difficulty in filling: altogether I did not desire or seek any alteration.'

The ball-room at Culverton House is tolerably filled for a country district. Lydia walks in on the arm of her father, still spry, and still wearing hair-powder. Ladies' gowns have waists: the musicians wear wigs. She is aware, without looking, of the tall lean figure advancing towards her.

'However, I was a young woman: it was expected that I should marry. What else is there to do? And the Templetons being an old established family, it was expected that I should marry suitably to my position. If I was no great heiress, I was still a very proper bride for a gentleman of family and

146

property. Did you ever see a coal-mine, Phoebe?'

'Oh! Miss Templeton—I was all engrossed in that story—why are we down a coal-mine?'

'Because they have wagons that are pulled along iron rails. Very smoothly, and only one way: along those rails. I began to feel like one of those wagons.'

'Dear me. Was Dr Templeton very eager for you to marry?'

'Well, my father never pressed me: that is not his belief, and not his way, thank heaven. I dare say he thought it would be a very good thing if I *were* to marry, and he has always esteemed Mr Durrant; but still, it must be only of my own free choice. George, my brother, was rather more pressing: likewise Lady Eastmond, in her kind way, for she would like to make matches for everyone. But above all it was the sheer force of society—of what was expected of me. There is no greater tyranny, Miss Rae, than convention.'

Phoebe nodded thoughtfully. 'I am sure you are right.'

Lydia was not sure that Phoebe ought to be so quickly and completely accepting her rightness: but there was no denying it was pleasant.

'And so, who more suitable than Mr Lewis Durrant of Culverton? The rails were taking me straight to him. Mr Durrant was so highly eligible—Lord, I remember hearing those words so often they seemed to lose their meaning.'

'Oh, yes—like when you are writing a letter and you look at a certain word and wonder if it's spelled right, and then the more you think about it the stranger the word becomes.'

'Just so. And since—'

'Like "sugar", which when you look at it for a long time seems horribly unlikely and like an anagram or something made up . . . Sorry. But really, I do ponder this—what *is* the meaning of eligible? Does it merely mean being rich, and settled, and the right age, and no madness in the family?'

'For many people, that is precisely the meaning. Indeed, you echo the very questions I was asking myself at the time. Of course I do not, you may have gathered, like being told what to do in any case. But it was more than that. Mr Durrant—and I speak of the past, with no reflection on our current situation, where we rub along pretty well as friends—Mr Durrant shared the general opinion of his eligibility. He could not remotely conceive that I might not wish to marry him: it was a matter of ask, and it shall be given you.'

Faces loom and fade in the candlelight: young men, beseeching the honour of this dance, arranging the fire-screen, fetching ices: offering here handsomeness, there good humour. Lewis Durrant does not excel in either. He only acts as if he does.

'I understand . . . And yet—I'm picturing it, you see, Miss Templeton, and the picture is lacking something,' Phoebe said, with one of her little tangential insights, which Lydia found very slightly alarming. 'There must have been something more than just eligibility. Is that a word?—never mind. Something—I hope I do not offend—something on both sides.'

'Oh! well, as to that, I hope I should never even consider the addresses of a man to whom I was wholly indifferent. There was, and is, certainly

148

nothing insipid about Mr Durrant: one could always talk with him and find something of interest, even if it was only material for a good argument. There was never dullness, at least. And if I had been absolutely set upon getting a husband, I might have done a lot worse, and I dare say we would have made shift to get along, as people do.'

He is leading her to a sofa, and she is reproaching him: he might put a little more animation into his dancing. He might, he replies, if he considered dancing anything other than a meaningless absurdity, dictated by convention: as well to talk of putting animation into his shaving. Lydia: You are so very sure of everything! Mr Durrant: Anyone who makes that reproach is sure of everything likewise: all they mean is that they disagree. And between Lydia's amusement and irritation a firmer, sharper feeling arises: a conviction that she could never endure being continually snuffed out like a candle in this way. Yes, she always looks for that dark head and taut figure amidst the anonymity of maleness, and yes, there is always a certain relish in striking her mind against his. But only relatively, comparatively. For some that might be enough, but for Lydia merely enough is not enough.

'Oh, Miss Templeton, I see what it is. The picture is complete: and I am sorry I was so behind-hand with it. Of course, you were not in love with Mr Durrant: and that is the sadness of the whole story.'

Lydia stiffened, and found herself inhaling noisily in just the way she had always deplored in the headmistress at Fulham. Then she laughed.

'My dear Miss Rae, I think you are right. You do see the picture complete; but I would not exactly call it sad. If Mr Durrant had been in love with me, then it might have been sad indeed—but on both sides, thankfully, there was so much solid indifference beneath our superficial partiality that the result was both happy and inevitable. I settled to the single life, which I must have known even then would suit me best, and time has vindicated my choice.'

A wet November day, and at Heystead Lydia stands gazing into the fire in the winter parlour, and listening to the sounds of Mr Durrant's horse being brought round to the courtyard just outside the window. Chock of hoofs on gravel: some cheerful remarks by the groom, unanswered: sharp trot quickening and dwindling into a gallop. The fire smokes, making her eyes sting as new-minted memories drift before them: the way the raindrops stood out like beads on his crisp black hair, the tense tapping of his riding-crop against his leg, the look he gave her after her answer—sharp, even contemptuous, as if he had caught her out in some particularly despicable lie. Her feelings are complex, as is to be expected: few pleasant: disliking agitation above all things, she is already looking forward to their subsidence. Especially this quite unexpected one, which certainly ought to have nothing pleasant about it: the feeling of power.

'Well, I must admire your resolution,' Phoebe said, with a wistful shake of her head. 'To have such a command over yourself . . .'

'Alas, self-command is the only one we can be sure of. We cannot command the weather, or the affections of others, or the health of our bodies. Why not avail ourselves of the one power that is truly ours?'

They had come to an avenue of lime trees, with a delectable prospect of the lake and the woods beyond, and paused to admire it: though Lydia felt that both were looking inward as well as out.

'And now that is quite enough about me,' she said at last. 'And at the risk of *my* appearing a gossip, I confess that I too have heard something from Lady Eastmond—about your own conquests, during your late London season. If it is a secret, I hope you will forgive her making me privy to it.'

'Oh! no, I knew she had told you all about it, because she said so. "Miss Templeton is the one to advise you," she said, "and so she must know all." '

Lydia took a deep breath. 'Well. That is certainly very—very direct of Lady Eastmond. Again, I hope you are not offended.'

'Not at all, for I badly want advice,' Phoebe said earnestly. 'I was only afraid—with all respect to Lady Eastmond—that you would find it rather an annoyance and a presumption. And all the more, when she said she would persuade you to be my companion for a stay in Bath.'

Lydia stared, gasped, and at last burst into laughter.

'I am glad you are able to laugh about it,' Phoebe said, smiling doubtfully, 'because I—well, I have had such pleasure in your company, Miss Templeton—indeed, I hope, friendship—that I would hate it to be spoiled by something that to you may be an irksome duty. Rather than that, I would happily drop the subject altogether.'

After a short struggle, punctuated by an image

151

of herself once more running on rails, Lydia squeezed Phoebe's hand and said: 'Friendship is my hope too. But it is a poor sort of friendship where the concerns only of *one* are to be talked of. Still, I would not press you, if I had not felt several times that you had something on your mind, which it would be a relief to let out.'

'You are very perceptive! I have set myself not to be mopish about it: I have told myself it is better for the present *not* to think about it,' Phoebe said, closing her parasol as they entered the shade of the trees. 'Still, it is like one of those tunes that fixes itself in your mind and will not be driven out—and isn't it odd that they are usually tunes you do not particularly like?'

'The two gentlemen in question, though, you *do* like—is that not so? And the unpleasant tune, as it were, is the difficulty of there being two of them.'

'I must seem like the completest idiot,' Phoebe said bleakly.

'I would have to meet the two gentlemen to pronounce on that,' Lydia said; then, feeling this to be a step too far, added quickly: 'However, Lady Eastmond has told me something of them, and of the manner of your meeting, and so on. And my first thought—if you will allow me—was that there should be no haste in the matter. You are young—I know, by the by, how vastly irritating it is to be told that—and I understand the acquaintance has not been long; and in short, there is all the time in the world.'

'Also, I have not met many men,' Phoebe said promptly, as if these arguments were familiar to her. 'That is why Lady Eastmond feels Bath may benefit me, as I will see more society. And perhaps choose another man altogether. Dear me. Now I sound like a—a light o' love.'

'As to the variety of men,' Lydia said, laughing, 'I fancy it is a little exaggerated. You are sure to encounter pretty much the same types of men wherever you go. But yes, time, reflection—I'm sure, you know, your own good sense has already recommended these things to you.'

'I'm afraid my good sense works rather fitfully. Else I would not be in this ridiculous position.'

'Why ridiculous? Two eligible gentlemen—yes, we must have the word—have paid their addresses to you: you have discovered in yourself a liking for them both; and you have the perplexing responsibility of choosing wisely. I would call it difficult rather than ridiculous.'

'You have put the case as it ought to be—as if Miss Templeton were in it, and not Miss Rae,' Phoebe said, very mournful. 'Perhaps instead of ridiculous, I should have said dreadful.'

'You do not mean,' Lydia said, with a quiver of alarm, 'you have made some undertaking—given some promise—'

'No, no—nothing so sensible even as that. That at least would imply some sort of intent. The fact is, Miss Templeton, I am in love with both of them.' Phoebe aimed a very creditable fencer's jab at a tree-trunk. 'Yes! There. Now you really will regret not dropping the subject, as I have revealed the full extent of my absurdity, and you must wish to retreat from the acquaintance as fast as politeness will permit.'

A little of this had, indeed, flickered in Lydia's mind at Phoebe's avowal: enough to make her start guiltily, and reply with willed firmness:

153

'Nonsense—nothing of the sort. My dear Miss Rae, you must think me quite the termagant. If, as you say, you are in love with both of them, then—then the difficulty is merely increased . . .' She floundered.

'What you wish to say,' Phoebe sighed, 'is that one cannot be in love with two people at the same time.'

Lydia prepared a spirited contradiction; but it would not do. She pressed Phoebe's hand again. 'I do wonder at it,' she said simply.

'So do I—when I think about it, that is; but most of the time I am not thinking but feeling, and that is such a very different matter. Lady Eastmond hoped, and yes, I hoped too, that being away from them would bring some clarity to my feelings. I fear it has only confused them more. "Absence makes the heart grow fonder," says the proverb—and then the other proverb says, "Out of sight out of mind," which makes nonsense of it. Indeed I dislike proverbs very much, don't you?'

'My dislike of them is proverbial. Miss Rae, I don't in the least mean to make light of your feelings: I can see that your situation—your dilemma—is thoroughly uncomfortable. The one question I would raise is, I suppose, of definition. Have you mistaken for love what are simply feelings of liking and attraction?'

'Exactly what Lady Eastmond says,' Phoebe replied, with a faint shrug.

'Well, of course the question is subtler than that,' Lydia went on, a little nettled. She had not wanted the role of counsellor, but if she must play it she would show herself expert in it. 'I dare say there are degrees and gradations of love also. One may be a little in love, with a sort of delicate hesitation about it: or deep in, beyond all thought of anything else.'

'That is me, I fear: deep in.'

'But my dear Miss Rae, surely not in both cases. Surely it is the nature of love to be exclusive.'

'Well—not always—after all, I loved both my father and my mother.'

'Ah, familial love: that is different from romantic love, entirely different.'

Phoebe was silent; and for a moment Lydia thought she was going to ask her how she could know, when she had never been in love herself. If so, then she would have to end the conversation. There were limits.

But instead Phoebe said, with her most beautiful pensiveness: 'You are right, of course: it is an entirely false comparison, and I think I have known that even while trying to soothe myself with it. What it all comes down to, I fear, is that I do not have that self-command I admired in you. I have—and I loathe myself for it—whatever is the opposite of self-command.'

Which makes you very vulnerable, Lydia thought: any man who admires you, you will conceive as doing you a great favour: because you insufficiently value yourself. She thought of Phoebe's upbringing, and caught the whiff of Calvinist brimstone. Miserable sinners ye are. From Lady Eastmond's account, the two gentlemen, whatever their other qualities, were honourable: Lydia hoped so with a fierceness that surprised her.

'Well, let us turn to specifics,' she said. 'You will not mind me making free with the names: there is a Mr Allardyce, Lady Eastmond tells me, who is in the diplomatic service, and a Mr Beck, who is a—a man of letters. You met them both in London, and came to know them very well.'

'Yes—but not together. Not, what's the word?, concurrently. Hooray, I'm on the letter *c*. There were different social circles, you understand.'

'Just so. And you conceived an attachment for each of these gentlemen. And—forgive me, I must be harsh as a lawyer—this attachment was mutual in each case?'

'Both Mr Allardyce and Mr Beck—' Phoebe's voice grew thin with emotion '—were very particular in their attentions to me.'

'Very well. I must continue forensic, or even scientific, and assert that nothing in nature can be identical. No two pieces of string can ever be *exactly* of the same length. Therefore, your feelings for these two gentlemen cannot be exactly equal. One must be stronger, even if by a tiny amount, than the other.'

'Oh, assuredly,' Phoebe answered, 'but I don't know which.' She smiled with a rueful tenderness that made the devotion of her suitors, in spite of everything, wholly understandable. 'I told you you would wish to drop the subject.'

CHAPTER ELEVEN

The subject was not so much dropped as hurled aside by Mrs Vawser, who at that moment disengaged herself from Mr Paige's arm and turned wildly upon them.

'Oh, this heat! Miss Templeton, do you not feel it?—absolutely killing heat—Miss Rae, is it not?— I am fagged half to death—' she swayed dramatically '—really afraid I shall fall down in a faint—don't know how I am to contrive—if you wish to go on, you must leave me . . . leave me here . . .'

There was a good deal more tottering and groaning, before an application of hartshorn from Mrs Paige's reticule effected a partial recovery. Still Mrs Vawser was at the end of her strength— could not go on—could not even put one foot in front of the other. What was to be done? Lydia longed to propose that they start breaking branches from the trees and constructing a litter; but instead Emma's anxious suggestion that someone should go back to the house restored Mrs Vawser's energy. The house—yes, she was sure she could manage to walk back to the house— there would be cool, and something to drink, and the mere thought of it would, with luck, sustain her . . . In short, she was bored with the beauties she had yearned to see. She set off on the return journey at a vigorous pace; and was soon drawing ahead, and merrily calling back to the others that they were shocking laggards, to be so knocked up by a mere walk around the park.

'So, Miss Rae, my scientific talk of lengths of string has done no good,' Lydia resumed. 'Perhaps the feelings cannot be analysed and measured in that way. Tell me, do you correspond with the gentlemen—either, or both?'

'Oh, good heavens, no, neither,' Phoebe said, with a shocked look. 'That would be most improper without an engagement. And besides, I

157

already feel I am being duplicitous—there, I am on the *d*s—horribly duplicitous, in receiving the attentions of both gentlemen.'

'Why, I have known many a young woman delight in having a whole flock of lovers at her command.'

'But that, I suppose, is mere flirtation. I wish I could think like that, but I can't. Which is why I have even thought it might be better if I broke off all connection with both of them.' Phoebe's voice trembled a little, and she forced a cough. 'And now this is all very silly and tiresome, and I think we should go back to Johnson's *Dictionary*.'

'No, no: but I do not see the need to turn Gothic, and talk of renunciations. I would simply ask—well, where do you see happiness in life, Miss Rae? Does it lie only in meeting the right man, and marrying him?'

'It ought not to, I dare say. But it is where most women place their happiness, after all.'

'And is that a reason for doing something—because it is what everyone else does?' Lydia asked; it came out more sharply than she intended.

'You are right, of course,' Phoebe said humbly.

'Women may *place* their happiness in the prospect of marriage, but it is debatable how often they find it there. Mrs Vawser is married to a worthless, foolish rake: doubtless when she married him she did not find him so, or expect that he would make her unhappy; or indeed that unhappiness would make her foolish in turn. For a woman without means, marriage may wear a different aspect: it is her only hope of maintenance, and protection from poverty. In that sense marriage is like drawing a bad tooth: a

158

necessary prevention of a greater evil, which one must hope will be as little painful as possible. But your fortune, Miss Rae, secures you against any such necessity.'

'You think so much more clearly than me!' Phoebe said admiringly. 'And I do hope I am not rushing towards marriage—on rails, so to speak. I know it is a profoundly important choice. But—I think you and I feel differently about these things.'

In Phoebe's thus quietly standing her ground, Lydia found more to like and respect than in constantly being agreed with. Still, the girl is romantic, she thought—indeed, downright romantical, as her old nurse used to put it. Just what she expected, in fact. Lydia made herself be bracing. Come: Phoebe Rae is healthy, she has a great deal of money coming to her, and as long as she does not choose to marry an absolute brute, she will surely do tolerably well in life: there is, after all, only so much interest and sympathy one can extend to her situation, and I have extended it.

But this left aside the fact that Phoebe was charming, that she was by no means stupid, and that she was alarmingly innocent. Also something Lydia had not bargained for: her own reluctant but undeniable curiosity about Mr Allardyce and Mr Beck.

'We feel differently,' she said, smiling, 'but there is the true mark of civilisation, when people can do so without pummelling each other. You anticipate, I think, seeing both gentlemen in Bath this summer?'

'I do,' Phoebe said, on such a deep, tremulous note as gave 'anticipate' a new meaning. Such as, desperately and wretchedly and passionately long

159

for.

'In that case, nothing can be better,' Lydia declared, as they came to the ivied wall that admitted them to the gardens. 'The separation, as you say, has confused your feelings, and suspense has heightened them. The relative merits of the two gentlemen will become clearer once the acquaintance is renewed. You will be able to compare the reality of each with your memory of them: assess again their manners, their looks, their conversation. Surely then the pieces of string will not remain equal. One of them will grow and lengthen.' She stopped: the image was, at best, unfortunate: the expressive gesture she was making with her hands even more so. 'Good Lord, I think we must have come the wrong way—I wonder where—'

'There,' Phoebe said, pointing to the house, elusive as a mountain. 'Miss Templeton, are you quite well? I hope you have not caught the sun like Mrs Vawser . . .'

She had not, but she was glad all the same to reach the terrace, and step again into the cool of the breakfast-room: by which time she had also composed herself, and mentally banished the lengths of string, and was fit for company. She was happy to find her father comfortably seated there, with a full glass of wine unregarded at his elbow, and a volume from the library on his knee. The cold luncheon stood ready, and Mr Paige was soon doing the honours of the table, and aggressively helping everyone to ham and Madeira.

Mrs Vawser, however, was discontented. Really it was too provoking of her dear monster not to be here to welcome them back—one of those whimsical creatures who could not bear to be thanked, no doubt, but still, she did not like to taste a crumb unless her host was present—she was fastidious in that way, all her friends would say so; and at last Lydia, knowing the house, and feeling that the servants had been busy enough, and wishing above all an end to the woman's noise, undertook to go and find him.

It was pleasant to be alone for a little space: to dawdle along the familiar beeswax-scented passages, and enjoy a renewal of that feeling of mellow tranquillity: even to congratulate herself. She had withstood the assault of memory: she had done her duty to Lady Eastmond, in interesting herself in Phoebe Rae, and giving her considered advice. Indeed, Lydia felt she had talked a good deal of sense.

She found Mr Durrant in his study: a manservant was just coming out with a bundle of letters for the post, and Mr Durrant, still at his desk, beckoned her in.

'Don't tell me: I am wanted.'

'By a certain party.'

Growling, he rose. 'I do not think I am equal to any more shrieks. If she shrieks, I am off.'

'Such a budget of letters. Are you writing off to Bath, to bespeak lodgings for your great adventure?'

'No, I shall go to my friend at Clifton first,' he said neutrally. 'He undertakes to find lodgings for me. He knows about these things. The letters are mostly to do with the school I am founding. Here—' he thrust towards her a building plan '—this may be of interest to you.'

'On your land?'

'Over towards Pickworth. For the children of the villages thereabout. There is no other provision. I have been writing to those few whose opinion I respect, as well as those who would expect to be consulted.'

'Tut, teaching the poor to read,' she said, in a parsonical voice. 'They will only be saucy and get above themselves.'

He smiled grimly. 'Yes, that's what most people will say. For my part I like the saucy poor: they have spirit at least: it is the poor who creep to church and profess themselves contented I cannot bear. But I shall have the school, whatever they say.'

She knew that this was no empty boast. Mr Durrant was an exemplary landlord, and a friend to all schemes of improvement; but sometimes she felt there was something altogether too showy in his hobnobbing with tenants and workers. Lady Bountiful in reverse, she thought with faint malice.

'It looks like an admirable project,' she said. 'And if I were to be consulted, which I won't be, I would lay down only one stipulation: that the girls should receive the same education as the boys.'

'Certainly: perhaps more. They stand in greater need of it.'

'You had better beware, though,' she said, brushing this aside, or trying to, 'of being too much the friend of the poor. They might take it to the ultimate conclusion. What if they decided they wished to have Culverton, and divide it among themselves?'

'I would resist it, of course—because I am selfish, and it belongs to me, and so on. But it would be an interesting experiment, though I can foresee the result. They would not divide it among themselves: they would talk willingly of doing so, and then the strongest of them would take the whole lot for himself.'

'An excellent excuse for keeping it in your own hands. But, Mr Durrant, such a dim view of human nature—I cannot believe you really hold it, else why build a school at all?'

'Human nature is not incapable of improvement: it is only very resistant to it. It is like a sickly patient, liable to weaken and sink the moment his treatment is neglected.'

'Hm. Mind, I suspect you would let the poor, saucy or sanctimonious, have Culverton before your nephew.'

'Good God, yes,' Mr Durrant said, going to the window and opening it to let out a drowsy bee. 'If the law of the land allowed—but Culverton is entailed. And as I cannot change the law, I must change something else.'

'You really do hate Hugh Hanley, don't you? Why?'

'I hate him,' he answered with cool consideration, as if discussing a badly written book, 'because he is part of a strand in the human race that has always caused trouble, and inflicted pain, but is always forgiven and indulged; because its members are superficially attractive. They talk well, and fit into society neatly, and find nothing in the scheme of the world that they would protest against, except the necessity of their having more money, and being allowed to do what they want even more than they do already. Hugh is a careless young coxcomb now, craving indulgence for his

163

follies, and even asking that we admire them: and there is nothing more certain than that he will end up as an elderly magistrate handing out stiff sentences and saying, "Youth is no excuse."' He did not look at her: his angular profile against the window showed no disquiet; but she sensed that there was a relief for him in pronouncing this speech, as if it had been revolving in his mind. 'Well,' he said turning, 'the school. Sit, sit. Boys and girls, certainly: and I shall insist on reading *and* writing. Religious instruction there must be, else it will never be approved, but I will not have it excessive. Now, what else do you recommend?'

'I cannot say until I know whether I am one of those people you trust, or one of those who must not be left out.' She received a quelling look. 'Very well—I refer again to the girls. Their education, no doubt, will include a deal of sewing—but please, let them be taught also to be sensible and rational creatures.'

'Aha!'

'Spare me your masculine aha, Mr Durrant.'

'I did not suppose it had a sex. I am merely making a supposition—though almost certainly a correct one. This has come from your encounter with your young charge.'

Lydia did not deny it. 'What do you think of her?'

He shrugged. 'Very pretty: and she looks good-tempered enough. But I have only exchanged a few words with her. You are much better placed than I to give an estimate of Miss Rae. She is your responsibility, after all.'

'She is nothing of the kind,' Lydia said, aware of her jaw tightening. 'Lady Eastmond wished me to

164

befriend her—and that I have been happy to do, as Miss Rae is altogether delightful.'

'Aha!'

'You're doing it again.'

'So she's delightful, is she? Delightful enough for you to turn chaperon after all?'

She glared at him: she did hate it when he was pleased with himself.

'Perhaps,' she said, taking a pen from his desk, and beginning to mend it. 'Who knows? I may do as I please. I am—thank heaven—a free and independent woman.'

'Heaven is certainly to be thanked for that. Well, you may do as you please, as you remark; but if you were to go with Miss Rae to Bath after all, I would know there was another reason behind it.'

'To have the pleasure of *your* company there, of course.'

'Not that. You would do it simply because I said you could not do it: that you were unsuited to it, and not capable. So generally accomplished as you are, *that* suggestion is unbearable to you, I think; and so you would have to prove me wrong.'

'You live too much by yourself, Mr Durrant,' she said, as collectedly as she could. 'It encourages you in the habit of believing that every question, every decision is referable to you. I regret to inform you that when I choose what soup we are to have for dinner, I do not ask myself: what would Mr Durrant like?'

'No, you are more likely to ask yourself what I would dislike.'

Lydia plied the penknife rather vigorously. 'Whether I accompany Miss Rae to Bath or not—and whether I am any use to her or not—still the project is well meant. Some might consider me unsuitable—but no one would consider my going an absurdity.'

'An absurdity—oh, I see: you still cannot accept the notion of *my* going to seek a wife.'

'I accept it, but I cannot help laughing at it.'

'You're ruining that pen.' He came away from the window, awkward about the arms as ever: folded them at last. 'You doubt my success?'

'No, no,' she said lightly, 'I am sure there are women who would consent to marry on such terms as yours.'

'You do not know the terms.'

'Well, is it not merely engaging a wife as you would engage a servant, or a farm-steward? I cannot imagine, from all you have said, that you go with any more romantic intention than that.'

'You assume too much.' His face remained darkly immobile, but there was a shift in his voice, like the drop into coolness when a thunder-shower begins. 'I am resolved to marry: that does not mean anything will do. I had much rather marry happily—yes, with true regard, affection—love: why not, if they are to be had? I shall certainly seek them. Do you find that a matter for laughter?'

'No: only for disbelief,' Lydia said; and saw at once he was offended.

'I wonder why you credit me with this insensibility—this incapability of feeling. Because I once proposed to you, and was declined, pray do not suppose I have been wearing the willow ever since, and have forsworn marriage because of it.'

Very much what she had said about him to George in London: but she preferred it when she said it. 'I do not suppose that, Mr Durrant,' she

166

said, putting the pen and knife down, and then picking them up again. 'I never think about the matter.'

He roamed to the window—where the bee, with deplorable lack of judgement, was trying to get in again—and presented his stiff high-shouldered back to her. 'After all, one might lay the same charge against you: for you have shown no inclination to marry since then either.'

'Because I am very happy as I am, Mr Durrant: no more nor less.'

'Exactly so with me,' he said with composure.

'But not *exactly* so, surely—as you are now proposing to take a wife.'

'For sensible reasons this time,' he said, on a half-yawning note, 'rather than stupid ones.'

'You refer to your proposal to me, of course—and, of course, you are trying to provoke me with it. A vain hope, as I view that past event with the purest detachment. So I will not ask why your reasons for wishing to marry me were, in your exquisite phrase, stupid. Indeed I do not have to. It is simply because I refused you. You comfort yourself for not getting what you wanted by pretending you did not really want it.'

'My reasons then belonged to the blind partiality of youth, which is seldom productive of lasting happiness.'

'Very well: but these *sensible* reasons of your maturity are really no different. They are still rooted in your self-regard and arrogance, and that general cold determination of always having your own way.'

He turned with a polite attentiveness, as if a piece of music had just ended. 'Well, and what if

167

they are? You are detached, as you say: whatever I do cannot trouble you.'

'Not directly: but if some poor woman does accept you, I feel for her, in loyalty to my sex.'

'Oh, I don't think so. Women are generally cruel to each other: their sympathy only takes the form of pity, which always has a little triumph in it, and the consciousness of being better off.'

'Oh, I pity her, I do indeed pity her, whoever she may be: and my only triumph, as you call it, is the knowledge that *I* had the sense to refuse you.' She flung the penknife down on the desk: it would have been very satisfying if it had thudded into the wood like a quivering dagger, but it didn't.

'Upon my word, you are curiously interested in this whole matter. You protest that it has nothing to do with our past association—but any unprejudiced observer would surely doubt that. I think rather they would conclude your vanity is at stake. Whatever you do, all must do. Because you refused me, you are piqued at the idea of anyone else accepting me. You too, Miss Templeton, are very much addicted to having your own way—to keeping everything under your hand, and in your control; and because you *once* had the power of making me happy or unhappy, you wish to arrogate that power to yourself in perpetuity.'

'Good God, you have a more conceited opinion of yourself than even I could have believed. What will it take to convince you of the simple truth, Mr Durrant, that I do not care in the least about what you do?'

'I do not flatter myself that you *care*—any more than the spoiled, selfish child really cares about the toy he keeps clutched in his hand, and will not

168

share with others.'

'Believe me,' she said, getting up, 'the toy is long relinquished, and there was never much amusement to be had from it. I congratulate you on the school, Mr Durrant. Whatever your motives for it—whether truly philanthropic, or a mere wish to make yourself appear so—still it is a good project, and good will come from it. I cannot say the same of your other project, but I *have* lost my fears on that score. My opinion is altered. You will not find a woman to marry you—not in Bath, not in Clifton nor Brighton nor all the watering-places of the kingdom. You may go where you please, the result will be the same: you may go to the ends of the earth: indeed, Mr Durrant, to speak candidly, you may go to hell.'

Some moments later she was walking quickly down the passage, with no memory of having left the study, and only a tardy realisation that she was going the wrong way. She stopped. From a portrait on the panelling some ancestral Durrant was looking down his long nose at her. Spoiled and selfish, he said. She scowled, turned and retraced her steps, slowly. She was loath to return to the conviviality of the breakfast-room, irked and flushed as she was: Lydia hated to appear in company other than in perfect calm and self-possession. Irked. I am on the *i*s. It was precisely the word for Mr Durrant's effect on her: the word was like hairs down the neck or grit under the eyelid. He had irked excessively today: but she must have caught the sun also, to be in this knotted, queasy, almost tearful state of feeling. So much for mellow tranquillity. Perhaps she could quietly hint to her father that she wanted to go home at once: oh, but she detested that sort of thing—Vawserism, call it: my precious feelings must always be made room for, like a cripple's crutch.

Turning the corner into the hall, she bumped into Phoebe Rae.

'Oh! Miss Templeton, there you are. I hope you don't mind, but I came to see if . . .' The storm-cloud-coloured eyes searched, but gently: Lydia felt no prod of intrusion. 'I just wondered. So I came to see if—if all was quite well with you.'

'All,' said Lydia, after a moment, taking her arm, 'is quite well, I thank you—or will be, when you leave off "Miss Templeton" and begin to call me "Lydia".'

Phoebe's face shone. 'I shall be glad to, if you will do the same. Well, not call me "Lydia", of course, because that isn't my name, Phoebe is. Can you imagine the trouble I had learning to spell "Phoebe" when I was a girl? I remember getting quite angry and saying, "I am not Pu-ho-eeb" and never will be . . .'

She talked on, not from tactlessness but from its opposite, as they made their way back to the breakfast-room; and if Lydia's composure was not quite perfect when they arrived, it was near enough so to satisfy her; and to deepen significantly her friendly feeling towards Phoebe. That simple act of coming to look for her had done much. In fact Lydia found in it—like unwrapping a surprising parcel—more than she could have guessed.

Mr Durrant was not long in joining them, and there was something hasty and nearly obliging about him that Lydia was pleased to think of as discomfort. Mrs Vawser, true to her word, had eaten nothing in his absence: but she had drunk several glasses of wine, which rendered her almost operatic in her response to her host's return. Lydia vengefully enjoyed the aria of flirtation and recrimination for a while, and then stepped out on to the terrace: her father was genially declining to agree with Mr Paige on the necessity of more hangings, Phoebe was listening with troubled attention to Emma's account of her children's illnesses, and she herself was free to steal away and indulge the luxury of solitary reflection.

She did not wish *always* to be alone: but she wished that the wish to be so was a little more respected. The requirement of lovers to be undisturbed was always an occasion of much sentimental indulgence—yet let a single person desire it, and swift gathered the clouds of disapproval and speculation: what are you *doing*?

What she was doing was looking further into the surprising parcel. And here at the bottom was the very decision she had steeled herself against. How had it happened? The reproachful ghosts of the past: Phoebe's gentle intuitive concern: curiosity: resignation: conscience: pride—perhaps they had all played a part. And, yes, Lewis Durrant's insinuations too. He could still affect her: that had not been a pleasant revelation, but there, it was an addition to self-knowledge, and for Lydia all knowledge was good. Of course, he would take the credit for her change of mind to himself. Well, let him do so. If she was to be an effective chaperon— wise, self-effacing, dispassionate—she must rise above petty annoyances.

A footstep sounded on the terrace. Damn it all, was she not to have a moment's peace?

171

'Miss Templeton.'

It was Mr Durrant, carrying a small tray with wine and glasses. He set it down on the balustrade, and frowned out at the gardens.

'Cooler now,' he said.

'Yes.' It was, a little: but the remark might equally have referred to their tempers, though neither would have admitted it.

'Will you take a glass of wine with me?'

Presumably he meant her, and not the rosebush to which he apparently addressed the question.

'Thank you.' *With pleasure* would have been a little too much.

'Of course,' he said, after they had sipped in distant silence for a while, 'the gardens are not at their best. Late June is the best time to see them— late June or early July.'

'I know,' she answered, with a carefully calibrated minimum of cordiality.

'Yes . . . I, of course, shall not be here then.'

'When do you leave?'

'Monday next, all being well.' He shook his head. 'There is a great deal to see to. Especially as I don't know precisely when I shall be returning.'

It was no good: her eyebrow would not be restrained: it would go up. 'No? I had thought your campaign planned to the last detail.'

He submitted a short smile, as if to say he would allow her that. 'Fortunately my steward is very capable.'

Lydia finished her wine, and as he came forward to take her glass she said: 'I shall not be here either, by the by.'

'Indeed?'

'Indeed.' She put the glass into his stiff

172

outstretched hand. 'Pray don't drop that, Mr Durrant, it's very good crystal. Yes, I am going to accede to Lady Eastmond's request, and be Miss Rae's companion in Bath for the summer. So: perhaps we shall see something of each other.'

'It is—possible,' he said slowly, as if peering into a deep well of doubt.

'Depending, of course, on whether either of us can tolerate a situation so alien to our natures, and does not come running back home at once.'

'That I do not anticipate in my own case. I do not easily give up on a resolve.'

'No more do I. Do put the glass down, Mr Durrant, you make a very indifferent waiter. No, I do not give up easily either, and so we might argue it out until Doomsday. You think I will fail as a companion to Miss Rae, and I think you will fail in seeking marriage; and only time will reveal.'

'Just so,' he said, faintly uneasy, 'and so I would suggest we let the matter rest there.'

'Well: to return to the school, then. Would fifty pounds, as a gift, help in its establishment?'

After a moment's surprise, he said: 'It would be useful indeed. But I hope you do not think I was canvassing for subscriptions: I always intended to bear the whole cost myself, and—'

'You may do yet. What I am proposing, Mr Durrant—as a way of letting the matter rest, comfortably and finally—is a wager. Fifty pounds on whoever succeeds in Bath.'

He lifted his head. 'Ah.'

'That was not quite an aha, so I will forgive it. Fifty pounds: the loser to donate the money to your school. This gives the wager a moral cast, and removes avarice from the equation of motives.'

173

He studied her: thoughtful, suspicious, and reluctantly amused.

'The terms of this wager are decidedly vague,' he said, weighing the glass in his hand.

'A thing can hardly be *decidedly* vague. The essence of vagueness is indecision—oh, very well, don't glare at me. Come, the terms are surely fair enough. One hears of gentlemen in the London gambling-clubs laying bets on which raindrop will reach the sill first, or whether the maid who brings the candles will be pretty or not. I dare say your nephew Mr Hanley has known many such.'

'I dare say he has,' Mr Durrant agreed gloomily, 'and lost a small fortune on them . . . Still, Miss Templeton, one needs to know what constitutes *success* in this matter.'

'Think of it the other way: to decide the wager, it requires only one or other of us to acknowledge failure. Now this is something we both hate—yet I believe we are both honest also. When the game is up, you may count upon me to say so; and I trust the same with you. There is no sadder spectacle, you'll agree, than a person who refuses to admit the truth about himself.'

'Or herself.'

'Which is what I meant—I would say "themself" if grammar would allow me. Pedantry will not divert me, Mr Durrant: what do you say?'

'Tell me first: what made you change your mind? About going to Bath?'

She took the wine-glass from his hand and set it down on the tray. 'Caprice, Mr Durrant: sheer womanly caprice. Does that answer satisfy you?'

'It must, as I see it is the only one I shall get. Very well, I accept your wager—subject to one

174

condition. There must be no interfering with the result.'

'Interfering—what can you mean?'

'I mean that if I were to make a bet with you on a horse-race, I should hope you would not creep round to the stables and hobble my fancy.'

Lydia suppressed her laughter. 'The poetry of your language is overpowering as ever. But you have my word: if I see you in the Pump Room making strong love to a moon-faced heiress, I shall not take her aside and whisper slanders about you. I shall let your recommendations speak for themselves. You being subject to the same conditions, of course, Mr Durrant. You will not complicate my task by making Miss Rae fall in love with you, for example.'

He gave her a long hard look; but there was a thawing in it.

'Well, it is no worse than betting on raindrops. Your hand on it, then.'

They shook hands; and in the breakfast-room Phoebe, looking out, smiled and said to Mrs Paige: 'I have heard about their past association—and I do think it is admirable how easy Miss Templeton and Mr Durrant are with one another.'

CHAPTER TWELVE

Sydney Place, Bath, Friday, 21 June
My dear Papa
Never let it be said the Templetons do not keep their promises—
I promised you a letter the moment we were

175

tolerably settled, and the moment I think is here. The last trunk, after a curious diversion at Devizes, has rejoined us at last, and is unpacked, and none the worse for its adventure. Mary Darber has examined the house throughout for damp, and pronounces herself satisfied. I was sure that as Lady Eastmond's careful steward had the choosing of our lodging, there would be no difficulties in that direction; but Mary suspects all Lady Eastmond's household, on the evidence of the maid and manservant who have come from Osterby with us. They tend to talk privately, and gaze at each other. Mary disapproves of that sort of thing.

The only truly good journey, you will agree, is a short one—but ours was as comfortable as a journey of a hundred and fifty miles may be. To be shut up together in a carriage for such a time was a good test of how Phoebe and I will rub along—and the omens are fair. We fell neither to quarrelling nor silence. She is, I freely confess, a delightful and excellent young woman: too good for me, no doubt. Which brings me to my other promise—that to Lady Eastmond—the promise to undertake the guidance and protection of her ward—the promise that, dear Papa, you know I strongly resisted making—and which I can still hardly believe I am fulfilling at this moment! Do I regret it, you ask—am I indeed fully reconciled to it—do I not, you ask, tremble at the prospect ahead of me? (And do you dislike as much as I do being impertinently told in a letter that 'you ask' something, when you probably do not ask anything of the kind?)

Well, time must tell as to the fullness or otherwise of my repentance or vindication—let me say only that as I sit here quite comfortably situated, and with no great apprehensions of the morrow or indeed of the eight weeks to follow, it occurs to me that I have been guilty of the worst sin in my private theology: I have dramatised *this whole business to a shocking degree, which you, Papa, have been indulgent enough not to point out. It is true that the first view of Bath, on our entering the town, answered all my gloomy expectations, and confirmed all my distasteful memories: a place of elegant stupidity, resembling nothing so much as a great set of genteel sentry-boxes, from which so many guards of mediocrity periodically emerge, to repel anything that does not smack of polite dullness and self-satisfaction. However, I begin already to bend a little—to mellow—for, after all, a person has little to complain of, whose sufferings extend only to the toleration of boredom and insipidity. The house is all one could wish: we stand directly opposite Sydney Gardens, which makes for a much more agreeable outlook than those nonsensical crescents and circuses in the upper town, all staring each other out of countenance like mausoleums squaring up for a fight. The drawing-room is sufficiently large and airy, and below it is a decent dining-room, and an arched hall that leads back to what the inhabitants of Bath are pleased to call a garden—meaning a scrubby yard, a piece of grass the size of a handkerchief, a water-butt, a rat-hole, and a revealing view of the neighbouring back-*

premises, all as lop-sided and dingy. I delight in this absolute admission at Bath that show and front *are all; and wonder mightily what would happen, if I were to set a corresponding fashion in dress, and let out a panel in the back of my gown so as to exhibit a patched old shift behind.*—*I am so sorely tempted to try it in the Pump Room that I had better stop thinking of it.*

There, I have writ the dread words—the Pump Room, to which no doubt tomorrow, now we are settled, we shall repair to write our names in the book, and so commence a true Bath residence of dawdling idiocy. (Forgive me—like indigestion, that came over me and could not be suppressed.) Phoebe to her credit is very pleased with everything, but not absurdly so: she has simply a great relish for every sort of experience, which is not to be disparaged.—And besides that, of course, she is in the place where she expects to renew her London acquaintance: the two gentlemen about whom her feelings are so desperately exercised—and again to her credit, she has refrained from talking about them: she has about her only a shining *look of anxious anticipation, which only a monster could reprove. (I have no consciousness of monstrosity* as yet.) *I do not expect her suspense will be long maintained. A letter from Lady Eastmond awaited me on our arrival. In it she remains so insistent that the rent, wages, victualling &c., of the house be at her charge, that I fear, Papa, there is nothing you can do: it is all fixed, and I dare say she would have persisted in her design of paying all my daily*

expenses also if we had not stood our ground.—
The substance of the letter, however, relates to
the Grand Design. The renewal of Phoebe's
London campaign has been carefully overseen
by Lady Eastmond. The foreign-service
gentleman Mr Allardyce, you may remember,
resides here in any case for the summer—his
mother lives at Queen Square; and Lady
Eastmond having numerous acquaintance in
Bath, has already written to spread the word of
Miss Rae's arrival, in such a way as must come
to Mr Allardyce's ears—leaving aside the fact
that she solemnly promised him she would
come to Bath this summer, or perish. As for the
other gentleman, Mr Beck the scribbler: Lady
Eastmond informs me that he has been
peppering Osterby with ardent letters ever since
London—letters that she has prudently
intercepted; and while much deploring their
extravagant character, she has maintained what
I believe is called (in Mr Allardyce's diplomatic
terms) an exchange of notes, and so has alerted
him to Phoebe's presence in Bath from this
date, on the understanding that any renewal of
acquaintance must be in circumstances of
strictest decorum.

I think she has done pretty well.—In London
both these gentlemen, it seems, exacted positive
promises from Phoebe that they would meet
again at Bath: awkward result for a guardian,
from youthful impetuosity!—but Lady
Eastmond has turned the matter to true Bath
decorum. Our hall table stands dusted and bare
and ready for the leaving of cards. I would
almost be inclined to lay a wager with Phoebe

*on who leaves a card first—Mr A or Mr B—
though I do not think Phoebe would be
receptive to matters of the heart being treated
so. I dare say she is right, though it is a pity.*

*—Which reminds me, do you hear anything
from Mr Durrant? His setting out for the west
three weeks ahead of us, and his stated
intention of relying on his friend at Clifton to
secure him a Bath lodging, makes me wonder
whether he may already be established here.—I
do long to see him trying out his bows in the
Pump Room, and glaring at everyone.*

*—I have just glanced back at this letter, and
have hit on a curious thing—Mr Allardyce and
Mr Beck I referred to quite unconsciously as Mr
A and Mr B.—Now this must be more than
happy accident. It reconciles me quite to my
task to know that there is no greater burden
placed upon my judgement than pronouncing
for Phoebe on the relative merits of Mr A and
Mr B—for I feel myself inserted into the
spelling-book—or even the mathematics-
book—if A equals B, &c. (and let us be
honest—in life there is usually not much to
choose between A and B)—and so all must be
well.*

*I look forward, dear Papa, to seeing you and
Heystead again, once my term of servitude is
over: but I am glad in the meantime that Mr
Shipley has decided to retire from practice, and
will be keeping you company disgracefully
during the summer.—Emma, I know, will also
be much with you, now that Mrs Vawser has
decided to return to the abode of matrimonial
bliss.*

180

—Cynical, what do you mean, sir?

I have decided by the by that I do not wish to be known as a chaperon to Phoebe: I prefer to be a 'duenna'. Yes, I know it is the same but consider—does not a duenna sound just faintly spicy, as if before her descent into mature chaperonage she had rather a Past?

My love to you in any case,
Lydia

Edgar Buildings, Bath, Friday, 21 June
Hugh Hanley Esq.
Dear Sir,
Your mother may have informed you of my intention to remove to Bath for the summer: I write to confirm the fact. Any communications should be sent to the direction on this letter, until further notice. I hope it is unnecessary to add that communications of a certain sort—requests for money, referred bills, &c.—will not be acknowledged.

My business here is my own: but it is as well to notify you that I anticipate a change in my personal and material circumstances, which may have a bearing on our future relation.

In the meantime I remain, &c.,
Lewis Durrant

Sydney Place, Bath, Saturday, 22 June
My dear Lady Eastmond,
We are just returned from our first thorough exploration of Bath—that, is first for me: Lydia, of course, finds no novelty in the place, but she is kind enough not to betray it—and I must not neglect this opportunity of writing to you; to

181

convey my warmest wishes, and above all my thanks to you, for indulging my desire of coming here. Also for your securing for me such an excellent friend and protectress as Lydia. I shall be sure to be guided by her in all matters of custom and conduct.

I like Bath extremely: it seems to combine so many excellent qualities within a small compass. There is something of Edinburgh in its look, but without the greyness and severity. There are views of green hills and cliffs from almost every opening in the streets, so that one does not feel entirely cut off from the country as in London; but then as in London, there is every civilised amenity. There is not, it appears, a great deal of company here, being the summer season—but for myself I would never have guessed it: the town seems quite full. There are the invalids, of course—the sight of whom inspires such pitiful reflections—but any number of elegant well-looking people besides; and the abbey bells are forever ringing in new arrivals—that is, those who come in a coach-and-four, as Lydia tells me—and as you must know. It does seem to me a curious distinction—four horses meriting this tribute; and Lydia was rather satirical about it, and wondered what a clangour would be set up if Bonaparte's cavalry entered the town. I think she is a little Radical in some of her sentiments; and I did have to remind her of the necessity of church attendance tomorrow; however, I know there is no harm in it. And then though the chief entertainments, the Lower Room assemblies, &c., do not begin until the autumn, there is still a great deal going forward—music at the New Rooms, and a gala at Sydney Gardens, and any amount of private balls and routs. And then there are the most agreeable circulating-libraries, and shops such as one only sees in London—in short, I do not anticipate we shall be bored for a moment.

We have paid our first visit to the Pump Room: where, Lydia tells me, we were thoroughly quizzed, this being an essential Bath amusement. She was for talking in French, and putting our names down in the book as viscomtesses, but I was afraid I could not carry it off. I felt I must complete the visit by drinking the waters: Lydia gently advised against it, but I was determined: at the pump-bar I chose one of the tallest glasses, and drank it off stoutly. I cannot say I found it pleasant. Lydia remarked, in her candid way, that it seemed to her like drinking a gentleman's shaving-water; and then took me over to the windows overlooking the King's Bath, where there were numerous people immersed, and wearing peculiar caps and smocks—more decent than comfortable; and Lydia said how odd it was that we should drink the same water people had been bathing in. Certainly this made me thoughtful for some time after.

I am sure I should tire even your patience, dear Lady Eastmond, if I were to go on with everything I have seen and done.—But I cannot omit this piece of news. Mr Allardyce left his card this morning. I hope I am not so nonsensical as to be very agitated by this circumstance; but nor can I be insensible to

183

such a very prompt mark of his regard—typical
though it is of a gentleman who, I believe, is
more agreeable and estimable than any I have
ever met.

I hear nothing of Mr Beck.—But then he is
perhaps less attentive to such conventions as
calling-cards.

We dine soon.—My dear Lady Eastmond,
please present my compliments to Sir Henry. I
hope his old indisposition is not rendering him
too uncomfortable—nor you neither.
Yours very affectionately
Phoebe

CHAPTER THIRTEEN

Lydia would have been guilty of an untruth if she
had pretended no curiosity to see at last the two
gentlemen on whose account she was prepared to
endure a summer in Bath. While she had privately
christened them Mr A and Mr B—and in her less
patient moments was even wont to think of them
as two peas in a pod—she was far from indifferent
at the prospect of meeting them. One at least must
soon be expected at Sydney Place: Mr Robert
Allardyce's card would, in form, be followed by
Mr Robert Allardyce. The very first rap at their
street-door, the Monday after their arrival, sent
Phoebe rushing to the drawing-room windows, and
even Lydia had to resist the urge to follow.

'Oh! Oh, it is Mr Durrant,' Phoebe said, and was
good-natured enough to hide her disappointment.

For her part Lydia, after less than a week's

residence in Bath, was already sufficiently wistful for home—its employments, its comforts, its associations—to feel a certain lift of the heart at that name. Their last meeting had been, even for them, less than cordial: still, when Mr Durrant walked in he did bring a little of Heystead with him, as well as a refreshing absence of Bath elegancies.

'Miss Templeton—Miss Rae—how d'ye do—miserably hot, is it not?' was the extent of his compliments, and he sat down looking very strained and cross, as if, instead of choosing to pay a morning-visit, he had been summoned there against his will at some unearthly hour. He was dressed exactly as in the country, in well-worn riding-coat and unpolished top-boots, and his restless eyes took in the dimensions and furnishings of the room with a baleful lack of interest. 'I saw your names in the book. You're comfortably situated, I hope.'

'Very much so, thank you,' Lydia answered. 'And you, Mr Durrant?'

'Oh—' he shrugged '—Bath is much of a muchness, is it not? I have been above a week in a suite of rooms in Edgar Buildings: there is an idiot woman learning singing next door and the chimney smokes, but all in all they will do.'

'I am so very glad to hear it. And do you have a large circle of acquaintance in Bath, Mr Durrant?'

He allowed her a small sharp smile. 'That is how we are talking, is it? Well, I suppose we must, now we are here. In truth I know hardly a soul; but I am on nodding and simpering terms with a good many people already, so I may conclude I am going on pretty well. Perhaps, though, I should be a little

185

more pushing, and lay on a turtle-dinner at the White Hart for two dozen choice cultivable boobies—what say you, Miss Rae?'

'I have never eaten turtle,' Phoebe said, in her serious way, 'and do not think I could fancy it: the manner of cooking it seems so very cruel. Of course it is always cruel in a way, when we kill a pig or sheep for eating, but it seems different somehow. Which perhaps makes me a hypocrite.'

'Lord, if that were the extent of hypocrisy in the world, we should do well,' he said. 'But I do see a kinder way to slaughter our meat: drive the pig or sheep on to the South Parade of a summer Sunday, and the beast will very soon die quietly of boredom.'

Mr Durrant was obviously both bored, and ill at ease; and Lydia was sorely tempted, despite Phoebe's presence, to twit him on the bullish confidence with which he had embarked on his enterprise, and to query whether he was equal to the further tedium of finding a bride. But she was not entirely without sympathy for him: she at least had Phoebe for company; and when he had sat out his half-hour, exhausted his mechanical civilities, and gone away again, Phoebe seemed to manifest something of the same feeling, asking after a thoughtful minute: 'Lydia, shall we entertain here at all, do you suppose?'

'I see no reason why we should not, on a small scale. We might give a dinner, or even—' she got the detestable words out '—a card-party.'

'Oh, yes, I don't mean anything grand. Something like a dinner would do very well. I thought it would be nice to invite Mr Durrant.'

'It would certainly be a nice thing to do, as I fear

he is a little at a loss: whether the experience would be nice, for you or me, is a different matter.'

'Oh, I think I am used to his manner now. It is indeed surprising that he has chosen to come to Bath—not that I know him very well, of course: only that it does not seem to suit him.'

Lydia had felt it right, for some reason, only to touch barely on Mr Durrant's purpose in Bath to Phoebe; and yet, after all, he had made no secret of it—quite the reverse. 'Certainly it is not, as it were, his natural habitat; but as others come here seeking a remedy for ill-health, so Mr Durrant has come to seek a remedy for his solitary state.'

'Oh!'

That 'oh', and the searching look that accompanied it, lingered a good deal longer than Lydia liked. 'Well, now, it is not so very strange,' she said briskly. 'Mr Durrant is still a relatively young man: he has a great care for the future of his estate, which as it stands is entailed to a rather unpromising nephew: so he concludes it is high time for him to marry. I wish everyone approached these matters so sensibly.'

That last sounded unfortunately pointed; but Phoebe was wrapped in thought. 'Well,' she said finally, with the waking-from-sleep look that deep reflection produced in her, 'I feel sure he will have no difficulty in that: no difficulty whatsoever.'

'My dear Phoebe, never tell me you think to add a third string to your bow.'

The flippancy was really the spray from a little wave of irritation; but Phoebe was grave. 'Oh, Lydia, pray don't suppose that I—really that was not my meaning. And as for my bow, I wish only to—to reduce the number of strings, if you see

187

what I mean.'

'I do, indeed I do,' Lydia said, pressing her arm. 'And now, as it continues so fine, should we not take our walk?'

I shall return from Bath, she thought as she put on her bonnet, a magnificent athlete with the hindquarters of a greyhound. For never was there so much walking. Strenuous walking too, so many of the streets, especially in the Upper Town, being steep; but for that same reason a carriage was more a hindrance than an amenity, unless of the light high-perch kind, which required a good hand at the ribbons. Walking—or rather strolling—was a social requirement here: there was no being at Bath without sauntering about the Parades, or (most dismally for Lydia) the lawns before the Royal Crescent, Sunday afternoons being appointed particularly appropriate for this most vacant and stultifying exercise.

But for Lydia walking was a requirement of a more urgent character. To walk meant to be out of the house in Sydney Place: which was perfectly acceptable, perfectly comfortable to return to, eat in, sleep in—but which resembled to her mind, if she were too long confined there, a well-appointed prison. Her fingers itched for music, but there was no instrument: the trouble and expense of hiring a pianoforte for their short stay was excessive, and she was besides here to be of service to Phoebe, not to indulge her own enjoyments: still the lack was keenly felt. Walking at least brought her to the excellent circulating-libraries of Milsom Street— oases for the parched mind, where there were not only books but all the latest newspapers, periodicals and reviews; even if she created a certain stir by actually reading them, instead of using them as accessories for lounging in her best dress. Walking varied the scene: failing everything else, it supplied her with people to watch. (A dangerous development this, however: would she turn into a Bath quiz, an old tea-drinking quadrille-playing tabby, speculating on this one's breeding and that one's fortune?) And walking tired her—preventing that flat, wide-eyed repose in the dead middle of her bed that had characterised her first few nights: wondering what she was doing here, and listening to the watchman cry the hour: *twelve of the clock, and only another eleven hours before you go back to the Pump Room, amble about, and despair of existence.* He did not say this, of course, he only seemed to.

Remorse: as they stepped out into the sunshine, Phoebe's face was lit with such a reciprocal glow of cheerful anticipation that Lydia mentally threw a handful of ashes on herself. Spoiled and selfish. Could she not for once be happy in another's happiness? (Dear God, even the phrase faintly nauseated her.) Perhaps thirty had been more of a milestone than she recognised. Perhaps her spirit was already beginning its transformation into a sour, wrinkled, crab-apple thing. Perhaps what she saw as the emptiness of Bath life was really an emptiness within herself.

Alternatively, perhaps she had drunk too much Madeira last evening. Her hands were a little shaky—and the invariable other symptom of over-indulgence was an apocalyptic mood. She entertained a theory about some of the prophetic books of the Bible having been written after a bumper of rather rough Canaanite red, but it was

189

not for Phoebe's ears.

Coming to the river, Phoebe lingered at the shops that lined Pulteney Bridge: she sought a stationer's, and had heard of a good one here. She wanted a small calfskin writing-book. 'Only for jottings,' as she said, going in; but Lydia had a strong suspicion, at once fond, melancholy and amused, that she meant to diarise in it. (Lydia remembered as a girl keeping a diary for a while, but she had caught herself out in so many lies in it that she had left off.) Presently Phoebe emerged from the stationer's satisfied, with parcel in hand; and the next moment promised the even greater satisfaction of having something to write in the precious book, as she delightedly cried: 'Mr Allardyce!'

Lydia was surprised to find that Mr Allardyce was merely one of a group of people chatting outside the print-maker's shop, on whom she had been idly resting her gaze while she waited. (Why surprising?—perhaps because his appearance had been so much a matter of anticipation: still one could hardly expect him to descend from on high, or burst out of a large drum.) He turned, made his excuses, and detached himself from the group: not alone, however: a very handsome young woman was on his arm.

For an instant Lydia feared that the diary was not only going to be used, but miserably filled. But the mutual smiles reassured her even before Phoebe's excited words: 'Oh, Lydia, let me introduce—Mr Allardyce, Miss Allardyce—my very good friend Miss Templeton.' Lydia remembered now, from Phoebe's account of her London season, that there had been a sister, naturally every bit as agreeable as Mr A himself.

While the usual compliments and exchanges were going on—including amiable wonder at their running into each other like this, as if in Bath it were possible not to, short of digging a hole and climbing in it—there was time for a preliminary assessment of Robert Allardyce, and of Phoebe's response to him. Miss Allardyce was a decided beauty: which perhaps accounted for her brother, of similar colouring and stature, appearing beside her no more than a moderately good-looking man—well-dressed, slim, fair, with a keen and intelligent and rather long face. As for Phoebe, she throbbed with such shy excitement, and hung with such devoted attention on his every word and look, that Lydia would have supposed her ready to approach the altar with him at that very moment, if she had not known that Phoebe was simultaneously in love with another man altogether.

'And are you comfortably settled at Sydney Place?' Mr Allardyce was entirely the gentleman, and careful to include both Lydia and Phoebe in his glance of enquiry. 'After leaving my card I was all for calling on you at once—but Juliet reminded me that there can be nothing worse than being plagued with callers when one's bags are only just unpacked.'

'Oh! we are perfectly settled—indeed you need not scruple—' faltered Phoebe, with an anxious smile at Lydia. Too forward? Too backward? Lydia gave her a calm look. This was Phoebe's ground, and she must learn to take possession of it.

'And are you quite well now, Miss Rae?' put in Miss Allardyce. 'You had such a very bad cold

191

when you left London; and though we called on Lady Eastmond some days later, and received a good report of you, we were quite concerned.'

'Absolutely well, I thank you—never better. The country soon set me up—it is a very good air in Lincolnshire, as Miss Templeton will tell you. Miss Templeton is god-daughter to Lady Eastmond, and of the same country. Oh, I am thoroughly well, indeed.' And she demonstrated it with her most brilliant smile, the effect of which on Mr Allardyce was plain: or, rather, plain to the observant eye. For where Phoebe's look was habitually intent, Mr Allardyce's seemed the opposite: there was no actual reserve, but he seemed to hold his own expressions, like an opera-glass or a vizard-mask, at a little distance.

'I hope the Bath air may agree with you as well,' he said. 'I am never convinced that its situation, ringed by hills, is of the healthiest, for all its reputation. Though to be sure there is variety in its climate: for it is either raining, or too hot.'

'These are the arguments with which he loves to tease our mother,' smiled Miss Allardyce, who had the same well-bred inclusive manner as her brother, 'for she would think of living nowhere else.'

'I am afraid she believes I have been corrupted by foreign parts,' Mr Allardyce said, 'and my only hope of redemption is never to go abroad again.'

Lydia said: 'You have lately been at Vienna, I think, sir?'

'Yes, I was attached to the British Ministry there: a fortunate posting.'

'Is it not rather dangerous,' Phoebe asked earnestly, 'with the war, and the French armies and everything?'

'No more dangerous than anywhere else in Europe just now, I would judge,' he said. 'And, after all, Juliet accompanied me, and I would never see her exposed to peril—not that I could stop her if she set her mind to it.'

Lydia experienced a feeling like a nasty rasping tongue that went from her nape to the crown of her head, and which she identified after a moment as pure envy. 'Vienna,' she said, 'that must be—there must be a great deal to see, and hear . . .'

'To hear especially—you are musical, Miss Templeton?' Mr Allardyce asked, with civil interest. 'Certainly it is a great city for music: Juliet may tell you more of that than I. We were often at the opera, but I am old-fashioned and tend to stick at Handel. But we are in the way, I see—' glancing over his shoulder, and drawing closer to Phoebe '—at least I assume that rather large gentleman, by glaring and snorting at us, intends a suave hint to that effect. Are you for the Lower Town?—Shall we go together?'

Much as he might have wished to, Mr Allardyce was too well-mannered to relinquish his sister's arm and take Phoebe's, let alone take both and leave Lydia stranded. (Not that she supposed herself likely to fall over sideways without a gentleman's arm: but the politeness was felt.) Still, as they all walked on together he contrived to give Phoebe a great deal of purposeful attention, without leaving anyone out: memories of their time in London were tactfully revived, and future prospects discreetly invoked, including a wish that he might introduce her to his mother, on whom he laughingly said he had been unjust. By the time

193

they parted at Milsom Street, the Allardyces having an engagement at the Paragon, the deep satisfaction on both sides at the meeting was as evident as their reluctance to end it.

Left alone with Lydia, Phoebe was a little quiet for a time, in a way that did honour to her good sense. Some girls would have shrieked, giggled, and professed themselves about to die on the spot: still others would have retreated into a high dramatic silence, from which the common claims of social intercourse could not reclaim them. The sun was strong now, bouncing mercilessly off the endless stone: Lydia was overheated, and proposed ices at Molland's the confectioner's; and still Phoebe restrained herself until they were seated in the dark, cakey-scented interior.

Then: 'Oh, Lydia, what do you think of him?' burst from her; and Lydia was obliged to push aside the growing tendrils of a headache, and properly consider the question.

'Well, I am very glad to have met him: and glad for you too, as this was, after all, a great part of our purpose here. Of course, all I can give you are the impressions of a very short, a very superficial introduction. But he appears agreeable, his manners wholly unexceptionable and pleasing, his air good . . .' She wilted for a moment. Really she could not do this: it was too much of a responsibility, and nonsensical besides: if the girl liked him, then let her get on with it . . . But a glance at Phoebe's eager, solemn, trusting face restored her; and she was forced to admit besides that after this encounter the notion of Mr A, the interchangeable cipher, would not do. He seemed a sensible man—and indeed, did she really suppose that Phoebe, with all her truly valuable qualities, would fall in love with a mere dummy in a complicated cravat?—and there had appeared much to like about his sister also. No, she must be honest. 'Yes, Phoebe, thus far I am very well inclined to Mr Allardyce; and it is clear that he is exceedingly well inclined to you. But, really, I am alarmed at the idea of your being influenced by me in these matters.'

'Oh, but, Lydia—I *want* to be influenced by you.'

'Flattering—and even more alarming. For the time being, Phoebe, I insist that you regard me as a sort of accompanying statue—no, not even that—a figure in a frieze on the wall, in the background, looking stern in profile. Trust me, as soon as there is anything in Mr Allardyce that I very much dislike, or that seems to threaten your happiness, I shall step down from the wall, and influence you like anything.'

Phoebe appeared satisfied; but Lydia was less than content with her own hyperbole. If the idea of offering benevolent encouragement was alarming, how much more so was the notion of advising her *against* an involvement, of whatever degree: it was fairly watering the ground for the seeds of reproach and recrimination. Not that she could imagine Phoebe turning very viciously upon her, or upon anyone: but still her young friend was a sharer of human nature, which had an invincible tendency to resent being told not to put its hand in the fire, and to maintain that if only it had been allowed to, the sensation would have been very nice.

No, Lydia must confine herself to the sympathetic ear, the temperate approval: not a finger would she lay upon the scales of decision. Anyone who could undertake such a thing must be confirmed in the most monstrously high opinion of themselves. Indeed the only person she could conceive capable of it was Lewis Durrant: which was sufficient warning in itself.

CHAPTER FOURTEEN

The call was paid: and Lydia thanked heaven for Miss Allardyce's coming too. She feared she could not have endured with patience the role of mere auntlike observer, while the lovers' armoury of looks and nothings was deployed. She must have wanted some other occupation than benignly smiling—not her forte in any case—through their eager nods, ready agreements and stifled sighs; and not being a sewing woman ('But where pray is your *work*?' Miss Beaumont had once demanded, in Lydia's own parlour) she would have been hard put to it for an alternative that combined mild attention and manual occupation. It might have been a good time to learn juggling. ('Don't mind me!') She had often fancied juggling.

Fortunately there was Miss Allardyce to take a share of the conversation. And if Lydia were honest, Mr Allardyce and Phoebe might have comported themselves a good deal worse. The consideration of the gentleman was not overcome by the absorption of the suitor; and Phoebe was constitutionally incapable of making anyone feel ignored or unwelcome. (Part of the trouble, Lydia reflected.) Still, it was a relief to let them feel they had paid her enough attention, and have some talk apart with Juliet Allardyce.

For some reason Lydia felt that Miss Allardyce would be very formidable when she was old: she would walk indefatigably without a stick, and suffer no fools gladly, and stooping urchins would drop their handfuls of mud at one glance. Her strong-boned beauty, emphasised by hair cropped to the nape and enclosed in a bandeau, was more striking than amenable: there was a good deal of style about her, but few could have carried off the severity of that dark grey gown and mantle. Absolute self-possession: such, without the least haughtiness or unfriendliness, was the impression she created: that there were places within her strongly and securely fenced off.

'I wished very much to go,' she said, talking of her accompanying her brother to Vienna, 'and held to my wish, against all opposition.' A slight, salty smile. 'We had rather a bad sea-crossing to Hamburg—so bad, that the decks were awash, and there was a good deal of praying, and I thought for a moment that here was a just reward for my pig-headedness.' She renewed the smile. 'Only for a moment.'

'She ate a good dinner,' put in Mr Allardyce, in a marvelling tone. 'Not only was she not sick, she ate a hearty dinner of salt beef and capers.'

'Are you not a good sailor, Mr Allardyce?' Lydia asked.

'I like to consider myself so. I keep my groans to a decorous volume, and refrain from calling on the Almighty too insistently; and when I reach dry land I do not fall down at once and kiss it. I wait a few minutes.' He turned his look to Phoebe. 'Is this not, Miss Rae, as much and more than a man need claim, to call himself a good sailor? It is, after all, unnatural to us to bob about on the waves in a giant nutshell: we are creatures of the solid earth, not finned or winged. Is not a man who boasts of his sea-legs really demonstrating his monstrosity?'

'I was never on the sea in my life,' Phoebe answered, with a smile, 'but I should dearly like to be. Whenever I have seen it, I have longed to know what was on the other side. I am sure I should not mind a little sickness. Mountains too: I would give a great deal to see some real mountains.'

'Ah! the Alps—I had hopes of an Alpine excursion when I was at Vienna, but it came to nothing. But Scotland, now—if there are no Alps, there are assuredly mountains: I have heard much of the grandeur and beauties of Scotland, and now you can tell me if they were exaggerations . . .'

Their harmony was so complete, their ability to interest each other so well developed, that Lydia could comfortably direct her conversation again to Juliet Allardyce, and to her own fascination: the music at Vienna.

'Well, as to the opera, the Italians still reign, though there have been attempts to foster a native German style. Some of the best music is to be heard in the houses of the nobility; though of course people will still talk through it. I think they should be knocked on the head at once.'

'And Haydn is still at Vienna?' Lydia asked wistfully. 'I saw his concerts at the Hanover Square Rooms in 'ninety-five: I wish he would return.'

'I fancy his travelling days are done. He has turned to oratorio now—that last infirmity of noble mind. I heard some extracts. *"Und Gott spracht"* this and *"Und Gott spracht"* that: a great bore. But I brought a deal of music back from Vienna, of all sorts, and have hardly begun to look through it. You play, I am sure?'

'The pianoforte, and the harp,' Lydia said: liking and respecting Miss Allardyce, and so with no reason to hear that faint sword-clash of competition.

'Then you must indeed borrow as much as you like. When you come to us, as you surely will—' with a flicker of her cool grey eyes at her brother and Phoebe '—let us investigate it thoroughly, and—'

'You are very kind; but we are only lodging here for a short time, and I am without an instrument, and so it would be more of a torment than an enjoyment.'

'Ah. You play for pleasure—not to *please*,' Miss Allardyce said, with her smiling crispness. 'All the better. You assuredly must come, and make use of our pianoforte. It would make me very happy— Robert too. Robert is an excellent listener. At least, he never taps his foot or says, "Splendid," at the penultimate chord.'

'I think I hear myself faintly praised,' Mr Allardyce said, turning, 'and I must be grateful for it. I require only a reciprocal gratitude: for while you, my dear Juliet, and Miss Templeton, I collect, are proficient in music, may I not claim the credit of being proficient in admiring it—and admiring, moreover, without the least practical understanding? I can hum along with a tune, and even remember a good one, but your music-sheets are to me perplexing hieroglyphics, and I tremble at the mention of scales and arpeggios. And yet I love to hear you play: so when I applaud you, I really think you should applaud me back.'

'Fie, Mr Allardyce,' said Lydia, laughing, 'is this admiration, or simply gaping wonder?'

'With respect, Miss Templeton, I must question the distinction. When we gaze up at a lofty cathedral, do we not simply wonder at how such a magnificent thing could ever have been raised, and feel it to be quite beyond us? And if we thoroughly understood engineering, and elevations and whatnot'—he appealed to Phoebe—'would our emotion not be a little hampered—a little deflated?'

'Oh, the world would be dull indeed without mystery,' Phoebe said, with her most heartfelt gaze. Very warm, soft and rich her looks appeared beside Mr Allardyce—slender, pared, a little angular in his refinement: but the wedding-portrait, Lydia thought, would work beautifully, and the children of the combination would be irresistible.

'Besides, in music an innocent appreciation is all that is required of we men, domestically at least,' he pursued. 'Men who sing well, or play the flute, are for some reason always deemed socially a little suspect—unless, of course, they are entire professionals like Mr Haydn.'

'And women,' Lydia said, 'are always commended for such accomplishments: but if they seek to become entire professionals like Mr Haydn, they are shockingly unsexing themselves.'

Mr Allardyce regarded her with interest. 'Yet there are women whose profession is music. Singers—'

'Oh, but if a woman is a singer,' put in Phoebe,

200

'it means that—whatever her virtues—still she must parade herself on the public stage.'

'And yet what does this amount to?' Lydia said. 'Exposing herself to the regard of many male eyes: which is precisely what every girl's mama intends for her, when she dresses her up for the assembly ball.'

Mr Allardyce looked his unobtrusive amusement. 'True: but I fancy the mama's reply would be, that at the ball she can be sure of the spectators, whereas in the concert-room it is a matter of that most direful phrase, "all and sundry". You know, Miss Rae, I should never like to belong to *sundry*. *All* at least has a sociable sound; but I can see a nightmare vision of two doors, and a demonic entity sternly pointing me to the other one that is marked "sundry" . . .'

Lydia was amused again, but attentive to an inner voice that told her to stop it. Chaperons or duennas did not go thrusting in their heretical opinions. If they could not sew smilingly, or smile sewingly, they should at least refrain from exhibitions of independent character. In other words, don't scare off Phoebe's suitor by showing Phoebe's friend and companion to be a tiresome bluestocking parlour-politician.

As soon as it was put like this, even by herself and in her own mind, Lydia's spirit rose in Bastille-storming mutiny—but fortunately, and to his credit, Mr Allardyce seemed not put off at all. The visit coming to an end, he was warm in his hopes that Miss Rae and Miss Templeton would do him, his sister and his mother the honour of calling at Queen Square, at any time they chose. He was clearly not a man to go in for a lot of mopping and mowing, but the bow he tendered to Phoebe on leaving was as full of meaning as a bow could be.

Meaningful, too, must be the insistence on meeting his mother. Lydia saw plainly that there was more in it than mere politeness, and so it appeared did Phoebe, who subsequently spoke of the prospect with a touch of apprehension. The momentous introduction of future bride to parent stood behind it, shadowy but distinct. Equally distinct, to Lydia at least, was a certain extra significance attaching to the figure of Mrs Allardyce. From various hints dropped by her son and daughter, Lydia began to suspect a matriarch. In Robert, the hints tended to an amused indulgence: in Juliet, to a dry restraint; but both sides suggested a woman who must be made allowances for.

At that, her mind leaped on the swift steed of prejudice and galloped away. She esteemed people who possessed character, but she greatly disliked those who set themselves up as Characters: they generally knew very well what they were about, and sought to secure themselves an exemption from the normal duties of civility by presenting as helpless idiosyncrasy what was really a cultivated selfishness. She let herself be carried such a way that she was on the point of hating this poor woman she had never met before she reined in. Whatever the lady's qualities, she reminded herself, Mrs Allardyce was nothing to her, whose sole concern here was Phoebe; and Phoebe's sweetness of temper, and readiness to think well of everyone, must surely armour her against the most aggressive onslaught of personality.

The younger Allardyces, at any rate, Lydia

found very acceptable company, and they reconciled her a little more to Bath. Her heart did not sink quite so low at the sight of the Pump Room that day; and there her eye lit with quickened interest on Lewis Durrant. He was with a mixed group of people gathered below the statue of Beau Nash: he was actually talking—if not with animation, then without visible effort: and he had exchanged the shapeless old riding-coat for a new cut-away with tails. Her longing to satirise what was, for him, a transformation of peacock extravagance was tempered by her acknowledgement that, lean and long-backed as he was, he looked rather well in it; and she was stayed from further aspersions by the good nature of Phoebe, who remarked that it was very pleasant to see Mr Durrant gaining some acquaintance.

'Yes: even for Mr Durrant, who does not mind being alone, it must be dull indeed to be solitary at Bath, where everything is designed for society.' But she could not help adding: 'He is certainly capable of being pleasing in company: it is only a pity that when he does so, he makes such a great favour of it.'

They were seated on a rout-bench beneath the north windows, and a string sextet was playing in the gallery: strain as she might, there was no hope of overhearing what the group by the statue were saying. And was there a marriageable young woman amongst them? A close bonnet hid, frustratingly, the face of the only likely candidate. Lydia had the wager made at Culverton to stifle any inner protest that it was none of her business; but her curiosity soon met with a dull sort of satisfaction. Whatever the attractions of Mr

Durrant's present company, they were insufficient to prevent several mouth-filling yawns; and when Lydia and Phoebe left the Pump Room, he appeared so far from captivation as to have turned his back on the group, and was watching through the window the passing of sedan-chairs across the flagstones of the abbey churchyard, with more hope than expectation of interest.

Again Lydia was not without sympathy. She was adopting her own remedy against tedium by viewing everything in her current life as a mere scene with which she had nothing to do: except mentally to note it, to describe it, as if perhaps composing a letter about it to her father. Before dinner she liked to take a short walk alone— Phoebe being sensible enough to understand rather than resent this—and as she went, she subordinated her mind to her impressions. The seething flush of setting sun on the roofs of the crescents: the various smells of roast and boiled meat wafting from basement kitchens and oozing through the area railings: the sound of the abbey bells seeming, in its expansive echoes, to dart about the town and issue from a dozen places at once: the glimpsed stories, like the riffled pages of a book briefly opened and shut, in the faces of other solitary walkers—retired officers with the deck or the parade-ground still in their step, paid companions thin-lipped with their wrongs, dancing-masters poised exactly between the dapper and the shabby. The effect was somehow refreshing: although today on turning for home— back, rather, to Sydney Place—she was conscious of carrying still a little oppression, as slight and as unignorable as a stone in the shoe.

There was no occasion for delay: the Allardyces' call was to be repaid the next morning. On their leaving the house, Phoebe again consulted the cards on the hall table. There were several: from friends of Lady Eastmond and, most direfully, from two prosy ladies whom Lydia had met on her last stay here, and whom she had hoped to include in that happiest category of people, those you will never see again. But there was no card from Mr Beck. Lydia detected in Phoebe's glance of disappointment a flash of pique; and wondered briefly if her task was going to be made easier by the dereliction of one of Phoebe's suitors—whether, in the geometry of courtship, a Mr A present was equal to two Mr Bs absent.

However, on their setting out Phoebe's look and tone became wistful. 'Mr Beck must surely not be in Bath as yet,' she said, 'though he did engage so definitely for coming, if I was to be here: he was so very definite.'

Lydia murmured something soothing, while feeling anything but soothed herself. Yes, I see how it will be, she thought: Phoebe must be romancing over the one who is missing. Now if it were the other way round—if Mr B were here, prompt and attentive, and Mr A mysteriously absent, she would be sighing for Mr A: no wonder men deplore the changeable folly of the female mind, when some of us supply them with such a thorough pretext!

It was her first moment of real irritation with her young charge. She had forcibly to summon what she thought of as her duenna-self—that calm watercoloured lady, all bovine serenity—and in this guise turned the conversation to the Allardyces, and what the house in Queen Square would be like, and so on: to such good effect that by the time they reached the High Street, Phoebe's brow had cleared, and she was talking rationally.

Then came the cry.

'Miss Rae! Miss Rae—up here!'

'Up here' was a first-floor window in the Christopher Hotel, flung open by a gentleman in shirt-sleeves, who was leaning out at some peril to himself, and to the general notice of the crowded street.

'Oh! it is Mr Beck,' Phoebe breathed, gazing up.

'I'll come down,' he shouted. 'Wait—wait there.'

'Oh, Lydia, it is Mr Beck,' Phoebe repeated, turning in pleased agitation. 'What shall we do?'

'Do as we are told, I suppose,' said Lydia, who did not much care for the stares they were attracting.

Within a few moments the gentleman came running down the steps of the hotel. He was no longer in shirt-sleeves: he had thrown on a coat: indeed it looked so very conspicuously thrown on that Lydia could not help composing a mental line to her father. *Mr Beck, having paused only to dishevel his hair a little more, came forth to greet us . . .*

'Miss Rae—I chanced to see you go by—I saw you from my window, and could not help but—I am at the Christopher, you see—just put up there last night. What great good fortune that I happened to be looking out— But how do you do? I am so glad—let me show you this.' Unceremoniously he thrust a bundle of printed sheets into Phoebe's hands. 'The very thing we were talking of in London—just printed, you see, and not yet sewn . . .'

'What a piece of luck indeed,' said Phoebe, pink and smiling, 'just at the moment we were going by—Lydia, is it not amazing?' Lydia's face must have shown that her amazement was not such as to overpower her: Phoebe collected herself. 'Lydia, let me introduce—Mr Beck, the acquaintance from London, of whom you have heard me speak: Miss Templeton.'

He gave Lydia a glance, and a short, impatient bow: then it was back to Phoebe. 'Please forgive me—I had intelligence of your coming to Bath, and I meant to be here earlier: but first the printing of this was a little delayed—and then my father was ill—'

'Oh, dear, I hope he is better.'

'It was nothing really. You know how old men like to cosset themselves. But look here—my new periodical—I so wanted you to be the first to see it. Oh, I have closed the one I began in London—ill-planned, ill-written, ill-printed. I mean to publish hitherto from Bristol, and then seek a London distribution. And you see I have abandoned the title The *Intelligencer*—too much like a news-sheet.'

'The *Interlocutor*,' Phoebe read out, innocently mispronouncing. 'Well, it is very handsome—'

'LOCutor,' he corrected hastily, with a faint frown. 'That is how it is—but then perhaps I have chosen rather an obscure word. Unsuitable for a properly memorable title—tell me, what do you think?'

Phoebe hesitated. 'Oh, I . . . Well, Lydia, what

do you think? Miss Templeton, you know, is a wide reader: you cannot do better than ask her.'

Mr Beck did not look as if he were very solicitous of knowing what she thought; but Lydia answered levelly: 'Very good. Interlocutor—one who exchanges talk with another. So you mean the paper to include a broad range of views, sir?'

'Oh, to be sure, it will be no narrow party magazine,' he said dismissively. 'This, of course, Miss Rae, is only a proof copy—I think to make some substantial alterations yet before it is offered to the public. More verse, perhaps: there is a preponderance of prose . . .' He suddenly glared about him, as if rudely accosted. 'Well. I am sure I must be detaining you. Unless—where are you going?'

'We have a call to make,' Lydia supplied, pretending he had asked a polite question.

'Oh, well, in that case . . .' He looked searchingly into Phoebe's face, and said, with deep-toned emphasis: 'Never mind. At least I am here: I am here, now.'

Self-evident: but perhaps he considered the fact called for general celebration. One was hindered from being fair to Mr Beck by his excessive good looks, which secured him such an advantage as enabled him, it seemed, to dispense with common courtesies. Fine shaggy head set on the sort of white columnar neck that was just made to stand proud of a careless neckcloth: broad shoulders, strong jaw, full lips, coal eyes—really, it was too much. He belonged on a plinth. *The Irritable Apollo*.

'Will you be staying at the Christopher?' Phoebe asked him. 'I hear it is very elegantly appointed—

quite as much as the York.'

'I dare say it is. I don't notice such things. Miss Rae, when can I see you? It has been so long since London—I never knew time to drag so intolerably. May I call? I mean—no doubt I should leave a card—all that—but I don't have a card. Was there ever such nonsense—' he flung out an arm, eyes wide '—as the *leaving* of *cards*?'

'It is rather nonsensical.' Phoebe smiled.

Meanwhile Lydia had reached into her reticule and brought out a card. Mr Beck looked down at it.

'Nonsensical, I know,' Lydia said. 'But at least you will know where to find us.'

He took the card, gracelessly stuffing it into his pocket. 'No no no,' he said, frowning, as Phoebe was about to hand him back the *Interlocutor*, 'it is yours. I must know what you think of it. And I want you to be absolutely, unsparingly truthful and honest with me, Miss Rae: will you promise?'

'Oh, certainly,' Phoebe said solemnly, while Lydia winced: when someone made such an appeal as Mr Beck's, they were really announcing their intention to go into a pet at anything but the grossest flattery.

'Then—then goodbye.' He did some impressive backwards walking and gazing, then stopped and cried: 'But, Miss Rae, you do remember—you must remember—that evening at Mrs Mansfield's. The dreary little pedant who cried down Cowper— how we vanquished him! And then the great fierce tom-cat—I shall never forget it.'

'Nor I,' Phoebe said, with equal parts warmth and restraint. 'Good day, Mr Beck.'

At least she had eschewed the drama of *goodbye*;

but she was in a visible and, when she took Lydia's arm again, palpable flutter. Lydia waited until they had gone on as far as Cheap Street before suggesting: 'If you folded that, it might go in your reticule.'

Phoebe looked at the sheaf of papers under her arm. 'Oh! yes. I suppose I must look rather like a lawyer's clerk . . . *Do* you think it a good title, Lydia?'

'Before properly deciding, I should have to read the contents.'

'Oh, yes, to be sure—and I hope you will. Mr Beck will be very glad to have your opinion.'

Mr Beck having done his best to reduce her to invisibility, Lydia rather doubted that.

'It was very curious Mr Beck seeing us like that, was it not?'

'I don't know: if he had taken up lodging in a lonely lighthouse, our passing before his window might have been a marvel indeed; but in the busiest thoroughfare in Bath, there is rather more of probability than curiosity.'

'I am intensely relieved that he is here—that there was nothing amiss, I mean, that prevented his coming. I confess I was growing a little concerned . . . It *is* strange he should mention that evening at Mrs Mansfield's,' Phoebe said, turning on Lydia her most dazzling look of happy discovery, 'for I was thinking of it just the other day. Mrs Mansfield gave literary evenings, you know—and she read out some Cowper, and a very disagreeable gentleman said it was poor stuff, and Mr Beck rose up full-armed. I cannot remember half the things he said, but they were very powerful. And it was such an interesting evening, we hardly wanted it to end, and when Mrs Mansfield said that the servants would be wanting to clear away Mr Beck said they must go to bed, and we would take the tea-things down to the kitchen ourselves—and so we did—only in the kitchen there was the biggest tom-cat you ever saw, and not knowing us he spat and menaced us quite like the fiercest guard-dog, and we could hardly stop laughing . . . Are you fond of Cowper, Lydia?'

'I admire him very much, and wish I could love him—but his habitual melancholy gets in the way. I could wish him a little more spirited.'

'Could you? Oh, for my part I think there is ample spirit—and then there is such beauty in his melancholy . . .'

Lydia had a strong feeling that it was no longer Cowper they were talking about. But she was relieved to find Phoebe sinking into the abstracted silence of recollection, as it saved her for now from the question that must come: what was her opinion of Mr Beck?

Judging by first impressions was an odious practice, of course: indeed there was nothing to be said for it—except that everyone did it, and they were usually right. But Lydia doubted that further acquaintance, no matter how long or intimate, could alter her estimation of Mr Beck's character. There was that degree of fascination with his own feelings, which was surely incompatible with attention to the feelings of others: there was a great show of disdaining the conventions of social intercourse, which seemed less like independence of mind than a simple desire of having his own way; and as to the business of the tea-things and the kitchen, she longed to ask whether Mr Beck's

211

egalitarianism had extended to staying there to wash up, make the fires, and empty the chamber-pots, or whether he had gone comfortably back to a hotel just as expensive as the Christopher.

Nor could she like the slighting way in which he had referred to his father. Then, remembering that Mr Beck senior was a Bristol sugar-merchant whose wealth came from slave plantations, she wondered if he deserved slighting: but no—there was still a place for filial feeling. Altogether, there was so much to say against Mr Beck that his uncivil manner to *her* hardly figured in the account.

She would say none of this unbidden, however: even if Phoebe were to ask her the question, she was resolved to be moderate in her expressions, as she feared that if anything could magnify Mr Beck's attractions in Phoebe's eyes, it would be to hear him disapproved. But there was one matter she felt she must mention.

'Well, I cannot help but remark that we have now run into both Mr Allardyce and Mr Beck. Exactly the kind of encounters that Bath is made for, of course—people come because they know they *will* run into their acquaintance. But it does set me to wondering about any future occasion at which both Mr Allardyce and Mr Beck may be present.'

'Lord, yes,' Phoebe said, not uncomfortably, 'whatever shall I do? Well: introduce them, I suppose. Mind, Mr Beck does know of Mr Allardyce.'

'Does he? How?'

'Well, in London I spoke of him to Mr Beck. Simply that—there was another gentleman who was particular in his attentions. We were very open with each other in that way: somehow you cannot be otherwise with Mr Beck. He sets a high value on candour: I think that is one of his admirable qualities.'

'But Mr Allardyce does not know about Mr Beck?'

'No,' Phoebe said readily, 'but then it is different again talking to Mr Allardyce. He is not at all pressing: you feel you are allowed to say just as much or as little as you like. And that is one of *his* admirable qualities.'

Phoebe smiled. They had to stop at that moment to allow a dray to come lumbering out of Bear Inn Yard; the delay allowing Lydia to muster up a smile in return, and the noise of the iron-shod wheels covering up her small, heartfelt sigh.

CHAPTER FIFTEEN

Mrs Allardyce lived in a pillared corner house on the grander north side of Queen Square—old, for Bath, and unimpeachably respectable. Phoebe, who had been lost in thought again for the remainder of their walk hither, licked her lips a little nervously as they mounted the steps. Lydia was not displeased to see that: to be nervous was, after all, to be conscious of important issues at stake; and Lydia's own thoughts since Cheap Street had been rather severely fixed on Phoebe's seriousness, or lack of it.

Her sheer affection for Phoebe, her pleased surprise at her many excellent qualities, had led her perhaps to forget the girl's youth, inexperience,

213

and naïveté. Today had furnished a reminder that while Phoebe had a fund of good sense, it was not the whole extent of her mental capital: she had ample reserves of silliness as well. The Miss Rae who could talk and behave with such understanding and discretion was also professedly in love with two men at the same time; and in the case of one of them showed less than creditable judgement.

Still, direct comparison could do much. Surely Phoebe must feel all the force of contrast, in being greeted in the drawing-room by Robert Allardyce—cheerful, civilised, and not at all inclined to open his eyes so that the whole pupil showed like the centre of a target.

He was prompt and eager to introduce them to his mother—his glance, as he did so, seeming just to graze Lydia with a little wry plea for indulgence.

Mrs Allardyce was a neat-figured, well-preserved woman, some way past fifty, but showing in her fashionable dress, her spangled turban and coral bracelets, that she was not ready yet for caps and mittens. There was nothing haughty or remote about her: her unrouged face had a certain dewy softness that was rather inviting; but her small pebbly eyes were anything but soft, and Lydia saw a long-moulded sharpness in her lips.

'Ah, so here you are, Miss Rae—how d'you do?—I have heard so much about you, without seeing you, that it is almost like meeting a fabulous monster at last. A pretty monster, mind: decidedly pretty: Robert, why did you not tell me Miss Rae was so handsome? Men have no idea of *describing* a person. "Oh, Mother, I met an old acquaintance of yours in town," says he, "only I have forgot her name." "Well, what does she look like?" "Oh," says he, "she has brown hair."' She snorted. 'No, I will tell people what you are like, Robert: you know me, I don't care.'

Her greeting to Lydia was polite, but without such marked interest—as was natural, there being no prospect of Lydia's shortly becoming her near relation. However, when Juliet rose with her cool smile and suggested that Miss Templeton, as she had proposed, might like to come to the pianoforte and look over her new music, Mrs Allardyce snapped: 'What is this? Nonsense, we don't want to be fussing with that. Sit down, Juliet. I want to talk to my visitors, not hear a lot of jingle-jangling.'

'Your visitors will have little enough to say, if you persist in trying to frighten them,' Mr Allardyce said, seating himself close to Phoebe: smiling on his mother, and quite at ease.

'You need not give me that look, as if I were a curious exhibit,' Mrs Allardyce said, frowning, pursing her lips, yet all enjoyment. 'You see I do not hesitate to tell him what I think of him, Miss Rae: that's my way.'

'As I return the favour,' he said, 'and always tell you when you misbehave shockingly—which is a good deal of the time.'

'Was there ever such a son? What do you think, Miss Rae? What do you think of us?'

'I think . . . it is the kind of freedom that proceeds from strong affection on both sides,' said Phoebe—to Lydia's admiration: she felt that if she had been confronted with such a question, posed with Mrs Allardyce's piercing, pouncing look, she could have done nothing better than whistle like a parrot.

Presently, when Mr Allardyce and Phoebe were engaged in a mutual reminiscence of London—Juliet putting in a word here and there, but apparently content to inhabit her usual circle of self-possession—Mrs Allardyce beckoned Lydia to draw her chair nearer.

'Now, Miss Templeton, you must tell me of yourself. It may sound impertinent, but that's my way. You, I collect, are Miss Rae's companion.'

Lydia bridled a little at that, thinking of the paid companions who trailed their browbeaten way after the superannuated dragons of the Pump Room. 'I am happy to call myself Miss Rae's friend,' she said, 'and her companion, during our stay in Bath.'

'And a very sensible notion of Lady Eastmond's I call it, to place a woman of mature years at Miss Rae's side: I approved it at once when my son told me about it. I know, of course, about Miss Rae's position: her orphaned state: her substantial expectations. There is a great need of protection. I see far too many giggling chits in Bath, walking arm in arm: no decorum: no one to teach them it.' Mrs Allardyce directed a speculative, not displeased glance at Robert and Phoebe. 'I never knew the Raes—but I hear that Sir Alexander Rae was a model of probity: besides being very rich.'

Her expression seemed to convey that the latter virtue carried more weight with her. 'Yes, Miss Rae always speaks with great respect of her late parents,' Lydia said blandly.

'Let him in, Jane, let him in,' Mrs Allardyce cried, as the door was nosed open by a pug-dog, with a maid in pursuit. 'He is missing his mistress, I

216

think. Come here then, you droll creature. You won't mind, of course,' she added to Lydia as the pug, with much snuffling and scattering of moisture, jumped on her lap. 'In the country, I suppose, you keep numerous dogs.'

'Not one,' Lydia said, 'though many of our neighbours do.'

She thought she had spoken agreeably: but Mrs Allardyce did not seem to like her supposition being contradicted. 'I am not fond of country retirement,' she said, with a shrug, and a look away. 'The late Mr Allardyce kept only a London establishment—and a very good one: but in his later years he took a fancy to purchase a place in the country. It was not at all my fancy: I told him so. "Bath," said I, "is the only place." That was how we were. I have always been plain-spoken, and I don't care who knows it. Now my son, in time, may wish to make such a purchase—but that time, if it comes, must be *much* later in his career.'

'To be sure—in the foreign service, he must always be going from place to place, and so—'

'My dear Miss Templeton, you have taken up a very wrong idea. There can be no reason for entering the foreign service except what it may lead to—high office at home. *There* is my son's future. It is what his father always designed for him: it is particularly suited to his talents. When that comes, a good town establishment is the first necessity. A public man must entertain, he must keep up a certain style. When he marries, his wife must understand that. She will have an exacting role as hostess and helpmeet. Taste, even fashion there must be—but no flighty, self-willed notions.' She scratched the pug's head punishingly. 'I suppose you are not fond of London.'

'I spend a part of every season in London, and like it very much.'

Mrs Allardyce sniffed. 'That is a very elegant gown Miss Rae has on. Bath-made, I suppose.'

'From London, I believe,' said Lydia, growing weary of these suppositions, which had the effect of making her appear continually contrary, 'though I cannot pretend to an intimate knowledge of all Miss Rae's wardrobe.'

'People have an entirely wrong idea about attention to dress. Within due bounds, it is not vanity: for a woman of any standing, indeed, it is an absolute requirement. At the theatre last month I saw an extraordinary creature in the next box. There she sat, in public, in the evening, in the drabbest day dress that you might at a pinch have put on to inspect your stores and closets. Some people might have contained themselves: I could not: that's not my way. I could not help but stare and exclaim, though my son tried to call me to order. Very shocking in me, but I can't help it. Such affectation, such impudent flouting of decorum demands to be challenged.' Mrs Allardyce leaned close and fierce, so that Lydia could see a little peachlike bristle of whisker on her upper lip. 'It *reveals* something about a person. I don't miss such things, Miss Templeton: not I. Oh! Lord, I see my daughter is still fussing about that music. You had better go and oblige her.'

It was the first time, Lydia observed, that Mrs Allardyce had said the words 'my daughter', though 'my son' was often enough on her lips. Joining Juliet at the pianoforte, she felt not only relief but a certain solidarity: not that Juliet

218

seemed in any need of it. That self-possession, Lydia divined, was really a necessary self-sufficiency.

Meanwhile Mrs Allardyce interrogated Phoebe, Mr Allardyce standing by with his look of judicious tolerance and putting in a reproachful word here and there. It was plain that he was the only person who opposed, or had found a way of opposing, his mother's will: plain too that she found a coy relish in this, which she would not have tolerated from anyone else.

Presently he was coming over to the pianoforte: his mother being too busy laying down some gimlet-eyed law to Phoebe to notice for a moment.

'Juliet—do you have that Arne song you played in London? It was a particular favourite of Miss Rae's. We—that is, I should so like to hear it.'

'Robert—Robert, what do you do there? A song? Nonsense, come away. The place for music is at an evening party.'

'Then we shall have to close the curtains, Mother, and call it evening: for I must have this song.'

Mrs Allardyce threw up her hands, smiling archly. 'There, Miss Rae—do you see how he rides roughshod over me?'

Dear Papa, wrote Lydia in her thoughts, *it is very curious: I'll go bail that Mrs Allardyce would have the greatest contempt for such disreputable creatures as actresses: yet she is acting her own character all the time.*

'You must play,' Juliet softly urged, with a touch on her arm. 'Do, while you have the chance.'

Lydia was certainly glad to feel the warm ivory beneath her fingers again, even in such

219

circumstances. The Arne song was a slight, fetching little piece that she had often heard sung at Vauxhall Gardens, though seldom with such grave purity as Juliet Allardyce's excellent contralto gave to it. The piano part was simple enough for Lydia to spare some glances for Phoebe and Mr Allardyce, who had gone back to a seat by her side; their identical look of conscious attention, and the way their eyes did *not* meet, seeming quite as significant as any amount of mooning. As for Mrs Allardyce, her attention was all on them: there was none for her daughter's superior performance, which she seemed only glad to have done, so that she could be talking again.

'Well, Robert, you have had your precious song: I hope you are in a way to be rational now.'

'Thank you, Juliet, Miss Templeton,' he said, a little spur of earnestness showing awkwardly through his habitual light manner. 'You did it justice—ample justice—did they not, Miss Rae?'

'Oh, I never heard anything more lovely,' said Phoebe, for whom earnestness was only a step further than being awake. 'The only feeling it does not rouse in me is surprise—for I do not believe there are two more accomplished women in England than your sister and Miss Templeton. Indeed, if you were to hear her play on the harp, you—'

'Who has the dressing of your hair, Miss Rae?' put in Mrs Allardyce.

'My maid, ma'am,' Phoebe said, after a surprised moment.

'Then you may tell her from me that she does it very well. The little coil at the crown—that is the London fashion, I suppose, and very becoming.

What do you say, Robert?'

'You should know better, Mother, than to ask a man such a thing. We are blind in these matters: we do not know what to look for. A woman may come downstairs in one gown, and then in another, and ask the man which one he likes best; and it is as certain as the rising sun that *he* will say they both look very well, and *she* will fall out of patience with him.'

'Very true,' said Lydia, 'and is this not because he cannot be troubled to make the comparison?'

'With respect, Miss Templeton, it is not,' he said, with his dry, slightly crooked smile. 'The real fact is, he has already forgotten what the first one looked like.'

'Tut, Robert, such nonsense,' cried Mrs Allardyce. 'You should not encourage him in it, Miss Templeton. The truth is, after all, that men have something else to think of.'

'Happy and fortunate for the men,' Lydia could not help saying.

'Pooh, no bluestocking notions here, if you please. I don't care who hears me say it, I have no patience with those clever women: they are forever envying men: and they are always such shocking dowds.'

'Now, *you* should not be encouraged in such nonsense, Mother,' Mr Allardyce said. 'Mind and elegance can, indeed often do, go together. And after all, you would surely wish to be thought a clever woman yourself.'

'I have sense, Robert, which is vastly different from mere cleverness and book-learning. I know how to recognise sense when I see it, and to value it; and I do not see what more one needs to know.

221

You will understand me, Miss Rae—you Scots are a prudent set.'

Even Juliet joined in her brother's laughing protest at that.

'No, no, I say what I think: that's the way I am— and Miss Rae does not mind it, do you, my dear? I have always found the Scots perfectly sensible and well-bred. Irish, that's a different matter. Have you connections in Scotland?'

'Only very distant, ma'am. Sir Henry Eastmond is my nearest kin.'

Mrs Allardyce looked thoroughly satisfied with that. 'I have not the pleasure of knowing the Eastmonds, but Lady Eastmond I know by report: a woman welcome in all good society, I hear; and of course my son has told me about her, from your acquaintance in London. Robert approves her: and for all he is a provoking creature, that is good enough for me.'

'And of course you also, Miss Allardyce,' Lydia said to Juliet, who had taken a music-book into her lap, and was sight-reading it, 'had the pleasure of meeting my godmother in town.'

'Oh, yes: she is all openness: delightful,' Juliet said, in her succinct way.

'Well, she must be if *you* say so, my dear,' Mrs Allardyce sniffed, 'as you are very little inclined to like people generally.'

'I like a good many people, Mama,' Juliet answered, with composure, 'just as there are a good many I find intolerable.'

'Well, *you* are fond of society, Miss Rae, I know. My son has told me all about your triumphs in town last winter. And it was your first out?'

'Yes, ma'am—but I fear Mr Allardyce has

222

flattered me. My—my "triumphs" I cannot pretend to be anything greater than not falling down any staircases, or forgetting people's names.' She exchanged a brief sparking look with Mr Allardyce. 'Or, at least, only a few.'

'Oh, I am shockingly bad at remembering names, and I don't care who knows it,' cried Mrs Allardyce, subjecting the pug to another pulverising caress. 'It is easily managed: I just say to them, "Now who *are* you?" People usually have sense enough not to be offended.'

'Or, perhaps, sufficient politeness not to show it,' Mr Allardyce suggested.

'It comes to the same thing,' Mrs Allardyce said, with her cosseted shrug. 'Now what age are you, Miss Rae? Not yet one-and-twenty? I came out when I was sixteen. But then I was ready. I had no fear of society. If there is fear in the case, thinks I, they shall be afraid of *me*. But then you lived retired, of course—which I never did—and you are an heiress. Your family showed sense in keeping you back. Throw a young girl with fifty thousand pounds into the world too soon, and there is bound to be trouble.'

Lydia, with much greater knowledge of Phoebe's situation, was beginning to feel exactly the opposite: that Phoebe should have begun to know society earlier. Of course it was no use saying any of this to Mrs Allardyce, who had set herself up as a woman of strong opinions, meaning that she never listened to anyone else's. There was more to be gained for Lydia, during the short remainder of the call, by silence, observation and reflection.

Certainly she did not envy Phoebe her future mother-in-law, if such were to be the case; but then much must depend on Robert Allardyce, and how he stood between them. He showed more forbearance to his mother than Lydia thought was due—but then, she *was* his mother. Mrs Allardyce's attitude to her daughter was instructive too. Plainly Juliet was not a favourite: just as plainly Mrs Allardyce was a man's woman, who would always find as much to condemn in her own sex as to condone in the other. It was to the credit of both of them that Juliet seemed so attached to, and unresentful of, her favoured brother.

Luckily, if any prospective bride for her son could please Mrs Allardyce, it would be one of Phoebe's type—well-dressed, gentle, unassuming, and incapable of thinking ill of anyone. And having been made privy to Mrs Allardyce's ambitions for her son, Lydia surmised that Phoebe's fifty thousand pounds weighed heavily in her favour also. Besides, even at the worst, there must be an eventual remedy for the disadvantages of Phoebe's situation: Mrs Allardyce *looked* as if she would live for ever, and doubtless would trumpet her intention of doing so, but sooner or later the happy moment must come that saw her finally contradicted.

None of this mattered, of course, if Robert Allardyce were sincerely and profoundly attached. Lydia thought he probably was: certainly she did not believe that the smooth lightness and urbanity of his manner rendered him incapable of deep feeling (as she suspected would be the opinion of the professionally tousled Mr Beck). But it was hard to be sure; and there was the added dubiety of Phoebe's own feelings. They were written with

224

all apparent plainness on her as the two of them came away from Queen Square: subdued smiles, blushes, remarks that Mrs Allardyce, though a little intimidating at first, seemed very good-natured (the blindness of love indeed), and long rapt silences. But then came the High Street, where Lydia could fancy a great brooding throb issuing from the Christopher Hotel, darkening the air and making the sedan-chair men droop in Gothic melancholy as they passed; and it was noticeable that Phoebe did not talk any more of Queen Square, and surreptitiously put her hand to her reticule to make sure the precious papers were still there.

In spite of herself, Lydia could not help but be curious about the contents of the *Interlocutor*. (No, that title was not quite right. The *Examiner*? No, too scholastic.) Back at Sydney Place, Phoebe fell greedily to reading it; but when dinner approached, and she went upstairs to dress, she left it behind, and Lydia pounced.

She took in the bulk of the contents quickly: essays, reviews, political articles—unsigned, but in their uniformity of style suggesting that Mr Beck had written most of them himself. She gave him credit for his energy, and even a brief glance showed them to be full of ideas—even if the ideas were not so much set out as poured in like a shovelful of chestnuts on a fire. But there was anonymous verse too: much apostrophising of landscape with many a 'Hail rugged spot' and so on. (Lydia always wondered about that—what made you want to Hail a spot, rugged or otherwise, and how did you go about it?) But there was one poem, prominently displayed, which was signed

WM. BECK: the signature denoted pride, and demanded attention.

The following is extracted from a much longer Work, a poem in Heroic Measure, to which the author tentatively assigns the title, 'The Open Field: or, a Reverie Upon A Rural Prospect With Figures'. N.B.—The Speaker of the poem, is supposed to be a young man of Parts and Talents, but a prey to Melancholy, engendered by the Objects of Pity and Tenderness operating upon a Nature too much framed for Sensibility for its own Peace.

See where the milking maid, with mantling blush
Her squeezish task a moment sets aside:
With care her lacteous bucket safely stows
Beyond the reach of bovine hoof, and turns,
Half pouting, half delight, her swain to view:
The glovèd hedger—who, at this regard
His wonted steadiness surrenders quite:
With am'rous shakes his heavy load he drops,
Though as her glances roguish still invite,
He firmer grips his needful implement . . .

'Miss Templeton?' Mary Darber's alarmed face appeared at the door. 'Oh, miss, are you quite well—I heard such a noise—'

'Me. Coughing.' Lydia wiped her eyes and tried with deep breaths to compose herself. 'Me coughing, Mary, that's all. So dry and dusty today . . .'

'Dry and dusty sort of place,' Mary said, with settled antipathy. 'I declare it's made you quite red in the face, miss. I'll get you some water—no, I'll

226

tell you what's best for soothing a throat like that—milk. There's a fresh half-pint downstairs—'

And it came from a lacteous bucket. 'No, no, thank you, Mary, really it's not—' *Not needful, like the hedger's implement.* 'Really, I do very well, thank you.'

When Mary was gone Lydia placed the sheets of the *Interlocutor* back on the table with a sort of guilty haste, as if she had been nearly caught reading someone else's letters, or a private diary. Not so wide of the mark, in truth: there was a good deal of self-exposure in laying your verses open to the public like this. The effect, in her case at least, had not been an increase of esteem for William Beck. Of course it was wrong to judge him on the merits, or otherwise, of his writing. (It was wrong to judge him altogether, she reminded herself: she was here only to be a sort of neutral invigilator. A title, perhaps: the *Invigilator*? No, too stern.) But putting together his writing with what she had seen of him, Lydia formed a dispiriting impression of a man living within thick walls of self-regard, unpierced by any ray of humour.

Could Phoebe really wish to join him within those walls—handsome and romantically battlemented as they were—for a whole lifetime? If that was what she should *choose*, of course, then there was no more to be said. But choice, Lydia reflected, was not a simple act. It depended not only on what you thought and felt, but on things you were quite unconscious of thinking and feeling, and to which only an outside agency could alert you. Choice implied a clear view of the object before the chooser: but whose view was not impeded, not smeared a little by the careless accretions of self? Surely to polish up that glass to perfect transparency was not to *interfere* with choice: really it was doing a service both to the chooser and to truth.

And besides, he wrote 'squeezish'.

CHAPTER SIXTEEN

'Why do you say I must be bored?' asked Lewis Durrant, calling at Sydney Place the next morning.

'Because,' Lydia said, sitting down, 'you have nothing better to do with your time than pay a dull visit to two maiden ladies.'

'Oh, as to that, I chiefly came to ask if you have had a letter lately from your father, and to enquire after his health.'

'I had a letter yesterday, and he is in good health and spirits, thank you.' She left a pause. 'Your enquiry after my own health I shall take as read.'

'Why, you look well enough. Actually you are hardly ever ill, are you?'

'No: I must be blessed with a good constitution. But if it will please you, I shall try to cultivate a little indisposition. It might be interesting to have one of those antique ones, like Rising of the Lights, or a Surfeit.'

Mr Durrant twitched a smile. 'Apparently Daniel Defoe died of *lethargy*. He must have contracted it in Bath . . . No, it's curious your saying I must be bored. It is exactly what I have been saying to myself, or rather asking myself: *am* I bored? And, oddly enough, I don't know how to answer. Perhaps eventually boredom itself ceases

228

to be boring, because you stop feeling it. The other day I found myself sitting in Sydney Gardens for a full hour, contemplating a single tree. When there is nothing else to do, it is surprising how much tranquil interest you can find in a tree.'

'Now I know you are not suited to Bath. Here you must confine your staring and gazing to its proper object—the dress, hair and probable bank-book of other people.'

'Oh, never fear, I am taking the social waters now. I have dined at two houses, and attended evening-parties at three.'

'And which do you like best, or detest least?'

'I prefer the evening-parties,' he said consideringly, 'as there you only smell the dinner instead of having to eat it.'

Lydia repressed a smile. 'Mr Durrant,' she said, as he roamed about, peering disdainfully into cabinets, 'in case it has escaped your notice, this maiden lady is sitting down: feel free to do so.'

'Oh, I don't much care for sitting down. One only has to get up again. Where is the other maiden lady, by the by?'

'Writing letters, I think.'

'Ah, shouldn't you be supervising her? Yes, unworthy, I know. Speaking of letters, I have had the favour of an excessively impudent one from Hugh, telling me that the news of my Bath adventure is the best joke he has ever heard, that he dines out on the strength of it, and whatnot. It has rattled him, in other words; and so I collect from a letter from his mother, who laments that her poor boy is dreadfully cut up with regard to his prospects. Which proves there is light in the darkest sky,' he concluded, with grim satisfaction, picking up a book. 'What's this, a novel?'

'Yes, the third volume. I have just finished it.'

'When did you begin it?'

'Yesterday . . . Has Bath turned you into a novel-reader, Mr Durrant?'

'Oh, with a vengeance,' he said, skimming the pages. 'A very tolerable way of passing the time. It is different from history or poetry: one is reading, but without any uncomfortable sensation of using the brain to do it.'

'Borrow it by all means—the other volumes are on the window-shelf. As long as you remember to return it to Meyler's, next to the Pump Room.'

'I will, thank you—as long as you can assure me of the absence of two things, which I cannot abide in a novel. There must be nobody who lives in the town of Blank, or belongs to the Blankshire Regiment; and there must not be a couple who are in love with each other all the time without knowing it, and who signal it by constantly quarrelling.'

'For once I agree with you: there is nothing more unlikely, or more destructive of the illusion of reality. I can assure you the book has none of that; and what is more, the descriptions of places are helpfully indicated by the length of the paragraphs, so you may jump straight to the dialogue without trouble.'

'An author who knows his business.' There was a knock below: Mr Durrant swept up the other volumes. 'You have another caller: I'll leave you.'

'Really, you don't have to.'

'I know, but I want to. Pray give my compliments to Dr Templeton when next you write.'

'Certainly. I suppose, Mr Durrant,' she added,

on irresistible impulse as he strode to the door, 'that I am not yet to wish you joy?'

He eyed her coolly. 'No, your fifty pounds is safe yet. But tell me—*would* you wish me joy, in that event?'

She was prevented, or saved, from answering by the manservant, who opened the door to announce Mr Beck.

'How do you do, Mr Beck?' Lydia began. 'This is—'

'Oh, Mr Durrant, hullo,' Mr Beck said, with mild surprise.

'Mr Beck. I hope I find you well. Please excuse me, I have another errand.'

The exchange, perfectly easy and polite, set Lydia wondering mightily about their previous acquaintance. She might even have asked Mr Beck about it, if he had shown any receptivity to normal conversation—instead of advancing to the centre of the room, staring, turning with his arms hanging sculpturally at his sides, and tonelessly declaring: 'I thought to see Miss Rae here.'

But here she was: she must have hurtled downstairs on hearing his name. The *Interlocutor*, dog-eared from reading, was cradled tenderly in her arms.

'Mr Beck, how do you do?' she said breathlessly. 'So good of you to call.'

He uttered a sort of crumbling laugh. 'You surely could not suppose I would *not* call—could you?'

'Yes, indeed. Or no, rather,' Phoebe said, with faint, smiling perplexity, inviting him to sit down. He did so, flingingly; and shot a frowning look at Lydia.

231

'Mr Beck,' she greeted him, with a portion of a smile: fully aware that he desired her instant disappearance up the chimney much more than her courtesy.

'Well—Miss Rae. You must tell me, you must tell me at once what you think of it. And I must remind you of my injunction: absolute honesty.' He sat forward, arms on his potent thighs. Lydia meanwhile understood what a pet bird must feel like when a cloth is thrown over its cage.

'Dear me—this is a very great responsibility,' Phoebe said. 'You would do much better to seek Miss Templeton's opinion—'

Lydia pantomimed an urgent negative. (Besides, she was going to put her head under her wing and go to sleep in a moment.)

'Well—first of all I must confess that I have not yet read it *all*,' Phoebe continued, 'so whatever I say must be incomplete. That is no reflection on the material or the style—only on my own slowness of comprehension. And beyond that you must know I have no understanding of politics or philosophy; and though I like to read, I cannot call myself well-read, or properly versed in literature, so my judgement—'

'Your judgement must be for that very reason all the more valuable,' interrupted Mr Beck, 'for it is spontaneous—not dulled by familiarity with the classics—not stifled by dusty prejudice.'

'That is kind of you to say so,' pursued Phoebe steadily, 'but still I insist you must not place too much weight on my word: please, do not make a virtue of my ignorance.'

'But that is precisely what it is,' Mr Beck said—not actually interrupting this time: it was just that everything he said sounded like an interruption. 'It is a virtue: the greatest virtue of all, because of its sincerity. There is more of truth, worth and wisdom in honest ignorance than in the greatest parade of learning: infinitely more!'

Though she knew Mr Beck to be unconventional, still Lydia felt a passing surprise at his way of being complimentary: lovers were usually ready to praise everything in their mistresses, from ready wit to dainty foot, but to hear a woman commended for being a dunce was a little disconcerting. What chiefly occupied her mind, however, was the fascination of discovery: it was not equal to religious revelation or falling in love, no doubt, but still there was a certain awe in coming across a statement you so vehemently, wholeheartedly and lastingly disagreed with.

'Well, you are determined on making me your arbiter,' Phoebe said, smiling, 'but I fear you will get nothing more discerning or useful from me than that it is very clever, and very interesting, and I am sure it will do very well. Now if you were to ask Miss Templeton—oh, but, Lydia, have you not read any of Mr Beck's review? I'm sure you must have—'

'Really, I have scarcely had a moment,' Lydia said, throwing up her hands, and hearing more shrillness in her voice than she liked.

'Now Miss Templeton really is well-read,' Phoebe went on. 'Not only in English but in Latin, and in French and Italian—and not by any means light literature. She understands poetry and essays with the greatest correctness—and she makes sense of opera—and perspective in drawing too, which I could never comprehend. When I drew a wall or a fence my drawing-master used to keep talking about the vanishing-point on the horizon, but I couldn't see how a wall *could* vanish. It just stayed there. Oh, and she knows politics too—'

'Please, stop, Phoebe,' Lydia said, with discomfort, 'if this monster is me, then I am dismayed—you describe a perfect prig and bore.'

'I shall always, I hope, be prepared to lay my tribute at the feet of true learning and accomplishment,' Mr Beck said, with rather muddy cordiality.

'Oh, yes: I have never met anyone as clever as Lydia.'

'It is indeed seldom met with,' Mr Beck went on, in his ploughing way, 'at least in its genuine state. More often this learning is mere pedantry— affected superiority—and, what is that wretched expression?—elegance of mind.' He gave his first full laugh: Mr Beck *could* laugh; but it took the form of a harsh shout of disbelief. 'God preserve me from ever having an elegant mind.'

This prayer seemed to Lydia very likely to be answered; but she felt she had better say no more.

Phoebe's encomium, however, had the effect of turning Mr Beck's attention to Lydia—if not with friendliness, then with a specific curiosity. He began, with more determination than grace, to speak to her: enquiries about how long she had known Bath, how she liked it, whether the air agreed with her, and so on, made with an effort as obvious as his indifference to her answers; but just as plainly, to Lydia, leading to a certain end. He must know where she fitted in. Was this woman who stood between him and his goddess a stern preceptor, a guardian in all but name, ready to cast a chill of watchful propriety over his ardent wooing? Or perhaps, in spite of her ancient years and her pedantic ways, a potential ally who would make fond allowances for the impetuosity of young love?

For Lydia soon divined that a conventional courtship did not suit Mr Beck's notions of romance or of himself. There was nothing to prevent his meeting Phoebe Rae on perfectly normal terms: he was known to Lady Eastmond, he had clearly received, if he had not benefited from, a good education, and there was no vast disparity of wealth or status to count against him—the labour of slaves having rendered him as eligible as the labour of his own hands would have damned him. But Lydia suspected that as a lover he must be Romeo or nothing. If there were no opposition, he must imagine some.

So, she was to be either vengeful Capulet or soft-hearted old Nurse. It was far more her inclination to cry, 'A plague on both your houses,' but let him find that out for himself.

'Lincolnshire I do not know at all,' he was saying, 'but I fancy it a dull, flat sort of country.'

'It is true that there is a deplorable lack of mountains in Lincolnshire,' Lydia said, 'but it manages a few beauties nonetheless.'

He looked sceptical. 'Of the park-and-meadow sort, no doubt: any county can claim those. But no one can appreciate beauty in landscape until they have stood before great bold hills and wild prospects—the Lakes, now. All is tame beside the Lakes. If you were to see them, Miss Templeton—'

'I should like to see them again, certainly.'

He gave her his widest eyes. 'You have seen

them—then you will concur, you must concur, in their being magnificent, wholly magnificent and sublime.'

'A beautiful part of the country indeed: so much so, that it is *almost* worth the trouble and inconvenience of going there.'

This concluded what they had to say on the relative merits of landscape. Phoebe, smiling a little fixedly, put in: 'So, Mr Beck, are you tolerably settled in Bath? Have you attended the Pump Room yet?'

'The Pump Room—good God, no. Was there ever anything so ridiculous and insipid? I know you must feel it so, Miss Rae—' he made a great tenderly confiding business with his eyebrows '—even if you are forced by convention and circumstances to go there.'

It was very vexing, Lydia thought, to hear something of your own sentiments crudely echoed by a person you found so unsympathetic; but not half so vexing as the implication that *she* was the strait-laced Bath tabby drilling her young charge in the ways of genteel boredom.

'Well, there is still very agreeable music to be heard there,' Phoebe said. 'That is one of the real pleasures of Bath. There is a concert coming on this week at the Upper Rooms—'

'I am not overfond of music, unless it truly stirs the heart,' Mr Beck said, 'and what one hears at Bath is generally very trivial, artificial stuff. I know from coming from here often with my father in my youth.' (Lydia estimated Mr Beck's age as at most twenty-four.) 'He tried the waters for several seasons, to no effect.'

Phoebe asked: 'Your father does not enjoy good

health?'

'Oh, it is simply that he has too much time on his hands to brood about it,' Mr Beck said, with all the confidence of a robust physique. 'Since my mother died he is rather the recluse.'

'Mr Beck is a West India merchant, I believe?' put in Lydia.

'Was: he is pretty much retired now.'

'You have never been to the West Indian islands yourself?' Phoebe asked.

'No, not I. My father last sailed to Antigua ten years ago. It is one place I have no desire to visit.'

'I am glad of that,' Phoebe cried, 'for what one hears from the wars lately—the way the soldiers die of fever there—it seems as if those islands are a perfect graveyard for white men.'

'They are somewhat less than healthy for black men also, I fear,' Lydia remarked.

'Oh, slavery will go,' Mr Beck said, with an expansive gesture. 'It will end—when other evils end—when there is a great reform all over: when there comes the great change in the minds and hearts of man. That'—with a swelling sort of modesty—'is what my writing is for, I hope: to contribute to that great end, by ever so little.'

'It is a noble, noble aim,' Phoebe murmured, with a soft rasp of emotion.

Yes, it was: and Lydia's own feeling was a faint sadness: the aspiration so large and real, the ability so weak—as, even leaving aside the absurdity of lacteous buckets, whose would not be? However, it seemed that Mr Beck could always be relied on promptly to destroy any sympathy one might begin to feel for him; for he turned to Lydia and, with a tolerant look, declared: 'Well, well, I am not helpful: I have now dismissed the Pump Room, and concerts; and I fear poor Miss Templeton must wonder what there is left in the social life of Bath that she can safely recommend to me.'

A recommendation that he depart forthwith and boil his head was, perhaps, more tempting than prudent: Lydia only replied: 'I would not presume to dictate, or even suggest, sir. I only wonder at your being in Bath at all: its amenities, as you say, being of no interest to you, and the printing-house, and your work on your review, being based at Bristol.'

'I am in Bath for one reason only,' he answered—not so much speaking as vocalising a shudder.

Phoebe could not miss the import of that, and did not at all appear to dislike it; but she only asked: 'When do you anticipate the *Inter*— The magazine going on sale?'

'Oh, not yet. There must be revision, in the light of . . . In short, Miss Rae, I await your approval: your blessing on the enterprise. Oh, yes, yes, you must, for I consider it our—our own offspring—after those happy times in London, when you were kind enough to lend an ear to my effusions—to hearken to my dreams.'

Lydia doubted that there was any way of not hearkening to Mr Beck's dreams, short of locking yourself in a cupboard: but she supposed Phoebe was not the first nor would be the last young woman to be fascinated by a man with an excessive propensity for talking about himself. Indeed it promised a certain compatibility; for while her fascination lasted, at least, they would never lack a topic of common interest.

'But before you give me your final opinion,' he said, jumping up and seizing the proofs from the side-table where Phoebe had placed them, 'there is one place—a horrible *bêtise* of style, it has been preying on me.' He took a stub of pencil from his pocket and scribbled vigorously. 'There—consider that as permanently erased.'

Lydia hoped, in a half-regretful way, that it was the hedger's needful implement.

'I have come to the end of that miserable convention, the half-hour call,' Mr Beck said, with a dark glance at his pocket-watch, and a darker glance at Lydia, as if the miserable convention had been invented by her. 'Never mind. It can—it must—sustain me until the next time.'

'And besides,' Phoebe said, meeting his burning look with bright good sense, 'we are all staying in Bath, and will lack no opportunity of meeting. If you should reconsider the concert, Mr Beck, it would be . . . well. Good day.'

He went all molten and twitching out of the room: leaving Phoebe to fall once more on the *Interlocutor*, and at length to carry it away with her upstairs; and leaving Lydia to reflect on the invidiousness of her position. Here was Mr Beck despising and resenting her for being a chaperon— the very role she had never sought or wanted in the first place!—it was rather unfair.

There was, of course, something else besides: irrespective of roles, she and William Beck did not like each other. The fact that they had large areas of common ground did not alter this: it was always the borders of countries that were fought over. But she felt he should be careful about regarding her as the vinegary and obstructive companion, alert to his every failing. He must surely know the proverb about giving a dog a bad name.

CHAPTER SEVENTEEN

The presence in Bath of the beautiful Miss Rae, and her still more beautiful fifty thousand pounds, was now sufficiently known for a regular deck of calling-cards to appear on the hall table at Sydney Place. Shuffling, Lydia found a viscountess and her honourable son—perhaps the ace in the pack—besides several esquires, a pair of reverends, and a solitary lieutenant R.N. gamely hoping that even a deuce could take a trick now and then.

Phoebe was not interested—or rather, only as interested as she was in everything. She would be very glad to make the acquaintance of all these people; but Lydia could not foresee any of them being added to the equation of Mr A and Mr B.

From one point of view—the selfish—this was a relief. Lydia reeled at the thought of having to counsel Phoebe on the relative merits of Mr C, Mr D and Mr E . . . Yet still she felt that Phoebe was being too precipitate in trying to add up the sum at all. Where was the need for hurry? She was not yet twenty-one, and the world was wide. This was what she tried to convey to her friend the next day, when Phoebe, by various hints, revealed her anxiety to know what she thought of her two suitors.

'Well. Now that I have had the pleasure of meeting both gentlemen, I can say that I see nothing absolutely to object to in either. I am assuming, of course, that you do value my opinion on the matter. And despite what Lady Eastmond says, I am far from convinced that it is my place to speak on it—'

'Oh, but you must!' Phoebe cried. 'That is— Lydia, I have never had a true friend before. A friend I can speak with openly, and in confidence. It is what I have so wanted. And this is what friends do, is it not? They are not afraid of offending, or being too familiar: they know that each has the other's best interests at heart.'

Lydia was touched; not only by this but by the brushing thought of her mother, and the friendship she had needed at the most vulnerable time of her life. 'Well, then, as a friend, I would only urge you not to be hasty in *any* decision you may make. It is simply unnecessary. Consider: soon enough you will be twenty-one, and in control of your whole fortune. You will have an enviable degree of independence. You may well find that that in itself is a satisfaction, for now: being your own woman, and able to do as you like. It may allow you to realise better who you are and what you want in life. You remember the magnificent cedar at Culverton? It grew so splendidly because it was planted on its own, with no other trees to crowd it.'

'That is true,' Phoebe said; and then, after a thoughtful pause: 'But I always think there is something rather melancholy about those solitary trees.'

'Do you? Well, I am a solitary tree, if you like. No specimen cedar—more a common beech with a touch of worm—but not, I hope, a melancholy sight.'

'Oh! no, no, indeed,' Phoebe said—with such

energy that Lydia did wonder, just for an unpleasant moment. 'You are right, of course: I should do nothing hasty. But I am glad to hear you say you like both gentlemen.' Before Lydia could protest she went on: 'I was a little afraid that you did not entirely take to Mr Beck. And yet I am sure now that that cannot be so. You and he are much alike, after all.'

Lydia was so silent and rigid with horror she might have been a tree.

That morning Phoebe had a fitting for a new gown at a dressmaker's in Milsom Street—one recommended by Mrs Allardyce. Lydia waited for her at Duffield's circulating-library. Seeing one of those prosy ladies she had been avoiding enter the reading-room, she snatched up the largest newspaper she could find, and hid behind it until she was sure the familiar droning voice had gone away. The fact that the newspaper was upside down perhaps rendered the subterfuge a little obvious, but no matter—or it would not have mattered, if she had not lowered it to find Lewis Durrant seated opposite her with a look of choice amusement.

'I'm trying to see the reasoning behind it,' he said. 'Does it make the bad news good, perhaps? But then that would make the good news bad. Not that there ever is any good news. The alternative, that you are trying to avoid me, is too wounding to contemplate.'

'Sometimes one wishes to remain quiet and unmolested; and we are not all in your fortunate position, Mr Durrant, and able to scare people away merely by facial expression.'

'You are too kind: I used to flatter myself that I

242

had that gift, indeed, but I fear I am losing it. I have read of certain priests of the ancient world who covered their face with a great brass head, and could only be spoken to when they took it off. I think that would do very well for me, though it might excite comment in the Pump Room.'

'Well, I am glad I have seen you, anyhow—oh, only because I want information from you. When you were calling yesterday, and Mr Beck came in, you spoke as if you knew him.'

'So I do, though not well. His father is a near neighbour of my friend at Clifton, and they often dine together: I met young Mr Beck there.'

'Ah, so you know the old slave-driver! There's an elegant addition to your acquaintance.'

'Oh, I confess I thought the same, at first; but old Beck is rather an interesting man. He inherited the West India estates from *his* father, and now he is sold up, and something of a philanthropist: endows schools and charities, and is setting up a scheme to train poor boys to the sea.'

'Ah, the late workings of conscience. I'm sure the slaves would be delighted to know they laboured for such admirable causes.'

He raised an eyebrow. 'You do not believe in the reformed character, Miss Templeton?'

'A reformed character usually means a rogue who has been scared into hypocrisy.'

'But may not a person genuinely change for the better?' he said, faintly smiling.

'Seldom, I think, outside the pages of religious tracts. After all, would you be in Bath now if you believed that a suppressed heart of gold beat beneath Hugh Hanley's silk waistcoat?'

He screwed up his face in a sniff. 'Oh, as for me,

243

I make it a rule to expect no good of humankind at all. That way one is never disappointed. Misanthropy, indeed, is the true recipe for happiness. Every time a fellow walks by without kicking you, you experience a delightful surprise. But come, what is this information you seek?'

'Oh, merely how you came to know Mr Beck, that's all.'

'I see. He, I collect, is one of your Miss Rae's admirers. Well, good luck to him. There seems nothing much amiss with him except foolishness, and I'm sure she is his equal there. And on that subject, Miss Templeton, you must confess that I am a little nearer winning our wager.'

'How? What do you mean?'

'Dear me, I had no idea fifty pounds meant so much to you,' he said, with a narrow look. 'I mean that you are already growing tired of constant chaperonage—is that the word? Constantly being at your charge's side, I mean. Quite understandable—but it gives me hope that you will admit defeat at last.'

'Oh, Phoebe has only gone to the dressmaker's, and will be meeting me here presently. You cannot count that as dereliction of my duty.'

'Not that. I mean allowing her to meet our friend Mr Beck alone. Again, it seems to me quite understandable: there can be nothing more tedious than making a third to a pair of drivelling lovers. Still, it promises—'

'Mr Durrant, what *do* you mean? Phoebe has only met Mr Beck when I . . .' Lydia felt her own face fall. Her mind's eye presented, with a mocking flourish, the image of Mr Beck scribbling an alteration on a page of the *Interlocutor*. Alteration,

244

or assignation? 'You mean you have seen them alone together.'

'Late last afternoon, in the abbey. I turned in there for a little peace, not knowing it was such a popular trysting place I might as well have been in the Dark Walks at Vauxhall Gardens. When I saw them, I assumed . . . Hm. It seems I assumed wrongly.'

'I did not know.' Lydia was assailed by such a host of feelings that she could say nothing more: as for Mr Durrant's inevitable triumphing over her, she could only sit numbly and submit to it.

After studying her for a moment, however, he said quietly: 'I am always prepared, of course, to be thought poorly of by you, and indeed I should be quite disturbed if it were otherwise. But in this case, Miss Templeton, I hope you will believe I did not speak with any intention of mischief.'

She blinked. 'Yes—yes, I do believe you, Mr Durrant. Not that it is any great matter, to be sure. I did not know, but no doubt Phoebe intended to tell me, and besides I think those strict notions of propriety are the greatest nonsense . . .' She felt the shabbiness of this, but could only hope that, like a torn petticoat or a pimple, it would go gallantly unnoticed. 'In the abbey, you say?'

'Aye, walking arm in arm and talking in that chap-fallen loverish way, as if the world is about to end; and well chaperoned by a dozen others, a verger and any amount of funerary monuments. My only thought was that Miss Templeton must be having a welcome hour's respite from nonsense— and, yes, that I might be on my way to winning the wager. Tell me—you don't doubt the honour of Mr Beck's intentions? For what it's worth, when I met him I thought him rather choke-full of honour, fine sentiments, and whatnot, even to a bilious degree.'

'Oh, yes, he is—full of it, certainly.' Late yesterday afternoon. When Lydia took her usual walk alone. How had it gone? A scribbled note: *When can I see you without the old dragon in attendance?* And Phoebe's reply, smuggled out to him somehow . . . Lydia found her foot rapidly tapping.

'Well, I say if Miss Rae is struck with him, let them go on as they like, and give it up and go home,' Mr Durrant went on. 'Yes, I am trying to press my advantage and win the wager, but I am serious also.'

'So am I,' said Lydia, equipping herself with a smile. 'Thank you for the information, Mr Durrant; and yes, so am I.'

*   *   *

She had betrayed nothing, she hoped, when Phoebe had rejoined her at Duffield's: she had been calm, natural, she had enquired pleasantly about the fitting at the dressmaker's, and in the same easy way she had asked if Phoebe minded going home alone, as she simply must pay a courtesy call on one of those prosy ladies and have it over with, and she certainly did not intend putting Phoebe through the ordeal as well . . .

Phoebe had gone away looking only a little perplexed. Very good: though Lydia, after what she had learned, felt she could no longer take the transparency of Phoebe's expressions on trust.

In fact she was only mildly disappointed with

Phoebe. If she had had to choose just one word from the dictionary to describe the girl, it would have been 'suggestible'; and she had no doubt that the tryst in the abbey had been Mr Beck's proposition, to which Phoebe, being Phoebe, had acceded in good faith. It was such a small request after all, and he would have been so hurt if she had refused, and so on—and Lydia was sure that when William Beck was hurt, everyone knew about it. He would be baring his breast to the lightning. It would be King Lear on the blasted heath.

No, if she was angry, it was with Mr Beck—for the image he had made of her. Two brief meetings had apparently been enough to convince him that she was an obstacle to be evaded—the vinegary old protectress out to trample with her great flat feet on love's young dream. Fury sang in her head. Did he really suppose she gave a tinker's damn about love's young dream? She had a thoroughly interesting and rewarding life waiting for her, when she had finished with this tedious interlude. She was not hovering harpy-like over a succulent romance, ready to stoop and tear the heart out of it.

But that was how he had treated her, by persuading Phoebe to a secret meeting. And she did not like it.

The coffee-room of the Christopher was empty except for a family in travelling-cloaks, arms full of parcels, waiting for the Gloucester coach that was making ready in the innyard. Leaving Bath. Lydia suffered a stab of envy for them, but her indignation quickly smothered it. No, she was not going to turn tail and run. She had undertaken this task, and she would damned well fulfil it.

247

'There is a Mr Beck staying here,' she said, to the waiter who attended her. 'Would you see if he is in his rooms, and tell him there is a lady downstairs who wishes to speak to him?'

The waiter pocketed the shilling. 'What name, ma'am?'

'No name. Just—no, wait a moment. Miss Rae.'

She had hardly seated herself before Mr Beck burst heroically into the coffee-room. Such speed seemed hardly possible, unless he had slid down the banisters. She thrust away the entertaining thought.

'Mr Beck.'

He glared wildly all about the room before allowing his eyes to rest on Lydia. (Not that Mr Beck's eyes could ever really be said to *rest*.)

'The man must have been mistaken,' he muttered. 'I thought to see Miss Rae.'

'Well, never mind. Perhaps you can make do with me instead. Will you sit down?'

He sat at an angle to her, nursing a well-filled hessian boot, glowering and suspicious. 'I think you have played me false, Miss Templeton.'

'Shocking of me, I know. But I thought we should have a little private talk—and the name of Miss Rae certainly brought you in haste, Mr Beck: you were very ready to meet her. Even without having made a secret arrangement beforehand.'

'Ah. So, we are discovered.' He rolled it out with lugubrious satisfaction. 'No doubt, ma'am, you have your spies.'

'This is precisely the sort of melodramatic nonsense I expected. Bath, sir, is hardly the sort of place where spies are needed. Everything is remarked by everyone. And nor is our situation—

248

Miss Rae's situation—of the kind that entails spies, and assignations, and hole-in-the-corner meetings. You know full well that you are welcome in our society: that you have Lady Eastmond's leave to pay your addresses: in short, that there is no necessity of treating Miss Rae as if she were a captive in a Gothic castle.'

'There are many forms of captivity,' he said, with a shrug.

'To the over-active imagination, no doubt there are. But my prosaic imagination cannot conceive why you should insist on a secret meeting in the abbey with Miss Rae—it *was* your idea?'

He tossed his curls. 'Certainly.'

'Then I cannot conceive what dreadful prohibition you were seeking to evade, Mr Beck—except myself. And really I had no notion I was so formidable. I gave up wearing snakes in my hair and carrying a spear when the master of ceremonies pointed out that they were inappropriate for formal evenings, and I have got quite out of practice at curses and hexes. You must have formed your conclusions about me on quite other evidence.'

'Miss Templeton, what would you have?' he said, with a twitch of his massy shoulders. 'I do not deny—I have made no attempt to deny—that Miss Rae and I met in the abbey. Nor do I deny that to a certain class of mind this must appear a fearful transgression—'

'You presume a good deal too far, sir, in ascribing to me that class of mind, or *any* class of mind. You know nothing of me.'

'Very well,' he said, pursing his lips, 'let us proceed on the evidence. You are here to reprove me for meeting Miss Rae in secret. That means, surely, that you disapprove: also that you do not understand the reasons for it.'

'Explain them to me,' she said icily.

'There you are, you see,' he cried, with his barking, impatient laugh. 'It must be explained to you why two people, between whom there exists the most tender and sacred attachment, should wish to meet alone, without all the miserable meddling fuss of chaperonage. Lord! What hope is there?'

'Obviously, sir, you have already satisfied yourself as to my position here as well as my sentiments. It hardly seems worth attempting to put my own side of the case—but perhaps you will humour me. I undertook to accompany Miss Rae to Bath at the request of her guardian, Lady Eastmond: out of respect to that lady, and also, perhaps more importantly, out of the firm friendship I have formed with Miss Rae. The fact that she is young, and inexperienced in the ways of the world, does not alter the character of that friendship: it does not turn us into schoolmistress and pupil, nor even gaoler and prisoner. It does, perhaps, intensify that element of protectiveness which is present in any friendship. It does not, decidedly not, render me a mere dummy of straw, to be thrust aside as an encumbrance, incapable of feeling.'

Mr Beck gnawed his lip. 'I did not suppose you any such . . . But surely, Miss Templeton, the matter need hardly concern you. You do not, as you say, stand as any sort of guardian to Miss Rae—'

'Nor am I an irrelevance, Mr Beck. And I

cannot help but wonder, if you can prevail on Miss Rae to meet you in secret, what other commitments you might prevail upon her to enter.'

'Now you do me an injustice,' he said, with the alacrity of someone who likes that best in the world.

'Do I? If you had not seen fit to go about things in so underhand a manner, I would be better able to judge. *Have* you persuaded Miss Rae to enter some sort of secret engagement?'

'There you are, you see,' he cried again. (She would allow him two of those. At the third, she would break her parasol over his head.) 'The way you speak of her—as if she had no independent mind of her own. But I will answer your question. No, I have not. Nor would I do so. It would be a profanation of what should be pure and true and open. All I have done, Miss Templeton, is lay my heart at Miss Rae's feet. It is there for her to take—or to scorn and spurn and trample on—as she chooses.'

Mr Beck's voice was loud, and the lady waiting for the coach peered over her shoulder with interest. Scorn and spurn, forsooth. Lydia couldn't be sure, but she believed she had never before heard a person not actually on the stage use the word 'spurn'.

'And I know very well,' Mr Beck pursued, taking her silence to mean she was impressed, 'that I am not the only aspirant for Miss Rae's hand. How could that be, indeed, when one look at her—one word from her lips . . . But I know, and accept, there is another gentleman in Bath who is paying his addresses to Miss Rae. Yes, we have no secrets from one another.'

251

'None at all? Really, I should keep a few, else you will be bored with each other within a twelvemonth.'

That remark seemed so perfectly to suit his conception of her that he smiled, pityingly. 'Well, well. I think I see my way clear now. Very revealing. You, Miss Templeton, are this other gentleman's advocate. He has, as it were, a friend at court, while I am out in the cold. Isn't that it?'

Lydia gathered up her mantle. 'Plainly you have not listened to anything I have said, Mr Beck. So I will not even address the question of why you should suppose me an advocate for the other gentleman, or any gentleman—except to remark that you must think me sadly lacking in things to occupy my mind.' She rose. 'Unless you suppose I do it for a fee?'

His arms went out. 'There you are, you see—'

She spared his head: instead walking smartly away from him. The parasol would probably have bounced off anyway.

*   *   *

'Lydia. Oh, Lydia, I have a confession to make.'

Phoebe was waiting—all pale solemnity—all wax, ivory and marble—in the hall at Sydney Place. It was no wonder, Lydia thought, that the young were so inclined to tragedy: they looked so beautiful in it. Their elders just couldn't wear it, and had to don serviceable cheerfulness instead.

'I cannot bear it any longer,' Phoebe went on. 'I must tell you—but I am afraid you will think very badly of me . . . But no, I am not afraid, because you would be *right* to think badly of me; and we should never fear what is right.'

Such a mixed dose of romance and Calvin was rather much to swallow when you had scarcely taken off your bonnet and had an urgent appointment with the decanter.

'My dear Phoebe,' Lydia said, taking her arm and propelling her upstairs, 'if we are to consider ethical questions before dinner, let us at least do it in comfort. And besides, unless this confession refers to a body in the dining-room with a knife between its shoulder-blades, I think I know what it is to be, and really it is nothing so very dreadful.'

Phoebe's mournful look suggested otherwise, but Lydia meant what she had said: her opinion of Phoebe had not been very much lowered, and this spontaneous admission had gone a long way to restoring it. It was an open question, of course, whether Phoebe would simply deceive her again, and confess it afterwards; but a glass of canary convinced her to let the question lie.

'It is to do with the abbey, I presume,' she said. 'Yes, I have seen Mr Beck, and spoken to him about it.'

'Oh—so *he* told you. Oh, that is so very like him. His nature is so frank and open, he cannot bear any sort of concealment—'

'Not Mr Beck. You were observed, Phoebe. It was by Mr Durrant, as it happens, which is why I credited it at once, as he considers himself much too important to gossip. But really, it might have been anyone. The whole point of Bath, you know, is that it has no sequestered spots. Here you live life as publicly as poor Louis XIV, putting on his nightcap in front of a crowd of courtiers.'

'Well, in a way I am glad,' Phoebe said, looking

253

very forlorn. 'It is right that your sin should find you out.'

'Come, if we are talking of sin, then there must be a good deal more to this than either Mr Durrant or Mr Beck said. But I am sure there is not. If anything it is a matter of propriety or etiquette, for which I hope I am no great fanatic. I was only puzzled, Phoebe, as to why you should feel it necessary to—to go behind my back, even to a little degree.'

'Oh, Lydia. That is exactly why I did not want to do it. But there's a prevarication, because I *did* do it.'

'Mr Beck pressed you, of course.'

'Oh, yes—and he is so very earnest and persuasive. Not that that is any excuse.'

'My dear Phoebe, I am not seeking excuses. I only want to know that you do not see me as a sort of enemy, whose surveillance must be evaded. Very well if that is how Mr Beck sees me—we have had our talk out on that subject—but I cannot be happy to bear such a character in *your* eyes.'

'Oh, no! And that is precisely what I said to him: that this must be the *only* occasion, and that I was being very unfair to you in giving in to it. I told him that there was nothing to prevent our meeting in the proper fashion: that it could never be misconstrued: that it was what Lady Eastmond would wish.'

'And what is due to you as a woman whom, I hope, he respects as well as adores.'

'I did not think of that.'

No, she wouldn't: a thousand pities!

'Did Mr Beck—' Phoebe wincingly hesitated. 'Was he—amenable?'

'We had a frank talk.'

Phoebe looked less than reassured. 'What he wanted to do, you see, was to be sure that I knew of his profound, his unalterable attachment. It has been some time since London—and affections, as he said, have been known to cool; but I must know, before we renewed our acquaintance, that it was not so in his case—that he brought to Bath an undimmed and ever-lambent flame.'

That certainly sounded like Mr Beck, Lydia thought, with an inward sigh. Perhaps if the flame got too hot, he could dip it in his lacteous bucket.

'And so I said very well—I understood, and was very flattered—but now we must conduct ourselves properly. There would be ample opportunity to meet in Bath—indeed you heard me mention the concert to him the other day, did you not? And then there is the gala night at Sydney Gardens: there, I suggested, we might go together—that is, make up a party . . .' She looked timidly at Lydia. 'Was that wrong?'

'Not in the least,' Lydia said gathering herself: she was only envisaging the prospective effect on her nerves of fireworks and Mr Beck in one evening. 'Very sensible. And now that he has, as you say, made his flamings—I mean feelings known, there is no reason why he should not be sensible also.'

'I do not at all mind you thinking badly of me,' Phoebe said, with her mistiest gaze, 'well—that's not true, I do, because everyone wants to be thought well of; but what I mean is, I know very well the fault was mine, not Mr Beck's.'

Lydia smiled. 'Well, I'll say no more: except that he is very lucky to have you as his defender.'

She had nearly said 'advocate'.

No, Mr Beck, she thought, as she went up to dress for dinner, I am not Mr Allardyce's advocate. If anything, I prefer to think of myself as a member of the jury, who has not the responsibility of pleading or passing sentence. But certainly in the case of Mr A versus Mr B, I am finding Mr A's case much the most convincing.

CHAPTER EIGHTEEN

Presenting daily at BATH, a new Comic Opera, entitled THE SUITORS, or THE DUENNA DISTRESS'D. Principals, Miss RAE, Mr ALLARDYCE, and Mr BECK: with Miss TEMPLETON in the celebrated comic role of the Duenna. All new scenes, costumes and decorations. Patrons are respectfully requested to take their Seats before the Commencement of the Performance.

Thinking of it in this way helped, Lydia found, a little. It was better, at least, than trying to make any sense of her current life.

Thus: a morning call from Robert and Juliet Allardyce. Much pleasant talk. Juliet agreeably dry on the subject of the Prince of Wales's debts, and how curious it was that a man went to prison for owing fifty pounds, whereas if he owed a hundred thousand they gave him a palace by the sea. Mr Allardyce transfixing Phoebe with an account of snowy midwinter in Vienna, and the grand ladies taking their exercise in horse-drawn sleighs in the shape of swans and scallop-shells. Then, an invitation to dine at Queen Square on Saturday. Phoebe luminous with pleasure. Lydia drawing conclusions: suggestion that exclusive Mrs Allardyce did not often give dinners: much meaning in the compliment. Before that, however, there would be the concert at the Upper Rooms this evening: agreement to make a party. Lydia and Juliet talking of the featured singer—known for the Italian repertoire—not *all* Handel they hoped, those endless *da capo* arias. Mr Allardyce looking on in alarm: beseeching Phoebe to take pity on him tonight, and give him a nudge when there was something very fine, and requiring that peculiar staccato *Br-vo!* that sounded as if you had been stuck with a pin. Exit of visitors, warmth all round, Phoebe in bright, buoyant, Allardyce mood.

Soon afterwards (suspiciously soon—had he been loitering in the street, observing, waiting?) entrance of William Beck. Visible effort at being cordial to Lydia, hindered by sighs, frownings, evidence of unconquerable resentment. Phoebe a little constrained after late confession of her own delinquency, but soon relaxing and easing into Beck mood: devoted attention to anecdotes of his childhood (bitter-sweet innocence, moments of poignant revelation, sensibility, loneliness, attachment to inevitably dying cage-bird) and, when allowed, anecdotes of her own, with much breathy amazement at their coincidence of feeling. Mr Beck eagerly seizing on Phoebe's remark that they would be walking to the Pump Room presently: he would accompany them: be their escort and protector against the savage beasts of Bath (with his exasperated laugh). All along Great

Pulteney Street, more visible efforts at not leaving Lydia out: walking beside her for several paces at a time, remarking frequently, 'Isn't it so, Miss Templeton?', and even, occasionally, looking at her: the total effect being to make Lydia feel like a child being given an old half-full pack of cards to play about with while the adults got on with their whist.

In the Pump Room, much company: including that very same viscountess and her honourable son who had left a card, and now, presuming on rank, introduced themselves with the air of conferring a great favour. Speculative, hard-up glint in glaucous eye of viscountess, all skin and rouge. Honourable son a gaping duffer, probably as deep in debt as the Prince of Wales. Mr Beck torn between lofty amusement and jealous scowling: adoration of Phoebe apparently not unqualified, when it came to her unfailing politeness to other people. A little relief for Lydia in Mr Durrant's entering the room, and talking apart with her under the great tompion clock, and making disgraceful comparisons between the viscountess and a plucked pullet. Retreat at last of viscountess and duffer, defeated but in good order: Mr Beck's mood now requiring a good deal of soothing. Phoebe mentioning again the concert at the Upper Rooms: Mr Beck angrily laughing, and declaring that he had had enough of social insipidity—long walk into the country more his line—renew himself—necessary to him sometimes—untied a sort of knot within—not a knot though—difficult to explain. Phoebe: 'Oh, do try.' Explanation lasting all the way back to Sydney Place, whither he had, unprompted, chosen to escort them: and where he would surely have invited himself back into the house if Lydia had let him.

Evening: concert at the Upper Rooms. Scantiness of summer entertainment bringing a vast deal of company to gather beforehand in the Octagon Room, where Lydia and Phoebe waited to meet the Allardyces. Crowd exacerbated by that incorrigible tendency of people at busy social occasions to consider, against all the evidence of their senses, that just to the rear of them was a great open space, and to step loungingly backwards as they laughed at their own jokes, and glance with surprised annoyance at the person they had just trodden on. Arrival of Robert and Juliet Allardyce, their look of sprightly intelligence pleasantly conspicuous amongst so much well-dressed vacancy. Mr Allardyce brushing a few speckles of water from his sleeve, and remarking that it was coming on to rain—and what an extraordinary expression *that* was—no one spoke of its coming on to be sunny or windy, and why not? because no one had started to do so: 'Miss Rae, we must begin it tomorrow, and then we may change the course of history, at least as far as speech goes: our descendants in future ages will say, "Dear dear, it is coming on to thunder", all unknowing that we first struck that path'. Bell ringing: movement towards the concert-room: sudden appearance at Phoebe's side of Mr Beck, ignoring everyone else: declaring that he was here, yes, he was here after all, her persuasions had worked and he was here— inclined indeed to go on congratulating himself on the fact, until aroused to unpleasant awareness of the rest of the party.

Phoebe delighted, but her delight not

uncomplicated. Lydia, unkindly perhaps, leaving it to Phoebe to perform the introductions. Phoebe, with her limitless goodwill, actually doing it very well: Juliet Allardyce smilingly unreadable: Mr Allardyce easy and polite: Mr Beck, inevitably, understandably, not doing well. So here it was, the meeting of the rivals. Lydia wondering mightily what Phoebe was feeling: appreciation at last of the absurdity of it? Sudden realisation, on seeing both of them together, of where her heart really lay? Sheer exultation at having two eligible gentlemen in train—somewhat like a pagan queen with a pair of leopards on the leash? Scarcely time to assess the evidence, as the awkward party must be moving into the concert-room. Question of seating arising. Delirious vision, for Lydia, of a sort of desperate game of musical chairs (Mr A and Mr B pouncing either side of Phoebe, comfortably ensconced old ladies being elbowed on to the floor) but in the end Mr Allardyce quite content to take his place on the bench between Lydia and his sister. Lydia amused at his wondering aloud, as he contemplated the stage, why a large, dusty potted plant was always deemed so necessary to a public musical performance: trying meanwhile to eavesdrop on Mr Beck, who was whispering to Phoebe in a dark, rapid, urgent flow, as if he had taken a bet that he could not tell the whole story of *Hamlet* in two minutes. Evident irritation on Mr Beck's part at having to stop talking for the music: on Lydia's part, enjoyment heightened by relief at everyone's having to stop, just for a while, being so insistently themselves.

Interval, and Mr Allardyce coming into his own. Tea to be had in the Octagon Room: Mr Allardyce

260

undertaking to brave the crush and get some, and Phoebe, displaying what must have been for Mr Beck a disappointing interest in such soulless conventions as eating and drinking, going to help him. Juliet, in her strong-minded way, walking off to talk technicalities with the pianist. Mr Beck left alone with Lydia, and making the most of the opportunity.

'Well, Miss Templeton. Well, well.' He gave the sort of skewed, distant smile that those who do not understand irony suppose to be ironic. 'A very agreeable evening, indeed. Certainly a revealing one. I am glad I came: it has opened my eyes to what is going on. My appearance on this occasion, I fear, must have been an unpleasant surprise for you.'

It was in Lydia's mind to say that Mr Beck's appearance on any occasion would be an unpleasant surprise for her, even if she were at the bottom of a well and he were at the top with a rope; but she held her peace.

'As I told you,' he pursued, 'I knew of Mr Allardyce. I accept him. I have nothing to say against him. I hope I have nothing to say against any human creature. But I see now that I am indeed—as I put it to you the other day—out in the cold. Plainly this party was formed at your instigation. Plainly you are seeking to throw Miss Rae in Mr Allardyce's way as much as possible. Plainly, in every moment of my absence, you are seeking to favour him: to further his cause: to influence Miss Rae's mind in accordance with your own ideas. But I am not put out, Miss Templeton: not at all! You may spin your webs all you like.'

'Well, that's what we spinsters do, you know,' she said: absolutely weary of him, and despairing of rational argument having any effect. 'How do you like the music?'

'Artificial,' he snapped, 'miserably artificial,' and he stared away: leaving Lydia to the interesting philosophic exercise of imagining what music with no artifice would sound like. A man falling off a step-ladder, perhaps, as long as he did it spontaneously, and with no soul-destroying preparation.

Re-emergence from the crowd of Mr Allardyce. Not only tea secured but seats—Miss Rae was guarding them—this way. Awkward squeeze of five people around a little table, awkward handing of lukewarm cups: discovery that there were only four, and Lydia without: Mr Allardyce promptly surrendering his to her: Mr Beck, a frowning moment later, deciding to do the same, which left her with two cups that she did not want, and a faint feeling of being a nuisance. Juliet attempting to make conversation with Mr Beck: he all prickly suspicion—another conspirator. Bell ringing: crush back into the concert-room. Unforeseen variation on the seating: Juliet so intent on pointing out something in the programme to Lydia that she ended up sitting next to her, leaving Phoebe symbolically placed between her two suitors. Juliet at last glancing up at Lydia's distracted expression: a measured smile and whisper: 'Oh, let them get on with it.' Lydia wondering whether Juliet—level-headed, observant—might perhaps be consulted, to clear some of her difficulties. Were Robert Allardyce's definite *attentions* indicative of definite *intentions*? Was that face, of which the profile was currently presented to her—elegant concave cheek, alert grey eye—the face of a man in love? Difficult to raise such a question, though, against the concert-room babble: might place her also in exactly the position Mr Beck accused her of adopting—projecting, meddling: finger on the scale.

Music again, to put an end to her fretting—yet failing to do so. Envy of Juliet, seated at ease, following the words—the endless caras and sospiros—in the programme, all contented concentration. That used to be me.

End of concert: audience as thrustful in getting out as they had been in getting in. Phoebe in the Octagon Room managing her pair of leopards very well: all ingenuous gratitude for their company— delightful evening—assurances sought that they would all make a party again at the gala evening in Sydney Gardens. Mr A cheerfully compliant— perhaps a little narrow wryness in his glance?— Mr B with the look of a man girding on armour. Return to Sydney Place, Lydia absently replying to Phoebe's effusions, mind guiltily reverting to the waiting decanter: reflection that Bath, supposed to cure the liver, would end up putting hers out of order. Curtain, until the next performance.

*   *   *

'I declare you are becoming quite as much a fixture here as Beau Nash's statue,' Lydia said, coming upon Mr Durrant in the Pump Room.

'The place exerts a dreadful fascination. Daily attendance makes the stupidest matters important. I gape at a new face, however commonplace. I am

263

troubled by absences, or alterations in habit. Old Sir Barton Scrimbleshanks, over there, takes a glass of the waters every day at eleven without fail—but today he has omitted it: what can it mean? My mind, or what is left of it, reels with speculation.'

'Sir Barton—dear me,' Phoebe said, 'what an unfortunate name.'

'It would be, if it was his real one,' Mr Durrant said readily. 'I make up the names to suit them. I've been deliberately avoiding an introduction to Sir Barton, to avoid disappointment. People are much more tolerable as fictional characters.'

'How very singular!' Phoebe said—smiling, but with reserve, as at something doubtfully moral.

'What about those two rather languid ladies, over there on the rout-bench?' Lydia asked.

'Miss Fannaway, and Miss Henrietta Fannaway. Their brother has a country place in Kent called Groynes. It isn't very nice. The gentleman with the young hair and the old face, plucking up courage to speak to them, is Captain Overbold, Retired.'

'I wonder what names you would have thought of for us, if you hadn't known us already,' Lydia said.

His eyes lit mockingly on hers for a moment. 'Ah, that is one of those things that can never be told. Now, over there by the gallery you'll see—' he caught his breath '—Mrs Vawser.'

'Oh, Mr Durrant, surely that doesn't count,' Phoebe exclaimed, 'for we know a real Mrs Vawser.'

'We do indeed,' Lydia said, through her teeth, 'and there she is.'

There she was, very fine, very sweeping in silk

pelisse and feathered hat, strolling the Pump Room like a queen amongst subjects, and on her arm a consort—an abbreviated man with more neckcloth than neck, a square head like a box, and small features like holes in it. They were spotted: Mrs Vawser and her appendage bore swiftly down on them. There was no possible escape, short of climbing on to the window-sill behind them, and plunging into the King's Bath below—a possibility Lydia saw flicker vividly across Lewis Durrant's face before he surrendered to the inevitable.

'Well, and here we all are! Is it not the most—? Was there ever anything so—? Lord, I was just remarking to Mr Vawser that if we met any *more* of our acquaintance, I should be almost fatigued with it—arrived in Bath just yesterday, and nothing but greetings and invitations from that moment to this! But how do you do—Miss Templeton, Miss Rae— and Mr Durrant, I declare!'—this with a very airy look. 'I must be my own master of ceremonies and introduce my spouse—mind, I am used to that, all my friends will tell you, "Penelope", they say, "you are a perfect Beau Nash . . ."'

Mr Vawser, bowing as much as his starch would allow him, declared himself enchanted, but looked only conceited. This then was the perennial betrayer and destroyer of Mrs Vawser's happiness—but for the present, at least, plainly the rake reformed and forgiven. Her arm tenderly gathered in his, Mr Vawser basked in his wife's smiles, seeming to concur in her opinion that she was the most fortunate of women.

'You will be mightily wondering how we come to be in Bath,' Mrs Vawser went on, 'and you will laugh when I tell you. I had hardly returned to

town from Lincolnshire—dear sleepy Heystead!—
one cannot help but be fond—before Mr Vawser
declared: "My love, I fear you are mopish." "My
love," said I, "I fear you are mopish too. What
shall we do?" And so we fell to laughing, and
agreed we needed a change, and I saw to the
packing at once. No dallying—all my friends will
tell you: "Oh, Penelope—no dawdling for her—
that's not her way"—and only then did we
consider, where is it to be? Oh, you would have
laughed to see us.'

'Her, her, her,' remarked Mr Vawser. For a
moment Lydia took this as an ungallant if accurate
reference to Mrs Vawser's habit of talking about
herself, until she saw that Mr Vawser's negligible
eyes had all but disappeared in creases of mirth;
and realised he was laughing.

'We turned it over—Brighton—Lyme—Bath.
Now we are both excessively fond of Bath—but
then, of course, it is *hardly* the fashionable season,'
pursued his wife. 'And then we laughed again, and
said: "What does it matter? Can it hurt us to live
for a time without a little fashion? Shall we not
survive? Then let us be off!" Oh, you would have
died of laughing, Miss Templeton, to hear how we
went on.'

Lydia offered a smile that, while polite, was a
good way off hilarious expiry; and said: 'I hope you
were able to find comfortable accommodation, at
such short notice.'

'Oh, as to that, it was only a matter of sending a
letter ahead of us, to our dear woman at
Marlborough Buildings who always provides us
with the most excellent lodgings—it is positively
embarrassing, I dare swear she would turn anybody

266

out on the street rather than let us down. Quite the best air in Bath up there, you must know. I have heard, of course, from poor Emma about *your* being settled at Sydney Place—which is not at all a bad air, all things considered.'

'You say "poor Emma",' Lydia said. 'Is Mrs Paige not well? I thought—'

'Oh, well enough: but Emma's temper, you know, is her trouble—nervous, and over-sensitive, though I have always tried my best, as a sister, to brace her up. Well! I said to Mr Vawser, "I shouldn't wonder if we run into Miss Templeton and Miss Rae"—but I am very much amazed, Mr Durrant, actually to see *you* here—you who never go anywhere.' Again her look was lofty, even cold, and she made a great business of affectionately toying with her husband's fingers.

'Oh, I was mopish too, ma'am,' Mr Durrant said. 'So, like you, I was off: in fact I came to Bath even *before* I had packed, which caused me some difficulty afterwards.'

'Her, her, her,' said Mr Vawser.

Mrs Vawser thinned her lips in a smile. 'I am amazed nonetheless. Setting up in Bath quite alone, and I dare say not knowing a soul—for you must know, my love, in Lincolnshire Mr Durrant makes quite a point of shunning society, and even *I* was forced to give up bringing him out as a bad job. Where are you staying, Mr Durrant?'

'Edgar Buildings, ma'am. I don't know whether it's a good air there: I just breathe it in and hope for the best.'

'This way of his, Miss Templeton!' Mrs Vawser sighed. 'Really we shall have to try and cure him of it, for while it may do in the *country* . . . Lord, my

267

love, only look there, I do believe those are the people we ran into at Cheltenham—do you recall?—I declare we really will not have a moment's peace.'

'Where?' said Mr Vawser, essaying the difficult operation of turning his head.

'Oh, they've moved on now.'

'Talking to Sir Barton Scrimbleshanks, I think,' Lydia said, craning. 'And isn't *he* a wonder for his age? I know everyone says so, but still one marvels.'

'Oh, indeed—everyone knows Sir Barton—and I might tell you a tale or two on that score,' agreed Mrs Vawser, with roguish vivacity. 'We are sure to see something of each other in Bath, of course— that is, you and Miss Rae: as to Mr Durrant, who knows? I am sure you are quite the hermit, sir— but all the same, I know Mr Vawser will join with me in wishing to help you to a little company. We are already engaged to be part of a large party at the gala night at Sydney Gardens—and I can positively vouch for there being no difficulty, at *my* recommendation, Mr Durrant, in including you also. One more can hardly make any—'

'There you place Mr Durrant in a difficult position, as he has already promised to join our own party for the evening,' Lydia interrupted her. 'Not a large party—exclusive rather—but I fear we must claim first rights upon his company.'

Phoebe eagerly seconded her: Mrs Vawser shrugged and pouted: Mr Durrant only looked neutral. Lydia was not sorry to have spoken. Mrs Vawser's behaviour was comprehensible—it was that implacable malice we always show to those who have seen us at our most foolish—but that did not mean it was to be easily forgiven. Only when the Vawsers, with much farewell laughter, mutual caressing, and self-consequence, had moved away, did it occur to Lydia that Mr Durrant might suppose her guilty of pitying him. She was pained: she had felt many things about him, most of them disobliging, but never that.

However, he merely filled his chest with air, as if he had been submerged in water for an uncomfortable period; and said: 'A kind thought, Miss Templeton—more than kind, indeed, as it stopped her talking. But I am quite capable of telling Mrs Vawser to go to blazes myself.'

'I know that: but the trouble with Mrs Vawser is, she won't go there even when she's told. To think of that ridiculous woman proposing to take you under her wing!'

'And the only relief her husband's sparkling wit: a shocking prospect. But come, I hope you have not perjured yourself on my account, and that your party on Friday is a real one.'

'It is,' Phoebe said, 'and our pleasure would be very real, if you were to join it, Mr Durrant.'

This was spoken with all Phoebe's instinctive warmth. Mr Durrant studied her as if seeing her for the first time.

'Bearing in mind, of course,' Lydia could not help adding, 'that you are not *obliged* to.'

'If you want me to come, I shall,' he said, looking into the distance; and English being English, there was no telling whom he meant by 'you'.

269

CHAPTER NINETEEN

Vauxhall came back vividly to Lydia on entering
Sydney Gardens for the gala night. There was
more gentility here, if less vitality—no Dark Walks,
no roistering bucks, and no prostitutes, or if there
were, they were discreet in true Bath fashion—but
there were the same groves and strings of coloured
lanterns, the same arbours and grottoes, the same
smell of bruised grass. Since coming to Bath she
had hardly thought about that last night in
London: Hugh Hanley lounging in their box,
Susannah smiling in poisonous innocence, George
getting drunk on rack-punch and talking his
blundering nonsense about all head and no heart.
Yet the fact that every detail presented itself to her
mind so clearly suggested that she had, perhaps,
been thinking about it without knowing it.

Then, of course, the Bath project had been
newly proposed by Lady Eastmond, and she had
been in a state of violent opposition to it. Now
here she was, and—well, was it so bad after all?

Not bad, but not pleasant. Where she had
feared dullness, she was finding increasing
perplexity. The duenna was distress'd indeed. The
party that gathered outside the Sydney Hotel was a
strained one, and she saw no prospect of its being
otherwise. Well-meaning and guileless Phoebe
might be—though Lydia had not forgotten the
abbey—but still she had created an infernally
complicated situation; and Lydia was afraid that
such knots and tangles, such lashings and
tightenings, could not be undone without some

270

pain to someone.

But then tonight no one seemed to be in spirits—herself included. From the beginning she was put quite out of patience by Mr Durrant's failing to meet them, at the time arranged, outside the Sydney Hotel. The Allardyces and Mr Beck were here—Mr Beck, indeed, giving the appearance of having solidly planted himself at the spot since daybreak; the strains of music could be heard beyond the gates, through which a stream of people was already passing. They waited, Phoebe murmuring her concern that Mr Durrant might be unwell; but it was Lydia at last who said they should go in, and let Mr Durrant find them. Having been in charity with him lately, she had barked her shins against his old capacity to frustrate and annoy, and surprise made her more vehement. He is not ill, she thought—he is merely being Lewis Durrant: capricious, and supposing himself above the normal claims of society: liking the idea of being waited for, so that his arrival would give him the supercilious pleasure of conferring a favour.

However, she kept these thoughts to herself, and the general low spirits of the party must be attributed to other causes—though the abstention of Mr Durrant at least highlighted one of them. They were lop-sided. Mr Allardyce, naturally enough, did not wish to be always giving his arm to his sister: Mr Beck, more mulishly, would not do so at all. Juliet meanwhile, perhaps in protest at either of them being turned into the superfluous woman, tended to walk with Lydia. The result was a straggle, with no one at ease. The gardens had been decorated very prettily—that was the word,

271

and quite right in the context: no one entered a Bath pleasure-garden looking for rugged sublimity. But where Phoebe was inclined to admire the illuminated cascades and Chinese bridges, and Mr Allardyce to smile on them with tolerant amusement, Mr Beck could not or would not stifle his disgust. 'A waterfall! Was there ever such a gimcrack travesty? And what have they done to that splendid tree? Festooning it like that—as if it has its hair in curl-papers.'

'The illumination is a little excessive,' Mr Allardyce ventured, 'but it does prevent that unfortunate hazard of dark nights—falling over.' Mr Beck only gave a triumphant snort, as if he considered himself fully vindicated. ('There you are, you see.') Mr Allardyce kept his composure, but he seemed to retreat a little further into that inner distance. Phoebe, in turn, appeared uncomfortable: frequently the exquisite neck turned, as if appealing for Lydia's help in her distresses.

This Lydia was no more willing than able to supply. If the sheer impossibility of her situation was striking Phoebe, then Lydia felt it was high time. Youth, naïveté and romanticism were all very well, but surely they need not be so closely allied to folly. Then she remembered, with a curious start, Mr Durrant's saying something very similar at Heystead; and then, more sombrely, she remembered the fate of her mother.

Perhaps, indeed, she should be *more* the chaperon. Phoebe had actually said she wanted advice, after all; and Lydia had no such low opinion of herself, of her own mind, experience, and taste, as would hinder her from offering it. If anything tended to prevent her, it was that propensity of people who asked your advice to act upon it, and then blame you if it went wrong. But just now the evils of that seemed negligible, compared to a continuance of this indecision, which could be tending to nobody's happiness.

A shriek of laughter made her turn her head in alarm; but there was a genuine note in it, which reassured her that it did not proceed from Mrs Vawser. The place was so well filled, indeed, that they stood a fair chance of escape from her. A fair chance also, she thought as she scanned the faces, that Mr Durrant would not find them; and from anger with him she shifted to a sudden disquiet. Suppose, after all, that he *was* ill, or that some accident had befallen him? Raging torrents and wild bulls were admittedly scarce in Bath, but still she would be easier if he appeared—if only that she might give him a set-down.

'What does he look like?' Juliet said in her ear, startling her.

'Who?'

'This missing gentleman—Mr Durrant.'

'Oh . . .' She found it curiously difficult to answer. 'Tall—very tall. Gentleman-like, but rather dark and grim.'

'You make him sound like the very devil. And I feel like the very devil tonight. Shocking language, I know. Mama would be horrified. Though not surprised . . . That's why both Robert and I are a little out of sorts, Miss Templeton—a certain familial disharmony. Are you equal to that greatest of bores, a confidence?'

'Certainly,' Lydia answered: for she doubted that with Juliet Allardyce these were either

273

habitual, or trivial; and she was curious.

'I had better start with the usual high-minded things about Mama meaning no harm, and so on. Indeed, I am quite prepared to believe them, now I have cooled a little. But the fact is we did get thoroughly at cross today, and the occasion of it is not likely to go away. It concerns my future—our future. Robert is to return to London in September, and expects thereafter—depending on the war news—to be dispatched again to the ministry at Vienna. I made the assumption that I would be going with him again. To London certainly—he has very decent lodgings there, which I have shared these past few seasons—and then abroad. It is what I very much wish.'

Lydia, thinking of Mrs Allardyce, could entirely understand that.

'Mama, it transpires, is set against this plan. It was with the greatest difficulty that we persuaded her to my going to Vienna last time. And now I learn that that was enough of indulgence—that I should have got that nonsense over with: in short, that I should settle to a regular life, and make a good marriage.'

There was enough that was familiar in this to bring a wry smile to Lydia's lips. 'And even London is not to be considered?'

'Well, Robert is not expected to be there long— this is Mama's reasoning—and so it is hardly worth the stir of removal—and of course I cannot remain in town alone—and furthermore, as Mama is careful not to say, once I am in London there is nothing to prevent me skipping off abroad with him.'

'I see. Mr Allardyce, presumably, agreeing to . . .'

274

'You are looking for a delicate way of asking, what is Robert's position? Excessively difficult. In essence, he is on my side, and will do everything he can to help me. But on the other hand his impulse is always to humour Mama, of whom he refuses to think ill; and he is after all the man of the family, and must weigh its responsibilities and so forth. And then, as Mama is kind enough to remind him, there is his own future to think of. He promises great things, and I believe deserves them; but in the meantime he must be prudent. Papa was more distinguished than greedy, and Robert's fortune is not great—at least—'

'Not so great that it should be burdened with the maintenance of an unmarried sister,' Lydia put in.

'Somehow I knew you'd understand,' Juliet said, tapping Lydia's arm in her brisk way. 'So, time for Robert to forge ahead with his destiny, and for me to accept mine. I sound like the most miserable carper and complainer, don't I? Over-educated, my dear, too many high-flown notions. I didn't give in, of course. Neither did Mama. The decisive battle is yet to be fought. Queen Square is rather like Europe in miniature just now. Hence the clouded brows. I fancy Robert suffers the most, because he always wants to please both sides.'

In that he certainly resembled Phoebe, Lydia thought; but Juliet's words had prompted further reflections, and in an unexpected direction. She began to wonder whether Mr Allardyce—honourable though he undoubtedly was—were not a little influenced in his partiality to Phoebe by her considerable fortune. Certainly Mrs Allardyce seemed to approve her for that very reason. And indeed if he were so influenced, why not? It was surely a very nice thing if the person you loved had fifty thousand pounds: indeed it seemed a positive incitement to devotion. Still, she felt that if she were to be an active chaperon, she ought to examine the question—ensure that in the sum of her attractions, Phoebe's sweet nature, charming manner, soft eyes, lithe figure, and money should be ranged in due proportion. And she had to admit that, distasteful as she found Mr Beck, no such suspicion of his motives was allowable. He was all too sincere. That was his trouble.

The question was all the more urgent in that Mr Allardyce must surely be settling his affairs before his departure in September. She wished she might ask Juliet where, in her opinion, Phoebe fitted in with her brother's plans; but this seemed carrying confidence too far. Nor could she easily state her own opinion, that Phoebe might well be ready to accept whichever gentleman asked her first: somehow it placed no one in a flattering light.

For now she could only commiserate with Juliet—for whom her sympathy was very real: though the tilt of Juliet's determined chin suggested that there was only so much sympathy she required or would accept. Meanwhile the ill-assorted party had drawn near one of the two stages, where a small orchestra was playing. Dissatisfaction with themselves and with each other could be for a time dissolved or masked in listening, or pretending to listen.

The time was short. Mrs Vawser found them. She was dressed like a shepherdess of expensive, even exotic tastes, and she did a great deal of carefree laughing and fond gathering of her husband's arm while the introductions were made.

Her eyes were busy; and presently she found an opportunity to draw Lydia aside.

'Well, well, Miss Templeton, here is a happy report for me to send to poor Emma! When next I write, I may assure her that she need fear no dullness for Miss Templeton and Miss Rae in Bath—for how prettily situated the two of you are, with your attendant beaux!'

Lydia suffered a start, in which several unpleasant emotions were mixed. 'Pray write nothing of the kind, Mrs Vawser—you have taken up quite a wrong idea.'

'Oh, you needn't be coy with a married woman like me, Miss Templeton—you may be assured, I know a little of the world. And whatever you do, don't mistake me for one of those narrow-minded people who suppose that only very young girls take pleasure in having a beau. I dislike that sort of prejudice excessively. It is never too late, I say; and even if it comes to nothing in the end, what woman can resist a little admiration if it should come her way?—especially, you know, if her life has been rather retired. It would be *too* inquisitive of me, I suppose, to wonder which of the gentlemen—'

'Neither, ma'am, just as I told you.'

'I see what you are about—you are wanting me to hazard a guess. Well, I warn you, I am a very good eye at such things—all my friends will tell you—'

'Mrs Vawser, as I see nothing will convince you that neither of these gentlemen is my beau, it would be even more futile to say that I do not want a beau at all.'

'Which is exactly what a woman says when she does want one!' shrilled Mrs Vawser, archly

277

nudging her husband. 'Alas, you will agree, Mr Vawser, that we women are like that.'

'Say one thing, and mean another,' he said, squeezing the words through his grin.

'This may be so—but duplicity is surely not the sole preserve of the female sex,' Lydia said. 'Don't tell me, Mr Vawser, that you have never been guilty of a fib.'

'Her, her, her.'

'Oh, come, this will not do,' Mrs Vawser cried, a certain tightening in her gaiety. 'Abusing the male sex, you know, is too revealing. You must be careful, Miss Templeton, or you will end up sounding like an old maid.'

'I am not much frightened by the character of the old maid. She is always figured as contemptible; but I would sooner apply that term to the kind of woman who must have a man, at any price to her pride and dignity.'

'Lord, such things you think of! I may as well tell you, Miss Templeton, that you will never catch your beau with *that* sort of clever talk. I fear that may have been your trouble!'

'Perhaps so. I confess I have always preferred cleverness to its alternative; but if the art of stupid talk should turn out to be an essential requirement for my happiness, be assured I shall know where to come for instruction in it.'

'Her, her, her,' said Mr Vawser, not entirely to his wife's pleasure.

Her grip on his arm grew more custodial than fond; but she presented Lydia with a corroded smile, remarking sorrowfully: 'Indeed you really must be careful, Miss Templeton—it is the absolute hallmark of the old maid that she flares up at the slightest thing.'

'Hallmarks?' said Lewis Durrant, appearing at Lydia's side. 'I know a thing or two about hallmarks. Someone been buying dubious silver?'

'Oh! you are here, are you?' Mrs Vawser said disdainfully. 'I supposed you had cried off.'

'No, I am only late.' Mr Durrant gave Lydia a short bow: Mrs Vawser a shorter.

'And not in the least sorry for it, I see.' Mrs Vawser sniffed.

'Oh, I always ration my company: it is too strong a dose for people otherwise. My apologies, nonetheless, where they are due, to Miss Templeton. Now where are these hallmarks?'

'We were talking of human ones,' Lydia said.

'Ah. I was going to suggest turning the thing over and having a good look at the bottom, but in that case . . .'

Lydia covered her smile; but Mrs Vawser looked with suspicion from one to the other, and then elevated her head in sour triumph. 'Oh, I see how it is. Oh, now I see why we are a little *de trop*, my love. We should rejoin our own party. Always rise from the table when the play becomes too deep.'

'What did I say?' Mr Durrant asked, when she had tripped away. 'I'm disappointed. I was just going to ask where she had left her sheep.'

'Hush, you must have a care: Mrs Vawser has been arranging my affairs, and she will presently be doing the same for you. Affairs of the heart, needless to say.'

'Oh! those,' he said drably: then, after seeming about to say something more, fell silent.

From relief at seeing him, Lydia fell back on her earlier irritation. 'It is fortunate you were able to

279

find us, Mr Durrant. We waited at the gate as long as we decently could, but—'

'What?' he said, coming scowling out of abstraction. 'Waited, what for? Oh! yes, that. Never fear, I wasn't detained by anything pleasant. I was about to leave when my landlady came up with a letter she had forgotten to give me earlier. Been sleeping off the brandy, probably. Or else she had some occult suspicion of how unwelcome it would be. It was from Hugh, of course. The most scampish and impudent yet.'

'Ah. And you needed a little space to tear your hair and chew the furniture.'

'Does that help, do you find?' he asked seriously. 'No matter. I sat down and wrote a prompt reply, which was probably too intemperate even for me to send . . . The young pup is coming to Bath.'

'Indeed? And not for his health, I presume.'

'No, alas. He is visiting some fellow-wastrel at Cheltenham, and declares his intention of coming on to Bath to see whether it is true that dear old Uncle Durrant has lost his wits and is actually setting up for a gallant. His words, of course.'

'Of course. Well, in one sense you are to be congratulated, Mr Durrant. He may phrase it how he likes, but the plain fact is you have shaken him. Which was part of your intention, was it not?'

'Aye, so it was . . . But I cannot like the prospect of the young whelp descending on me to, as he put it, talk some sense into my head.'

'No, I can see that: especially as you have, after all, no success to show in your project as yet.'

His lips twitched. 'Hugh cannot be sure of that; and what is more, Miss Templeton, you cannot be

280

sure of that either.'

'No, I suppose not,' she said, aggrieved at his tone, in which she found something sharper than his familiar rudeness.

Phoebe turned to them just then, and with a smile of welcome introduced him to the Allardyces. Soon the party was complete—and no less uncomfortable than before. Mr Durrant took just as much notice of them as suggested he would have difficulty recognising them again in the morning. Preoccupation made him more distant than ever. He walked about dutifully, offering no one either his arm or his conversation. Lydia understood that he was brooding on Hugh Hanley's arrival—the news did not lack its piquancy of interest for her—but she resented his so blatantly not caring to disguise it. He was here because he was her acquaintance, after all. Whyever did Miss Templeton bring along that stuffed dummy? It was nonsense to suppose the Allardyces thinking any such thing, no doubt, and nonsense to care even if they did; but still, something had touched her upon the raw. She did not like to think it was the idiot aspersions of Mrs Vawser.

It was Mr Beck who proposed that they go into the maze. His companions being spiritless made him sparkish; and the protests of both Mr Allardyce and Juliet that it was best tried in daylight, that they would only be blundering about, made him more insistent.

'This is precisely the point of a maze—to be deliciously lost,' he cried. 'And look, they have hung those ridiculous lanterns at the opening, so there must be more inside. Miss Rae, you will not shrink from the experiment, I know. There is always some amusement to be found even in the greatest dullness, and here it is.'

'Well—' Phoebe hesitated, smiling '—I dare say if we do become very lost, we can always shout.'

'And what is to prevent us being heard, save the noise of half a thousand people and an orchestra?' Mr Allardyce said lightly.

'Oh—that is a consideration indeed,' Phoebe said. 'If you really think—'

'Shout, nonsense,' chuckled Mr Beck. 'If it comes to that, there is a key to all mazes, and that is to keep bearing either left or right.'

'Well, let us try it,' said Lydia, who felt that there was little material difference between wandering aimlessly round the open gardens, and trooping aimlessly between tall box hedges.

They went in, Mr Beck and Phoebe leading the way. The maze was very dark. Snatches of laughter from further within suggested that they were not the only ones to make the attempt; but they soon faded, and so too, uncannily, did the noise from the gardens. The smell of thick leaves and rich earth grew stronger, until it hardly seemed possible to Lydia that the town of Bath lay all around them. Their own voices took on a husky, furtive note that blended with the shushing of gravel underfoot to make something oddly suggestive of poachers and danger. In daylight there would have been ample room to go two abreast, but in the darkness the brushing prickle of twigs—imagined cobwebs and moths also—nudged them into single file. Somewhere behind her, she knew, was Mr Durrant: ahead of her, Mr Allardyce. She could hear his breathing, a little sharp; and when she

282

bumped into his back, he gave a start.

'I do beg your pardon,' she said. 'At least, if you are Mr Allardyce. If you are a stranger, I don't much care.'

He gave a short, impatient laugh. 'Not at all. Inevitable consequence of, if you'll forgive me, a very wrong-headed notion.'

'I dare say you have often been in this maze—in the daylight, that is.'

'Once or twice. And in the daylight, as you say. Juliet!'

'Yes, I'm here,' came a voice from somewhere ahead.

'Mr Beck is still confident of leading us out, I collect?' Mr Allardyce called out.

'Not at all, sir!' came Mr Beck's laughing voice from further on. 'But let me just find the next right turn, and then I think I shall know where we are.'

'Curious modes of pleasure we do think up for ourselves,' Mr Allardyce said, with a thin sigh. 'Rather like sticking pins in one's hand for the novelty of it. Really one would suppose they would hang more lanterns. Mr Durrant is still with us, I hope?'

'I'm here,' came Mr Durrant's voice, gruff and bored, but surprisingly close behind Lydia. She had forgotten how noiseless a tread he had for a large man.

They shuffled on, led by the sound of Mr Beck being spontaneous and irrepressible, and Phoebe joining in his laughter, if a little more quietly. Lydia's eyes, adjusting to the darkness, made out Mr Allardyce's slender shoulders raised high and taut. From Mr Durrant behind her came an intermittent noise that she could only suppose was

283

his characteristic sniff of contempt. Well, she understood: as they rounded yet another featureless corner, she found herself rather tired of the amusement.

But not as tired as Mr Allardyce who, stopping so short that she nearly collided with him again, called out in a hard-edged, glinting voice: 'Very well, Mr Beck, we have gone around and about, and done all the things that people do in a maze: I think now is the time when a man who says he can find the way out begins to prove it.'

'Upon my soul, sir, I am trying,' came Mr Beck's voice, a little yelping and dog-like in his hilarity, 'but I am quite at a loss for the moment. Is it not monstrous refreshing, though, not to know where you are? Just for once, eh? We mortals pride ourselves on that knowledge, you know, but I think it does us no end of good now and then to be lost—absolutely lost. Does it not, Miss Rae . . . ?'

'This fellow will lead us nowhere—nowhere,' lamented Mr Allardyce, his shoulders more angular than ever. 'Juliet—can you get some sense from him? I doubt it. Miss Templeton, can you? Of course not. We must suffer it until—Lord knows—until the sun rises, perhaps. And hark—no one else in the maze at all—ample evidence of the nonsense of it . . . Well, my apologies, at any rate, Miss Templeton, for this wretched situation.'

'No need, sir: you did not build the maze, I assume, and you certainly did not bring us into it,' Lydia said. She understood Mr Allardyce's irritation, though she found its extent rather excessive. Mr Beck was simply as silly as she expected him to be: Mr Allardyce was less sensible than she had hoped. To be so thoroughly put out

284

of temper by such a thing . . . Of course, it was not equal to Mr Beck's fatuity, but it disconcerted her. Let Phoebe choose Mr A or Mr B, she thought, there was still something lacking for her own tastes in either case.

Not, of course, that her own tastes mattered: these were Phoebe's suitors, and *she* was not in Bath to make any sort of choice. Reminding herself of this, she found that she had come to a stop: that Mr Allardyce's vague silhouette was shimmering away from her, and that there was a close presence at her back.

'If everyone can be persuaded to turn round,' Mr Durrant said, 'we can all go out of this thing at once, and be back in the gardens: the fireworks are beginning soon.'

'What do you mean?' she said, turning, and for the moment as irritable as Mr Allardyce, trying to make out Mr Durrant's face in the gloom.

'I mean that I have copied Ariadne, and have been laying a trail ever since we entered the labyrinth.' Mr Durrant found her elbow, and briskly turned her around to look back at the path by which they had come. Drops of white, like a trail of solitary blossoms, were dotted along the gravel.

'What—where did you . . . ?'

'Hugh Hanley's letter,' he pronounced, with spidery distaste. 'I loathed it so much that, as with most such things, I had to bring it in my pocket; and then as we came in here I saw a use for it, and began ripping it into little pieces.'

Lydia was surprised at her own relief—at how oppressed she had been by the maze, by the exhilaration of Mr B and the complaining of Mr A and her being trapped in the darkness with them.

285

Everyone else, it seemed, was glad likewise to learn of Mr Durrant's ruse, and began retracing their steps with alacrity—except Mr Beck, who was still in exhaustingly high spirits. 'A cheat—oh, a shabby cheat. We should soon have found our own way—and there was something so delicious about being lost—something so very liberating . . .'

While Mr Beck continued unabashed, Mr Allardyce's looks showed that he was conscious of his loss of composure. Giving Lydia his arm as they made their way to the stage where the fireworks were preparing, he said, with a faintly forced note of urbanity: 'Curious—curious thing. I have never been fond of enclosed space. Yet I have found myself quite comfortable in a ship's cabin on many an occasion. Perhaps the difference is, there one may always leave the cabin, if only to stagger up on deck and be ill. They do say Admiral Nelson suffers from seasickness, which is another curious thing.'

'Perhaps that is why he achieves his dashing victories. He can hardly wait to have the battle over so he can get back to dry land again.'

Mr Allardyce laughed so extravagantly at this that she concluded he was still not quite himself. Well, they none of them were; and she was glad of the roll of drums that announced the fireworks, for the fireworks signalled the end of the evening— and that, she felt, could not come too soon.

Unlit, the array of rockets, catherine wheels and fizgigs was impressive—the handbills had advertised them as having been brought at great expense from China; but when the liveried servants of the town corporation began lighting them, it appeared that the fireworks had suffered

286

something in their long passage. There was more sputtering than grandeur. Rockets rose lethargically, popped and plopped. Lydia was just reflecting on the aptness of this conclusion when the display suddenly and accidentally turned much livelier. A lit rocket came off its mounting at an angle, skittering and bouncing through the rest of the array and setting off everything at once. Now came the appropriate gasps, as the night sky bloomed in brilliance—then cries of alarm. The rogue rocket had made an explosive consummation with a large firecracker, and a shower of papery, gunpowdery sparks was falling into the crowd on this side of the stage. Heads ducked, resourceful ladies flung up parasols as the hissing gobbets landed in the grass. One came down near—very near. Lydia saw Mr Allardyce seize Juliet's arm and pull her aside. It missed her—but not quite. Phoebe shrieked, pointing. A smell like ironing. The short train of Juliet's white muslin gown was blackening—then crackling into flame.

Mr Allardyce beat desperately at it with his bare hands. Phoebe screamed. Someone called for water, someone else cried to Juliet to roll, roll. Then Mr Durrant, in waistcoat and shirt sleeves, was thrusting Mr Allardyce aside, flourishing out a great blanket. Where—? His coat, of course. He flung it down on the burning train and then flung himself bodily on top of it. Lydia's paralysed mind registered, inconsequently, that it was the handsome new cut-away.

Mr Durrant rose. In an instant, where there had been peril and panic, there was only a scorched smell and two ruined garments.

'Thank you, sir—a thousand thanks.' Juliet's voice shook, and she was as white as her gown, but she and Mr Durrant seemed the calmest people there. Phoebe was in tears, Mr Beck was trying ineffectually to soothe her: a gentleman arrived with a jug of water, and Lydia with difficulty dissuaded him from throwing it over Juliet to be on the safe side.

'No harm done, I think,' Mr Durrant said, picking up his coat and shaking it out. 'You are not hurt, Miss Allardyce?'

'I—not at all—are you?'

'Getting up again was the hardest part. My old bones. But, Mr Allardyce, I am afraid you have burned your hands.'

'That's nothing—nothing—my only regret is that I cannot shake yours, sir, in profound gratitude.'

'In a way my tailor is to be thanked,' Mr Durrant said, bundling his coat under his arm. 'An old-fashioned fellow who will not cut tight across the shoulders, which means I can take my coat off without the aid of two strong lads and a winch.' He glanced back at the stage. 'The conflagration seems to be over, but we had better move away to be sure.'

'And my dressmaker assures me that trains are *de rigueur*,' said Juliet, shaking out her skirts: trembling, but very nearly composed. 'No: all my thanks are to you, Mr Durrant, but I will not embarrass you with them. Miss Rae, please be easy. Robert, you must go home at once and see to your hands. Take a chair. Butter or goose-fat—'

'I take a chair? *You*, my dear Juliet, you must take a chair—I shall fetch one directly . . .'

288

'Good Lord, I have never taken a chair in my life, and don't propose . . . Well, if you insist . . .'

It was the breaking up of the party, and its exceptional circumstances, that finally made them natural with one another. Phoebe rallied herself, Mr Beck was genuinely anxious in his hopes that no one had come to hurt, and Mr Durrant had ceased brooding over Hugh Hanley. Lydia, shakily, was glad of it; but she doubted that harmony was sufficiently established for anyone to make the customary jaunty suggestion: *we must do this again!*

CHAPTER TWENTY

Phoebe had many misgivings about the dinner at Queen Square appointed for the next day. After such a shocking event, the Allardyces might be unequal to company—for her part she had been dreaming of fireworks and flaming dresses all night; and then besides there were poor Mr Allardyce's hands—for she recalled burning her fingers on a pair of curling-tongs once, and how painful they had been the next day; and then some superstitious part of her, untouched by the kirk, saw ill-omen in their meeting together again so soon. Lydia was kept busy with reassurance. There was a note from Mr Allardyce, assuring them of their health and spirits, and looking forward to their company later, and, as she pointed out, written in as elegant a hand as ever. As for further disasters, they were surely most unlikely at a dinner party, certainly compared with a firework display.

'There is always the peril of a splash of hot gravy, or a fishbone in the throat, or an apoplexy brought on by the sudden popping of a cork—but these, you know, are risks we run every time we go into dinner,' Lydia concluded, and was rewarded with a smile at last. She might have added that if there were any danger to be apprehended at Queen Square, it was that of being talked to death by Mrs Allardyce; but as Phoebe persisted in thinking well of her, and actually looked forward to meeting the old harridan again, Lydia held her peace.

The optimistic note was confirmed by the fortuitous arrival of Phoebe's new gown. Diaphanous silver and white, it was in the purest, most waistless and Grecian fashion, to which Phoebe needed to add only a plain necklace and her beauty to suggest a classical maiden rustling through a grove while the gods battled each other for her favours. Thankfully Lydia was secured by wisdom and experience from the futile vanity of envy, for otherwise it would have made her sick to look at her.

'Well—I will do, I suppose,' Phoebe said, looking doubtfully in her mirror. 'I am glad it has come, for the dressmaker was Mrs Allardyce's recommendation, and she would be sure to ask about it. Also—' she swallowed nervously '—also I suspicion dinner there will be a rather grand affair.'

Lydia had no doubt that it would be: Mrs Allardyce would make sure of that, both in honour of Phoebe's fifty thousand, and as a declaration that her family was worthy of it. She was not wrong. Quantities of flowers, wax candles, and ice, foot-men to wait at table—one or two of them evincing a certain unfamiliarity with the layout of the dining-room, suggestive of the hired waiter—choice wines and Frenchified sauces: all declared a desire to impress, quite at odds with Mrs Allardyce's brazen declaration: 'You must forgive my asking you to such a plain family dinner, Miss Rae, Miss Templeton. Living quietly as a widow, I have quite got out of the habit of anything else.'

Whether the two high-cravated and interchangeable gentlemen and the ageless female in crêpe counted as family Lydia was not to discover; they were plainly there to make up the numbers, and to show a becoming subservience to their hostess. A much more important addition to the party was Mr Durrant.

He had called that morning to enquire after the health of Mr and Miss Allardyce: had been loaded with thanks and compliments, and an absolute insistence made on his joining them for dinner in the evening. So he confessed to Lydia, in an awkward mutter, when they gathered in the drawing-room before going in. It was very natural: he was the hero of the hour: Mr Allardyce's cordial looks, and Juliet's warm attention expressed it; so, more volubly, did Mrs Allardyce, though not without some hints that if *she* had been there, she would have taken the situation so thoroughly in hand that the fireworks would never have gone wrong at all.

Lydia was not displeased to see Mr Durrant made much of. For once he had certainly earned that respect, which he was too often inclined to regard as his due without doing anything to merit it. She admired his quiet discomfort with the subject, as she had admired his presence of mind last night. It would not do to be admiring him too much, of course; but she was saved from that by amusement at his awkward attempts to speak of something else—which, given his habitual scorn of small-talk, resembled the efforts of a hound to perform the little tricks of a lap-dog.

Juliet, who was able to talk quite coolly of her misadventure, presently saw his unease with the subject, and turned the conversation to the war news, on which they were still engaged when he gave her his arm to go in to dinner. At table they continued solidly in talk. Lydia, looking on, felt a mild pity for Juliet, who had yet to learn that bringing Mr Durrant out was a disappointing process, and that he would soon go in again as smartly as a mechanical figure on a Swiss clock, with a snap of the door behind him.

No such difficulty with Mrs Allardyce: her peremptory tones could be heard all along the table, though it was Phoebe, on her right, who was being chiefly favoured with her discourse. There was much on her son's future career, which she had taken as far as an under-secretaryship before the soup was removed.

'Oh, as to his Parliamentary seat, of course, that had better be in the borough interest. Links with the county interest may always be forged later, when he is settled. Tell me, Miss Rae, was your father ever a Parliament-man?'

'No, ma'am: I think his friends urged it once, but he felt his health was unequal to the travelling it would entail.'

'Oh, well, wise in that event: but Robert's health

has always been excellent. He is blessed with my own sound constitution. Of course, when he *is* settled, it will be at no great distance from London. A public man cannot afford to bury himself in the wilds. Hertfordshire or Bedfordshire will do very well . . .'

'It must be a great comfort,' Lydia ventured to Mr Allardyce, who was on her right, 'knowing the course of your future life so very precisely.'

'Oh, no, you see there is a little uncertainty,' he answered readily, smiling, 'Hertfordshire *or* Bedfordshire. That is rather disturbing: but I am sure before long she will have fixed upon the very spot of ground where I am to raise the familial standard, and then I may rest easy.'

He seemed quite happy to talk of this: Phoebe, on his other side, was wholly engrossed by her hostess: Lydia seized her moment.

'Well, be assured I mean no disrespect to either party when I ask—being hopelessly inquisitive—do your own plans coincide with these?'

'My own plans are not half so comprehensive. And such as they are, they share a debatable border with my wishes. For the present, I look forward to nothing more than a return to Vienna. Whatever the chances of the war, I think it is there that the great matters will be decided. But talking to my fellows in the service has given me a hankering for other postings too—I dream of St Petersburg, or even Constantinople. Ambassador to the Sublime Porte: could anything have a more splendid ring? I dare say the place is quite as dingy as sublime, but never mind. Beyond that, Paris: that would be the ideal, if ever we can come to peace with France again.'

'That I can understand. I was there before the Revolution. I wonder what it is like now. It cannot all be guillotines and unshaven *sans-culottes* mutilating statues, can it?'

'The Directory has put an end to the excesses, and it seems that wealth is flourishing again, though at the expense of corruption. Of course it will not be the old Paris of the Bourbons—but I hope no one pretends to see perfection in that. You have been much on the Continent, Miss Templeton?'

'Only France, with my father. My dream would have been to make the proper old-fashioned Grand Tour—dozens of trunks, and letters of introduction, and a pompous tutor pointing out the antiquities and shuddering at the habits of foreigners.'

'And when you get home, a crateful of Old Masters, painted last year in a Neapolitan workshop and stained with tobacco. With relief you tuck into plain roast and boiled, and consider yourself a finished man of the world.' His eyebrow lifted, ironic, also sympathetic. 'At least, if you are a man. As a woman, of course, you have never left home.'

'Just so. Though there are hopeful exceptions, like your sister. Tell me, what do they eat in Vienna?'

'Just now, with the pinch of the war, the fare is a little restricted. But a dish I was very fond of was liver dumplings with sauerkraut, which is much nicer than it sounds. Not that I am averse to plain roast and boiled now and then; nor indeed to settling in England at last.'

'And Mr Pitt—should he be looking anxiously

over his shoulder?'

'Oh, I do not lack respect for Parliament; though my respect would be greater if it were more of a parliament, and less of a club. Nor do I doubt that I could learn to talk endlessly in a see-saw voice while not believing a word I was saying: not much different from training for the Church or the law, after all.'

'Mr Allardyce, this is shocking. You will be calling for reform next.'

'Only politely. Reform, in the sense of making better, is a very good thing: it is something I have been urging on myself for years, but without much result; and if a man cannot improve himself, he should at least be circumspect about demanding improvement from others.'

'Shocking again. Without a little good firm hypocrisy, what is to become of decent private life? Of course, without reform, it will always be a monstrous expensive business getting into Parliament. It was once suggested to my brother, who calculated he could hardly afford to do it and educate his children—much to his own relief.'

'Ah, so you are an aunt, Miss Templeton!'

'I am, twice over, though I cannot help it. Does that modify your view of me?'

'Oh, it must do. There is a certain gravity in the title of aunt—it suggests judicious good works and sensible advice. Did you not feel these tendencies stealing over you when the happy event took place?'

'A little: I resisted them. Though I do not know how I shall be equal to great-auntdom, if the day should arrive. Nature, no doubt, will have supplied the *embonpoint* by then, but there is the added requirement of being grand and formidable.'

'I should not think being formidable beyond you, Miss Templeton,' he said, with a shrewd look.

'Thank you: I shall take that as a compliment, even if it is not meant so.'

'It is certainly meant so, though there are women aplenty who would shriek at it.'

'Oh, I have not shrieked since my fourteenth year, when I came across an error in the marginalia of *Religio Medici*. But what about becoming an uncle? Does that entail a change in the character?'

'I fear so, and whenever Juliet turns me into one, I must be ready. An uncle positively must have creaking boots, and a jingling watch-chain, and no frivolity in his system, alas: perhaps as a result of being, as a rich uncle, always applied to for money. Well, I appeal to you: did you ever hear of a poor uncle?'

Lydia laughed, reminded of Mr Durrant's complaints. Glancing over at him, she saw him still deep in talk with Juliet Allardyce—actually laughing, with that rare boyish lift of the mask, at a remark she had made; and for the space of five seconds, the sight of them combined with Mr Allardyce's words—happy events—uncles—to produce the most peculiar vision. There was no other name for the unheralded, unbelievable idea that sprang into her mind—except, perhaps, sheer absurdity. She had recognised it as such by the end of the five seconds, and dismissed it.

'People can hardly be blamed for prejudice, when words are so full of it,' Mr Allardyce went on. 'Was not a gossip originally just a god-sibling? Or is that an error to make you shriek?'

'It was,' she said, smiling. 'And I wonder whether

296

you felt any such prejudice when you learned that Miss Rae was coming to Bath with a *companion*.'

'If I did, I deserve whipping—at least, not whipping—that would hurt: but some severe punishment, like asking someone how they are, and then having them actually tell you. But really, Miss Templeton, I hope I have never given you any reason to—'

'No, no—in truth I am reflecting on my own feelings.' There was something about Mr Allardyce's very lightness of conversational pressure that encouraged frankness: just as she would never have spoken of her feelings to Mr Beck, knowing with what a ghoulish appetite he would fasten on them. 'When Lady Eastmond first proposed my being Miss Rae's companion, I fear—I realise now it was just such a prejudice that fed my reluctance. A part of me must have thought: Am I come to this? Companion has a direful sound, does it not? But that was before I met Miss Rae, of course.'

'Of course,' he said, thoughtful. 'I am trying to imagine myself in such a position. I think I would have been alarmed. However informal, however warm the relation, there is a degree of responsibility in it, after all.'

'Exactly.' It was pleasant to be so swiftly understood. 'I felt, selfishly no doubt, that nature did not intend me for a chaperon.'

'Not nature perhaps—though to be frank I have no high opinion of nature as a guide. Nature frames us for little more than looking for our next meal, and does not object if we make it out of our neighbour: it is civilisation that does that. But if not nature, I would say education—

297

accomplishment—good sense: these, I am afraid, doomed you to your task, Miss Templeton. And to continue complimentary, and at the risk of making you conceited, I may as well say you are doing it very well.'

'Am I? Just the right combination of the governess and the Gorgon, would you say?'

'None of either: but the proper degree of care and caution. After all, you have just been establishing my *bona fides*, in regard to Miss Rae's future.'

Lydia hardly ever blushed, and when she did it was as painful and incommoding as heartburn. Glancing away, she found Mr Durrant across the table looking at her curiously, which forced her to collect herself. 'Again it is a question of terms,' she said stiffly. 'I hope—Mr Allardyce, I hope nothing so obvious—'

'You mistake me,' he said gently touching her arm. 'I speak in admiration, and out of my own esteem for Miss Rae. You would be no true friend to her if you did not have her interests at heart, and I honour you for it. You have besides an obstacle to judgement in my mother, who does have a deplorable habit of speaking for me, and giving a full account of my intentions. At least, she *thinks* she speaks for me, and I am too fond of her to disillusion her: but she does not, I assure you. And please accept my word that neither you nor Lady Eastmond need have any anxieties about the nature of my attachment to Miss Rae. Believe me, there is nothing to fear on that score.'

'Well,' Lydia said, floundering out of awkwardness, 'I shall risk making you conceited also, Mr Allardyce, and say that I really did not doubt it.'

'Thank you. Look at that, we have arrived at a very good understanding through mutual honesty of dealing. If we represented two warring countries, who could doubt that the soldiers would soon be sent home, and peace restored?'

'A woman in the diplomatic service—now there is a fabulous impossibility.'

'More's the pity: I have always contended they would do it superlatively well. Many the wife of an indifferent ambassador, indeed, carries a good deal of her husband's burden, and carries it easily. But tell me—you knew little or nothing of Miss Rae, I collect, before Lady Eastmond introduced you. It was the *idea* of doing the office of a companion, you have hinted, that was repulsive. But when the introduction was made—when you saw and began to know Miss Rae herself—was that the moment of change?'

'I would not go so far as to say a *moment*,' Lydia said, and then stopped: she had thought her motives for coming to Bath very neatly established in her mind, but just now she found them curiously disordered and obscure. 'There were—many considerations. But yes: not to quibble, I very soon found so much to like in Miss Rae that the question took on a different aspect altogether.'

He was nodding eagerly, though it seemed less in agreement with her than in some internal confirmation. 'Yes, it is curious how life takes us by surprise—or rather, how it suddenly reveals some surprise about ourselves.' His look was so pensive that it caught the attention of Mrs Allardyce: who, no friend to thought in any form, called sharply out to him, and demanded his opinion on the vital

299

matter of whether buff breeches were acceptable as Court dress.

Lydia's momentary embarrassment was over, and she was not sorry to have acted upon her resolution to be more the chaperon, and pin Phoebe's suitor down a little. She had found nothing in Mr Allardyce to suggest the fortune-hunter: only a seasonable mixture of sense and feeling that seemed to promise fair for the prospects of Phoebe, in whom the ingredients were less felicitously mixed. Not that she had actually pinned him down on those prospects—the ifs, whethers and whens—but she was satisfied that this was a man serious in intent, and scrupulous on the occasion of declaration. A duenna could do no more—except actually say to her charge, 'This is the one to choose, and not the other': and whatever her own inclinations, Lydia thanked her stars she was not so foolish as to do that.

She was pleased again, after dinner, to find that Mr Allardyce did not linger over the port, but promptly rejoined the ladies, and devoted his attention to Phoebe—as if Lydia's talk had cleared his thoughts and concentrated his mind. Mrs Allardyce and her pug had claimed the sofa, but Juliet placed a chair close to hers, and as soon as Mr Durrant appeared invited him to it. Lydia looked on with an inward, tolerant smile. Here was a very natural state of things: her gratitude and obligation must be making Juliet attentive to Mr Durrant; and certainly Juliet's sensible, unaffected, even crisp manner was the sort he would respond to. But Lydia doubted he could long bear the strain even of rational gallantry; and her surmise seemed confirmed when presently

Juliet rose and went to the pianoforte. Either he had asked her to do so, or she had found his entertainment so difficult she had proposed it. The hour had struck, and the clock-figure was trundling back in.

Juliet began to play, with such superb taste and execution that Lydia sat transfixed and hardly breathing. She listened with the ear—and faint envy—of expertise, but anyone must have felt the same, unless they had the sensibility of a pig's head.

Almost at once Mrs Allardyce leaned over and began talking to her.

'So, Miss Templeton, your mother was a Holdsworth, I discover.'

Lydia could hardly think of a reply to make that did not involve the fire-irons. 'You are well informed, ma'am,' was the warmest she could manage.

'Oh, I make it my business to be so. Come, one cannot be too attentive to matters of family. The Templetons also I have heard about: Heystead Priory is a very good old house of its kind, I hear. For my part I am not fond of these Gothic places: they are too often inconvenient. When my son settles, it must be in a tidy, newish sort of property, suitable to his position. There must be sash windows and a proper carriage-sweep. People are very wrong when they suppose these things to be unimportant.' Mrs Allardyce darted a glance of impatience at the pianoforte, as if at a servant making a clatter with the crockery. 'Well, I find your neighbour Mr Durrant a very gentleman-like man. Not in the first flight of fashion, perhaps, but these things do not matter as they do for a woman.

He has a very good property at Culverton, I understand—the largest in your district?'

'It is, ma'am, and much improved—though I cannot swear to the sash windows.'

'Oh, it's no manner of use making repartee with me, Miss Templeton: I take no notice of it: that's the way I am, and I don't care who knows it. Now Mr Durrant has not been in Bath before, that I can swear to. I would have remembered. There is nothing in Bath that does not come to my ears, even though I seldom stir abroad now. The fact is, no one can make an appearance in the Pump Room without my getting to know about it. Is that not remarkable?'

The fact seemed less remarkable to Lydia than the sheer vacancy of mind of which it was evidence. But she contented herself with agreement, hoping that acquiescence might be the shortest route to silence, so that she could hear a little more of Juliet's playing. She was allowed to hear the end of that piece, and the beginning of the next, which Mr Durrant called for eagerly; before Mrs Allardyce turned to Phoebe and remarked loudly: 'Juliet will have done soon, Miss Rae, and no doubt we must have Miss Templeton too. *You* are not all a-quiver to give of your all, I think? Good for you. One can have enough of these women who are always straining to show off their accomplishments.'

Very well, thought Lydia: but the wife of Mr Robert Allardyce, diplomat, public man, under-secretary and whatnot, would do well to possess certain accomplishments, as Mrs Allardyce might perceive if she ever turned her gaze beyond the visitors' book of the Bath Pump Room. Which was not to say that Phoebe would not manage very

302

well. Her innocence was only a negative, a lack that could be made up: whereas, as Mrs Allardyce proved, there was such a thing as positive stupidity.

On Lydia's taking her place at the pianoforte, she found amongst the music-sheets a copy of the fiendish Clementi sonata she had bought in London. Well, if her hostess was set upon turning the deaf ear of rudeness and indifference, then at least her teeth would rattle for it. Lydia played two movements: having lulled her audience with a sighing *Andante*, she launched demonically into the *Presto*. One of the makeweight gentlemen jumped so hard at the first crashing chord he nearly disappeared into his cravat like a tortoise. Juliet watched and listened avidly and, as it were, professionally: the odd slip of the finger that would have escaped the notice of the others would be obvious to her. There was a certain additional spur to flamboyance in this, and Lydia ended more *prestissimo* than *presto*, and with the agreeable consciousness that Mrs Allardyce was finally not talking.

At least, not for a moment. Soon her voice was sailing over the applause: 'Hm, very pretty. What a great *labour* it must be, writing down all those notes, and just for something that lasts a few minutes. I suppose these composers somehow find it worth their while.'

'Art should be pursued for its own sake, Mother,' Mr Allardyce said, with a little bite of asperity in his tone, 'rather like good manners.'

Secretly Lydia felt she had been more showy than artistic: but she did possess one skill too often lacking in the amateur musician—knowing when to leave off. Smilingly, she declined Mr Allardyce's entreaties that she play more; and rising, found Mr Durrant had come forward to hand her to her seat.

'Thank you, Mr Durrant. Now make the expected compliments on my playing, and I shall not despair of your becoming a drawing-room exquisite at last.'

'We have been royally entertained. Indeed I would say that you have surpassed yourself, Miss Templeton—or rather, surpassed someone else, which may after all have been the intention.'

Lydia strove to control her expression without thinning her lips. 'So much for the expected compliments.'

'Oh, there is nothing wrong with a little emulation—a little competition,' he said, sitting down beside her. 'Certainly it can do you no harm—you who have been accustomed to being considered the most accomplished of women—to have your superiority put to the test.'

'Well, it is at least capable of being put to the test, Mr Durrant—it has grounds, on which judgements can be made, opinions canvassed. Contrast your superiority, which is based entirely on your opinion of yourself.'

He shrugged. 'I would trust no one else's opinion on so important a matter. Come, would you? If some absolutely infallible sage and seer undertook to tell you the whole truth about your mind and heart, would you still not turn him away, and say, "No thank you, I know that best"?'

'Perhaps: but I will confess that there are some things about ourselves which others are better placed to see. We must all beware complacency, Mr Durrant. Your friendly civilities to Miss

Allardyce, for example—you may well consider them no more than that—'

'And you do not?' he said sharply.

'I speak only as a neutral observer, Mr Durrant.'

'Pooh, there's no such thing, least of all when a woman is doing the observing. She will build a feud on a cool glance, and construct a romance from a pleasant exchange of chat.'

'I said nothing of romance. But perhaps you should have a care, lest Mrs Allardyce be on the watch for a match.'

'Extraordinary world,' he said, sitting back with a look of bitter surrender. 'To be subject to these wild suppositions—romances—matches—simply for enjoying the company and conversation of a rational, intelligent woman: no more, nor less.'

His displeasure was plain and profound—she thought it could hardly be more so, until Mrs Allardyce beckoned him to the sofa beside her. Well, that would do him no harm either. Privately Lydia shook her head over Mr Durrant's obtuseness. She congratulated herself on being too polite to point out to him that romances and matches were precisely what had brought him to Bath; and as for the company and conversation of a rational, intelligent woman—no more, nor less— why, if that was all he sought, why come all this way for it?

Mr Allardyce was at her side. 'Miss Templeton,' he said urgently. 'Miss Rae and I have been talking of the future.'

'Oh, yes?' she cried—unable to restrain her eagerness: *The Duenna's Distresses Ended!*

'Yes, and we are agreed that this fine weather surely cannot hold much longer. Soon enough there will be that rain and greyness which always makes people stare miserably out of the window and wonder why they did not make an expedition into the country when they had the chance. I have been telling Miss Rae of the delicious views round about Lyncombe and Widcombe. They are all the more delicious in that when you are tired of them, you have only a short ride back to Bath, and so rapture is not overtaxed. We are agreed that it would be shameful, even criminal, not to make a picnic party—say, early next week. But it must be the *right* party. For one thing, if you do not consent, the idea is abandoned for ever.'

'It sounds delightful,' said Lydia, turning over the coin of her disappointment.

'And then we must have Mr Durrant too. Though I'm sure Juliet—' with a smile '—will be able to persuade him. Now, nothing very formal— no servants in gloves laying a trestle table on the hillside. Just a meal when we want it, and in the meantime everyone to ramble about as they please. At the risk of declaring myself that most unbearable of beings, a child of nature, I do have a fancy for the open air now and then. Somehow— somehow one can think and speak more freely.'

'An excellent notion,' Lydia said, answering his smile. This was promising indeed: even more so, in that he had not been so punctilious, nor Phoebe so vacillating, as to suggest the addition of Mr Beck to the party. Her flicker of sympathy for Mr Beck on that account was soon extinguished by a vision of him let loose in the country—tirelessly tramping, drinking from streams, and knowing the names of all the wild flowers.

CHAPTER TWENTY-ONE

Though Lydia was not superstitious, she refrained, when writing to her father the next day, from alluding to her hopes that her duty might soon be over and Phoebe's dilemma resolved. She preferred to postpone any hint of that, until the moment of definite announcement; and wrote instead of the enlargement of their Bath acquaintance, actual and potential. The Vawsers here, alas: and, more interestingly, Hugh Hanley soon expected. The arrival of this young man, whom she did not much like, and did not at all respect, was a matter of anticipation for Lydia only for its effect on Lewis Durrant; and in that she found a certain tart enjoyment. She sincerely wished him well of his temporary celebrity at Queen Square—of his basking in the smiles of the rational, intelligent Juliet Allardyce: it was simply that she found about him now something just a little too smug, and requiring deflation; especially as she was so much nearer winning their wager than he was. The presence of his nephew could always be relied on for that. But this feeling also she omitted to mention to her father—who, besides his general benevolence, was always unaccountably indulgent to Mr Durrant.

The country picnic was set for three days' time. The weather was, indeed, of a perfection that to any inhabitant of England must appear almost sinister; and when Lydia took her customary walk alone that afternoon, she sought the green freshness of Sydney Gardens, just down the street from the house, and free at this time of day from the perils of rogue fireworks.

But not from all perils. Approaching the gate, she saw Mr and Mrs Vawser coming out of it. If she proceeded, they must meet. There were worse things than having to talk to a person you detested; but just now, at the hour consecrated to solitude, Lydia could not think of any. She turned, and keeping herself well hidden beneath her parasol, loitered back the way she had come. Risking a glance, she found to her frustration that they were strolling the same way, along the south side of Sydney Place. She debated whether to carry on, and make the whole circuit of Sydney Place in the hope of losing them; but a simpler solution presented itself. Doing artful things with the parasol, she crossed back to the house, went in, and stationed herself discreetly at the dining-room window to watch the Vawsers away, and await the moment of safety.

The moment came: Mrs Vawser's opulently feathered bonnet, which had the unfortunate effect of making her husband appear even shorter than he was, disappeared from sight, and Lydia prepared to resume her interrupted airing. The sound of voices from the drawing-room upstairs stilled her. Phoebe's, and another.

An odd hour for calling; and the urgent agitation of their speech did not suggest a polite exchange about the weather. Then came a kind of despairing hollow laugh, and she recognised the other voice.

Lydia walked upstairs, neither creeping nor stamping.

'Oh, dear God,' came William Beck's voice,

'surely—I thought you said she—'

'Good afternoon, Mr Beck,' Lydia said, going in. She laid down her parasol and took off her gloves. Phoebe was standing at one end of the room, clutching the back of a chair: white-lipped, angular with tension, but not wholly uncomposed. Mr Beck stood at the other end of the room, his back against the bookcase: looking about as composed as a man who had thrown himself off a cliff and found himself at the bottom unharmed.

'I'll go,' he said, ignoring her. 'Miss Rae—forgive me—I'll go—'

'Not on my account, I hope,' Lydia said, seating herself.

'Oh—dear God—what's the use?' he said brokenly, or more brokenly than usual. 'This is efficient spying indeed, madam—how do you do it? Do you put hounds on my scent?'

'Mr Beck, please,' said Phoebe, painfully, 'you should not speak so—'

'Pure coincidence, Mr Beck,' Lydia said, 'as no doubt it is pure coincidence that brings you here at the very time of the day when I am always out. Certainly it cannot have been intentional, as you made it plain to me, in our previous conversation, that you would not seek to do this sort of thing again.'

'You see?' he cried, with a sweeping gesture towards Phoebe. 'Hearken to the language. "This sort of thing". It is no wonder . . .' A brief fit of roaming, staring, and half-laughing prevented him saying what was no wonder. 'Miss Templeton. You may as well know, as *you* are sure to find out anyhow—' with a very unfriendly look '—that I came to see Miss Rae—I *had* to see Miss Rae, alone, for the most pressing, the most undeniable and sacred of reasons.'

So that was the way the wind blew. Lydia might have realised it at once, from a certain charge in the room, suggestive of the momentous; but Mr Beck's habit of imparting momentousness to a request for a glass of water had diverted her from the proper conclusion. She made a mental adjustment—there was no adjusting her feelings, which were hopelessly mixed—and looked from one to the other: but especially at Phoebe. She saw acute discomfort, unease, trouble—but could not for the moment see beyond them.

'I understand, at least I think I do,' Lydia said carefully. 'You might, Mr Beck, have simply asked to see Miss Rae privately on a matter of such importance and delicacy, but never mind that—'

'Aye, never mind that,' he grated. 'I'll go, Miss Rae. It is of no use my staying for an answer now—now that your sainted protectress is in place.'

'Mr Beck, please do not speak so,' Phoebe cried, with an anxious glance at Lydia. 'My answer—I have told you that I cannot give you an answer, at least—not at the present moment.'

'The present moment is indeed miserably inopportune,' he said, heading for the door, then stopping to glare at the fireplace just to Lydia's right. 'I can only hope, Miss Rae, as the matter is now out of my hands, that you will not let *her* dictate your answer too.'

Lydia had tried to make allowance for the young man's feelings, but this was too much. 'Sir, I have put up with being a spy, and a sainted protectress, and setting hounds on you, but I cannot consent to

310

be talked *over* in this way. Have the goodness to talk *to* me, if you have something to lay to my charge.'

A moment's confusion passed across his face. 'You must forgive me,' he said—but he made it sound more like an order than an appeal. 'I am unable to say any more—my heart is so full I hardly know . . .' He wrenched himself round to bestow an anguished look on Phoebe, wrenched himself back in a sort of bow to Lydia, and then with no apparent damage to his spine stalked out of the room.

Phoebe sank into a chair; and they sat gazing at each other with a kind of deliberate suspense of emotion while Mr Beck's rapid footsteps faded into the street.

'Lydia,' Phoebe said, 'I am so very sorry.'

'Are you? I cannot see you have done anything to be sorry for. But I am sorry too—for coming in so—but then I did not mean it either. I was escaping the Vawsers. Believe me, please, I did not design it.'

'Oh, Lydia! Of course I believe it,' Phoebe said, with her most luminous and steadfast look.

'Thank you: I fear Mr Beck does not.'

'He was—very overwrought. But that does not excuse . . . I didn't know he was coming, Lydia. I hope you can believe that—after last time. He simply burst in and—and spoke.'

'Of course. And the subject of his speech was, I presume—that is, I assume . . .'

'What *is* the difference between them, I wonder,' Phoebe said, passing off a sob as a laugh, and scrabbling for her handkerchief.

'My dear Phoebe, I am very stupid. You perhaps

wish to be alone just now—to reflect in peace, to consider—'

'Oh, please no! Don't go. I shall be better in a moment—not so nonsensical. To tell the truth, when Mr Beck began—speaking, my first thought was a wish: I wish Lydia were here.'

Lydia opened her mouth to speak, but got no further. Phoebe, gentle Phoebe: who ushered trapped flies out of the window with patient care, and who also possessed the ability to be quite terrifying.

'Well,' she managed at last, 'I am flattered; but such a moment is, as Mr Beck hinted, usually reserved for the tête-à-tête, and is not improved by the presence of a third party. Though I still wish he might have openly sought the audience, instead of feeling he must go behind my back to secure it. Never mind. That *was* the question he came to ask—was it not?'

Phoebe nodded, examining the hem of her handkerchief. 'He asked me to be his wife.'

Lydia sat back, then sat forward: there was no bodily position that could ease the discomfort of her mind at this moment. Its acuteness surprised her. That Phoebe would receive a proposal had always been a probability, and the fact that Lydia had begun to expect its coming first from Mr A and not Mr B did not render this event at all astonishing. Indeed, reviewing Mr Beck's conduct since their arrival in Bath she found it appeared thoroughly likely that he would throw down such a declaration. Still she could not shake off her perplexity. It was as if she saw for the first time what a great matter this was: no parlour-game, no comic-opera complication, but a crisis of decision that would determine the future course of Phoebe's life. And we have only one life, she found herself thinking insistently, as if that, too, were a new and startling apprehension: we have only one life. Beneath all this lurked, sulky now but still combustive, her anger at Mr Beck for the way he had treated her: indeed, for the way he had treated them both.

But it was not her part, she reminded herself, to bring any of this forward. It was alarming enough that Phoebe had wished for her presence during the proposal. But she allowed herself a little measure of relief that Phoebe had not, at least, answered it with a definite yes.

'I see. I shall not press you for details of what is, after all, an entirely private transaction. But I hope I did not march in *just* at the moment of—'

'Oh, no no,' Phoebe said, with a weak smile. 'He asked me at once—it was as if he were terribly burdened with it. He flung himself down, and said he could not bear it any longer, and that I must answer his question—whether I would make him the happiest of men or the most miserable.'

The happiest of men, thought Lydia before she could stop herself: not the freshest of figures.

'He was most—impassioned,' Phoebe went on. 'A few minutes before, I had been looking in my work-box and wondering what had become of the gold thread that I bought the other day, or at least I was almost sure I had bought it—and then, suddenly, this. I am afraid I was very awkward— very stupid. I did not know what to say or do: it was in my mind, absurdly enough, to ask him to go out and come in again, and begin in a different way— or not begin at all . . . This *is* very nonsensical,' she

313

burst out, biting her lips, and frowning at the clock on the mantel as if it were telling some fantastical time that had never been heard of.

'It might be, if the occasion of it were something trifling; but, my dear Phoebe, that is not the case. It is entirely natural to be agitated, to be at a loss for words—'

'Was that how it was for you?' Phoebe asked, with a hopeful look: then dropped her eyes. 'I'm sorry—that is not my business at all.'

Lydia took advantage of Phoebe's embarrassment to deal with her own. It was curious, and not pleasant, to dip suddenly into the well of her past, and remember the moment of Lewis Durrant's proposal: especially as she was forced to confess, if only to herself, that she had certainly not been at a loss for words: that she had had, if anything, a gratifying surplus of them.

'That was exactly how it was,' she answered briskly. 'Though of course nothing can be exactly comparable in such a case. For one thing, I was quite certain of my reply, and I have the impression that you were not.'

Phoebe shook her head. 'It is very difficult. I struggled with all sorts of feelings—so many, so confusing that I hardly knew myself. But I knew that a definite answer was not in my power—though I felt it dreadfully unfair on him—and I said so. And you heard me repeat it, did you not?'

'I did. And I think it very sensible, when you had been so taken by surprise.'

'Yes,' Phoebe said, on a melancholy note; then threw down the handkerchief, as if it were a seductive distraction, and met Lydia's eyes. 'And I felt it to be sensible, and right, absolutely right,

314

when you came in and he was so rude to you. That I cannot excuse: nothing can excuse it.'

'No, no: it was a difficult situation, and he was not in command of himself,' Lydia said, with that most luxurious feeling of having been wronged and being generous about it.

'Perhaps: but I cannot like the way he spoke to you, Lydia. What he said to me at last—"I hope you will not let her dictate to you", or something like it: I am so sorry for that. I know he is impulsive in the way he talks, but that—'

'That was regrettable, I would say, Phoebe, only for the disrespect it showed to you. I do not mind his suspicion of my influence: I am used to it: but I do mind when he suggests that *you* are too susceptible to that influence. There is a dismissiveness about it that—for the moment at least—does not speak the lover.'

'Is there?' Phoebe said wonderingly. 'I dare say . . . But then the strength of his feelings, you know—I can allow for that in my own case. With you, it is a different matter—'

'Phoebe, I insist that you do not take this into account. Mr Beck's feeling for you and his feeling for me are entirely separate things.'

'But they aren't—not to me. I cannot bear to think of the people I care for not liking each other.'

'Can't you? Then you must live alone, Phoebe. Whoever you may choose to marry or not marry, this one certainty remains: that you will think your husband's friends contemptible fools, and wonder how he tolerates them, and he will think the same of yours.'

'Oh, Lydia—you exaggerate, surely.'

315

'Well, yes. There are exceptions: occasionally the husband likes his wife's friend so much he runs off with her. Or vice versa. But generally the rule holds good. It is curious, as presumably the same taste makes one choose friends and spouse.'

'I suppose . . . But I cannot think of things in the way you do, Lydia—in the abstract. I have tried, but it's no good.'

'About things like this, you should certainly not think in the abstract. But if anyone should think— well, call it objectively, then it should be me. After all, that is what I am here for.'

'Yes—and I am very thankful for it. I hardly know what I should do, left to myself.'

This, too, was a rather alarming utterance. As brightly as she could, Lydia said: 'Now, surely not. You would do—as I am sure you are doing, as far as the shock of the moment allows: think, reflect: consult your feelings as well as your reason: consider the proposal in all its aspects, in every way that it tends to your happiness or disquiet.'

'Yes . . . but the one consideration I keep coming back to is that I did not say yes at once. And surely that is revealing: surely if one were certain, the yes would come unbidden—without thinking—straight from the heart.'

Lydia hesitated. The fact that Phoebe had not said yes to Mr Beck at once was, to her, a hopeful sign—because she felt that Phoebe should never say yes to him at all. This, of course, could not be said. But nor could she simply sigh and agree with Phoebe that it was all too revealing. Intellectual honesty would not allow it.

'It reveals, if anything, your great surprise and confusion,' she said, 'and that *perhaps* reveals the approach was a little hasty—a little soon—no more. But as for things coming straight from the heart, I am not sure they are always to be so implicitly accepted. I fancy they should at least pass through the head on the way out, to receive the impress of reason, before they can be accepted as legal tender. It makes them more valid, not less.'

Phoebe gave that a good deal of thought. 'Well,' she said at last, 'I am passing it through my head—but I am afraid it comes out no clearer. Still, I am glad to hear you say that: that I was not wrong in hesitating.' She walked to the window and gazed out, fixedly, mistily. 'It is dreadful to think of Mr Beck's feelings just now—not knowing what his answer is to be: whether he is to be happy, or . . .' She turned abruptly. 'Oh, Lydia, I must accept him. Mustn't I? It is too cruel—to think of him being made miserable, when it only needs a simple answer—'

'To make him happy. Quite so. Nothing simpler. But that is to consider only his feelings, and not yours. A thief may declare that he will be enormously happy if you give him all your money, and miserable if you do not: is that a reason to hand over your purse?'

'No: to be sure, no,' Phoebe said, but without total conviction: Lydia feared that she was picturing the scenario of the beseeching thief and finding it problematical. Quickly she took up a more promising line.

'Your position, Phoebe, is a difficult one, and it is no use pretending it isn't: especially as there is a third person to consider. I'm sure he has been present in your mind all the time.'

Phoebe nodded, and with a subdued smile came

317

and sat down beside her. 'Of course I did not say anything of that to Mr Beck. But at the back of my mind was the thought of Mr Allardyce, and how there was *his* happiness or unhappiness to consider. Though to be sure, if a thief—'

'Never mind the thief,' Lydia said, stopping her with an affectionate, or at any rate powerful squeeze of the hand. 'We are talking of Mr Allardyce. We must establish how far he is a factor in your decision, and what it means. For example— if there were *no* Mr Allardyce, would your response today have been different?'

Phoebe took a deep breath. 'That is a very difficult question. My heart has an answer, but I had better pass it through my head first.'

'Let us just hear the heart,' said Lydia, beginning to regret her tendency to metaphor.

'Then yes: I think I would have been much more decided. I fear that when Mr Beck knelt before me, I felt: This is not right, a woman in this position should not be—should not be *divided*. I felt unworthy, somehow.'

'Well, now we are getting somewhere: though I assure you, Phoebe, you are quite worthy of Mr Beck, or indeed—' Lydia was going to say 'or indeed ten Mr Becks', but caught herself in time. 'Or indeed anyone.'

Phoebe shook her head as if to say she doubted that. 'Well: the fact remains, there *is* a Mr Allardyce, and my feelings must take account of him . . .' She frowned. 'Lydia, I declare this must be dismally tedious for you, hearing me prate of my feelings. You should not have to bear it. Perhaps— perhaps I ought to write to Lady Eastmond: tell her all, and wait.'

'By all means do that as well. Certainly if you do wish to accept a marriage proposal, it will have to be referred to Sir Henry and Lady Eastmond, as your guardians, for their consent: but that we need not think of yet.' And it would have little material effect, she thought, as the consent was sure to come: Lady Eastmond had made it plain she had no objections to either gentleman. 'But my dear Phoebe, none of this talk of tedium. It would be a poor sort of friend who could complain of it, or indeed feel it, when the question is of such profound importance. Now let us try another supposition. Imagine it had been Mr Allardyce making the same proposal. What do you think your feelings would have been then?'

Phoebe stared resolutely at a certain spot on the floor, which Lydia presumed was where Mr Beck had performed his prostration. Then she shook her head again. 'Really I cannot imagine it, Lydia. It is quite a weakness of mine. You are very good at that—picturing things that didn't happen but might have: I really think you ought to write a novel. Yes, why don't you? I borrowed the most insipid thing from Duffield's the other day, and I'm sure that you could—'

'Thank you, I shall bear it in mind,' Lydia said, restraining a smile, 'but just now it is your story I am concerned with, and how it is to be continued to a happy resolution. Mr Allardyce proposing— think of it as a possibility, then, rather than a picture.'

'You do ask difficult questions. You see, in the first place I know Mr Allardyce would never have made an approach with such—with so little decorum. Also—' Phoebe's colour rose '—I know

319

he would never have behaved with such rudeness to you, which I have not forgotten, by the way. but beyond that . . . Lydia, I cannot quite imagine it because I do not feel, somehow, that Mr Allardyce's regard for me is such that . . . well, I do not think it reaches so far.'

'Phoebe, this is modesty beyond reason. Mr Allardyce's attentions—his so evident desire of renewing the acquaintance, after that time in London—'

'Oh, I do not say there is no regard: I should be a dull, ungrateful creature to think that. I even flatter myself that there is a degree of attachment—but as to the issue of it, I am unsure. Mr Allardyce's manners are so universally obliging, and there is such charm in his address, that one may be easily misled—'

'Phoebe, you do full justice to Mr Allardyce's qualities, but you err in how you value them, and still more in how you value yourself. Trust me: there is no question of the strength of his attachment: I have particular reasons for my certainty in this matter. The issue of it, of course, I cannot speak for—but if any doubt about his present sincerity is clouding your mind, then dispel it.'

'I confess there has been a little doubt,' Phoebe said, with a look half mournful, half glowing. 'But if I have your assurance—'

'You do. And I give it with no interested motive; only so that you may be quite clear about everything that affects your decision.'

'Yes . . . my decision.' Phoebe's eyes dwelled again on the spot of carpet: then she turned with a sudden uneasy flash of hope. 'That is—if I do have

320

to make one.'

'Well—you might pack your trunk at once, leave Bath incognito, and run away to sea; but I am not sure that anyone would find that a satisfactory solution.'

'No,' Phoebe said seriously, as if she had already considered it, 'but I must give Mr Beck an answer; and I do not know what answer to give—I am so torn—no sooner coming to one conclusion than thinking of another. And so I wonder if I might not say so to him. Tell him that I am gratified by his proposal, and so forth, but I cannot yet come to a decision on it; and if he will be so good as to accept a postponement . . .'

Lydia was shaking her head, partly in admiration at Phoebe's desperate resourcefulness, but chiefly in pity for Mr Beck, as she imagined him condemned to such a tantalising durance. She might wish some minor ills on him, but not that. 'Phoebe, I'm sure on reflection you will see that that is a hard thing to ask of Mr Beck. It offers him hope, but does not guarantee him against the ultimate pain of refusal—the worst of both worlds. A simple "No" would hurt, but it would not torture. I am afraid the decision must be made, no matter how hard it seems: a man accepts that risk when he poses such a question. That does not mean the decision must be made *quickly*—only that it is not fair to tantalise.'

'You're right, of course,' Phoebe said, with a deep, full sigh. 'You think, then, that I should refuse him?'

Lydia kept the closest rein on her own expression. No hint of alarm: above all no hint of the loud 'Yes!' resounding in her mind. 'I hope, I

321

devoutly hope, that I have said nothing so categorical on either side of the question. I think you should do whatever appears, on careful reflection, to offer you the best chance of happiness in the long life ahead.'

Phoebe's great rich eyes pinned her. She was waiting for more.

'If it should appear that accepting Mr Beck's proposal of marriage—and marrying him, of course,' Lydia went on, in what she feared was a rather lumbering fashion, 'if that is what you feel will secure your lasting happiness—leaving aside Mr Allardyce, leaving aside all other considerations—then, to be sure, you cannot do better than accept.'

'Leaving aside all other considerations,' Phoebe repeated trustfully.

'Yes. If on the other hand you entertain any doubts—any scruples—if you find that anything more than mere surprise and temporary flutter of the spirits is holding you back from accepting him, then—then you must give those doubts their due weight, put aside any squeamishness about wounding his feelings and . . . act accordingly.' Lydia drew breath: she felt rather as if she had had to deliver an extempore lecture on a difficult subject to an expert and hypercritical audience.

Phoebe was silent: she seemed to be making an effort not to look at that place on the carpet. I shall have to put a table on it, Lydia thought.

'Would it be acceptable,' Phoebe said, stirring, 'or at least, would it be right, to answer Mr Beck in writing? I am only wondering if it is an option—for I am such a coward.'

'It is quite acceptable,' Lydia said—electing not

to add that a letter tended to be associated with a refusal. 'But please, Phoebe, do recall that this must be your decision alone: that in matters of the heart you are your own best counsellor, and that even the most well-meant advice is not so very far off from mischief. Having said that, I will proffer one piece of advice, which I excuse by referring it to folk wisdom: that is, it is best to sleep on such a question, and see how it looks in the morning. Mr Beck can find no excessive delay in that, and you will find your own feelings much more manageable.'

'That would indeed be a relief. I feel I must stop thinking and thinking of it—as if that were possible . . . Do you think—would it be very bad if we were to drink some wine before supper?'

'I think it would be very good, not very bad,' Lydia said, almost bouncing off the sofa in her haste to ring the bell. 'A glass of wine fortifies, and you have had a—well, a tiring experience, which requires fortification.'

'Dear me, you make me sound like a castle.'

Lydia was glad to find a little lightness entering Phoebe's tone, even though her face remained grave and pale, and her eyes were elsewhere. 'Even two glasses will not hurt you,' she said, maintaining the same tone, 'and while we drink them, you can tell me what I should write my novel about. It is not a thing I have ever considered, and I am sure I could not do it, but you have whetted my curiosity. Is it to be Gothic? We are back to castles again. I must warn you, Phoebe, I have a healthy disrespect for ghosts, and my only response to a Bleeding Nun would be to offer her a piece of court-plaster.'

'Oh, no, not that sort of novel. That would not

suit you at all. I was thinking of the way you help me to see things, not by dictating—really, that was shocking of Mr Beck—but by reason. Persuasion. You could make a very good sort of novel about people simply facing these questions, and about what is best to do in life. I remember one of my governesses reproving me for indulging in sensibility. I think she felt I needed sense instead. But then how to reconcile the two? That is the sort of thing I mean.'

'Sense and sensibility—well, it has a certain ring. But I doubt, you know, that it would appeal. And a mere woman writing about moral questions— surely that is man's field—'

'Park,' cried Phoebe, 'that was the governess— Miss Park. Very austere: I was rather frightened of her. But I remember finding out by chance that her first name was Emma, and thinking how pretty it was, and wondering if there was a different person inside that stern lady I knew. But then who can guess at the feelings of others?' She sighed. 'It is hard enough to know our own . . .'

Phoebe's gaze was straying again to the carpet, and Lydia mentally urged Mary Darber to hurry with the wine.

*   *   *

Lydia woke in the middle of the night dry-mouthed from excess of wine and talk. Going downstairs to fetch water from the kitchen, she saw candlelight coming from the drawing-room. Phoebe was seated at the bureau in her nightdress, writing.

'Phoebe? Can't you sleep?'

Phoebe offered the outline of a smile. 'I have

324

simply been lying there composing the letter in my head. So I thought I had better get up and write it. Then John can take it to the Christopher first thing in the morning.'

Lydia sat down, hugging herself. It was a mild night, but two o'clock always has its own chill. 'Are you sure?'

'About writing?'

'About all of it.'

Phoebe wiped her pen carefully. 'I am very fond of Mr Beck. Indeed when I think of him my heart—my heart misgives me. But still I do not think I should accept his proposal. There is a suddenness in it—a rashness. It is too precipitate. Is that a good word?'

'It is exactly the right word.'

'Good, because that's the one I've used.' Phoebe glanced dubiously over her letter. To Lydia it already looked very long. 'I have also said that marriage is a very big step—which it is, isn't it?'

'Not only a step, but a whole flight of stairs. And so you must be sure that the two of you will toil up them in reasonable harmony.' Lydia got up. 'But I'll leave you, else I shall certainly appear to be dictating.'

'Oh, I have mentioned that too, in strong terms. But, Lydia—I must know that you approve of what I am doing.'

Lydia stifled a yawn. 'If it is what you want, then of course I approve it.' This was an evasion, as Phoebe's anxious look showed. 'But yes—I think you are doing absolutely the right thing.'

'Thank you.' Phoebe gave the ghostly smile again, and returned with fresh energy to her writing.

Lydia was late rising in the morning, and was only just finishing breakfast when the street-door shook with a violent knocking. She met, then evaded Phoebe's eyes as Mary went to answer it, and a familiar deep-chested voice spoke.

'I must see Miss Rae.'

Lydia nodded to Phoebe. 'Go on, my dear. Take him up to the drawing-room. I'll stay here.'

Well, it was after all to be expected. Mr Beck would surely wish to hear his answer from Phoebe's own lips. Abandoning her tea, Lydia suffered a little disquiet at the thought of Mr Beck's passionate persuasions and limpid eyes undoing everything, and causing Phoebe to change her mind: but there, it was out of her hands now. She would certainly resist the temptation to creep out to the hall and listen.

The temptation had taken her as far as the dining-room door when there came another knock. This time she heard the voice of Lewis Durrant.

'Thank you, Mary,' she said, stepping out. 'I will see Mr Durrant in here. If you don't mind the breakfast things, sir.'

'What's this, a new Bath fashion?' He roamed around the table. 'Rather like the *levée*, with butter and crumbs. That ham looks dry stuff. There is only one thing worse than the provisions in this town, and that is the price demanded for them. Where's Miss Rae?'

'Upstairs. Receiving a caller. Please sit down, Mr Durrant.'

'A caller? You are neglecting your duty again,

326

Miss Templeton.'

'There is something of an important and private nature going forward, which specifically requires my absence, not my presence.'

'Ah, now you're sounding like a chaperon,' he said approvingly. 'You'll be knitting before long. Important and private, eh? Sounds promising, or perhaps not.'

'I am not at liberty to say any more.' He was wearing his old loose country coat again, she saw. 'Mr Durrant—I do think it was a pity about your new coat.'

'Was it? Why?'

Somehow she did not care to say he looked well in it. 'Because—it was new. You must order another like it.'

'Two coats in one year? You'll turn me into Hugh Hanley.' He groaned. 'There, I managed to forget him for a few minutes. He's here. Put up last night at the York Hotel—naturally, that being the most extravagantly expensive in Bath. And came straight to my lodgings for a comfortable cose, as he put it. Also so that I might feast my eyes on his new uniform. Such was the treat that awaited me when I got back from Queen Square. Yes, the moneylenders have responded again to my name, and his commission in the Prince of Wales's Own is bought, though he is not gazetted yet.' He sat down moodily, digging his hands in his breeches pockets.

'And was your cose comfortable? Did you fall on each other's necks, and swear to renounce all your former animosity?'

'Not really: the only thing I wanted to do to his neck was wring it. Probably the feeling was mutual, though of course he kept the smile going to the end.' Mr Durrant produced a brief imitation, more grotesque than authentic. 'He tried to dissuade me, in the most insolent terms, from what he called my Bath folly. I replied that it was none of his deuced business: and so it went on.'

'Though of course it is, in a sense, his business. It is solely because of him that you are pursuing your f— your project.'

'Not solely,' Mr Durrant said, looking out of the window. 'Well, he may hound me all he likes: it only hardens my resolution. The sight of Hugh Hanley parading Bath in his red coat is almost enough to make me propose marriage to the first woman I see.'

'How enchanting for her . . .' Lydia cocked her head: she could hear agitated footsteps above, and Mr Beck's voice audibly raised.

'Important and private matters going forward— or backward?' he asked, studying her. 'I believe that's Beck I hear.'

'Yes . . . but really, Mr Durrant, I shouldn't talk of it. It is purely Phoebe's affair.'

'Hm? Well, it is plainly affecting you also. You look as grey as that ham. Come, tell me a little. Even a chaperon must have a confidant.'

'Well—I must insist that you adhere to the meaning of that word, and regard this as given in the strictest confidence.'

He sniffed. 'Miss Templeton, you know my character.'

'I do, and it reassures me. I need not fear looseness of tongue in a man who will seldom give himself the trouble to speak. The matters are—the matter is a proposal of marriage. That is, Mr Beck has made the proposal, and Miss Rae has declined

328

it.'

'Has she now?'

'Yes—and you need not sound so surprised. She is very young, after all, and an heiress, and she must give great thought to the disposition of her hand; and the proposal is rather—precipitate.'

Mr Durrant, irritatingly, was silent, regarding her with dry, heavy-lidded interest. 'Yes,' he said at last, getting up and roaming, 'to be sure, very true. Only I supposed Miss Rae was—well, I supposed her very ready to have him.' He glanced up at the ceiling. 'And is she, as it were, administering the blow now?'

'Her decision was communicated by letter. I imagine Mr Beck seeks to—to confirm it.'

'Yes, I shouldn't wonder. Well, I am sorry for him. He is something of a cockle-brain, to be sure, but still it is hard on the man, when he surely had good grounds for thinking his luck was in.'

'Now I am surprised, Mr Durrant. You hear of a man failing of matrimony, and you commiserate instead of congratulating him on his escape.'

Mr Durrant paused in his pacing, and looked at her with a kind of dawning of malicious delight. 'Miss Templeton. I believe I detect your hand in this. You wish her to marry her other suitor—you want her to take Robert Allardyce.'

'Good heavens, Mr Durrant, you do misread a situation. My wishes—whatever they may be—have nothing to do with the case, nothing whatsoever.' She lifted her teacup and drank, trying to repress her shudder at the taste.

'Yes, that must be pretty well cold and stewed by now,' he remarked. 'Come, I am sure you must have at least made your wishes known, and they must carry some weight with Miss Rae. It is plain to me, simply from observation, that you much prefer Mr Allardyce of the two.'

'Very well—privately, in my own opinion, yes,' she said, frowning. 'And what do *you* think? You are very thick with that family. You said you were at Queen Square last evening, after all.'

'So I was,' he said, smiling at her annoyance, 'invitation to cards and supper.'

'And so,' she went on, more annoyed than ever, 'you have become pretty well acquainted with Mr Allardyce, and I'm sure that even your misanthropy will concede him to be a very sensible man.'

'Yes: thoroughly sensible, I have no doubt of it. But what I beg leave to doubt is whether a *sensible* man would entirely suit Miss Rae.'

'You suppose you are revealing your insight, but in fact you are revealing your prejudice. I know Phoebe a good deal better than you: I know she has abundant good sense: indeed the fact that she has attracted the regard of such a man as Mr Allardyce is proof of it.'

'Perhaps: but good sense is not necessarily what every man looks for first when he chooses a wife. Which is just as well, in a way, as otherwise the human race would soon come to an end.'

'You are being deliberately provoking. I have nothing excessive to say for Mr Allardyce, or against Mr Beck. I would only urge against haste and thoughtlessness, and those I see in Mr Beck's proposal, and so does Phoebe.'

Mr Durrant grew sharply attentive. 'Do you mean he should have waited?'

'Yes—I don't know—perhaps,' Lydia said,

floundering, 'and besides, a man may always—well, ask again.'

'Ask again!' Mr Durrant repeated, with a very cool look of appraisal. 'Forgive me, but I discern a lack of insight *there*. For a man to ask again, after he has been refused, requires a great conquest of his natural pride—such a conquest as he may feel himself unable, at the price of all self-respect, to make.'

'Then that is his affair: but he should consider that, by and large, men are over-supplied with this natural pride, and it can do them no harm, and even some good, to dispense with a little of it now and then.'

'This is easy for a woman to say.' He sauntered to the window, and began feeling the stuff of the curtains. 'She has nothing to do in such a case: no efforts to make: no adjustments to her self-opinion to countenance. She may just sit there, nursing her favour like a miser's purse, and await the next approach.'

'If that is ease, it is the ease of the caged bird. You say she *may* just sit there, but in truth she *must* just sit there. It is not given to a woman to declare herself—to make proposals or counter-proposals: if she changes her mind, she is powerless to act upon her inclinations, and must merely hope: sit and hope.'

Mr Durrant dislodged the silk cord holding back the curtain, retied it with splendid awkwardness, and came smartly away from the window. 'All the more reason,' he said, scowling, 'for her to make the right choice to begin with.'

'Precisely. I am glad we are in agreement.'

He seemed about to say something more,

something as definitive as a sword-thrust, when there was a great clatter on the staircase, and then Mr Beck thrust open the dining-room door.

'Well, Miss Templeton. I congratulate you. Your object is achieved.' His superb cheekbones worked convulsively. 'You have turned Miss Rae against me in full measure, and I admit my defeat. While such influence continues to prevail, my suit is hopeless.'

Lydia rose. 'Mr Beck, I understand that your feelings on this occasion must be painful, but you are mistaken, grievously mistaken if you suppose that I—'

'I have been mistaken: oh, yes, mistaken in many respects. Not least in supposing that, in spite of our differences, you did in the last resort "understand feelings", as you phrase it. But you do not, madam. Your understanding is vast, admirable indeed, but there it fails, believe me, most miserably. This is uncivil: I know it: but you need not fear the incivility will be renewed, for you will not see me again.' His burning eyes finally took in the presence of Mr Durrant: he swallowed. 'Sir.'

'How d'you do, Mr Beck,' Mr Durrant said blithely, with a little wave.

Lydia said: 'Mr Beck, if you will just sit down a moment and—'

'Sit down, Miss Templeton, I have no intention of ever sitting down again,' Mr Beck cried heatedly; and then, after a moment's visible thought: 'That is, if sitting down is to be equated with rest—that rest which I shall never find this side of the grave. But no matter—I only came to say that you will not be troubled with my presence any longer. I shall leave Bath today.'

'I'm sorry you are leaving, Mr Beck,' said Mr Durrant, courteously. 'Where do you go—to Bristol? Please give my compliments to your father if so.'

'Bristol, yes. First. Then—heaven only knows. There are ships aplenty at Bristol docks, and I'm sure one will find a berth for me. And so—goodbye.' Mary Darber—an accomplished listener—had appeared soundlessly behind Mr Beck, tactfully holding his hat. He turned, jumped, and then with a drop from drama to naturalness thanked her. Mary smiled, and it occurred to Lydia, randomly, that she was in a room with the only two men she had known aside from her father who treated servants as fellow human beings. She was about to make a last appeal to reason, but he forestalled her with a guttural 'Say nothing, madam: for once, say nothing,' and was gone.

They sat for several moments silently contemplating the teacups.

'Well,' said Mr Durrant, 'he seemed to take it pretty well, after all.'

Lydia glared at him. 'You might have helped me.'

'I might, if it were any of my business.'

'Even so—you heard him insult me—traduce me . . .' She winced: Mr Beck's language was catching. 'There is such a thing, Mr Durrant, as chivalry on behalf of a lady.'

'No, there isn't: it always conceals a design. No knight ever swept a lady from a dragon's lair without expecting something more in return than a thank-you and a ribbon to tie on his helmet.' He coughed. 'As it were. You have too high an opinion of the male, Miss Templeton.'

'I assure you, my opinion of the male was never lower.'

He grinned. 'Besides, you defend yourself very ably. Not, of course, that there is anything that needs defending in your conduct. It's not as if you have done anything wrong, is it? Anything to cause you to reproach yourself?' He rose, stretching. 'And Beck will get over it.'

'To be sure he will.' She hesitated. 'If I had any doubt of that . . .'

'No, no.' He came and stood by her chair a moment. 'If there were less bombast, there would be more concern. Believe me, the men who run away to sea are very seldom the ones who talk about it. Well, I dare say you'd better go to Miss Rae, so I'll leave you. I must say, this has taken the dullness off the morning call.'

When he had gone Lydia sat for several minutes nerving herself to go up to the drawing-room. Never before had a flight of stairs appeared so imposing, and never before had she felt the weariness of tackling them alone.

CHAPTER TWENTY-TWO

There had been tears, and though they were over now, Phoebe's eyes shone drily with perplexity and grief.

'I never thought these things could be so difficult—so painful. I fear I have been a great fool from the beginning. In London—it was all so delightful, and I was flattered, and none of it seemed liable to come to any great issue. But of course I should have known. I have been careless and selfish.'

'These things are difficult, certainly, and there is something surprisingly—contorted about them,' Lydia said: nudged by her own memory of a November day at Heystead, the sound of hoofs crunching away on gravel, her eyes smarting as she huddled closer to the fire. 'But you should not reprove yourself, Phoebe. You have done nothing wrong.' She stroked her friend's fingers. 'Nothing wrong.'

'He was so very disappointed—so very bitter in his expressions. If I had known he would be so stricken, I would have . . . Well, no. That is not the way to think. I must remember the thief and the purse.'

'He is very disappointed now: but the feeling must moderate with time, as all feelings do; and perhaps, quite soon, he will begin to understand the reasons behind your answer, and even concur with them.'

'I hope so—indeed, I *did* hope so: that is, I thought I could help him to understand, because we would still see each other—remain on friendly terms. I did not think he would go quite away.'

'It is a frequent wish at such time,' Lydia said, 'the wish to remain friends, and go on as you were—but I am afraid it is very rarely managed.'

'But—but, Lydia, what about you and Mr Durrant? You managed it admirably—indeed I think I always took heart from that.'

'Well, that was different. In the first place, we were neighbours, and there was a family friendship, and so inevitably . . . And then, you know, Mr Beck and Mr Durrant are very different

335

people. Mr Durrant's temper is not so—impetuous.' Her own speech gave Lydia varying sensations of discomfort. Not so impetuous—was that another way of saying Mr Durrant simply hadn't cared so much? Certainly she hadn't expected him to run away to sea; but the sang-froid with which he had resumed his life after her refusal might be seen as deeply unflattering. It was strange, and disturbing, to feel the touch of her own hurt and resentment across the years, like coming across some painful, half-forgotten, unanswered letter in a drawer. And now, besides, she had led herself to the unpalatable admission that Mr Beck *did* feel deeply.

Oh, but he was so theatrical—surely there was as much pose as genuine emotion, as Mr Durrant had suggested. Lydia shook herself. 'But everyone says strong things in the heat of the moment, Phoebe; and Mr Beck's *saying* he will go away does not mean he will, at least not for any length of time. Indeed I think it is not unwise for there to be a little separation between you for the present: to meet now would only be to raise an agitation that can do no good on either side. Now, you do not wish him to be unhappy, because you care for him: is that not so? Then assuredly, if he cares for you, he would not wish *you* to be unhappy. It is hard, I know, to lift your spirits at such a time; but do not abandon the hope that they will rise, and sooner than you think.'

Lydia persevered: she could not have applied more effort of persuasion and ingenuity to soothe Phoebe's distress of mind if it had been her own; and she was rewarded at last with at least the appearance of composure in her friend, and a

336

declaration, apparently heartfelt and wholly sensible, that she would not dwell on the matter any more, as it could do nobody any good. It was almost more than Lydia had hoped, that Phoebe would then pronounce herself ready to go out on their daily walk: but so she did, with a certain impatience from which Lydia concluded that the house itself, with its painfully fresh associations, was oppressive to her. There remained the possibility that, going into the town, they might happen to see Mr Beck; but this was an evil that must be faced.

There was one other resource on which Lydia could call, and she employed it sparingly and judiciously as they took their walk. It was another serenely fine day, and she remarked on the fair prospects for their country expedition with the Allardyces tomorrow. Phoebe did not say much, but her face brightened, or at least something of the shadow receded from it; and Lydia had hopes for the restoration of her spirits from the thought of this, and still greater hopes from the event itself.

They reached the South Parade without incident—or, specifically, without Mr Beck materialising in the middle of any thoroughfare, cloaked, cadaverous and reproachful; but once there, Lydia suffered a start as a male voice called out: 'Miss Templeton!' Not Mr Beck, however: a young man who might have figured as an illustration of his opposite, as he came forward with studied grace and negligent elegance to make his bows.

'Mr Hanley, how do you do? Your uncle told me you were arrived in Bath. Let me introduce Miss Rae: Mr Hanley, Mr Durrant's nephew.'

'Miss Rae: delighted. I knew *you* were in Bath from the same source, Miss Templeton: my uncle actually found room to mention it in one of his sadly abbreviated letters. To be sure, I had a *hint* of it when we last met, at Vauxhall. But then the matter was undecided.' A bright, feline look passed from one to the other, then dissolved into a disarming smile. 'And now, most curiously, here we all are! And it's not so very bad, is it? Quite a deal of company here—and not *all* dowds and dowagers. London just now, you know, is a very desert. Not a soul there.'

'Not a soul?' Lydia said. 'Good heavens, who is minding the shops and sweeping the streets?'

'Oh, I have been keeping bad company, in which it is taken for granted that those sort of people do not possess souls. Now, please, allow me to be your escort to wherever you are going, which in Bath hardly matters, as no one goes anywhere to any purpose. One perambulates only to be seen.'

Certainly the figure of Hugh Hanley, dazzling in red coat, buff facings, sash, silver buttons, white breeches and iridescent boots, shako easily cradled under his arm, was one that attracted many glances as they passed along the South Parade; and Phoebe seemed a little in awe of him. Lydia felt no such thing: she thought he looked well in the uniform, in the way that a very convincing actor would: but she supposed she had better congratulate him on his commission, and the achievement of his desire.

'It is obliging of you to notice,' he said, with a mock-modest glance down at himself. 'In truth I am not really empowered to adorn myself thus until I properly join the regiment at Brighton—but

338

it all cost such a pretty penny, or confoundedly ugly penny, that I feel I ought to get the maximum wear from it. Miss Rae, have you ever heard of Schweitzer and Davidson's?'

Phoebe murmured that she had not.

'Well, you can find them at Cork Street, just off Bond Street. I offer the information in case you should ever need to perform a daring robbery, or even just take a fancy to it: for by the price they charge for tailoring this uniform, I dare swear they are worth a mint of money. And whoever your *modiste* may be, be assured she never did so much fussing and primping, so much sighing and tweaking, and altogether making you feel rather dismally conscious of your shape as those gentlemen. Now tell me, what are the excitements I can look forward to in Bath? I observe there is a Dress Ball at the New Assembly Rooms on Monday, and intend to subscribe at once—but what other pleasures should I anticipate?'

'That depends on how long your stay is to be, Mr Hanley,' Lydia said.

'I have not the least notion,' he said cheerfully. 'I came to see my uncle, and to try to work out what curious freak has got into his head to bring him here; and he is such a hard study that I scarcely know how long it will take to get to the bottom of it. Can you help me, Miss Templeton? Is it some rare distemper, and can the waters cure it?'

'It is not for me to answer your question, Mr Hanley—it is for Mr Durrant alone; and knowing him, I feel sure he has already done so, in the plainest terms.'

'Exactly—*knowing him*, which you do, I think, as well as anybody; and I am certain you must have seen something of him in Bath. Old acquaintance, after all, is the only acquaintance he can bear. I know he is seeking, or says he is seeking, a wife, but I am not sure how to take this astonishing information. It is rather as if one heard that the King has been discovered to be an impostor, and that all these years the throne has been occupied by an illiterate costermonger from Battersea.'

'The information is correct, as far as it goes,' Lydia said with a reluctant smile, 'but perhaps it should not be so astonishing, Mr Hanley: perhaps it only proves that you do not know him as well as you suppose.'

'I have never known him as well as I could wish,' Hugh Hanley said, with a slight frown. 'He is my nearest family beside my mother and sisters, and though a father, of course, can never be replaced, I have been accustomed since his death to look upon Mr Durrant with something of the same regard. For all our differences, which I do not deny for a moment, I have always tended to look up to him. Oh, yes,' he went on, at Lydia's glance, 'though I have often taken pains not to show it—perhaps from a young man's awkwardness—perhaps also from a contrary feeling that he is rather too used to being looked up to. Still, the feeling is there: and one would be glad to convert it to something warmer, if only there were some sign of will on the other side. You are acquainted with my uncle, I'm sure, Miss Rae: I hope you will not think me disrespectful when I say that to be always looking *up* tends to produce a pain in the neck.' He looked at her closely. 'But this heat is excessive, and my dry talk is making it worse. Let us cross to the shady side—and then, if I may presume to dictate,

340

refreshment is in order, and I know the very place.'

He led them on, up to York Street and into the town, talking volubly and lightly of other things, and requiring little in the way of reply: a style of company that, Lydia reflected, was fortunately suited to distract and divert Phoebe just now. At Gill's, the pastry-cook's, he was fastidious about their seating, and then as the serving-man hovered he held up an admonishing finger.

'Now, throw away your preconceptions. Ladies fagged with walking in the heat—no, you don't look it, but I intuit it—always refresh themselves with an ice. I urge against it. An ice is a deception: there is a momentary coolness in the mouth, but the subsequent shock upon the stomach is anything but salutary to the system, and the thing has no nourishment in it. You get up supposing you are restored, and in a moment you are wilting again. I recommend instead a basin of Gill's excellent vermicelli—piping hot. Nature cries out in outrage: will this not heat further? it will not. A friend of mine served three years with the East India Company at Bombay, and there he saw—to his bewilderment at first—that food in that fierce climate is commonly eaten raging with hot spices. He tried it, and discovered that its effect on the system is actually cooling. The vermicelli, besides, provides sustenance without apparent substance as it slips down so easily. Now, try it, and tell me afterwards if I have not missed my vocation.'

They tried it, and it was just as Mr Hanley said—though he took none himself, pleading a late breakfast. Lydia had a suspicion, from that rather full-lipped, soft-necked handsomeness of his, that Hugh Hanley had to be watchful of his weight. But

341

she was pleased to see Phoebe looking less wan and weary and, above all, more like Phoebe: prepared to be interested in everything that was new to her.

'I suppose it is made of the same thing as bread,' she said wonderingly, 'that is wheat, of course, but—how curious that people around the world should think of such different things to do with it. For my part, I doubt that I could ever have thought of *anything* to do with it—the way it just stands there in the field like stiff grass: it scarcely looks as if you could eat it at all.' She sucked in a thread reflectively.

'I am glad there is someone else who thinks of these things,' Mr Hanley said. 'Observe that carriage outside, bowling along—well, straining along as well as it can in Bath, but nevertheless—I wonder, who first thought of those round things we call wheels? He was certainly a benefactor to mankind, for the coaches must have bumped horribly without them.'

'Oh, but surely, if there were coaches,' Phoebe said, 'then there cannot have been—oh.' She flushed, and smiled ruefully.

'You do well to catch me out in my nonsense, Miss Rae,' he said, answering her smile, 'for you have surely divined that I am talking it as a diversion from what is really occupying my mind. Very well: I must bore you with this again, because it *does* fret me—what is my uncle about?' He turned to Lydia. 'I make no apologies for this question, because it is beyond apology—but really, is it all a piece of flummery, designed to bring me to heel? Or does he have a lady in view?'

'That is two questions,' Lydia said, with an

342

unaccountable feeling of sipping lemon or vinegar. 'But I can answer the one that is most troubling you, Mr Hanley, and assure you that there is no lady, as you term it, in view.'

'Oh, but, Lydia, surely,' put in Phoebe, coming out of wistful abstraction, 'Mr Durrant is on very friendly terms with Miss Allardyce.'

'Friendly terms—exactly,' Lydia said, with prompt firmness. It was not that she particularly wanted to relieve Hugh Hanley's mind—not at all: but she was particular about the truth. 'Miss Allardyce is a mutual acquaintance of ours and Mr Durrant's—merely one of many.' Not true, but never mind. 'But come, Mr Hanley, you know what Bath is like: if you wish to enquire into your uncle's affairs, you have only to open your ear to the latest gossip; a turn or two in the Pump Room should do it.'

'Precisely my thought, and you are right to reprove me,' he said, spreading his hands: though she could see him storing up the name of Miss Allardyce. 'I shall combine enjoyable leisure with observation. I wonder if he will attend the Dress Ball. I should so like to see Uncle Lewis dancing a cotillion.'

'No cotillions at the Dress Balls—only at the Fancy Balls on Fridays,' Lydia said—with a little plunge of the heart at the vacuous things that had been added to her knowledge. 'In fact Mr Durrant dances quite capably, when he chooses.'

'Well, if I am honest, that does not surprise me: for there you have the conundrum of my uncle. I am sure he can do many things when he chooses— but he does not choose! Now this, candidly, I cannot understand. Miss Rae, I appeal to you. Isn't life set before us as a banquet to be tasted to the full? Or is it a fire to be shunned in case it burns us? And if it is a fire—then should we not risk the burning, so that we can warm ourselves at it, and mull wine at it, and—well, I'm trying to think of something else to do with a fire that's pleasant.'

'See pictures in it,' offered Phoebe, with a kind of sad brightening of expression.

'Exactly. Miss Rae, I hail a kindred spirit. Never fear, I'm done with being poetical. Takes it out of you, rather. Now if only my uncle would see life in this way—and I speak with respect—I'm sure he would be a good deal less unhappy.'

'What makes you suppose that Mr Durrant is unhappy?' Lydia asked, with something of genuine curiosity, and something of vague offence.

'You are polite enough not to refer to my own effect on him—the vexations I cause him: but these I freely acknowledge, and I am not so vain as to claim that *I* am at the root of it all. No: there is, it seems to me, a want of relish for life in Mr Durrant, which is as melancholy as unaccountable.'

'He relishes different things from you, perhaps,' Lydia said. 'And I am certain that amongst all the things he does *not* relish, being an object of pity would rank high.'

'Really? Then there indeed we differ: I will accept any kindly feeling on offer, from adoration down to pity.'

'If that were to be taken seriously, it would suggest a man who has always been starved of kindly feeling; and that, I am sure, Mr Hanley, cannot be the case.'

'No: not at all,' he said, fixing her with a look at once jaunty and thoughtful. 'And from what you

344

know of me, Miss Templeton, you may well conclude instead that I am the spoiled child of fortune. Which I do not deny, to a certain degree. But consider: when we met at the South Parade, you introduced me as Mr Durrant's nephew. Apt, and revealing: for that has long been the sum of my identity. A very tidy sum, I do not quarrel with it: I only remark that being my bachelor uncle's heir has been, as it were, my place in life; and suddenly to face the prospect of losing that place is a little disconcerting—as if a parson should find the church door barred against him, and his congregation cutting him dead in the street.'

'The parson might well apply himself to the question of what he has done to deserve this fate.'

'Oh, deserve—what do any of us deserve?' he said, with a laugh. 'Probably a good deal less than we get. I do not propose quarrelling with Providence. Nor, in truth, do I propose quarrelling with my uncle: if he is really set upon this course, then I am the last person in the world to be able to dissuade him. I only want to know whether he is . . . serious.' He shrugged, and beckoned for the bill. 'An odd word to hear from my lips, perhaps.'

'And if you discover that he *is* serious—what then?'

Mr Hanley paused, sighed, and gave a smile of wry resignation. 'Why, then I shan't mind so much. Which is not to say I shan't mind at all.'

He paid the bill, tipped the serving-man handsomely, apologised for the tedious subject, and on their leaving the cook-shop talked pleasant nonsense until he parted from them at Pulteney Bridge.

'This will not be our last meeting, of course:

345

Bath does not allow of that. So permit me to say, though you are surely despairing at the grim prospect, that I am glad of it. I could go on— company of two ladies unequalled in elegance, grace, charm et cetera—but you would not believe it, even though it is the truth, so I won't.'

Lydia, aware again of the interested looks, the turn of bonneted heads, which followed the young man's departure, found her mind divided. She had looked forward to Hugh Hanley's arrival, simply as a stick with which to beat Mr Durrant's complacency: now she acknowledged that there was entertainment too, in his company, especially after so much Bath staidness, and he seemed to have done Phoebe good. Yet he made her uncomfortable. He was so far from awkwardness that he could adapt himself to any position, as a cat can curl itself tidily on the narrowest fence: she could not imagine finding anything he would disagree with, at least on the surface. Nor did he lack perception; and though it went against her nature to say so, Lydia felt he almost had too much of it: the effect was like a handshake held too long.

Phoebe's comment on the famous Hugh Hanley was predictable. A very different character from Mr Durrant—but thoroughly agreeable, she pronounced, as they crossed Pulteney Bridge. Lydia felt that the time had come for Phoebe not to find people so agreeable, even if it was not the time for her to say so.

'Do *you* think Mr Durrant is unhappy?' Phoebe asked her.

'Only about as much as he likes to be. Mr Durrant would not be himself if he could not be perennially at odds with the world. Being so hard to please is for him a sort of cultivation—he is a connoisseur of dissatisfaction.'

'Oh, I know that is how he behaves—even perhaps how he thinks. But I do wonder how he feels—deep down in his heart. There are such mysteries there—in everyone's heart, I mean; and the pity of it is they are so seldom brought to light.'

Lydia had a feeling it was no longer Mr Durrant they were talking about. Phoebe's eyes had misted again, and Lydia felt she was not seeing the view of the glittering river either. It was to be expected, of course, that she would keep sounding this melancholy note. It had been a sad business this morning, though for the best; and Lydia must look for everything that diversion and distraction could do, to prevent Phoebe's spirits relapsing. Here, tomorrow's picnic expedition must do much: not least as it would present Robert Allardyce before her—as contrast and example. Not necessarily as anything so crude as the natural alternative: it was to be hoped instead that Phoebe would now appreciate the ill-effects of haste, bear in mind her youth and inexperience, and be in no rush to the altar.

Although if Mr Allardyce *should* bring himself to a declaration, that would be a very good thing too; and Lydia could begin planning her packing with a feeling of satisfaction—of vindication—of a job well done: feelings not usually associated with intensity but that just now represented themselves to Lydia's mind as the most exquisite felicity.

'There's Mrs Vawser,' Phoebe said, extinguishing happy thoughts with admirable economy.

There, or here, she was, cooing at them from the

347

seat of an open carriage being driven by her husband. As he reined in the horses Lydia realised what sort of carriage it was.

'Well, and how do you like the barouche? Is it not the very thing? Such perfect weather for it—we have been on the most delightful drive up to Claverton Down. I said to Mr Vawser, "We must have a barouche—it is an absolute requirement with this weather—country expeditions are the very thing." You must be sadly in need of an airing, Miss Rae, walled up in Bath in such weather!'

'Oh, we are going on a country expedition tomorrow,' Phoebe said good-naturedly. 'Just to—'

'But how are you going? Have you a barouche? There will be no pleasure in it without a barouche, I assure you. And we were prodigious lucky to get this one. The livery-stable keeper had nothing else left—nothing fit to be seen in.'

'I think Mr Allardyce spoke of hired chaises,' Phoebe said, while Lydia groaned inside.

'Lord! I wish you joy of it, Miss Rae—stuffed up like that! A closed carriage!' Mrs Vawser stared and gasped as if they had proposed a pleasure-trip to a house of correction. 'I dare say you, Miss Templeton, will not mind it—you like being fugged up indoors with your books, after all—but it is a shocking pity for you, Miss Rae: youth and bloom locked up in a box! But never mind—you must come for a drive with *us* as soon as you are at liberty. Just say the word—you know where we are to be found. Now, promise you will: it will do you a great deal of good; and you will not be at the mercy of strange coachmen. Mr Vawser is an excellent driver, you know.'

'Say it myself,' uttered Mr Vawser, 'pretty good

348

hand at the ribbons.'

How shapely life is sometimes, thought Lydia. Her, her, her.

'Thank you, that is very kind of you,' Phoebe said placidly. 'I should not like to put you to any trouble—'

'Oh, my dear Miss Rae, I see you must get to know me better, if you suppose me the sort of person who sees a kindness as a trouble. My friends absolutely shake their heads over it. "Penelope," they say, "finds nothing a trouble." Now, mind, I consider it a promise.'

'Well,' Phoebe said, when the Vawsers had paraded on their way, 'one does not like to refuse absolutely. I dare say she is a well-meaning woman after all.'

Here was an aspect of Phoebe's character not to be changed by worries, distresses and love-problems; and even as she sighed, Lydia took heart from it, and concluded that she need not fear too much for the state of Phoebe's spirits. A girl who could find Penelope Vawser well-meaning could find good in anything.

CHAPTER TWENTY-THREE

Perfect weather—everyone agreed: a perfect day for the picnic—absolutely perfect. Such were the civilities that passed among the party as they climbed into the two carriages. It took Mr Durrant to point out the signal imperfection of the day, as they manoeuvred their steep, jolting way out of the town.

'It is too hot, and it will get hotter. Your housekeeper, Miss Allardyce, need not have gone to the trouble of roasting the chickens.'

Certainly the brilliance of the sky had a hard, enamel quality to it: the clouds were powerless fragments, and the trees, unstirred by breeze, might have been paintings on glass. Lydia, in thinnest muslin, was already perspiring. It was high-pitched summer weather: the kind that would not relent, but only perish in a storm.

Perfection was missing too in the human element of the party, for Lydia at least. Mrs Allardyce had joined it at the last moment: though the fact that she was already dressed for an outing—frizzed, straw-bonneted, gloved, shawled and booted—suggested that the sudden decision had been contemplated at least for a couple of hours. She made much of the fact that she was breaking her habit of retirement—spoke of it, indeed, at such length as must have exhausted the interest of even the best-willed person; but along with her impatience Lydia found gratification. There was surely in this an implied compliment to Phoebe, which she hoped her friend would not be too modest to perceive. To realise in what regard she was held in Queen Square must do her good: for Lydia was anxious that Phoebe should not learn the wrong lesson from the affair of Mr Beck, and mistrust her own feelings altogether. Here, again, she relied on the attentions of Mr Allardyce; and a promising beginning was made, as Mrs Allardyce insisted on Phoebe and her son riding in the first carriage with her, and surrendered her daughter to the second, with a parting hint that she should not bore her companions by talking dry stuff all the way.

They were not the only party seeking the air and space of the country heights. Carriages of various kinds overtook them, or passed them going the other way, and Mr Durrant remarked on the glazed stares they met with.

'Curious, this vague hostility with which pleasure-trippers habitually greet each other—as if the very idea of other people taking it into their heads to do what you want to do is an affront.'

Juliet laughed. 'As the Frenchman said, the English take their pleasures sadly, after the fashion of their country.'

'Sully. Henri Quatre's minister,' Lydia supplied.

'Ah, one enjoys the *mot* so much better when one knows exactly who said it,' Mr Durrant said, with a little straight-faced nod in her direction. Lydia was determined not to blush, and the impulse to kick him was restrained by the consideration that he would probably find satisfaction in it. Juliet only smiled. She was looking very beautiful today: the fine-boned, regal cast of her features, which could by candlelight appear a little forbidding, was splendidly equal to the strong sunlight, and the heat scarcely seemed to trouble her. Lydia momentarily felt that if Juliet were not clever, sympathetic and congenial, she might dislike her very much.

'Oh, Mr Durrant, I quite forgot,' she said sweetly, 'we had the pleasure of seeing your nephew Mr Hanley yesterday, on the South Parade.'

He gave an explosive grunt.

'Mr Durrant will have told you, I'm sure, about Mr Hanley,' Lydia said to Juliet, 'or I should say

351

Cornet Hanley of the Tenth Light Dragoons.'

'Oh! yes,' Juliet said, exchanging a glance with Mr Durrant, 'I know about him.'

'And about his being in Bath, no doubt,' Lydia went on, with a feeling of having taken a sip of champagne and finding it flat. 'He has not called at Queen Square, I think? Ah: Mr Durrant, you are remiss: you must indeed make the introduction soon.'

'I do not see the necessity,' he said, looking out of the carriage window, and manifesting an unlikely interest in a five-barred gate. 'If I contracted the plague, I hope I should have more care for my friends than to go calling on them, and introducing it into their houses.'

'You are only making me more curious to meet him,' Juliet said, giving him a searching look.

'Oh! it will happen soon enough, no doubt,' Mr Durrant sighed gloomily, 'and when it does, no doubt like everyone else you will be charmed.'

'Well, we shall see. It will be an interesting experiment, Mr Durrant,' Juliet said, causing him to meet her eyes, 'as I do not generally set a high value on charm.'

Lydia was not sure whether she was at the top of the see-saw, or the bottom; but she was prevented from pursuing the question as the carriage slowed. The first had come to a halt: Mrs Allardyce had spotted the perfect place for them to disembark, ramble, and lay out their luncheon, as the servant who had been riding behind came hurrying back to inform them. They were at the top of a broad green slope, with a view of Widcombe below, and pleasant hills all about: but Lydia, handed down from the carriage by Mr Durrant, and feeling the heat swaddle her at once, feared that they were rather exposed, and could have wished there were more shade than was offered by the thin copse that stood at some distance down the slope, beyond a stretch of sheep-pasture. However, Mrs Allardyce was now commander of the expedition, and there was nothing for it but to troop after her, listen to her being strong-minded and incorrigible, and perhaps, if you were Lydia, reflect on what a fine target she would present for a marksman with a reliable gun and a sense of philanthropy.

Mrs Allardyce's servants, sensibly, and grumbling only with their looks, began conveying the picnic-things at once towards the shade of the trees; but there was no such unanimity of purpose in the party. Mrs Allardyce claimed Phoebe's arm, and directed her to the highest part of the hill with sweeping gestures—probably referring to the many people she was acquainted with at all points of the compass, who knew what she was like, and she didn't care if they did, because she spoke her mind, and so on. Mr Durrant was claimed by Juliet—or the other way round: Lydia could not be sure, though she kept an eye on them from a sense of detached disquiet. Detached, because of course it was his business alone: but she did hope, from ordinary compassion for both, that he was not driven to such provocation by Hugh Hanley as would cause him to throw himself at Juliet Allardyce. There would be much to regret in that: a friendship spoiled—dignity lost.

That was supposing, of course, that Juliet should refuse him; and Juliet was certainly no Phoebe, ready to fall in love at a moment's notice. Still, she had her own pressures to contend with—the

353

stifling influence of her mother: might she not in turn be driven to look favourably on Mr Durrant, who was, after all, a very eligible man? The thing was true, even if the phrase was detestable. Again, not her affair; but Lydia had a sense of a looming mistake—she seemed to breathe it in the humid air. There was no question of her addressing Mr Durrant on the matter. The interference would be keenly resented: he would consider that no true motive could lie behind it.

Lydia thought she might perhaps broach the question, quietly, with Juliet when they were alone; but she reminded herself that her duty lay with Phoebe: and here the disposition of the party seemed to promise well. Walking with Mr Allardyce, she hoped to draw him out on his intentions, as she had done at the dinner in Queen Square—perhaps even gently lead him towards that conclusion, to which his heart must already be inclining him. Yet she found conversation difficult at first: he was too sensible a man ever to be called *brooding*, but there was an abstraction about him, a certain smothered short tension in his replies, which she had not observed before. Seeing the sheen on his brow, she attributed it to the stupefying heat, and pitied him. Where ladies could resort to thin muslins and parasols, the prison of the gentleman's coat and waistcoat was inescapable. Spying a shepherd boy in loose shirt and straw hat, she remarked: 'Now, but for convention, you might be as comfortable as him.'

'Hm? Oh! yes,' he answered, with a bare glance. 'But the lad would surely trade places with me, given the chance, and exchange poverty for a little stiffness and discomfort.'

'Very true,' Lydia said, with a feeling as if the heat were affecting her perceptions too: this was like talking to Mr Beck.

'There—my mother would be pleased: I am being stuffy and sententious, so a political career surely beckons.'

She smiled: he was himself again, or nearly: coolness would do the rest. 'Speaking of convention, shall we consider the beauties of the view duly admired, and go into the shade?'

It was better under the trees, though the flickering of the intense sunlight through the leaves was more dazzling than pleasant. Her thoughts seemed to scatter and dance with it—thoughts of Phoebe, of Juliet and Mr Durrant and Hugh Hanley, of Mr Beck. Her companion had lapsed into silence again, and suddenly it occurred to her that he might have seen Mr Beck—that there might have been some dramatic encounter. She pictured Mr Beck arriving with a baleful flourish at Queen Square: *I come to congratulate my adversary. Sir, the field is yours. Let me say only this—the interference of Miss Templeton* . . . The thought was so horribly plausible that she found herself blurting out: 'Mr Beck—whom you know, of course—has left Bath, I think.'

'Oh, yes, I am aware of that,' he said, in a curious, bleached tone. Phoebe must have told him so, on the journey here: well, that was surely encouraging. 'Isn't it odd,' he said after another unrestful pause, 'the things one says unthinkingly—how they can be more revealing than the most considered utterance? Just now I spoke slightingly of politicians: yet how much of real feeling I find there! All the dullness of such a

355

life rises up before me. Yet it would gratify my mother: which does weigh, though not so much, candidly, as she likes to think. And then it is the road, of course, to advancement: to the juicy plums of places and pensions and sinecures. Whereas the diplomatic service will not make a man wealthy.'

'A consideration only if wealth is your object.'

He shrugged. 'I shall not be poor . . . but this is to take into account only my own wants, as a single man.'

Ah, Lydia thought, with quickened interest. 'If you were to marry, of course, your bride would know this, and accept it.'

'That is exactly my thought,' he said—frowning, yet appearing somehow heartened. 'What she must also be prepared for, however, is an unsettled sort of life: subject to the vagaries of war and governments, travelling and living abroad, accustoming herself to the ways of foreign countries. This is a good deal to ask.'

'Of a certain kind of woman, perhaps: but if she has an open, enquiring mind, and an eagerness for experience, I should call it rather an inducement than otherwise.'

'If that were so, then I should feel . . .' He glanced at her with lifted brow, then looked away. 'I should feel able to—to proceed without impediments of conscience. Now that sounds absurd,' he added, with a little laugh, 'but I hope you take my meaning.'

'I do; and I think I can assure you, Mr Allardyce, that you may certainly consider there are no such impediments in your way.'

His relief was visible—and so, Lydia felt, must have been her own. This was propitious indeed:

356

she dared to hope that her anxieties over Phoebe, and the low spirits that occasioned them, might soon be at an end; and in the circumspection and delicacy with which Mr Allardyce approached his question, she found her judgement confirmed. Mr Beck might have his good qualities, but surely here was a man to whom Phoebe's future could be confidently entrusted. He seemed about to say something more; but they were interrupted by a loud halloo from Mrs Allardyce, wanting to know why they were lurking there, and demanding that they come and get some air on the heights.

Leaving the copse and ascending the hill, she found a skittish breeze beginning to blow—earnest of an approaching thunderstorm, perhaps; but for now a blessing: and with this, and her own lightened heart, she had no objection to a further ramble, or even to having Mrs Allardyce instructively point out the best views to her.

'After all,' said Juliet, slipping her arm through Lydia's, and urging her to fall back a little, 'without Mama's help, you might just stare at the grass, and wonder what all the fuss is about.'

Lydia smiled. 'How is the war news lately?'

'Call it a state of armed truce, with hostilities likely to break out at any moment. Never mind: I shall stick out for victory as firmly as Mr Pitt, and without the three bottles of port a day.'

'I heard it was six.' Up ahead Mrs Allardyce had claimed her son's arm, and Mr Durrant, with his easy, long-legged stride, was accompanying Phoebe. 'You are set upon going abroad with your brother, then.'

'My dear Lydia, you should know that Mama talks of taking me to Tunbridge Wells next season.

357

Just the proper sort of people to be found there, it seems: genteel assemblies—promenades—the right company. Now can you doubt that I am set on going with my brother?'

'Tunbridge Wells is a spur to action indeed . . . I merely wondered if there were nothing here to hold you back.'

'Oh, I see nothing at present,' said Juliet: handsome, smiling, and impenetrable.

Lydia watched Mr Durrant, and trouble stirred in her again. Suppose he did have Juliet in view—not just as the nearest solution to his difficulty, but seriously? Surely not: yet she must do him the justice to admit that he was not a frivolous man when it came to the great issues of life: far from it. If his heart were taken—well, that could not be; but if his heart were in danger of being taken, then he might be heading for a disappointment, and that she would not wish to see. Yes, she had spoken to him of men needing the odd blow to their pride—but that was between them: they always talked so, and there was nothing in it. Again she felt the need to say something to him, and the impossibility of saying it.

I had better be careful, she told herself: my success as a chaperon is going to my head, and soon I shall be settling everyone's affairs for them, like the worst sort of meddlesome old maid. And then she suffered a momentary protest of the spirit: yes, other people's affairs, and what about my own? The protest seemed to echo back at her, as if from some great hollow vast as the valley below, yet horribly within. Even thinking of Heystead and her father could not quiet it. Only by sternly admonishing herself that she was turning into Penelope Vawser did she regain her composure.

Juliet pressed her arm. 'Fagging, isn't it?' she said, though she looked fresh enough. 'Country picnics always *sound* nicer than they are. I think we should just have the idea of them, and be pleased with it, and then not go. The only true pleasures are indoors, artificial, and untainted with healthiness. Which reminds me, Robert has tickets for us all to the Dress Ball on Monday. Will you come?'

'Certainly—that is, Phoebe and I. Mr Durrant I cannot answer for.'

'Oh, he is coming: I have already asked him.'

Just then the Allardyces' manservant came up to tell them that the picnic was laid out, and he was afraid in this weather it would soon spoil. Such an example of plain good sense could not go unchallenged by Mrs Allardyce, who loudly upbraided him for his nonsense, declared that a little heat brought out the savour in cold viands, and proposed that they walk as far as the village. But she was firmly overruled by Mr Allardyce, who observed that Miss Rae looked tired, that he certainly felt it, and that the food was there to be eaten.

'Very well—Lord, you see how he tyrannises me, Miss Rae! Here, I yield you to him. Juliet, help me with my shawl, it's all in a tangle. Jane did not set it on right. Time was when servants knew their business . . .'

Lydia walked back to the copse with Mr Durrant. She repressed the immediate urge to ask him how he liked his future mother-in-law, and remarked instead: 'I understand we shall see you at

359

the Dress Ball. I am glad—but I should warn you that Hugh Hanley spoke of going also.'

'Yes, I shouldn't wonder. Well, let him come. He may follow my trail all he likes: he will find no satisfaction at the end of it.' Before she could answer, or interpret his look, he went on: 'Well, I have had an interesting talk with your Miss Rae, and I salute you: your task cannot have been easy, for she is a thoroughly romantic creature.'

'Was she—was it Mr Beck she was talking of?'

'No, not at all, or not in so many words. But it is plain she is choke-full of sentiment, one way and another: a girl who must always be falling in or falling out of love. One meets many such.'

'I see. Meaning she is not like, for example, Juliet Allardyce.'

'She is not at all like Juliet Allardyce,' he replied calmly. 'But I was about to salute you again: for in spite of all that, she does have a modicum of sense too, and at the risk of making you excessively pleased with yourself, I conclude that you put it there.'

Though she was pleased, she would not show it: and fairness to Phoebe made her say: 'I have always known she had plenty of sense. I have done nothing except, perhaps, to encourage her greater reliance on it. But yes, her feelings are very susceptible: all the more reason to have a care about where they may lead her.' The ground at the foot of the slope was uneven with old dried cart-tracks, and she chose her words as carefully as her steps. 'To be in love with love—that is a dangerous state indeed. I can hardly think of a more dangerous one—unless it be a determination, from whatever motive, to will oneself into being in love,

360

in the absence of any true feeling.'

He gave her a flat, puzzled stare. 'What? No one can do that. Either the feeling is there, or it isn't.'

Something—inattention—a struggle to think of an answer—made her clumsy: her foot jarringly struck a ridge of sun-baked earth, and she would have fallen if Mr Durrant had not caught her and held her up.

'Thank you. And this is before we get to the Madeira . . .' She winced in pain.

'You have hurt yourself. Here, let me carry you—'

'Certainly not,' she said, laughing distressfully. 'It would look ridiculous. Besides, it is not very bad—just a little jolted.'

'Set it down very slowly and gently,' he said, still holding her, 'just a little weight at first. That's well. One can never be too careful. Even a sprain . . . Does that hurt?'

'No,' she said, with almost complete truth, taking a step and then another. 'No, it's nothing. Not that I shall refuse the Madeira.'

He watched her carefully, released her at last, and shook his head, wryly smiling. 'How like you to consider that it would look ridiculous. What would you do if you had to be rescued from a fire?'

'Put on a veil and resign myself to mortification. What were we talking of?'

'Impossibilities. Ah, they have put out chairs. Sit down at once, and if Mrs Allardyce proposes another exploration, ignore her. You will not be able to dance at the Dress Ball otherwise, which would be a great shame.'

'Would it? Do you mean, Mr Durrant, you have set your heart upon my granting you the first pair of country-dances?'

'No: I mean that you will have to sit by the wall all evening, and be an object of general pity.'

Well, this was the kind of answer she felt at home with, at any rate: there was a reassurance of normality in it, like the diminishing twinges in her foot as they entered the copse, where welcome bottles were being uncorked. Welcome, too, was the sight of Mr Allardyce helping Phoebe to a seat in the deepest shade, and plying her with the best cuts of cold meat: likewise the faint metallic tang in the breeze, and stealthy mustering of cloud, which told of the storm coming: and even Mrs Allardyce could not for long oppose her stupidity to her son's simple declaration that after their luncheon they should go home.

If there was less satisfaction to be found in Juliet's inviting Mr Durrant to the seat beside her—knowing, or divining from what she had said today, that Juliet's affections were really not engaged—still it must be borne. He was, after all, a difficult man to help. It was a curious fact, Lydia reflected, that a person could be intelligent, cultivated, independent of mind even to the point of stubbornness—and yet still blind to the direction of their true interests, and intent on following a path where they must stumble and come to grief. She could almost have cursed Hugh Hanley for the perilously false position in which he had placed his uncle; and resolved that at the Dress Ball she would find a way of warning Mr Durrant of his danger.

This was the voice of disinterested benevolence—much more to be listened to than the selfish cry that had rung through her a few minutes ago. A glass of wine—well, two—the manservant was so prompt to refill—and she was soon picturing a pleasant return to Heystead, and her modestly admitting to her father that in Bath she had indeed bestowed Phoebe Rae's hand on the most suitable of gentlemen, and had prevented Mr Durrant from making a terrible mistake into the bargain. Add to that the winning of her wager, and there was so much prospective contentment that the first rumble of thunder sounded to her merely like the beginning of one of Mr Haydn's symphonies, with a great deal of enjoyable harmony to follow.

CHAPTER TWENTY-FOUR

It was long since Lydia had been excited by the prospect of a ball—the days of girlhood, when the prospect of a few hours in the Assembly Rooms of Grantham or Stamford, with a rather languid band, a smell of chalk, and a glass of tepid cordial at the interval, was enough to set the pulses racing for a week beforehand. Even then, she liked to think, her excitement had not equalled that of her contemporaries: she could enter the hallowed doors with pleasure rather than transports, and could admire the couple leading off the dance without feeling they had reached the summit of human ambition. She was content to talk of the event for only a few days afterwards, rather than a fortnight; and she could never quite contain her surprise at hearing a girl who had visibly had a dismal evening, with few and stupid partners, torn lace, and a sick headache, declare that it had been a famous ball, and she could hardly wait for the next.

But excitement there had been, and it was curious to find a measure of it returning now, at the serene heights of thirty, as she and Phoebe entered the Bath Upper Rooms on Monday evening. There might be no smell of chalk, but it was likely to be a sedate enough entertainment— no stronger stimulation than tea, and a sharp conclusion to the entertainment at eleven o'clock, an hour at which she was usually beginning to feel lively. The reason must be simply that, like the Lincolnshire maidens of years past, she had great hopes of the evening. Not for herself—and what a saint, she thought, being a chaperon made you— but for Phoebe. In the glowing looks and eager chatter of her friend Lydia found her first satisfaction of the evening; and in the banishing of the last shade of trouble from her beautiful eyes, and the restoration of their brilliancy, she looked forward to her triumph.

And yes, here was Mr Allardyce in the Octagon Room punctually greeting them, his elegant slenderness perfectly attuned to cream breeches and pumps.

'Tolerably well filled for a subscription ball out of season—in fact, quite filled enough. In November there is often a sad squeeze. I have seen a lady have her headdress knocked askew in the crush, and snatch the feathers from the hair of the lady nearest her in a wild impulse of revenge. Will you come and see my mother? And indeed, do you suppose you have a choice?'

Grand in silver and gauze, Mrs Allardyce was

ensconced in the ballroom on the bench nearest the one reserved for peers, with Juliet at her side. Juliet, however, was quickly dispensed with: Phoebe was to take her place.

'I must have you by me for a little, Miss Rae: there is rather a mixed set here, I see, and I can point out to you just who is worth knowing and who is to be avoided. I shall surrender you in time for the dancing. My son, of course, engages you for the first pair.'

'Of course,' he said, with a slight bow. 'But if you intend playing the master of ceremonies, Mother, had you not better dispose of all the other couples in the room?'

'I should do it very well, if I chose. I would begin by ensuring that that young man by the door should *not* be favoured with any introductions: his coat is light grey: corbeau is the only colour for dress. Ah, but here is Mr Durrant—how do you do, sir?—you see I am planning the disposition of the first dances, and you I am sure will claim my daughter for the first pair.'

'With pleasure—if the lady herself is agreeable,' said Mr Durrant, who had a peculiarly noiseless tread for such a tall man, and had given Lydia a slight start when he appeared at her side.

Juliet smiled. 'Certainly.'

'Oh, what has a lady to do at a ball, but be agreeable?' chuckled Mrs Allardyce, obviously in what she considered fine fettle. 'Now as to the second pair—'

'As to the second pair, I consider they should be at our own disposal, as you have dictated quite enough,' Mr Allardyce said, with a shake of his head. 'Miss Templeton, I hope I may claim the honour.'

'Thank you.' She did not care to be pitied, but this was done with his usual delicacy.

Mrs Allardyce shrugged. 'Now, Miss Rae, was there ever such an undutiful son? I quite despair— oh, now look there—there is a thoroughly elegant young man. Everything he should be—quite a reproach to that creature in grey. I detect the London mode. I wonder who he is . . .'

Mr Durrant, turning, announced bleakly: 'My nephew, ma'am. Mr Hugh Hanley. Never fear, you shall have an introduction: he will see to that.'

Hugh Hanley was immediately amongst them, and Mr Durrant was making the introductions, with the air of a judge reading out the names of the condemned. Mrs Allardyce was much impressed: though it would have required only the superfine coat and marcella waistcoat, with nobody inside them, to achieve that, even without his ease of manner and address. He spared no one his compliments—but it was on Juliet that his eye lit with real interest; and he took advantage of a moment when Mrs Allardyce was pointing out the instructive sight of a demi-train at least a year out of fashion, to ask with a bow: 'Miss Allardyce, I cannot doubt that the first pair of dances has already been secured, but may I venture to hope for the second?'

As she inclined her head Juliet seemed to flash a questioning glance at Mr Durrant; but he was now performing his unrivalled imitation of a graven image, and did not leave off until roused by the tuning of the violins.

Lydia would have been content to sit out the first pair of dances, and enjoy the liberty of observing her twin anxieties—Phoebe being led out by Mr Allardyce, and Mr Durrant leading out Juliet—and mentally urging on the one, and cautioning the other. But Hugh Hanley insisted on her hand.

'Really, you need not trouble, Mr Hanley: at my time of life all I ask is a seat near the fire and a rubber of penny whist.'

'If you really meant that, Miss Templeton, I should be concerned. I should not expect you to realise that you are as handsome as any woman in the room—that would be to fly to the other extreme of vanity—but beware of thinking such things, for one is apt to start believing them. And so, that is the family, is it? Well: Mrs Allardyce I fancy is a vain woman, who presents as plain-speaking what is actually a good deal of malice and meddling; and the gentleman is too habitually good-natured to restrain her.'

Lydia could not contradict this, nor even disapprove it. 'And Miss Allardyce?'

'Oh, really, Miss Templeton,' he said, with his most decorous smile, 'I could not presume to pronounce on a person's character after so short an acquaintance.'

It was curious to see the glances of speculation and envy directed at her dancing with Hugh Hanley, and consider how little they were merited—how little she cared for him as a man— how little she trusted him: though she doubted there was much actual mischief he could do, considering the characters of both Mr Durrant and Juliet. The only real evil she could foresee, indeed, was that in trying to dissuade his uncle from his pursuit of a bride, he would have the opposite effect. It was a relief to turn from him, and the tangle of thoughts he occasioned, to the solid virtues of Mr Allardyce, coming to claim her for the second pair of dances.

He seemed in high spirits. 'Now, Miss Templeton, how do you like your dancing talk? Solemn? Or shall we try idiocy instead—remark on what a very genteel assembly it is—height of elegance—nothing wanting—superlative dancing—many fine dresses—distinguished company—'

'Stop,' she said, laughing, 'this is too fast. Such remarks are meant to last the whole evening—there will be nothing left for you to say later.'

'Oh, I shall think of something,' he said, relinquishing her hand as they took their positions in the set.

'Solemn, or idiotic?'

For a moment she thought he had not heard her: but then he bowed and said: 'You alone must be the judge of that.'

Though thunder and rain had left a cool washed day, candles and bodies had soon rendered the ballroom warm and stuffy, and Lydia was glad to be free of the exertion of the third dances, ply her fan, and take a turn about the room. Passing near Mrs Allardyce's bench, she saw no sign of her being abashed: instead she was holding forth to two other matrons, in a voice loud enough to be heard over the orchestra.

' . . . Strictly it is not to be spoken of yet—but just between us, I may say that the engagement is all but a settled thing. An excellent match—I have favoured it from the beginning: I will not mention the fortune, but I can say it is handsome—very handsome. But I can say no more . . .'

This was interesting: she looked about for Mr Allardyce, wondering if he was in hearing, and what he would think of it; but he was right at the other end of the room, talking to some other acquaintance, of which he doubtless had many in Bath. Phoebe, she saw, was dancing with Hugh Hanley, and coming in for the jealous stares: doubly jealous, for they were unquestionably the best-looking couple in the room. Juliet was sitting out, but not unattended: Mr Durrant was seated closely at her side, their heads were close together, and he was nodding, with a sort of rapid decision, at something she was saying.

Lydia closed her fan so sharply that she caught the tip of her forefinger in it, and uttered a curse quite unsuited to a Bath assembly. She was inclined to repeat it when she saw, coming towards her, the Vawsers: he in a tightness of breeches scarcely to be contemplated on a full stomach, she in a filmy costume that included laced sandals and a plumed turban, as if an ancient Greek poetess had joined the circus. But Lydia was spared the infliction of vivacious greetings. Plainly something had happened. The only change in Mr Vawser was that he looked stupidly uncomfortable, instead of comfortably stupid; but Mrs Vawser had on her apocalyptic face, and passed by like a procession, seeing nothing. The fact that they were still arm in arm suggested that this was not a renewal of the grand tragedy—that Mr Vawser had not fallen prey again to the charms of a woman in an unlikely profession; probably it was a tragedy of a lesser sort—a slighting word, or an imagined one: perhaps a chipped fingernail. Still, there was sufficient unhappiness on view to make it a

369

cheering sight nonetheless, like a glimpse of a robin on the windowsill.

Lydia had wandered close to the dais, and was peering up at one of the musicians' scores, and wondering who had done such beautiful copying, when Mr Allardyce appeared at her side.

'Miss Templeton, this will never do. They are about to begin again—you may tell it by the way the second violinist starts scratching himself—and you, I believe, are unengaged.'

'Oh! yes, but quite happy to be so, sir.' She looked over for Phoebe, but could not see her in the milling crowd. 'What of Miss Rae—is she unengaged?' She saw a momentary embarrassment in his face at her smile, and understood. To dance repeatedly with the same partner, at so public an event as a Bath Dress Ball, was such an obvious avowal as would be talked about—as would be the subject, indeed, of definite conclusions. But the time for this discretion, she felt, was past. 'Mr Allardyce, I hope we are in a position from which I may speak frankly. If you are concerned with the matter of *appearance* . . .'

He nodded ruefully. 'I confess I am. A miserable stiff-necked sort of confession, but there it is.'

'No: I honour you for it. But please believe me when I say—well, I go further than I should, perhaps: but I can assure you, there is that degree of understanding—of warmth—of readiness— which renders this concern unnecessary.'

He blinked at her, breathing rather fast: then gave a short, rattling laugh of relief. 'Thank you— Miss Templeton, thank you for your frankness. I— well, I was never more glad of anything. And now they *are* beginning—and I cannot see Miss Rae—

370

and so there is nothing to prevent your dancing with me.'

She took his proffered hand, and joined the set: very happy in their understanding, and only a little doubtful that this delicacy might still retard him from the avowal that, as she had tried to convey to him, needed only to be made. That would be too bad. It was not that he had a rival now: Mr Beck was gone; but with all due respect to Phoebe, Lydia conceived that a girl who could fall in love with two men, could very easily fall in love with a third, if the suit of neither came to a happy issue.

Mr Durrant and Juliet were partners in the dance also—Phoebe, Lydia saw now, had been claimed again by Mrs Allardyce—and in their crossing, Lydia found Mr Durrant giving her such a searching look—unpleasantly searching—that she was impatient for it to be over, so that she might ask him what he meant by it. Of course she must first detach him from Juliet: but opportunity favoured her; as soon as the dance was concluded, Mrs Allardyce called Juliet over to do something trivial and demeaning for her, and with softer accents demanded her son's presence too. Lydia marked the deep bow with which Mr Durrant surrendered his partner, and then drew near.

'Oh! there you are,' he said, glancing down at her. 'I thought you looked as if you wanted to tax me with something. I don't suppose it's tea yet, is it?' He shuddered. 'Tea. Better than nothing is all one can say.'

'No, *you* looked at *me* as if— Well, never mind. Now you will deny it. This is the privilege of men, to give looks, often thoroughly unpleasant ones— yet to affect to believe them a mere nonsensical preoccupation of women, who are naturally always over-sensitive to such things.'

'Now I know you want to tax me with something. When a woman begins fulminating against men in the abstract, it usually means one particular man has annoyed her—or has failed to pander to her vanity, which amounts to the same thing.'

'Oh, please, Mr Durrant, do not squander these pretty compliments to the sex on me: save them for Miss Allardyce: but be aware that she also has a mind, and may not reward them with the requisite giggle.'

'I know she has a mind: and she never giggles,' he said, gazing with fathomless disgust at a blameless old gentleman going into the card-room. 'What's this? Has Hugh been talking to you? God knows he has been hard on my trail tonight, and Juliet's too.'

Lydia chose not to notice, or dislike, that 'Juliet': her aim was above such things. 'Yes, of course Hugh has been talking to me—he talks to everyone: it is like his job.'

'It's magnificent in a way, isn't it?' Mr Durrant murmured, with rapt distaste. 'The yawning servant who opens the door—the old lady he makes way for in the street—he makes sure they all remember him, as deedily as if he hopes for something from their will. When you or I get out of bed in the morning, our first thought—if we have one—is compounded of dryness in the mouth, and mild dread of the coming day; but Hugh's is "I am that delightful young man! The world requires me!"' Mr Durrant drew a deep breath. 'I'm sorry—what were we talking of?'

She hesitated. 'Something you will probably not

372

like—something I wish could come from someone else; because from *me*, you will suspect it. Could you not imagine that, say, Dr Templeton says this to you—that I am my father?'

'The relative absence of whisker detracts from the impression—but go on.'

'Does it not occur to you,' she pursued, trying to ignore this, 'that Hugh must now be sufficiently aware of the seriousness of your displeasure—even of your consequent intention, however distant its fulfilment: and that so much of your work has been done, as must make it a pity—even a folly—to hurry it through to a hasty conclusion?'

He eyed her narrowly. 'Is this about our wager? Do you consider your fifty pounds in danger?'

'I do not care for the fifty pounds. The dangers I see are much more important—more real. The dangers arising from your flirtation with Miss Allardyce—'

'Flirtation?' He snorted. 'I have never flirted in my life.'

'Well, the apparent intimacy, then. If Hugh goads you to increase it, think of the potential for misunderstanding, painful misunderstanding, on either side. This would be a sad result: and a sad confirmation of Hugh's power to make mischief—the very thing you wanted to undo.'

Listening attentively, eyes averted, Mr Durrant nodded at last. 'Yes . . . yes, that did sound tolerably like your father. Of course, the fact remains that it isn't him speaking: it is you. Now, wrong-headed of him it may be, but Dr Templeton does genuinely care for my welfare.'

'And you suppose I do not,' she said angrily. 'Too spoiled and selfish, perhaps. Thank you,

373

Mr Durrant, you have exceeded yourself in compliment.'

'I meant no derogation of you: only an observation. But I do thank you, Miss Templeton, for your thoughts; and I can assure you, in return, that I know very well what I am about.'

'But does Miss Allardyce know?'

He showed his teeth. 'That she must answer for herself. But your taking such a strong interest in my private affairs emboldens me to make a like return. You have elected to give me a warning— and I can only say, look to yourself, Miss Templeton.'

'I don't understand you.'

'I should hope so—for if you are aware of what is going on, and even encouraging it, you are placed in an unflattering light indeed. But I shall do you the justice of believing your sincerity in this, as I could not in my own case. And I repeat, look to yourself: for I fear Mr Allardyce's attentions grow particular.'

She stared at him in bafflement. 'Mr Allardyce's attentions—yes, to Phoebe, quite so, but there is nothing in that—'

'Not to Phoebe. Mr Allardyce's attentions to *you*.'

Lydia stood frozen; and when he touched her elbow to give a little room to a lady passing, she shook him off sharply. At first there was only this cold, drenching anger. Doubtless he was put out by what she had said, and was trying to give her the retort—but to snatch at *this*, something at once so shabby and ridiculous . . . After a few moments it was the ridiculous aspect that stood forth to her, and she wanted to laugh, if without pleasure.

Really he was not good at this: he was pitiably out of his depth. She felt a sort of shame for him: he had often been vexing—never contemptible; and he was not the man she had thought him, if he could stoop to such littleness of malice.

'If this suggestion is the fruit of observation, Mr Durrant, I can only call it observation very ill-employed. It is a warning, indeed, but a warning against self-opinion. You can have drawn such a conclusion only from a belief that whatever notion enters your head must be right, no matter how contradictory the evidence. And I am putting the kindest construction possible on what I am otherwise inclined to regard as an insult.'

'Insult? To whom? I certainly mean no insult to you. As to the evidence, it is there to be seen—has been for some days. Mr Allardyce seems strongly inclining to you: he seeks you out, he invites tête-à-têtes, and altogether there is an earnestness, a significance—'

'Now, Mr Durrant,' she said, unable to forbear a rueful smile, 'here is the unhappy result of a little knowledge being grossly misinterpreted. It is like the blind man feeling the elephant's tail. Oh, dear! I hardly know what to say now. To give you the right interpretation would be to break a confidence, which, as yet, I do not feel able to do. But I fear I answered you rather too sharply, and am sorry for it. I can only say that your time in Bath has been ill spent if you have not learned the arts of gossip and innuendo, and realised that they must work upon some small foundation of truth.'

His expression was watchful, but calm. 'Have it as you please. I should be glad to be wrong, for everyone's sake.' He bowed and left her.

Watching him go, she had an urge to renew her own warning to him; for anyone who could make such a blind error was surely at grave risk of miscarrying in their own affairs. But the heat of anger had not quite cooled. Mr Allardyce's attentions to her . . . ! There she had been, the perfect chaperon, diligent on behalf of her charge—and there had been Mr Durrant thinking— Well, she had done with what he was thinking. It seemed likely to sow new seeds of discomfort, and she must thrust it from her mind.

Another dance was beginning: she saw Hugh Hanley smile his readiness to partner her, but she was too irritated to respond. A little more responsibility on that young man's part, a little less stubbornness on his uncle's, and much of this unpleasantness might have been avoided to begin with. She walked about, impatiently refusing several introductions; and there was nothing in the sight of the set to please her. Mr Durrant dancing again with Juliet—to be sure, let him; but no Phoebe—this would not do. Mrs Allardyce had gathered her to her side again. Very well in a way, but Phoebe did not come to a ball to be talked at by an old woman. Mr Allardyce should see that, and whisk her off. There was such a thing as being too delicate.

The first interval coming, and the heat worse, she went out to the Octagon Room in search of a little air; and finding the outer door standing open for late arrivals, stood there for some time looking out at the wedge of starred sky, drinking the breeze, and politely rebuffing several hints that she would catch a chill or worse from the rheums of the night air. It was no chill she felt, but a certain

376

oppression that no amount of freshness could relieve: it proceeded from a place in her own mind, which very unusually for her she was reluctant to examine.

'Lydia! Oh, Lydia, there you are.'

Phoebe: high-coloured, excited—perhaps flustered.

'What is the matter?'

'Oh, nothing—only I wondered where you had gone to. Mr Allardyce did too. I was going to look for you. But then—oh, Lydia, I must tell you—I do not think I can tell anyone else. I said I would go and look in the cloakroom—and Mrs Allardyce said that I was to wait for her there, as my hair was coming down a little and she would help me with it, which was excessively kind in her, was it not? But never mind—I had just entered the cloakroom, and I saw you were not there—I thought there was nobody there, but I heard voices, and I recognised Miss Allardyce's, and then Mr Durrant's. Oh, this was shocking of me, but I could not help it: I was still behind the door, and they were at the far corner of the room, and I just put my head round. It was the tone of their voices that made me curious—and I saw Mr Durrant bending very low over Miss Allardyce's hand, and kissing it. Yes! It was so very surprising—and affecting too—the way he did it. And he said—I heard him say—I know it was shocking of me to listen: "I am glad—so glad to have spoken." Those were his words—and he thanked her—oh, that was affecting too—the way he thanked her. And then he straightened up, and I thought he must be about to see me, and I crept away. I felt very bad afterwards, but I couldn't help it; and I came away

377

to find you. Those were his words: "I am glad—so glad to have spoken." Oh, I know it is none of my affair, but what do you think? Is it not—do you suppose there is an understanding?'

Lydia found her voice. 'What did Miss Allardyce say?'

'Nothing—nothing that I heard. She smiled. She was a little pale perhaps—it is hard to say. Oh, Lydia'—Phoebe's eyes anxiously searched her face—'do you think very badly of me? I know I ought to have come away at once, and I *nearly* did.'

'There can be few greater temptations than eavesdropping, but there are many worse ones,' Lydia said, gathering herself, and patting Phoebe's hand. 'I believe—I think you are quite right in saying, however, that you should not tell anyone else. The thing has a—a certain appearance, to be sure—but that is all we can say at the moment.'

'You are right, of course,' Phoebe said, trustful, but faintly disappointed. 'One should not draw conclusions.'

'One should certainly not draw conclusions,' Lydia breathed, as they turned back to the ballroom.

'But I only thought—*if* it were the case, what a very good thing it would be. Such a match as everyone must rejoice in—so suitable: for I am sure, besides being so clever, they are both discriminating in their tastes, and not anyone would do. And there seems besides a sort of—' Phoebe's eyes grew lamplike '—well, a sort of fitness in it. But indeed I must not talk of it any more.'

Certainly this was as much as Lydia's patience could bear; and she was glad to surrender Phoebe to Mrs Allardyce's possessiveness, and be as alone as she could be in the crowded ballroom.

One should not draw conclusions—and she struggled against doing so, with all the strength of aversion; but they would not be denied. The meaning of the scene—well, there was no doubting that it *had* meaning. Mr Durrant, as he said, did not flirt: whatever had taken place in the cloakroom was no nonsensical exchange, to be forgotten next day. Phoebe's conclusion seemed indeed the likeliest—an understanding . . . But there was another possibility: an avowal, a proposal refused, and the dignity of sense and maturity on both sides . . . Yet Lydia could not contemplate either of these conclusions without the wretchedest of feelings—feelings she could make no sense of for some time, as they resounded dully against Phoebe's words: *none of my affair.*

There was the trouble. The scene had come so soon after Lydia's well-meant advice to Mr Durrant that she could not help linking the two. If Mr Durrant, instead of seeing well-meant advice, had seen provoking interference, could that have made him press ahead in a mere spirit of perversity? It did no honour to his feelings for Juliet Allardyce if so. And yet she was an intelligent woman, who would surely have recognised the hollow nature of any such proposal, and treated it as it deserved: there would have been no earnest voices, no kissing of hands. And it was no use grasping at the hope that Phoebe might have been an unreliable witness: she was a notably clear-eyed observer. Interpretation, of course, was a different matter. But then it was all down to interpretation.

Yet supposing her words had actually served to confirm his true feelings—had hardened inclination into decision—was that so much to be regretted? Lydia stared blankly up at the pilasters and mouldings of the ballroom: found herself loathing their assured symmetry. No: but still it could not be approved: it was skewed, it was not right. There was a lack of rightness to the whole evening, and she felt she could hardly endure to get to the end of it. The last pair of dances before the interval was signalled. A glance showed Mrs Allardyce leading Phoebe up to her son: the sight could not please: Mr Allardyce should be doing that himself. To evade the pester of applications, she hurried to the card-room.

Normally this was a place that nothing short of escape from a hungry lion, or perhaps Mrs Vawser, could have induced her to enter; but just now there was balm in the dullness, the flitter of cardboard on baize, the somnolent absorption of the players. Incredible as it had always seemed to her, people came not only to play but to watch over games, and she was able to feign doing this, until a curtained alcove at the end of the room caught her attention. There were seats: there was retirement and silence: nothing could be better. Or rather, many things could be better, but they lay outside her scope. She sat in a kind of numbness of reflection, in which her excited thoughts on arriving at the ball figured rather mockingly; and when she raised her eyes, Mr Allardyce was before her.

'Miss Templeton. I thought I was aware of all your many talents, but here is another—finding the quietest and pleasantest spots.' Uninvited, he seated himself beside her, and nodded towards the card-tables. 'You are not waiting to join a game?'

'No, no. I was just—seeking a little quiet, as you say, sir. But the music is beginning—were you not engaged to dance with Miss Rae?'

'Oh, I am not one of your determined dancers. A few sets does for me. She is dancing with Mr Hanley, I think.'

'Now, this is not gallant,' she said, summoning a smile—somehow it came with difficulty. 'You must consider not only what suits you, but what suits Miss Rae.'

'Why, it suits Miss Rae to be dancing,' he said, smiling much more readily, and shrugging. 'That is all that youth requires of a ball. Enviable, too, in a way: but one would not really wish to be so easily pleased.'

Lydia looked away: she found his gaze fastened too constrictingly on hers. 'Mr Allardyce, I don't understand—I fear you are not in spirits. Has there been a—a quarrel, a misunderstanding of some sort?'

'I was never in better spirits. Dear me, how puppyish that sounds. As if I am about to slap my knees and guffaw at every remark. In truth, when I am in spirits I am a little nervous, which must account for any strangeness in my manner. But in truth again, that cannot wholly account for it—as you surely know. It is more than that. Miss Templeton—this may be hasty, tell me if so and I will be guided by you, but after what we said earlier I cannot believe it is—I must declare myself now.' He had taken her hand in his, which was slightly trembling. Lydia looked down in pure astonishment, as if she had found him stealing her purse. 'This is the moment when a man should

381

make fine speeches. I cannot. I have thought of them—run them over in my head. No good. One of them—' he breathed a laugh '—one of them included saying I am yours to command. Dear God, what a phrase. Yours to command—and yet it is true. Miss Templeton—Lydia—'

'Mr Allardyce,' she said, with a firmness she did not feel, pulling her hand away, 'this is—this is a curious joke indeed. If you are making a sort of rehearsal for what should be said to *another* party, then you ought to have said so from the beginning. Otherwise—otherwise I can only suppose that your good spirits have led you into a moment's absurdity. Now pray, let us return—'

'A joke? Lydia, I know it is my habit to speak lightly—perhaps even at such a moment as this you are deceived into supposing I am not in earnest. My fault perhaps. But I must—I *shall* convince you of my good faith. I do not even ask for a definite answer now—though I long to. The encouragement you have given me makes me bold enough for that: but out of very love for you, I ask only that you consider that love as yours. Accept that, and I will accept your answer, my dearest Lydia, whenever it may be. There—I have lapsed into a speech in spite of myself.' Tense, smiling, excited, he reached for her hand again. 'But you know this is not a moment's absurdity. You know—'

'Mr Allardyce, this is strange indeed,' she cried, withdrawing her hand, and even hitching her chair away from him, through an exertion of muscles she never knew she had. 'Too strange to be pleasant. You speak of the—the *encouragement* I have given you, as if it were something quite other than what it is: a very sincere urging to make your suit to Miss

382

Rae, as your chances of success are—'

'Oh! I see—here is the misunderstanding,' he said briskly. 'Though I had thought that matter clear enough between us by now. My dear Lydia, believe me, you should not consider Miss Rae at all in the light of a rival for my affections. That time, I hope, is past, and obviously so. I apologise, if you still have some uneasiness on that score. But it must have been plain to you for some time that my interest in Miss Rae—well, she is a charming girl, and I esteem her all the more as your friend, and I heartily wish her well—'

'Sir, you talk of things being obvious and plain, but they are not—not at all. Rival for your affections! I have not for a moment sought your affections—my only concern throughout has been for Miss Rae.'

'I know it, and I admire you all the more for it. Lydia—'

'Stop. This—this freak of yours is not amusing. It does no honour to me, and what is more important, it does no honour to your attachment to Miss Rae.'

'My attachment to Miss Rae—well, I see that is still the sticking-point. You are scrupulous: you need not be. My attachment to Miss Rae, if such it may be called, is a thing that might have been, not a thing that is, as she has surely become aware. I was much taken with her, when we first met in London—even began to fancy myself a little in love; but that closer acquaintance, which you were good enough, and wise enough, to promote, has revealed the limits of my esteem. At the same time, my admiration of *you*—who have acted your part with diligence and discretion, sacrificing all to the interests of your young charge, and yet revealing your superiority to her with every breath and word—oh, Lydia, that admiration is boundless. I cannot help it—I must ask that you accept the offer of my hand—'

'No—no, Mr Allardyce, I cannot think of any such thing. You are not yourself . . .' Yet she knew, with a scorching mortification, that this would not do. Robert Allardyce was not a man to say wild things: he was not a tippler or a joker. He was serious, intensely serious; and she was tied to a stake of miserable realisation. Phoebe: the pain she felt for Phoebe at this moment was only bearable in that she knew she must prepare to endure much more of it. Her only solvent was indignation.

'Lydia—Miss Templeton if you will—I won't press. But I know this cannot be an entire surprise to you, and I flatter myself that what I feel—'

'I have heard quite enough about your *feelings*, sir—enough to convince me that they are no more to be trusted than your conduct. I can only ask what you suppose Miss Rae's feelings to be, she having been so shockingly misled.'

'Miss Rae's feelings, I am sure, will not be such as to incommode her. I have surely made it clear to her, by tactful and respectful means, that I do not wish our association to develop in any more intimate direction; and *her* conduct has convinced me that I do her no great wrong, and that she suffers very little from the alteration.'

'Her conduct? Now I know you are not in your right mind. Miss Rae—'

'Is your friend, and you show all the generous loyalty to her that I expect of you. There is the

384

integrity, the singleness of mind that I have come to love—which a man must hope to find in a future wife—and which Miss Rae, for all her qualities, cannot be said to possess. She has shown herself very ready to be courted by anyone who asks: you have shown yourself a woman thoroughly deserving to be loved.'

'These compliments, Mr Allardyce, do nothing—nothing but make me more indignant on behalf of my friend. I can only presume you are referring to Mr Beck—yet it was no secret, and can be no surprise, that you were not Miss Rae's only admirer. It is ungentlemanly of you to cast such aspersions on her character.'

For the first time his ardent look cooled, and his jaw grew tight. 'If there were justice in such a charge, I hope I should acknowledge it. Certainly I knew that Mr Beck had hopes in that direction; and from what I began to observe, they seemed not unfounded. Miss Rae seemed much more inclined to him than to me—a fact that, by then, I could not positively regret, even if I could still deplore the inconstancy of mind it demonstrated. I confess I was a little surprised at his leaving Bath—abandoning a suit I had thought tolerably likely to succeed—but on further reflection, and further information, I considered it no great matter.'

'Information? You mean Miss Rae has spoken of this?'

'Not at all. Indeed I am uncertain what information *you* may possess—but never mind—we are speaking confidentially. I heard about her meeting Mr Beck alone, and secretly. It was all the confirmation I required to acquit myself of any lingering sense of obligation: my heart was as free

385

to dispose of as she surely considered hers. But I knew—I *know* where mine is fixed.'

'The event you refer to—yes, it happened once—some time ago. She freely confessed it, and was I believe entirely persuaded to it by Mr Beck. It was wrong of him, and I told him so—'

'You must be referring to a different event. More than once . . . Well, I am not surprised. Miss Rae met Mr Beck alone the day before he left Bath—or rather, the evening. They were observed in the coffee-room of the York by a friend of mine.'

Lydia knew she should speak, but could not. Her throat felt like a wound.

'The indecorum is much to be reprehended,' he went on, in a more relaxed tone, 'but you, in your kindness, will surely urge the heedlessness of youth in excuse. And yes, I accept that; as you will accept that I am surely justified in happily surrendering any claim upon Miss Rae. Certainly it would be absurd for her to pretend to any claim upon *me*.' As she did not speak he moved closer, his voice soft. 'Does this distress you? Really it should not. I think Miss Rae's affections are generally of a superficial, undeveloped kind; and there can be little pain where there is no deep feeling. Her conduct has not been blameless—but *you* have nothing with which to reproach yourself.'

Dear God, how mockingly untrue those words seemed to her! She had done nothing right since coming to Bath: she had involved everyone in misery. But the anguished silence in which she suffered these thoughts seemed to inspirit Mr Allardyce. She found her hand imprisoned again.

'There will be time enough to pursue these explanations, in which I am sure the conduct of everyone may at last be found excusable, and no harm done. For now all that matters is that you understand me—and the truth of my feeling. Let us begin again, my dear, my dearest Lydia—'

She wrenched herself away from him and rose, trembling, but fierce. One or two of the card-players raised their heads.

'These expressions are offensive to me, sir. You have no right to make them: this feeling of which you speak does not confer it: it is a feeling of which I entertained no idea until this moment; and though it may be customary at a time to declare oneself flattered, I must speak the truth, and tell you I am not. I have never considered you in any other light than as a suitor to Miss Rae, and as such held you in the proper degree of friendly esteem; but now I cannot even maintain that much regard for you, and as for returning your feeling, it is impossible. If you wish me to speak plainer than that, I will, but be assured you will not like it.'

He had risen too: but he did not draw near her. Mr Allardyce remained his precise and composed self, and bowed. But he was white and meagre-lipped, as if he stood in a freezing blast instead of the fug of the card-room.

'Then I humbly beg your pardon,' he said, bowing again. 'My feelings have misled me, and I shall not allude to this subject any more. Yet I must express my perplexity. I trust I am usually in command of my feelings—and if I am to doubt them, then I fear I must begin to doubt some other things. To doubt, for example, whether you have not after all set yourself to provoke these feelings: and to doubt your professions of friendship for Miss Rae. If, as you seem to contend, she remains in any way hopeful of a genuine attachment between her and myself, then I am sorry for it; but she must have had some encouragement for such a hope, and that encouragement has certainly not come from me. Altogether I must begin to doubt, Miss Templeton, the part you have played since coming to Bath. If this has been a game, then I congratulate you on your success in playing it; but allow me to suggest that it is not one of your more admirable accomplishments.'

She did not see him go. Some helpless childish impulse made her cover her eyes; and for some minutes she stayed so, staring into the dry, dancing blackness: unable to move, or even conceive its possibility.

It was one of the card-players at last who roused her: an old lady, gently bending over her and enquiring: 'My dear, are you quite well?' The simple touch of kindliness made her flinch, and muttering something she ran from the card-room.

In the ball-room the candles, the music, the tripping dancers assailed her like the distortions of nightmare. She did not know what to do. Go: she must go, now, but somehow she could not even see the door: and then there was Phoebe . . .

'Lydia?' It was Juliet, looking with concern into her face. 'Lydia, whatever is the matter? Are you ill?'

'Yes. Ill . . . yes, I am feeling rather sick.' Yes, sick—it was no lie—sick with her own misjudgements, with the apprehension of the past: still more of the future. 'Juliet, I must go home at once. Will you tell Phoebe? Tell her not to worry, and I—I . . .'

'Certainly I will tell her, and if I know Phoebe

she will insist on coming with you, as I would. Are you feverish? You should have a doctor if so. Send for Dr Yates at Cheap Street—'

'No, no, nothing so bad as that. If I could just get home—rest . . .'

'You shall, and you shall go in our carriage. No, I insist. Sit here. I shall have it brought round directly, and I shall fetch Phoebe to you. Do you dislike smelling-salts as much as I do? Very well. I shall only be a moment . . .'

Useless to protest: the bitter irony of leaving in the Allardyces' carriage weighed very little in the balance of wretchedness. Much heavier was the look of tender concern on Phoebe's face, as she joined her, took her arm, and declared that she certainly would not stay at the ball without her, and would give her a thorough dressing if she even dared to think it.

There was, thank heaven, no sign of Robert Allardyce; and they were able to make their departure during the general scramble and hubbub of the tea-interval, when it would be least noticed. Curious, Lydia thought: the things one continued to believe important, even at such a time as this. Arranging one's hair while the ship sank. Juliet, capable and uninquisitive, saw them into the carriage.

'It was dreadfully hot in there,' Phoebe said, as they set off. 'Do you suppose that's what it was? I have been wondering about the cutlets we had at dinner. I didn't take any, so—no, wait, I did have one, I changed my mind. The one thing that *can* be relied on in this life, as you are too kind to say. So it cannot have been the cutlets. I wonder—'

'Oh, Phoebe,' Lydia cried, bursting into tears, 'I

have something to tell you.' But the tears were so uncontrollable that the telling must wait; and she could only let them have their way, while Phoebe— so patiently, so kindly, so unbearably—held her hand.

CHAPTER TWENTY-FIVE

'Quiet and airy situation' was how the house in Sydney Place had been advertised. Quiet it certainly was that evening, as Lydia and Phoebe sat gazing at different parts of the swept fireplace; but to Lydia it felt no more airy than a tomb.

At the last—as she had dried her tears, as they seated themselves, as Phoebe calmly declared that whatever it was she had to tell, it could not be so very bad—Lydia had clutched at a little hope. According to Mr Allardyce—and she had no reason to doubt this—Phoebe had secretly met Mr Beck the night before he left. Perhaps something had been forged anew between them then—something that would make Mr Allardyce's feelings for her of no account. But it was a feeble hope, Lydia knew: for had she not been assiduous, ever since then, in directing Phoebe's vacillating feelings towards Mr Allardyce? And had she not, God help her, lately been congratulating herself on her success?

There was no varnish to be put upon it: no easy disguise or evasion that could be anything but a despicable lie, and would not bring worse trouble and pain in its wake. 'Phoebe,' she had begun, 'I have had a conversation this evening with

Mr Allardyce, which leads me to question whether we have not been a little mistaken about his intentions . . .' It would not do. 'Oh, Phoebe, *I* have been horribly mistaken. He is not—what I thought him. He has declared himself in love with me.'

So it had come out. Trying—though often failing—to keep her eyes fixed steadily on Phoebe's, Lydia told her everything that had passed between her and Mr Allardyce in the card-room. Everything in substance: the slighting manner in which he had spoken of Phoebe must be softened, in tenderness to her, though it was making him appear better than he was. If there was room for any feeling beside humiliation, mortification, hurt pride, and pity, it was admiration for the courage with which her friend listened to this narration. Her face revealed nothing but solemn, profound attention: only her hands betrayed her—wandering, plucking, twitching, as if they sought something unaccountably gone missing.

And then, the unrestful silence. Lydia bore it as long as she could; at last rose, went to trim a candle that was smoking, and said, her voice feeling as hoarse as if she had been speaking an hour to a crowd: 'Phoebe—I feel I have no right to ask you anything. But I do not want to give Mr Allardyce any more credence than he deserves; and so—what he said about your meeting Mr Beck again . . .'

'It is true,' Phoebe said, drawing a deep breath. 'I am sorry to have deceived you, but I knew it would be the last occasion. The meeting was of my proposing. I wanted—it sounds rather pathetic, but I wanted to say goodbye to him, and above all to wish him well. I'm sorry.'

'Phoebe, please, I have nothing with which to reproach you—'

'Oh, I think you should; but there was reproach enough, or regret, in the meeting itself. He was still very angry, and he was not kind. He spoke hurtfully to me. I cannot blame him—but I did feel it . . .' She looked down at her quivering hands. 'Well. I see now—I see I am sadly to blame. Yes. I have been at fault from the start—grievously at fault. It is one thing to be flattered by the attentions of a gentleman—but to receive the attentions of two, and be unable to choose between them—and to suppose that no evil can come from such a selfish, light-minded state of affairs—really it is no more than I deserve, to . . . to . . .'

To lose both of them, was what she could not say, and it pained Lydia to think it. 'Phoebe, you are being much too hard on yourself. You have been well-meaning throughout: there is no evil in having a susceptible heart. I know you can draw no comfort from this, but yours is the true generosity and candour that I fear Mr Allardyce lacks. I have been reviewing his behaviour—trying to see it from his point of view—and it still seems to me that it has not been above reproach. He should have said something . . .'

Phoebe shook her head. 'In truth I am not surprised—at least, not wholly taken by surprise. I have begun to feel, in my heart of hearts, that I am not good enough for him.'

'You are a great deal too good for him,' Lydia said hotly, with his last chill, lacerating remarks leaping again to her mind. 'This too I cannot expect you to feel now—but in time—'

'Dear Lydia, you keep thinking of me: and it is very kind, and I do not pretend that I am not a little—knocked back, and dazed, and wondering where on earth I am . . . But I can still be glad for *you*—gaining the love of so estimable a gentleman.'

'Glad for me? Oh, Phoebe, we are certainly not understanding each other. I am not in the least glad: I am angry: the only feeling I have towards Mr Allardyce is indignation. I do not at all value his regard, believe me.'

'Don't you? Yet you have always said—that is, you have always maintained that he is the most creditable man, and—'

'I was wrong,' Lydia cried hastily, 'wrong in my estimation—and if in that respect I have influenced your feelings, then I bitterly, oh so bitterly, regret it. But I supposed—I thought he gave every indication of being most warmly inclined to you, and from what I knew of him *then*, I believed it a very favourable connection.'

'You never gave me any advice that I did not ask for,' Phoebe said, with spectral gentleness. 'The only thing you did, I fear, was something you could not help. You outshone me.'

'Phoebe, I beg you to believe that I never set out to impress Mr Allardyce, to engage his interest or his attention in the slightest—'

'I know, Lydia: but you did not need to. You needed only to be yourself.'

Lydia roamed about the room—rather as Mr Durrant did, she thought. Well, his warning had been right: not that it could have made any difference if she had heeded it. 'Phoebe, I will not

393

hear you lower yourself in this fashion. All the blame must lie with Mr Allardyce, who must surely have known that I had no interest in him or anyone—that I am more than content in my single state. He must have seen this, if he had half the sense with which I credited him.' But then she was forced to admit to herself that Robert Allardyce was not an easy man to read: he might have been drawing all sorts of conclusions, coming to all sorts of decisions, that did not appear on the surface. There was something to be said, after all, for not being so guarded—for having at least some of Mr Beck's openness. The thought of Mr Beck made her mind throb even more acutely, and her pacings more frantic. To think with what satisfaction she had seen Mr Beck packed off, in perfect confidence that his departing shadow would be banished by the bright light of Mr Allardyce!

And what an ill role, indeed, she seemed to have played in Phoebe's life. Mr Allardyce's parting hints had been, no doubt, the reflexive cruelty of a disappointed man—not that they did him any sort of honour; but Lydia could see that to a hostile observer, or even a casual one, her conduct and its motives might appear in all the cold yellow light of envy, coquetry, and malicious interference. She hardly knew whether it made it better, or worse, to find Phoebe still refusing to think ill of her.

'I cannot quite blame Mr Allardyce,' Phoebe said slowly, her head bowed, 'because to do so I must abandon the warm regard I feel for him. Oh, I know I must do that in any case, now—that is, I must abandon any hope of reciprocation; and as I said, secretly I had begun to doubt it in any case.

But it is hard—it is rather a wrench—to turn my heart wholly against him.'

Lydia felt a swarm of arguments against that, but she batted them away. 'I know,' she said miserably. 'I know, Phoebe, and I wish it could be otherwise. I can find no good in this evening's work except the distant one—the one that I trust will come at last: the realisation that you were mistaken in him, as I was. Mistaken not in your feeling towards him—that was the honest impulse of the heart, and so never to be regretted—but in your estimate of what *he* was feeling: and I still contend that the mistake was entirely understandable, and that he played you false.'

Fine words, but as with most fine words there was a hollowness at the centre: the hollowness was the omission of her own part in the affair. With intolerable pride she had trusted in her superior judgement of Mr A and Mr B: with a pretence of objectivity, which would have been far less reprehensible if it had owned itself to be the mere operation of prejudice, she had directed Phoebe's sentiments towards them, dismissing the claims of one, advancing the claims of the other; and to an effect that, for all her friend's studied calmness of manner, must be injuring her present happiness, and might be endangering its future, where trust and proper self-esteem were concerned.

But Phoebe listened, and nodded, her eyes fixed on the still smoking candle as if there were prophecy in it; and then, stirring with a kind of slow shudder, said: 'I dare say you are right: but I do wonder, Lydia—can you tell me, for it is a question that truly puzzles me—how *can* one know what another person is feeling?'

Lydia sat down heavily, with an expressible weariness on her. 'I don't know, Phoebe. And I think I am the last person who should even hazard an opinion on the matter.'

'No, no. I trust you. Yes, I trust you all the more, because you have not concealed anything about—about tonight.' The sketch of a smile appeared on her face. 'Some people would have, you know. They would have made the best of it, just to save themselves trouble.'

Somehow this tribute seemed the worst part of the evening to Lydia: she could have wept again, but she was conscious of the fact that she had already fallen into an indulgence that Phoebe, dry-eyed, had denied herself. She tried to think: but could only say: 'I don't know. If we always knew, there would I dare say be a deal less misunderstanding in the world. All I can think is, that if a person feels something, they should say so, directly. It would not solve every difficulty, but it might prevent a good many difficulties from beginning. For my part, I have done with hints and clues and implications.' Weariness and heart-soreness, like too much wine, were making her excessive. 'Feel it, and say it, and act upon it, and the devil take everything else. "Let your yea be yea; and your nay, nay." That's all.'

It occurred to her, too late, that the biblical quotation might be taken amiss by Phoebe, steeped in the solemnities of the kirk. But Phoebe only smiled: she seemed already drawing away from the question, into some inner retreat where Lydia knew she could not follow.

'I think that is very sensible,' Phoebe said, rising. 'I'm sorry—you will think me very strange, Lydia,

396

but I really must go to bed. Convention should dictate a wakeful night, I know, but I must defy it and say I—I want only to sleep.'

Lydia watched her go with deep misgiving—longing to say something more, but doubting the power of any further words of hers to effect a remedy. Indeed her own way with words, her fluency and persuasiveness, had done so much to create this predicament that she felt tempted to take a vow of silence ever more. Life would be duller, but it would be safer.

A glass of wine could not ease her mind, but it did make her sit down and review her thoughts instead of having them fly headlong around her. Phoebe's apparent calm was not reassuring—far from it. The silly trifling miss that Lydia had pictured when Lady Eastmond had first proposed her as companion would not have been calm: there would have been screamings and swoonings, smelling salts and sofa-beatings, and presently a sharp retributory hatred of Mr Allardyce, or Lydia, or possibly both, with at length an airy, healthy unconcern and a declaration that she never cared for him anyway. But though she might have her little absurdities, Phoebe's was not a trifling nature. She felt deeply—Lydia would have said too deeply, if she had not come so lamentably to mistrust her own judgement.

Her feeling towards Mr Allardyce remained unfriendly. Now that she had sufficient composure and leisure to look back over their association, she was able to discern the warning signs of his waning interest in Phoebe, even if his waxing interest in herself appeared scarcely more plain and no less surprising. No: she could not have known; but it was a grim thought that Phoebe must be looking back over the same events, with a wretched consciousness of their meaning—and, surely, a creeping suspicion of Lydia's own motives that not even her generous nature could suppress. Nor did she suppose that Phoebe could soon arrive at her own, decidedly lowered opinion of that gentleman. He was not a villain: but he had displayed a priggishness in his disapproval of Phoebe's conduct, and a pettiness in his reaction to her own refusal, that could never restore the respect, still less the liking, she had entertained for him before.

But there was no consolation in this—it only demonstrated afresh her wrong judgement. And there was another memory of that evening, which set the seal on her state of despondent contrition: Mr Durrant, and Juliet. She winced at the thought of her own presumption in pressing advice on Mr Durrant; and whatever had gone on in the cloakroom, whatever had been the outcome of that evening for them, she could only feel that through her intervention the same curse lay upon it.

*   *   *

Phoebe's ashen look the next morning suggested that the sleep she had craved had refused to be summoned, and after a bite of breakfast she begged to be excused and returned to her room. Lydia, having drunk a good deal more wine before retiring, had purchased rest at the expense of a liverish headache, and was unequal to conversation even if they had been able to find any. Talk there must be—of what to do now, whether they should remain in Bath, and what should be reported to

Lady Eastmond—but the time was not yet. Lydia's one hope was that there would be no morning callers—a most reliable device for ensuring a swift knock at the door. She wished she could simply tell Mary to say 'not at home'—but a remnant of pride prevented her. Much as she longed to, she would not hide her head.

The callers were Mr and Mrs Vawser. Lydia was by now too resigned to the malevolence of Fate to be surprised.

'Well, Miss Templeton, and so here you are— quite snugly situated, I declare!' Mrs Vawser, her flow of spirits quite restored, subjected the drawing-room to a thorough scrutiny; and it seemed she was prevented from actually peering under the sofa only by tenderness for her hat, which was so profuse with ribbons, beads, pearls and feathers that it looked as if a large bird had expired in a sewing-box. 'Quite pleasant indeed— though for my part I should not care to be so close to the river, with its damps. We are quite free of that in Marlborough Buildings. But where is Miss Rae?'

'She is a little indisposed this morning.'

'Now I call that a pity! I was saying to Mr Vawser earlier how we positively owed a call to Miss Rae and Miss Templeton—that what with all the demands of acquaintance and company, we had neglected them shamefully. And now we are here, and no Miss Rae! Really it is too bad. We wanted to repeat our invitation to take her for a drive in the barouche—nay, I meant to insist on it. Such a blooming young creature will positively wilt if she is not afforded the means of an airing. I confess I thought her not absolutely in her best

399

looks last night. A pretty enough sort of occasion, was it not? One did not expect a *great* deal of fashion, but all the same there was very little to blush at. And we made *one* thoroughly delightful acquaintance. Mr Hugh Hanley—an officer of the Prince of Wales's Own. The very pink of the *ton*, but not in the least affected—you know I have a horror of affectation. An altogether charming young man—and what is scarcely to be believed, actually nephew to that dry old stick Mr Durrant!'

'Yes, I know of their relation, as I know Mr Hanley.'

'Oh! well, I dare say you would,' Mrs Vawser said, with a shrug. 'But such a difference between them! Mr Hanley so agreeable—so entertaining—whilst between ourselves, I find Mr Durrant's company so heavy I would almost go out of my way to avoid it, if it were consonant with politeness. Mr Vawser is quite as taken with the young man as I am—indeed they have so much in common one might almost suppose them brothers.'

'Twins,' offered Mr Vawser, putting his head over the parapet of his cravat. 'Her her her.'

'He dances excessively well, as one might expect—and again between ourselves, I cannot have been the only one to remark on Mr Durrant's taking the floor so often last night. Nothing *against* a man of his years doing so, to be sure—but with his stiff standoffish ways, it was rather a curious sight. One could not help but stare. Mr Vawser'—with a playful slap—'was rogue enough to suggest he was in liquor. Of course *you*, Miss Templeton, did not dance at all, which was much more sensible.'

Lydia did not trouble to correct her, nor to exert

400

herself beyond bare civility throughout the length of their call; which ended with Mrs Vawser insisting that Miss Rae be given her friendly message about the barouche. 'For I do not take no for an answer, Miss Templeton—all my friends will tell you so. "Penelope", they say, "is like a dog with a bone—an absolute dog with a bone."' Lydia, mentally bestowing on her guest a canine comparison of her own, promised that Phoebe would be told, and heard the door close upon them with a gloomy relief that lasted perhaps five minutes before the knocker resounded again.

It could have been much worse—it was Mr Durrant; but such was her weariness of spirit that she could only say: 'Oh, hullo. What do *you* want?'

'To refresh myself at the never-failing springs of your charm, of course. Aren't you going to invite me to sit down?'

'No, because you never do.'

'Never let it be said that I am predictable,' he grunted, taking a chair and hitching up one long leg. 'In truth, I came to ask after your health, and not in the usual unmeaning way of the phrase. I heard from Juliet last night that you had gone home feeling ill. A Dress Ball is certainly enough to turn me sick, but I had thought your stomach stronger. Are you recovered? What was it?'

So, it was still 'Juliet'. 'Nothing of consequence. I am better now. Tell me—have you called at Queen Square today?'

'Not yet. My next call. Why?'

There was a certain peculiar pleasure—if any feeling could be termed pleasure on such a joyless day—in knowing that he had come here first; but a little disappointment too, for she was anxious to

401

know what, if anything, was being said at the Allardyce house. Her hope was that Mr Allardyce would never speak of the matter, but there were difficulties in the way of that. The close friendship with the ladies of Sydney Place must necessarily be at an end now—neither she nor Phoebe nor Mr Allardyce himself could possibly maintain it even as a fiction—and Mrs Allardyce, who had been so plainly anticipating Phoebe as a daughter-in-law, would want to know why.

'I merely supposed that you would call there today, because— Oh, Lord, I don't know.' Sunlight was vigorous at the window, and she shielded her eyes from its hateful stabbing. 'I suppose nothing. I have done with supposing.'

Mr Durrant moved his chair closer to hers. 'Miss Templeton—you really are ill.'

'Do you mean you doubted it?'

'Well . . . I did wonder if the indisposition was of the tactical sort. Indeed I confess to a certain sense of—not guilt—responsibility. I fear *I* may have spoiled your evening, with what I said to you about Allardyce. It was ill-considered. It was the result of one of those peculiar feelings, which may be uncannily accurate, or else mere gammon. But in either case, I should have reminded myself that you surely know perfectly well what you are about.'

She raised her eyes to his. 'As you do?'

'I hope I do,' he said, after an instant's hesitation.

'Well—it was ill-considered, certainly,' she said looking away: she was too raw for any touch of sympathy, and her inward flinching made her curt. 'But I didn't leave because of that. I hope I am not so weak.'

402

'I'm sure you are not. Where's Miss Rae? Is she indisposed too?'

'Yes—that is, a little. Mr Durrant, I fear I am rather indifferent company today. The Vawsers have been here, and—'

'Good God, after that you should be prostrate, not indisposed. I'll leave you. Try a glass of port.'

'Port—at this hour?'

'Yes, why not? We should not let the clock dictate to us: we invented it, after all, not the other way around. I have a very sharp way with my clocks, believe me.' He rose, stood irresolute a moment. 'I'm sorry you did not have a pleasant evening.'

She waved a weak hand. 'Thank you. But I hope you did, Mr Durrant.'

She felt him studying her—looking for irony, no doubt; but she was herself mildly surprised to find there was none. That too, it seemed, was exhausted.

'It was . . . it was all I could have wished,' he said, in a tone that seemed forcibly stripped of expression; and, with a brief good day, left her.

*   *   *

The afternoon brought two notes. One was from Juliet Allardyce, and was addressed to both Lydia and Phoebe.

*My dear friends—I thought I should tell you
that my brother leaves Bath for London
tomorrow morning by the earliest coach.
Sudden and urgent business, he says—I can get
no more out of him tho' it seems to me sudden*

403

and urgent to an almost impossible degree—
and he knows or will say nothing of his possible
return. I have made no preparations to leave
until September and so remain here—rather
perplexed—all the more so as I have urged him
to come to you and make his goodbyes—but he
pleads lack of time and asks me to present his
compliments and apologies! What think you?
And is it fair that our sex is always called the
inconsistent one? Mama's mood by the by is
even more singular—something brews—but of
course she will tell me nothing about that.
Hoping, my dear Lydia, that you find yourself
recovered—yours with all good wishes & c.,
Juliet

So, Mr Allardyce was leaving the scene at once!
Was this delicacy, or embarrassment—the wish to
avoid inflicting discomfort, or the wish to avoid
experiencing it? Whatever the case, avoidance was
the essence of it; and Lydia detected a pique that
did not increase her respect for him. She read the
note alone, but it must be communicated to
Phoebe, though its effect would surely be further
to depress her spirits: here was the man she had
believed warmly attached to her, taking off without
a word to her face; and it was with a heavy heart,
when Phoebe came down at last to dinner, that
Lydia placed the note in her hand.

'I suppose he could hardly stay,' was Phoebe's
comment at last. 'It would be too painful for him.'

Lydia hardly knew which was the more
distressing: Phoebe's tone, still of a terrible stifled
evenness, or the substance of her remark. She was
still pitying Robert Allardyce—and pitying him for

his unrequited love. This was intolerable. Lydia had been striving, during the tortuous reflections of today, to find some sympathy for him—here, after all, was a man making the most profound of avowals, and being rebuffed in the bluntest terms; but it was no good. Indignant loyalty to her injured friend would not allow it; and she had had, besides, no consciousness of being loved. He had merely presented her with the evidence of it, like an amatory warrant, and gone into a pet when she refused to accept it.

No such robustness of feeling, alas, could be detected in Phoebe, who was a quiet and distracted companion at dinner. Lydia had debated whether to tell her about the second note, but now she was convinced that reticence was the best course.

It was from Mrs Allardyce.

Dear Miss Templeton: Have the goodness to wait upon me at Queen Square tomorrow morning at your earliest convenience. I do not require a reply, only your presence.
Catherine Allardyce

'Well, Miss Templeton, well? What have you to say? I look to you, you know, for an explanation— a thorough explanation. Oh, sit down, sit down—I don't stand on ceremony: that's not my way.'

'I would gladly sit down, ma'am, but your dog is in the chair.'

'Lord, what a fuss! Shoo him away: he won't hurt you.'

The creature looked as if it wanted to—though if it did, Lydia had her response ready, in that she had already chosen which window she was going to throw it out of. But after some more snarling, the pug-dog waddled off, and Lydia was able to sit down in the limited comfort afforded by visible hairs and probable fleas.

'Now. First of all, no doubt, I should apologise for my summoning you here in such a fashion—but I shan't: the matter is too important. There is no shilly-shally about *me*, at such a time as this, and I don't care who knows it.' Mrs Allardyce was as carefully dressed, as grandly enthroned as ever, but there was a tautness about her lips, a glitter in her unkind pretty eyes, that proclaimed her ill at ease. '*Do* you know that my son left for London at first light this morning, with no hint of his possible return?'

Lydia inclined her head. 'Miss Allardyce was good enough to write me the news.'

'Oh! Juliet—we are not talking of Juliet. It is my son that concerns me—my son who has astonished me, disturbed me, by this unaccountable behaviour. Well, do *you* not think it so?'

'Mr Allardyce is a man of affairs, and as such may surely be required to make such sudden removals,' Lydia answered, with the coolness of mere recital; and she did feel cool, oddly enough: quite cool. 'Beyond that, ma'am, I can really say nothing: my acquaintance with him is not such as—'

'Nonsense! Miss Templeton, do not trifle with me. Those who try it come away with their fingers mightily burned, believe me: that's the way I am. Something has happened to make him act so, and I want to know *what*.'

'I dare say—but I do not see, ma'am, why you should ask me.'

'Because, Miss Templeton, I challenged him.

Others might not, but I did: that's my way: I spoke up. When he announced this extraordinary decision yesterday, and actually began his packing, I faced him: I demanded to know *why* he was going, just when everything seemed so propitious, just when his continued presence in Bath was surely of critical importance—what could it mean? And do you know the only answer he would give me? "Ask Miss Templeton." Just that—in a tone, in a manner quite foreign to him—and with a refusal to say anything more. "Ask Miss Templeton." And you may be sure, I *am* asking, and I demand nothing less than an answer!'

'I am not in the habit of complying with demands, Mrs Allardyce; but I shall suppose the question a civil one, and say in reply that it must refer to your son's making a proposal to me at the Dress Ball.'

Mrs Allardyce's head jerked back as if Lydia had actually thrown something at her, instead of merely wanting to.

'A proposal to *you*? What is this? Do you mean he conveyed his proposal to Miss Rae through you? A very unnecessary proceeding, though to be sure Robert is always a model of discretion—'

'Not on this occasion, ma'am. The declaration, the proposal, was to me, not Miss Rae, and I was as startled by it as you are.'

Such a livid flush suffused Mrs Allardyce's face that she looked as if she had been hanged by her jet choker. 'To *you*? Miss Templeton, this is a fantasy—or else a jest in the very poorest taste. I know you are one of those women who set themselves up as wits, but this is beyond anything.'

'Very well: if that is what you choose to believe,

then let us talk of some matter else. Will it rain, do you think?'

'What you say is impossible. *Robert* must have been making some sort of joke, and you took up the wrong idea. That is all I can suppose.'

'If that were the case, I do not see why he should have made this very sudden departure. Mrs Allardyce, there is no great mystery here: the matter is simple. Your son declared his attachment to me—a thing I had not in the least suspected—and proposed that I become his wife: an offer which I declined.'

'Declined! I should hope you did!' There was an admission in this that she was beginning to believe: but now her colour rose again, and still more fiercely she cried: 'But he must have taken leave of his senses! I must write him at once—recall him to Bath to set this matter straight. It has been my firm expectation that he is to marry Miss Rae. And he *shall*. I shall see to it. Whatever mischievous intrigue you have led him into—'

'That Miss Rae was his object was my expectation also, ma'am; and supposing him to be in love with her, and the match a promising one, I did all I could to encourage it. It has not been the most diverting occupation in the world, but I thought it good for my friend's sake. Your son informed me, however, that his feelings for Miss Rae had changed, that he no longer considered her as a bride, and that his affections inclined to me instead. I am afraid this communication held no pleasure for me. I felt nothing besides pity for Miss Rae's disappointment, and disapproval of the way she had been treated. I told him so, and we parted with very little cordiality on either side.

That is about all of the story, ma'am: it is not a pretty one, but no one is killed in it: my only concern now is to see my friend recover her spirits and happiness at last; and as for your son, I think he did very well to get quickly away from such a scene of embarrassment.'

Mrs Allardyce was quite still, her eyes hooded. 'You entrapped him. There is no other explanation. This is shocking—a shocking admission. My son Robert—my son—'

'I know he is your son, ma'am, the words are often enough on your lips for there to be no doubt of the matter,' snapped Lydia, in ungovernable irritation. 'And I tell you for the last time that I did not seek this, I did not want it, and I shall be heartily glad to be able to forget all about it.'

'Oho, you do not catch *me* with such pretty denials, Miss Templeton—I don't allow the wool to be pulled over *my* eyes. I know the world pretty well, and I know my son. He is no fool. It must have required a good deal of guile and cunning to lead him so disastrously astray. Nothing else could have so blinded him to sense and interest. He is on a way to a distinguished career, Miss Templeton— what possible reason could he have to throw himself away on a woman of thirty with nothing but ten thousand pounds?'

'That is a question that must await your letter to him, as only he can answer it. I only hope you will frame it in less unmannerly terms than you have used to me; and that whatever his answer may be, it will force you to the recognition that you do not know your son as well as you suppose.'

'I understand it now,' Mrs Allardyce grated, with a bitter shake of her head. 'This impulse to mischief and meddling—oh, I have seen it before. You are of that class of women who cannot get husbands, and so take a perverse pleasure in preventing others getting them. I pity Miss Rae indeed—a trusting nature so abused . . .'

For a moment Lydia felt herself back in the Royal Academy exhibition-room, hearing the wicked wiles of Miss Templeton deplored: but now there was no amusement in it. And a certain red rim to her vision suggested that Mrs Allardyce had chosen the wrong person, at the wrong time, to subject to her insolence.

'Abused, but not by me. The character you have given me is an insulting one, ma'am; and if I *had* accepted your son's proposal, it is an interesting question how you would have maintained it in your daughter-in-law, before the opinion of that society which is so important to you.'

'Ha! It would not have come to that, trust me— oh dear no—I would very soon have turned Robert's head back the right way, if he had come to me to announce such a folly. But there, I should not have been surprised: there was, after all, much in your mother's reputation that did not bear scrutiny.'

'My mother made mistakes in her life, ma'am, that I do not deny. But I felt towards her all the warmth and affection that a child must feel for a mother, whatever her deficiencies; and those deficiencies were never felt but as a past shadow, easily redeemed by her present grace, tenderness and goodness. I was never driven to shame, for example, by her behaviour in public: never blushed at her vulgarity, or struggled to make excuses for her ill-bred and ignorant self-assertion. My brother

410

and I were able to love her, with no such sacrifice of respect as you require from a son who eternally indulges you, and a daughter who must silently despise you.' Lydia rose to her feet, remembering Susannah comparing her to a giant. Very well: it was no bad feeling. 'You will, I know, be diligent in defaming me, in the tiresome circles in which you move, and where your parade of presumption is taken as consequence. I am helpless against that, but I am not unduly troubled. I take comfort in the fact that Miss Rae, unhappy as she is now, has been saved from the greater, the more lasting unhappiness of an intimate connection with you.'

Mrs Allardyce stared and mouthed, but no words came. It was a savage sort of satisfaction, no doubt, that Lydia took to the door—and incomplete, as the pug-dog had made itself scarce, and was unavailable for a kick: but it was the best that could be hoped for, until the blessed day that took her away from Bath.

Ah, blessed day—so it had always appeared to Lydia; but as she emerged into Queen Square and stood hard-breathing, blinking in the sunlight— gazing at the obelisk in the centre, and idly trying to remember which royal blockhead it commemorated—the blessed day somehow refused to present itself in its old glowing colours. There was something tarnished about it, as of a prize no longer valued.

*   *   *

Phoebe had seemed a little more herself that morning, and had declared, with a willed sort of lightness, that she was sick of being in her room;

411

and when Lydia returned to Sydney Place, she found her receiving a caller. Hugh Hanley was lounging elegantly in the drawing-room, and in the middle of some amusing anecdote to which Phoebe was giving a welcome, if faintly dutiful smile.

'Ah, I could tell you many a tale about Lady Desborough. Even the true ones are entertaining. Miss Templeton, I am concerned. Miss Rae tells me you are quite recovered from your indisposition of the other night, but I shall be glad to hear it from your own lips.'

'You may set your mind at ease, Mr Hanley. I was never better.'

'I am intensely relieved. It does not do to fall ill in Bath, you know: rather detracts from the purpose of the place. And look at my uncle: I wouldn't go so far as to call him as fresh as a daisy, but certainly fresh as a good strong thistle, say, and—I cannot repress an unearthly shiver at it— almost in spirits. He actually asked me to breakfast with him this morning. You must look to Hamlet meeting his father's ghost to picture my astonishment.'

'Except that Hamlet was a worthy young man with a wicked uncle,' Lydia said.

'You are too delicious for Bath,' he said, with an appreciative look. 'But now tell me—what and whence? My unwicked uncle—this sinister cordiality—what does it mean?'

'I can't conceive how *I* am supposed to know that, Mr Hanley.'

'Well, your past association—your close neighbourhood—your peculiar friendship: you are in a way his ally, surely. I doubt anyone holds the key to his heart, but you—'

'Mr Hanley, I am nobody's ally,' Lydia said, with a relapse into irritation, 'and I would be heartily glad if everyone would leave me out of their games. But if you are concerned that Mr Durrant has it in mind to marry, and disappoint you of your inheritance, then very well—that is what he came here for. I do not know his mind, but he is a man of determination—I say no more: except that if you hadn't wanted such a thing ever to happen, you should have conducted yourself better to begin with, and it is too late to undo it now.'

'Thank you.' Mr Hanley stood and bowed. 'You have spoken to me honestly and directly. It is a thing I never do, but I know how to value it. And please believe me, I shall not pester you with the subject again.' He looked at her closely—perhaps kindly. 'Miss Templeton, are you sure you are quite well?'

'I am perfectly well!' she cried, her voice breaking; and hurrying from the room, ran upstairs to her bedroom, where she flung herself down in a dry-eyed and stubborn misery. It was the interview at Queen Square, of course: vituperation had sustained her at the time, but it could not do so for long—as the blood cooled, the woeful reaction set in. After some time she heard the front door close; and soon after, Phoebe's light footsteps approaching her room, and pausing. But Lydia had not the heart to invite her in—she felt that even to take sympathy from Phoebe would be to rob her— and it seemed that Phoebe had not the heart to press either, and the footsteps went softly away.

CHAPTER TWENTY-SIX

The next day brought a letter from Lady Eastmond—usually an occasion to be relished, for she was as effusively likeable on the page as in person: but now, the kind thoughts, genial hopes, and eager speculations on their progress in Bath gave more pain than pleasure. It was hard to know what to write in return—what urbane phrases could be employed to convey that all was in ruins. The reply was best postponed, along with the larger question of what they were to do.

They had approached it, in some sort. Before breakfast Mary Darber had brought Lydia a question about the buying of provisions, which had made Lydia ask Phoebe, in a tone of fragile casualness: 'Do you—do you think, Phoebe, that you would wish to stay at Bath until the end of our lease, or—or perhaps make an early return home?'

'I don't much mind,' Phoebe said. 'We could go home early, if you like. But it depends how you feel.'

And that was how they went on for the next few days—raising the subject, only to drop it: as if neither had the will to confront the task of decision. At last Lydia did sit down at the writing-desk, sharpen a pen, and remark that she really ought to write to Lady Eastmond. Phoebe agreed; and fell into uneasy contemplation.

'I was thinking,' Lydia went on, 'that we need not go into a great deal of explanation—indeed, I feel that is much better left until we return to Lincolnshire, and see her face to face.'

414

'That will be better, indeed.'

'But what I might do—what I should do, after all, is inform her of when we are coming back. In other words, fix a day when she may expect us. We will need time to arrange matters with the house-agent and the tradesmen, and book our coach-places and so on; but if we fix a day, that will be— that will be something.'

'Yes . . .' Phoebe's shoulders slumped. 'I do want to see Lady Eastmond again—Sir Henry— Osterby—it is all so present to my mind. And yet I don't know how I shall be able to face it.'

'Face it? My dear Phoebe, you speak as if you have done something wrong, and you assuredly have not.'

Phoebe sternly shook her head. 'Oh, no. I have been foolish, Lydia. Foolish in that I have— vacillated. Is that a good word?'

'It is a . . . a good word to describe a certain way of . . . Oh, but, Phoebe—'

'A good word,' Phoebe said, still solemnly determined, 'for me. There, I shall use the whole dictionary at last. Well, no more vacillating. It seems to me now that there is no more criminal folly.'

'Oh, there are many,' Lydia began; but as so often now, she felt Phoebe was only half attending to her; and she was far from inclined to blame her for it.

It was a drifting, tail-end sort of life: the old companionable walks to the Pump Room or Sydney Gardens seemed to them both, by tacit agreement, out of the question; but its oppressiveness was alleviated by two things, both perhaps unexpected. Mrs Vawser was as good, or

415

as bad, as her word, and descended on Sydney Place to take Phoebe out in the barouche. To Phoebe's usual obliging nature was added this melancholy supine quality, in which one thing, alas, was as good as another. She went: she returned saying it had been very pleasant, and looking, at least, less papery of complexion; and Mrs Vawser insisted on the drive being a daily appointment. Certainly it had everything that could please a mind such as hers: she could indulge in ostentation in the fact of the barouche, condescension in taking Phoebe in it, and spite in never inviting Lydia to join them. But so low was Lydia's self-opinion that she thought it, if not a good thing, then a better one for her friend than anything she could propose.

The other ray of light, if it could be called that, was Hugh Hanley: in that he called often, never stayed too long, and talked in his trifling, sparkling vein of trifling and sparkling things. He was true to his word also—no longer quizzing Lydia about his uncle's intentions: not that she could have given him any information even if she had wanted to. She saw nothing of Lewis Durrant. He was, she supposed, much occupied in another direction. Not a supposition that gave her any pleasure, but preferable to the alternative: that he had heard something about her, something emanating from the Allardyce house, and was keeping his distance. She wanted to think that Juliet would not speak against her—but then, she was much attached to her brother; and besides, the loudest voice in that quarter would be Mrs Allardyce's, and there was no doubting what story she would be telling. To imagine Mr Durrant believing *that* about her was intolerable; but she lacked the heart to face him. Otherwise, she would have gone and handed him his fifty pounds at once. Indeed so acute was her consciousness of failure that she would have made it a hundred.

With Phoebe absent for most of the days, Lydia busied herself with preparations for their departure. At last came the visit to the coach-office, the bespeaking of a post-chaise for five days hence, the booking of coach-places for the servants. There was finality in this, but no satisfaction; and as she came away, and strolled idly down Milsom Street, she found in the broth of her emotions one unexpected flavour. Part of her would actually miss Bath. She had been rather happy at the beginning, even if she had not been aware of it. Or was that not the definition of happiness? If so, the discovery was as dispiriting as everything else. She turned into Duffield's, hoping that a draught of reading might revive her, as wine was so signally failing to do lately; and on the table exhibiting the new periodicals, a familiar title caught her eye: The *Interlocutor*.

So, here it was, the finished copy. Turning it over, she was unsure whether to admire Mr Beck's perseverance in completing it after the blow he had received, or to conclude that the blow could not after all have been so severe. The poem with the lacteous bucket and the hedger's implement seemed to have been withdrawn, she noticed with faint disappointment.

'My dear Miss Templeton, reading in a reading-room—how very gauche,' Hugh Hanley said at her side. 'Are there no bonnets to be stared at? No reputations to be impugned with a wink and a

417

whisper? The *Interlocutor*. Is that how you pronounce it?'

'No.'

'Looks dreadfully earnest anyhow. Will you have a seat with me for a minute? I have been *sauntering* about the town so long it has quite turned my legs to jelly. Surprising energy required for a saunter. Marching will be nothing to it.'

'Do dragoons march?'

'Only to the debtors' prison. I risk the gloomy phrase, as I judge that you are in no better spirits than I.'

'You don't look gloomy.'

'The curse of an amiable face! I could never play Hamlet, indeed, Miss Templeton: even when I got stabbed I would look no more than mildly discomfited. Besides, I don't really run to full-blown gloom. Call it resignation to fate.'

'The fate of the debtors' prison?'

'Eventually, eventually. Unless I thoroughly reform. I might give it a try. Virtue at least has novelty to recommend it. Well, will you be surprised to know that my uncle continues cordial? He secured me an invitation to dine at the Allardyce house with him last evening. Very Queen Square there, isn't it? Very genteel and just so. No ice, and the port rather indifferent—though plenty of it, thank heaven, as one must adjourn to listen to Madam Crocodile afterwards. I venture on the disobliging sobriquet as I am certain, from what she was saying, that she is not a favourite of yours.'

'Well, what was she saying? Oh, don't tell me: I can guess. No doubt it will soon be all over Bath in any case.'

'No doubt—Bath being a very small and very

418

trivial world. From what I could gather, she had great hopes of Miss Rae as a bride for her son, but now he has taken himself off, all seems lost, and Miss Templeton is to blame. I think there was some talk of lures and snares, which all sounds very county and gamekeepery and not at all like you.'

'Thank you.'

'You needn't. I think it must all be nonsense, not only because I doubt you would do any such thing, but because that old reptile said it: but I know you don't care for my opinion anyway. I would willingly discount the other theme of her rather *relentless* conversation, but there I fear the evidence is stronger. At the Dress Ball, you know, she made a great to-do about a forthcoming engagement in her family, and very neatly she is still contriving to do so. But on the distaff side.'

'You mean—Juliet and Mr Durrant?'

'Who else?' Hugh Hanley drew out a pristine handkerchief and applied it to a speck on his boot. 'Not that there was any corroboration from *them*, you understand. He was as about as easy and communicative as a sentry, and Miss Allardyce— well, you can hardly expect me to be fair about her, but there is just a little too much of the cat that got the cream for my taste. But certainly they are as thick as thieves—heads forever together—handing her to this and that—and in short, my uncle achieved his purpose. I went, I saw, and I confess myself conquered.'

Lydia tried to read his expression. Difficult, as he said: but she thought she detected something chill and stony in those long-lashed eyes. As for herself, she hardly knew how to respond to the

419

news. *It is wrong—it is wrong*—those were the words that seemed to repeat themselves along with her quickened pulse. And yet, she thought dully, who was she to say so? Who in their right mind would trust her judgement?

'There is nothing of certainty in this,' she said at last. 'Mrs Allardyce is, as you say, a boastful, loose-tongued woman—'

'And a shocking liar, I would add,' he put in, freshening. 'I fancy there are two kinds of nature that would always see through her: natures equally dishonest, like mine, and natures absolutely transparent, like Miss Rae's. I was with the Vawsers' exploring-party to Wells the other day— and aren't they a fantasy?—there is an endless fascination in their acquaintance, wondering at every moment whether they are *real*—and Miss Rae spoke of you with unhesitating affection and esteem.'

Lydia shook her head slightly. She had a strong feeling that Phoebe's opinion of her was much altered; and if what Hugh Hanley said were true, she could not feel it deserved. The whole subject was, indeed, too painful for her to pursue—which, observant as ever, he seemed to perceive.

'Heyo! Well, time will tell, and all the same a hundred years hence, and every other wise saw you care to mention. Tomorrow night I dine with the Vawsers, and expect entertainment enough to lift the blackest cloud. Mr Vawser seeks my advice on the latest fashion of tying the cravat. If you should see him parading the Pump Room with his cravat wound round his head like a bandage, you'll know that I gave in to an *unpardonable* temptation.'

'You intend staying in Bath, Mr Hanley?'

420

He shrugged gracefully. 'For the nonce, however long a nonce is. An immediate withdrawal in high dudgeon—can one have low dudgeon, by the by?—would give my uncle, I fear, far too much satisfaction. And what of you, Miss Templeton?'

'We leave next week.'

'Well, we two dispossessed idlers are sure to run into one another before then—but if it should happen otherwise, accept my wishes for a safe journey.'

Only when he was gone did she remark that word 'dispossessed', and think it odd that he should apply it to her: odder still, she found it, for no fathomable reason, entirely and frighteningly apt.

*   *   *

Lydia hardly knew on what impulse she said to Phoebe, that evening, that she had seen a copy of Mr Beck's review at Duffield's. Probably because *not* to say anything would be, in some measure, to hide something: and to hide something from someone suggested that one thought it would be best for them not to know it: and if one thought that, one was exhibiting a confidence in one's opinion, which she had forsworn . . .

Fortunately, Phoebe's reaction was much less complicated.

'Oh, I am so very pleased that he has seen it through! And Duffield's have taken a copy—that must be a good sign. They take only the best. I wonder if Godwin's has it too? I shall ask when I next go in.' She found Lydia watching her, and smiled. Not her old, radiant smile—that was

421

gone—but a good try at it: a sketch from memory. 'I always wish Mr Beck well, Lydia, and do not mind talking of him. Please don't be afraid of that.'

Lydia smiled too: reassured, yet mistrusting even reassurance. 'I am afraid of everything lately.'

'Oh, you mustn't be. That is the greatest of mistakes. I venture to say that *that*, at least, is something I have learned.'

Lydia longed to ask her more: but Phoebe soon sank again into quiet abstraction, broken only by neutral remarks: amongst them, a reminder that she was pressingly invited to dine with the Vawsers tomorrow, and would go if Lydia didn't mind. There was no objection Lydia could raise. Phoebe was probably right in feeling that they were better off apart for a little; and Lydia's self-opinion was so crushed that even the idea of Phoebe preferring Mrs Vawser's company to hers could only raise a thin howl, like a cat trapped down a well.

*   *   *

It was three days later, and Lydia was awake unusually early—actually up and stretching—when Mary Darber came knocking with the hot water.

But no—not hot water: Mary was holding out a letter.

'Good morning, Mary. What's this? Never tell me you're resigning because you want to stay in Bath. I shall have to . . . Good God, whatever is the matter?'

'Miss Rae's not in her room, Miss Templeton— and her clothes are gone—and there's this.'

Lydia went forward to take the letter, with the slow, treacly, dreamlike suspension—the curious

422

premonitory slippage of time that accompanies the receiving of bad news.

*   *   *

'Mr Durrant? To be sure, ma'am—only . . .' The woman wiped her nose apologetically with her apron. 'I don't know, ma'am, it being so early, whether he's at home, as you might say . . .'

'Who the devil is it, Mrs King?' came Mr Durrant's voice from a room down the hall.

Lydia spoke. 'It's me. I must see you.'

He came out hastily, in breeches and shirt-sleeves, towelling lather from his face. He met Lydia's eyes. 'Mrs King, would you be so good as to brew some coffee? Bring it into the drawing-room.' He flung open a door on the other side of the hall and ushered Lydia in. 'Come. Sit down.'

Numbly she took in the comfortably disordered appearance of his lodgings: books, a littered desk, his old coat on a chair. She had imagined him marooned in rented sterility, but this felt like Culverton.

'What is it?' His eyes lit on the letter clutched in her hand, and he fell on his knee beside her. 'News from home? Your father?'

'No, no. It's Phoebe. She's gone. She . . .' Her voice faltered on the word, which should have been absurd and was not. 'She's eloped.'

'The devil she has! Not with Beck? I didn't think he . . .'

She shook her head. 'Read it.'

He went to the window to do so, while Lydia re-read the letter in burning memory.

423

Dearest Lydia

I hope you can forgive me for what may appear a terrible desertion, and an ungrateful reward for all your care and solicitude on my behalf— and that of my kind guardians the Eastmonds likewise. Believe me, it is not meant so.

I am going away to be married. Mr Hanley has declared himself in love with me, in the most urgent terms. This is sudden—yes— though we have seen a good deal of each other lately: and at a time when I have, I hope and believe, been very little inclined to the idle dreams of romance. And yet now comes this— so overpoweringly. And I have decided upon decision, if that makes sense.

Mr Hanley throws his life at my feet. I am challenged to take it up, and I shall. I must no longer doubt my heart—else I shall remain a vacillating fool all my life. That is why we do it this way—running away to be married. To wait for consent—to listen perhaps to persuasions and arguments—is surely to court delay and disappointment. Happiness surely must be seized, even at some risk. Of my future happiness I have no doubt, and beg you to accept that assurance, and rejoice with me: that is the one request I have to make of my dear friend, who has already acceded to sufficient demands from me. I shall write Lady Eastmond myself as soon as I am able, and hope in time to present my husband to both of you—when, though my surname be changed, I shall remain as ever

Your affectionate Phoebe

The memory of it made her bury her head in her hands; and when she looked up, she was shocked to see Mr Durrant slumped in a chair and looking haggard—even shrunken.

'This is my doing,' he said, in an ashy voice.

'What?'

'I should have seen it. God, with my ridiculous folly I have thrown Hugh into a panic—driven him into the worst of all courses. He has set his sights on an heiress—young and impressionable, yes, he made sure of that—and seduced her. In single-minded cold blood, he has persuaded this girl to her ruin.' His eyes glittered. 'And it is my fault—'

'Stop, Mr Durrant—tell me what you mean. Her ruin? Do you think Hugh will not marry her—is that it? Use her, and desert her?' Oh, yes, she had thought it herself, or rather the thought was one of the many that had brushed her, cobweb-like, as she had run here to Edgar Buildings, wanting only his help, wanting only not to be alone.

'That is one outcome to be feared. It is always to be feared, when such a thing happens. It may not be his first intention—but he is so wayward, so little to be trusted, and she is so innocent . . .' The housekeeper brought in a tray of coffee. He thanked her, and when she had gone poured half a cup and topped it up with brandy.

'Here. Drink it, drink it, you're as pale as death. His first intention . . . well, that of course is what she says—marriage. Which is to say, marriage to her fifty thousand pounds. Is it fifty?'

'Yes. Fifty thousand pounds on her coming of age—early next year.'

'As he surely knows. Hence the elopement— which she, God help her, attributes to his ardour.

425

They must go to Gretna, as in England she cannot marry without her guardian's consent. And Hugh surely knew that Lady Eastmond would see him at once for the adventurer he is.' He sprang up and paced restlessly. 'Dear God, you and I would have told her so at the first hint.'

'And once married, of course, they cannot be unmarried.' The laced coffee made her gasp, but it seemed to brace her: Mr Durrant's presence also, perhaps. 'Next year Hugh will be a rich man, and Phoebe . . . But this is what I must ask myself, Mr Durrant. My immediate conclusion was the same as yours. Hugh Hanley is taking advantage of her, and she is making a dreadful mistake. But should I—should I not consider this also as Phoebe's own decision—and respect it as such?'

'What? What in heaven's name makes you talk like that?'

Lydia drew a deep breath. 'I fear I have had a hand in her decisions before—to unhappy effect. Indeed I am afraid this—this disaster is the ultimate result.'

He studied her, then sat down and went on in a gentler voice: 'I see we had better be frank with each other—as this matter concerns us both so nearly. But I am glad to hear you call it a disaster—as it is: and don't, for pity's sake, begin blaming yourself for it. First, your Miss Rae is a fool—a naïve rather than malicious one: and second, Hugh is a rogue, but a horribly plausible one. The combination is fraught with mischief. But as for their being driven together—no, I bear the responsibility for that.' He felt for his watch, then realised he was in shirt-sleeves. 'It must be getting on for nine now. When did you find the note?

426

When do you think she left?'

'Mary found the note early this morning. Phoebe must have slipped out some time in the small hours . . .' She thought back to last night: dinner, a little desultory conversation: Phoebe electing for an early bed. It all looked as pregnant and sinister now as it had looked unremarkable then. 'None of the servants heard anything. But the maid next door thought she heard carriage-wheels in the middle of the night. I suppose they must have made an arrangement. She took only two bags—'

'And he was waiting just down the street, in classic fashion, to carry her off in a chaise to a glorious future. Lord, I feel sick . . .' He frowned down at himself. 'I should dress.'

'Mr Durrant, wait. Tell me why you blame yourself. Do you mean you suspected something?'

'I suspected nothing,' he said grimly, 'which is where I am at fault again. I should have thought of it. But I was too busy being pleased with myself.'

'There is nothing wrong with being pleased with yourself,' she said, looking away and sipping the potent coffee. 'It is a sensation I would willingly experience again.'

'You've seen Hugh lately, of course. What has he said? About me, about Juliet Allardyce?' His voice was deliberate and hard.

'He—he believed that there is, or will be, an engagement between you.' Lydia coughed: the brandy.

'Damn it all,' he said softly. 'Well, now you see why I blame myself, Miss Templeton. Hugh sees himself cut out. He has looked to his prospects—or lack of them—and has taken appropriate action to

427

restore his fortunes. As simple as that. Dear Lord. Beware, always beware of your wishes coming true. They bring a curse with them.'

'No—you shouldn't think that,' she said, with difficulty. 'This—this is something separate, surely. It shouldn't spoil whatever you—you and Juliet have—'

'What?' His head jerked up. 'Oh—of course, I'm sorry, I'm not thinking . . . The point is, there is no engagement between Juliet and me. Nor is there any in prospect. I must break a confidence, but I think—that is, I know she will understand. Juliet is secretly engaged—has been some nine or ten months.'

Lydia was used to reading in novels of people's feelings being indescribable: but she had never before experienced it.

'It was when she was with her brother at Vienna,' he went on, his face set, masked. 'A Prussian gentleman, attached to the embassy there. It was kept secret, of course, because of Mrs Allardyce, who would never approve, and no doubt do all in her power to stop it. They are hoping to marry when she returns to Vienna. Allardyce knew of it too.'

Lydia licked her dry lips. 'When did you learn about this?'

'Not long ago . . .' The mask hardened, but his shoulders were restive. 'No need to talk of it now. Suffice to say that Juliet knew all about my situation with Hugh: she heartily sympathised—all the more, when she met him; and she was good enough to go along with the deception. Yes. This is the reckless game I have played. I do not blame her at all: she felt she was helping me—making it

428

appear that there was an understanding between us. It was exactly what I wanted, after all: to put my damnable nephew's nose out of joint. And it was—God forgive me, but this last week or so I have drawn an unholy satisfaction from it. Seeing that smile of his wiped off—well, not precisely wiped off, but most gratifyingly smudged. I should have known that no good could come from such an unnatural pleasure.' He snapped to his feet. 'I must dress. There's no time to lose. I'll not be a moment—take some more coffee. The brandy's there.'

'No, no, I shall be drunk.'

'Nonsense, you always had an excellent head for liquor.' With a brief bare smile he was gone.

She did take a little more; and in the fumes of it found, despite all the baneful misery of anxiety, a moment of pure joy in the knowledge that there was no engagement to Juliet Allardyce. Pure? Well, a little impurity in it, perhaps—picturing Mrs Allardyce's displeasure. But at least here was one direful mistake avoided.

Yet Mr Durrant's candour deserved no less from herself, and she could not let him take up a burden that was partly hers. As soon as he returned, waistcoated, booted, and muttering about his coat, she spoke.

'Mr Durrant, hear me now. You should not blame yourself. Your coat is on that chair. You should not, because it is going too far. Hugh got the unpleasant shock he thoroughly deserved, but you could not predict this result. There I am at fault: for Hugh would not have found Phoebe such an easy mark if it were not for me—for my failures in guiding her.'

'What do you mean?' He shrugged the coat on to his long, rangy back. 'You were not much impressed by Beck, I know—but still, it was she who refused him.'

'Yes—but influenced by me, I fear. And it was I who pointed her towards what I thought was the better course for her—Robert Allardyce. And I was wrong.'

He hesitated, wincing slightly. 'Ah. Hm. He—he is an odd fish, all in all, taking off like that. Yes, I heard a version of the tale from Mrs Allardyce but, like most things she says, I ignored it.'

'Did you? So much that you cannot remember what it was?'

'Oh . . .' He avoided her eyes. 'The gist was that you had spoiled Phoebe's chances with him by alienating his affections. I put it more neatly than her, of course.'

'What does Juliet say?'

'Nothing: her brother did not confide in her, it seems, and it is not her nature to speculate.'

'And what do *you* think?'

'I think,' he said carefully, 'that I may have been right after all, with what I said to you at the Dress Ball: and that's all I can say.'

She sighed. 'You *were* right—and I am sorry I was so dismissive of it. I fear we always do that with things we don't wish to believe—things that are beginning to dawn . . . Well, that evening he declared himself to me. He proposed. In the card-room of all places.'

He gave her a long, wondering look. 'And what did you say?'

'I said no, of course,' she said, faintly snappish. 'It was absurd. I had never shown the slightest interest in him, except as Phoebe's suitor. He was meant for Phoebe: that was why we were here, that was why I had done everything in my power to . . . And that's just it. I had led Phoebe to believe he was about to propose to her—and instead, *this*: this most wretched of reversals. I had to tell her, of course: and she was kind, understanding: she was Phoebe. Yet what she must have been really thinking—or suspecting . . . You see, I came to Bath, Mr Durrant, to help her with her choice: and I left her with none. And now—turned in on herself, surely mistrusting all influence, all careful counsels—now appears this dazzling man before her. He passionately proposes to whisk her away:—this minute. And why not? There is only wreck behind her.'

'A wreck not of your making,' he said firmly. 'Certainly, it was not consciously done: there was no design. Allardyce, after all, could not help himself. That is—you offered him no encouragement, as you say: it was a thing beyond your control.' Suddenly he was brisk. 'But it is all a damnable confounded business, I must say. And it makes me all the more apprehensive for Miss Rae. Plainly she is not thinking straight—if she is thinking at all.' He drew out his watch. 'And time is getting on.'

'What are you going to do?'

'Go after them. Stop them. Oh, to be sure, respecting her decision and whatnot is all very well—but let us be honest. Phoebe Rae? Gentle, good-natured as she is—*too* infernally good-natured—tying herself to that coxcomb? He'll bring her to grey hairs even before he's run through her money. No, if anything can be done to

431

stop it . . .' He grimaced. 'Pray God I can. It must be me, you see. I have already learned my lesson. I cannot see Miss Rae put to a much harder one because of my folly.'

She did not ask him what lesson he had learned. It was, as he said, the time for action. She rose. 'Very well, I shall come with you.'

'No. And don't look at me like that, I'm not alluding to feminine frailty. I know *you*'re not frail. I mean to pursue them—which surely means taking the coach-road north, as they must be heading for Scotland; but we must bear in mind the other possibilities. They have surely left Bath—but there is always the faint hope of a return: or they may send you some other communication, which means you must be here. I shall ask at the posting-inns about chaises hired yesterday—and at the York, when the charming Mr Hanley vacated his rooms. I'll go bail he's left his bill unpaid.'

'But wait—if they left some hours ago, how will you catch up with them?'

'A swift post-chaise, and no rest. They will surely halt for meals—for Hugh to order the choicest morsels, and to press her hand and tell her about her eyes.' He smacked his lips in disgust. 'I shall not be so hindered.'

'Then please, Mr Durrant, have a care . . . And if you do find them, what then?'

'Then—then I shall have to use my powers of persuasion. They are something rusty—but I do have them, somewhere. Where's my hat?'

'There—on the mantel.'

'So that's where the clock went. Now, go home, wait for news, and hope for the best.'

'This is a miserable prescription! The agony of

432

waiting—'

'I'll send you word as soon as I am able. Don't think. Occupy yourself. I am not such a fool as to suggest sewing. Read.' He searched among the papers on his desk. 'Ah, here. Beck's journal. Picked it up in Meyler's yesterday. Wish he had changed that title. Rather indigestible, but some nourishment in it.'

'That is the last thing I would wish to read,' she said, taking it. 'And I do not want to read at all. I only want—oh, Mr Durrant, I only want everything that's done to be undone.'

He hesitated, then briefly pressed her hand. 'That is more than I can promise. But I shall do what is in my power.'

CHAPTER TWENTY-SEVEN

Back at Sydney Place Lydia moved in an air of unreality. She eyed the familiar furnishings with a faint suspicion, as if someone had crept in and moved them around. Phoebe gone: Phoebe gone with Hugh Hanley: an elopement. Here was the greasepaint whiff of unreality: the stuff of stage comedies and schoolgirl gossip. It happened, though. Where there was a word for a thing, there must be a thing. It happened, and it seldom turned out propitiously.

And Lewis Durrant gone after them! Stranger yet, but undoubted: very soon after her return, he had sent a stable-boy with a note. Hugh Hanley had hired a post-chaise from the York yesterday, its destination Worcester, on the north road.

Mr Durrant had done likewise. That was all. She must wait.

Wait, and think. There lay the terrible task of endurance. Without thought, there would only have been the stretched ache of tension: but thought was a rain of needles. She tried to sit, to rest herself—to read: she followed Mr Durrant's advice with the trustful submission of a patient to a physician, and took up the *Interlocutor*. She tried and failed to anchor her mind in a fathomless essay on the metaphysics of the sublime. Leafing, she came across a poem: this must be the substitution for that regrettable rustic effusion. Her heart sank when she saw the heading: *For P***** R**.*

> *The infant who would clutch the flower*
> *As roughly as a favoured toy*
> *This lessons learns: his puny power*
> *May what he most desires destroy.*
>
> *The traveller who with holy greed*
> *His flag plants on the heathen strand*
> *Doth nothing but a desert breed*
> *Where slaves and sickness blight the land.*
>
> *I saw a vision—oh, so bright,*
> *So sweet and fair—I could not wait:*
> *I seized it—and it vanished quite.*
> *My fault, my loss, my fitting fate.*

Lydia laid down the paper with trembling fingers. Such an exchange for the lacteous bucket . . . yet she could almost wish the absurdity back. Had Phoebe seen these verses? It was likely: she had said she would look for a copy. The thought of

434

their effect on her—the adding of this tender regret to the bitter sum of her late experience—was, like every thought now, unbearable. She recalled Mr Durrant's first exclamation on hearing that Phoebe had eloped: *Not with Beck?* And if it had been bearable, she would have thought: *If only so!*

Had she been asked for just one word to define Hugh Hanley, that word would have been 'untrustworthy'. This did not rule out other qualities—charm, wit, good temper—and she could even imagine a woman being happy with him. But it would have to be a woman of his own shrewd, worldly sort, who could match him at every turn. That was not Phoebe. Lady Eastmond's brown, plain, kind face swam before her. Lady Eastmond who had not asked much of her, after all, as her father had gently suggested: only what was due to a woman who had been such a staunch friend to her mother. Her mother—who had run off with a handsome soldier. The wheel coming round. Elopements never propitious. No comedy here. Dear God. Unbearable.

By six o'clock it was literally so. Lydia packed a carpet-bag, put on her bonnet and spencer, and left the house.

*   *   *

The York could not oblige—not an equipage left for hire—and the Christopher did not seem to want to. The waiter fetched the livery-stable keeper, and he chewed his lip and hawed over her request. There was a chaise for hire, to be sure—but then there was the question of the lateness of

435

the hour: how far was she going? There, you see—
he would need to know, on account of driving at
night. Stagecoaches were always leaving at night,
she countered. Ah, but it was different driving
post, and there was the question of a postilion: he
had better speak to the hotel-keeper . . .

He left her fuming in the coffee-room, where
presently a gentleman entered with an armful of
papers, nearly dropped them in surprise, and cried
out: 'Miss Templeton!'

'Mr Beck.' Well, yes, let it come: let the bolts
and the brimstone fall on her.

He came forward, wrestling with his papers,
blinking rapidly. 'Miss Templeton, I—I am very
glad to see you.'

She waited for this to be elaborated with some
titanic irony and scorn. When it was not—when he
smiled tentatively, and asked if she would sit
down—she felt as if the world had momentarily
turned inside out.

'Miss Templeton, this is most favourably met. I
had thought of calling on you—supposing you still
in Bath—which, of course, you plainly are. I
arrived here yesterday on business to do with the
Interlocutor, and I thought . . . I wondered, but
then I hesitated. Oh, Miss Templeton, what I
wanted to say is'—he spread out his arms with the
old exultant glow—'you are Canidia!'

Now the world had turned the other way. 'I am
what—? Mr Beck, I . . . Oh! good heavens, that.'
Her letter about the translation of Horace: it
seemed an age ago, across a great sundering gulf of
experience.

'Yes—*that*—that most superb, penetrating,
valiant defence of poetry against the defacement
436

of a self-conceited literary vandal. Those noble lines tricked out into so much versified lace to trim a fine gentleman's cuff—I remember throwing the impudent book across the room—oh, but you put it much better than I could. It was stirring, Miss Templeton. I have only just come across it: my printer found me a back copy of the *Universal Review* at last, though Mr Durrant told me about your being Canidia some time ago.'

'Did he?'

'Oh, yes, he was always talking about you. And I was very interested—but then various events intervened, and when I left Bath I fear I was . . . a little disaffected towards you, and dismissed it.' Mr Beck blushed, as richly as a girl. 'This—this is an opportunity also, I hope, for an apology. I fear I was a little intemperate. My passions master me, as they will do, and it was—I think it was not handsomely done.'

Lydia waved a hand weakly. 'There are much worse things, Mr Beck: much worse.'

'I think not,' he said, with the familiar strenuous assertion. 'I have been inclined to dismiss manners as a mere superficiality, but it is borne in on me that they soften and civilise human intercourse just as much as the affections. Indeed I have an article in mind for the next issue of my review . . . But now this also is what I wanted to ask—to request. Miss Templeton, you must write something for it. If Canidia could only grace its pages—'

'Mr Beck, I am very flattered,' she said, half laughing, half tearful, 'and at any other time I should think it a thoroughly interesting project. But just now I—I have a terribly important matter on hand—'

'Good God, what's the matter?' He peered into her face. 'Tell me.'

Well, let it come: there had only been a postponement of the brimstone, after all. She told, as briefly as she could, wishing the hotel-keeper would come, wishing she could be gone, wishing Mr Beck's liquid eyes were not so desperately attentive.

'So you see: this—unfortunate news is all the recompense I can give you for your courtesy, Mr Beck. And now if you want to be intemperate again, I shan't blame you.'

He gazed for some moments at the window, where a mockingly pink sky exhibited itself. 'Intemperate? No. I am shaken . . . shaken with pity for Miss Rae. She cannot have been herself to have done such a thing—oh, I don't refer to the man, I can't speak there—but to have left her friends, to have thrown everything at hazard: it is not her. It is not her nature to give pain. And this, Miss Templeton, is something you can never have intended.'

'Dear God, no,' she groaned, 'but it has happened, and I feel my responsibility. I think of what might have been. Oh, Mr Beck, I read your verses. You still care for her greatly, do you not?'

'Oh, I shall love Miss Rae to the end of my life,' he said, almost conversationally. 'And besides that, I cannot think ill of her. When a man has been refused, I think he often finds a salve for his disappointment in turning against the woman who refused him: but I cannot do that.' For a moment he was lofty: then a shadow touched his face. 'This gentleman—this Hanley—you doubt his sincerity: his integrity?'

438

'I fear I must do: still more does Mr Durrant, which is why he makes such haste to follow them.'

Mr Beck folded his large, well-shaped hands, which were not quite steady; and seemed to pick his words carefully, delicately, as if they were twigs caught in a fast, swirling stream. 'Then I pity her the more. If I had heard she were engaged to someone else—someone of her true choice, worthy of her—well, no one could be that; and of course I should not like it, I should hate it with all my being—but still, it would be different.' He looked up at her in perplexity. 'I thought—I thought if there was a rival, it was Allardyce—'

'No.' Lydia shook her head, unable to say more. 'No.'

He seemed to draw back from some new and dizzying height of surmise: then made a fist, and said: 'Then God speed Mr Durrant, I say! And you are waiting here for news? This is the distillation of agony! Let me wait with you—or at least let me order you some tea—'

'No, no. I am waiting to hear if I may hire a post-chaise. Mr Durrant said I should stay at home, in case any news came there, but it is intolerable. I feel—I feel I must be doing something.'

'You mean to follow them?'

'I know it sounds absurd. But I might get a fair way up the Worcester road tonight—find out if there is any news at the post-houses on the way. It would be—'

'Better than this, yes. And there are servants at Sydney Place, after all, if any news comes there. Yes, why not?'

It was rather a relief to be with someone who

would never urge her to be sensible. 'The only thing that prevents it, I am afraid, is that the livery-stable is reluctant to hire me a post-chaise. Something about night travelling, and postilions—'

'Oh, there is nothing more thrilling than driving in the dark,' he said, very Mr Beck. 'And besides, this is a matter of utmost urgency. By your leave, Miss Templeton, let me go and speak to them.'

He went quickly away, and was quickly back, moving with a sort of modest swagger. 'The chaise is being made ready,' he announced, 'and there should be a moon later, so we may get along pretty smartly.'

'Thank you . . . We?'

He flushed again. 'I should not presume—but I shall. Miss Templeton, this affair does not perhaps concern me as immediately as it does you, yet I simply cannot stay and linger about, any more than you can. As Miss Rae's devoted, eternal well-wisher—if no more—' his magnificent Adam's apple bobbed convulsively '—I wish to help. It will be sad work for you travelling alone, in such anxiety. I shall only add that if you refuse, then I—I fear I shall become intemperate again.'

The realisation took a moment, but with his awkward smile it could not be denied: Mr Beck was being humorous. If the world were to keep turning inside out like this, she would be too giddy to travel. 'Well, that would never do,' she said; and part of her confessed that she did not want to go alone. 'And thank you, Mr Beck, for persuading them. However did you do it?'

Her thought was that he had probably made a radical appeal to the stable-keeper as a fellow-man bound by the sacred ties of human fraternity: but he replied with a shrug, offering her his arm: 'Oh, I gave them a bribe. It always works, alas. At least until the perfectibility of human nature is achieved . . .'

Soon they were in the post-chaise and climbing the steep road north out of Bath, with several pleasure-carriages bowling past them in the other direction. Country picnics: even that innocuous thought touched Lydia's mind like a goad, as she recalled the outing with the Allardyces, and her complacent attention to Mr Allardyce's talk of marriage, of the disposition he sought in a wife, and his hesitations in approaching his candidate . . . How blithely she had assured him that his suit would prosper—that he need only ask the question! A barouche passing by reminded her of the abominable Vawsers. *There* had been the means of bringing Phoebe and Hugh Hanley together. If only she had dissuaded Phoebe from accepting Mrs Vawser's friendship—but then had she not wisely given up trying to influence Phoebe altogether? Besides, she suspected now that Hugh Hanley had set his sights upon Phoebe from the night of the Dress Ball. No, there was no comfort to be found in any reflections, and she was glad when Mr Beck emerged from his own pensiveness and began to talk.

He spoke of the *Interlocutor*: Lydia's telling him that she had read the poem addressed to Phoebe led him to suppose that she had read the rest of it with equal attention, and the minuteness of his references to its contents left her floundering, and hoping that her eager nods would satisfy him. At last he mentioned his regret that 'The Open Field' had been omitted. 'I felt it had fine things—did

441

you not? But it needs, perhaps, a little more polishing.' Lydia contented herself, and him, with agreement, and was partially relieved when he broke off quoting from it, and began to talk of Phoebe. Here the new amity between them was, inevitably, threatened. He spoke of her at first with circumspection—then with awed, regretful tenderness—at last with powerful emotion.

'And to think of her led astray—deluded and entrapped by some villainous fortune-hunter—it is like an ill dream. I can scarcely believe such a thing can happen—can be *allowed* to happen.'

'Please, Mr Beck, there is no reproach you can lay upon me that I have not already heaped upon myself.'

'No, no, I mean no reproach,' he said hastily. 'This is no time for such things.' But as he went on to recall his acquaintance with Phoebe in London, and its unhappy renewal in Bath, he could not help himself: some murmurs against Lydia could not be checked, some little points must be scored. Lydia could not enjoy them, but felt he had a right to them; and he did not persist. The lamps of the first toll-gate, shining full into the carriage, must have shown the weary dejection in her face, and Mr Beck suddenly changed the subject.

After Lydia had paid the toll, the gate-keeper gave them a look of bored curiosity before returning to his lodge.

'Wondering who we are,' she said, 'and what can be our relation. If he knew, he would suspect something improper.'

'Aye, impropriety,' Mr Beck said, with his sharp-edged laugh. 'Lord, even to say the word makes one's lips go thin. People think very stupid things, do they not? Is it because they do not choose to think clever ones?'

'I fear society discourages them from doing that.'

He laughed again: then said abruptly: 'Or else they are hiding something from themselves.' And they fell into a curious, not unrestful silence, until the juddering of the wheels on cobbles announced that they had come to the first post-house.

While the horses were changed, Lydia made enquiries. The ostler she approached appeared not to speak English, or indeed any language except spitting, in which he was dismayingly proficient; but a chambermaid passing by with a laden basket overheard, and was more helpful.

'Fair young gentleman, fair young lady in a chaise, not much luggage? Aye, you're not the first to ask. Single gentleman was here this morning wanting to know the same thing. Aye, they passed through, going north. So did he.' She grinned. 'Any more a-coming after you, are there?'

Her words gave Lydia a sudden sense of futility. Was this not, indeed, like playing a ghastly game of ring-a-roses? It was Mr Beck who roused her: he brought her out a glass of brandy-and-water from the inn, assured her they were making good time, and urged her back into the chaise as soon as the fresh horses were in the traces. He was determined, righteous: and also, as she found to her shame that she was not, tireless. To the fatigue and anxiety of the day was added, at last, sickness from their rapid jolting pace. At the next post-house, there was only the same story—the same ring-a-roses: and the coming of full dark sank her spirits further. She had meant for them to carry on

443

travelling through the night; but when they rattled into the old quaint streets of Tewkesbury, and drew up in the yard of the Hop Pole Inn, she had to confess to Mr Beck that she could not go on.

'After midnight,' he said, consulting his watch. 'Well, we have made good time. You mean to stay here for the night?'

'I'm sorry. I have the greatest dislike for feminine frailty, but if we were to go on I fear you would not relish being in a close carriage with me. If I could only have a short rest—lie down for a little—and have them wake me very early, then we could go on. Oh, but you, Mr Beck—you have no luggage—'

'Oh! that doesn't signify. I can lie down in my clothes.' He handed her out. 'You do look fagged. Go and bespeak a room for yourself, and I'll make the enquiries.'

Yes, he was much changed towards her. He might perhaps change again, pricked by the memory of her wrongs—but that did not affect the new opinion she had come to about Mr Beck. Where previously she had deplored his volatile temperament, she now saw the virtue in it. To be changeable, after all, always entailed the possibility of changing for the better. It was certainly to be preferred to that rigidity, that narrowly unyielding quality that at the last she had discovered beneath Mr Allardyce's smooth manner. To be sure, it would not suit her—but then, what was the bearing of that? She had gone wrong from the start in even positing that question. For, after all, what *would* suit her?

I am unsuitable, she thought, as she followed the chambermaid's candle along a creaking passage:

444

which is not the right word, grammatically. Incapable of being suited. What *is* the word . . . ? Bone-weary as she was, she knew she would not be able to sleep. She lay down resigned to staring sandy-eyed at the tarry beams and the riotously floral bed-hangings, with words, wrong words and right words, playing ring-a-roses around her head.

What seemed only moments later, she was starting awake at the maid's knock, and cringing from a shaft of full morning sunlight.

She had forgotten to be called early. Cursing the loss of time, she dressed hurriedly, did something novel if efficient with her hair, and ran down the mazy stairs. Mr Beck was in the dining-parlour, looking perfectly fresh, if blue about the chin.

'Mr Beck, I didn't mean to sleep so long. Have you breakfasted? We ought to be—'

'I waited breakfast for you. And I fancy we may not be able to make a prompt start in any case. I went out to see about the chaise, and there was a lot of head-shaking about the left fore wheel.'

'Oh, no . . .'

She rushed out to the yard to see for herself. It was true: the carriage was propped on bricks, and a wheelwright had been fetched to make the repair.

'Oh, no, it won't be soon, ma'am. Nay, she'll be a while yet before she's right,' he told her, with the infuriating lovingness of the craftsman. 'You must bide a bit, ma'am. Take a bite, and watch the Worcester stage come in. That's always a handsome sight. Proper turn-out.'

She could think of nothing less interesting; but there was no help for it. She returned to the dining-parlour, and sat down in the wooden booth with Mr Beck, trying to stifle her impatience. Well, perhaps she should eat: she could do no good fainting on the road. But though she forced down a little ham, and a good deal of coffee, and tried to take heart from Mr Beck's robustness, she could not fend off the tuggings of despair. This was all hopeless. Even Mr Durrant's swift pursuit could do no good: Hugh Hanley was no fool. He would have known they would be followed, and made every possible speed. Ring-a-roses.

'That must be the Worcester coach,' Mr Beck said, rising and going to the window. The blowing of the horn, the rattling and rumbling and shouting, usually so pleasant a sound, struck her as almost insolently cheerful. Disconsolate, she went to join him. Yes, a proper turn-out, she thought bleakly.

Moments after the coach had come crunching to a halt, another vehicle careered into the yard at a lick—a post-chaise, the horses snorting and lathered. It had scarcely stopped before the door was flung open, and Mr Durrant jumped out.

'Miss Templeton—do you see?' cried Mr Beck. 'We shall have news—there's Mr Durrant . . .'

'And alone,' Lydia said huskily, and ran out to the yard.

She found Mr Durrant elbowing aside the ostlers and shouting up to the outside passengers of the Worcester coach. 'Miss Fowler! Is there a Miss Fowler there? Where is Miss Fowler?'

An elderly lady put back her veil and peered timidly down at him. 'I am here, sir. Whatever is the matter?'

Mr Durrant's face fell. 'Nothing—I beg your pardon, ma'am. A mistake.' He jumped as Lydia touched his sleeve. 'Great God, what do you do

446

here?'

'I could not bear waiting—and see, here's Mr Beck, he accompanied me. I had to follow you and—oh, Mr Durrant, what news? What has happened—who is Miss Fowler?'

'The news is good as far as it goes,' he said, drawing a hand across his face. 'Then perhaps not good.'

'By your leave, sir,' grunted an ostler, 'people wanting to get down.'

'Come.' Lydia took his arm: though he was brisk and upright as ever, she saw how exhausted he was, pale eyes glittering, cheekbones rawly prominent. 'Come and sit down. Mr Beck, will you order more coffee?'

In the dining-parlour Mr Durrant slumped down with a sigh and closed his eyes for a moment: then, as if that was enough of rest, snapped up and drained a whole cup of coffee.

'I found them. Their trail was easy enough to follow, as no doubt you have found: and yes, Scotland the destination. Last night—well, call it three in the morning—I came to the Crown at Worcester. Roused the innkeeper from his bed: he did not appreciate it, but I had to know if they had passed there—I knew from each report at the post-house that I was gaining on them. Yes, young gent and lady—but they had not passed through—they had put up there for the night. Gentleman's name—' his grin, sharpened by fatigue, was positively wolfish '—would you believe he was using the name Durrant? Travelling with his sister—yes, here is the first good news: separate bedchambers. Miss Rae's own sense, I suspect, because . . . Well: I wanted to know where the

447

gentleman's room was, and when I had found it, I asked for a chair, as I was going to sit there in the passage and wait. The innkeeper made a fuss, but I—well, I made it clear I would not be denied. Quite generous of me, really, not to drag him out of his bed at once. I waited until first light, and then I did it. In a way I should not have waited . . .' He shook his head. 'Hugh was no pretty sight—very seedy—a couple of empty bottles by his bed told the tale. And a good tale, an encouraging tale. Last night, he told me very sourly, they had sat down to dine together, and Miss Rae had flattened him. Not literally, alas. But she told him plainly that she had repented of the whole escapade—that it had been a moment of madness—that she was sorry, deeply sorry, but she could not continue. It seems he used all his persuasions—even, I gathered, some unpleasantly threatening ones—'

'Villain—unspeakable villain,' cried Mr Beck hotly.

'Quite so, sir: but Miss Rae was absolutely determined. She would go no further, and they must part on the morrow. That, it seems, was when Hugh gave up on his hopes of a fortune, and took himself off to his room, and applied himself to the bottles. You may imagine my relief.'

'Oh, thank heaven!' Lydia said, seizing his hand. 'And thank heaven that Phoebe came to her senses!'

'Here is the less hopeful part,' Mr Durrant went on, disengaging his hand gently from hers. 'It seems that after the second bottle, very late, Hugh made one last mutton-headed attempt to change Miss Rae's mind—went down to her room on the floor below, hammered at it, said no doubt a lot of revoltingly maudlin things. At last a servant came and told him the lady wasn't in that room: she had packed up and left—he didn't know where. Hugh's reaction was, apparently, very well—good riddance—and so to drunken bed.'

'Phoebe left alone? Where can she have gone? Can she have returned along this road? Surely we would have had word—'

'This is exactly what disturbs me. She did not take the chaise she and Hugh had been travelling in; and it appears she had very little money with her—she had given most of it to Hugh, for what he called expenses. Yes,' he said at Mr Beck's thunderous look, 'this is where I began to be a little impatient with him, as he made it quite clear that he did not care in the least what became of her. He concluded by ringing the bell for ice, and assuaging his disappointment by cursing Miss Rae as a light-minded—I won't say what—and laying a comprehensive curse on me, my future wife and all my progeny for destroying his prospects.' Mr Durrant looked faintly shame-faced. 'I confess then that I proposed a better cure for his distemper than ice—in short, I frog-marched him down to the inn-yard, and threw him into the horse-trough.' He coughed. 'I fancy I will not be welcome at that inn any more.'

'Mr Durrant, I abhor and detest brutality,' exclaimed Mr Beck, 'but in this case, sir, let me shake your hand on it!'

'Thank you—but in truth there was as much bitterness as satisfaction in it, for I had found Miss Rae only to lose her again. And now she was alone, with little money, and surely in some distress of mind—for a time I was utterly at a loss.

449

Then I recalled that the public coach for Bath left the Crown before dawn. I spoke to the clerk in the coach-office—there had been one very late booking, an outside place, a Miss Fowler. Here was my hope—that Miss Rae had enough money for that—that she might well give another name . . .' He sighed and slumped back again. 'Well, you have seen the result. I set off after the coach as fast as the horses could go, poor creatures. And here I caught up with it. And Miss Fowler is Miss Fowler, and Miss Rae . . . God knows.'

'You have done everything you could,' Lydia said, trying to conceal her own alarm. 'Wherever Phoebe has gone, it must be better than . . . Perhaps instead she stayed at Worcester—left the Crown, and took some other lodging in the town.'

Mr Durrant inclined his head. 'It is a possibility. Though how long she can stay there, without money . . .'

'Then we must go on to Worcester—search—search the whole town,' cried Mr Beck, jumping up and bounding to the window. 'Is that wretched, thrice-damned wheel mended yet? What are they about? I shall mend it myself—I shall . . . Good God.'

'What is it?' Lydia said. 'Mr Beck . . . ?'

He was gone, clattering into chairs, stumbling, almost falling: out to the yard. Mr Durrant strode to the window.

'What on earth is he . . . ? Good God. The carrier's cart.' He uttered a broken laugh. 'I never thought of the carrier's cart.'

Still laughing, he took Lydia's arm and guided her outside. The great broad waggon of the Bath and Bristol carrier, with its elephantine horse, its curiously assorted freight of sacks, odd-shaped parcels, caged hens, and patient passengers, had lumbered into the yard, and the carrier in his smock and gaiters was climbing down with infinite slowness. Half clambering into the cart, extending his hand, gasping out her name, was Mr Beck: one of the passengers, demurely seated beside a large string of onions, was Phoebe.

Well, there was so much to say, and so little to say: Lydia could only murmur, 'Phoebe,' and then embrace her fiercely as she got down. Mr Durrant was still chuckling ruefully; and Mr Beck looked like a man transported at least several post-houses towards Paradise.

It was Phoebe who found her voice at last: looking round at them all, and saying with resolute firmness, in spite of the tremor in her throat: 'I am sorry. I am so very sorry. I have better friends than I deserve.'

'Oh, we all do,' Mr Durrant said. 'Good God, the carrier's cart. I simply never thought of it.'

'Well—it was the most inexpensive means of getting back to Bath,' Phoebe said soberly. 'So I thought to save a little money. It is the beginning, you see, of my being sensible.'

CHAPTER TWENTY-EIGHT

'Did you ever see such bed-curtains?' Lydia said. 'I wonder I did not dream of being strangled to death by rampaging lilies.'

After the incoherent greetings, explanations, questions, and half-tearful replies, all accompanied by Mr Beck's burning and worshipful gaze, it had been Mr Durrant who suggested that Lydia might like to take Phoebe to her room to tidy herself, and proposed that Mr Beck be his companion for breakfast. He supposed, no doubt, that they would have much to talk of—and no doubt he was right: but Lydia, not normally at a loss for words, did not know how to begin, or even whether she wanted to. Relief seemed to have drained every other faculty out of her.

But while she was nervous and inconsequent, Phoebe was direct. She took off her bonnet, gave a level, unimpressed glance at herself in the looking-glass, and said: 'I am sure you had a troubled night, but it was not the curtains that gave you bad dreams. Lord: I am lucky—so very lucky.'

Lydia hesitated. 'Certainly I think it is fortunate that you—that you thought better of this scheme so quickly. But then, that is not so much luck as—well, your better judgement. Was it not so?'

'I thought better of it from, I think, about half a mile out of Bath. But then I could hardly think worse of it. I hated myself, and the whole business, as soon as I said yes. But then, in some terrible absurd way, I liked the hating. It was like eating a lot of sugar, a great deal of it, more than is good for you, but not caring. And then, all at once, I sickened of it.'

'Was he—was Mr Hanley altered to you?'

'In his conduct? Oh, not at all—not until last evening, that is, when I told him that I had made a mistake and could not go on with it. Then he was unpleasant, which I dare say was understandable: I didn't mind that. No, before that he kept swearing the same devotion. Only I realised I didn't want it.

That is, I do—I'm afraid that is my nature—but I didn't want it from him. There was the ridiculous, simple error.' She sat down heavily, in sudden weariness.

'Did you—did you read Mr Beck's review—before you went away?'

Phoebe nodded. 'His verses . . . They could not help but affect me. But it was in a strange, deadly sort of way. They added to the self-hating. "There you are," they said: "there's another folly behind you. Think of what you have lost there." Now, what other folly could be worse? What could possibly be worse?' She folded her hands, and fixed Lydia's eyes with her own. 'However, this has been my last folly, Lydia. And though I owe you a thousand apologies, I shall just make this one, because you will be tired of them.'

'Oh, Phoebe, I have no reproaches to make—none. Only a request that you don't do anything *quite* like this again soon, because your poor old chaperon's nerves won't stand it. You know, Mr Beck—' She stopped.

'He has been very kind, hasn't he? It is excessively good of him. When I saw him in the yard, I really thought *I* was dreaming. I hope I may thank him properly for his concern, though he may not much care for my thanks.'

Lydia shook her head. 'I don't know whether I should say this—but, Phoebe, Mr Beck is still very fond of you. Very. Lord knows I have learned my lesson about meddling, and giving false impressions—but this I know.'

Phoebe swallowed, and tore her gaze away. 'It hardly seems possible that he should—but I believe you. I was very angry with myself

453

downstairs—allowing myself to think, from the way he looked at me . . . Lydia, *is* it possible?'

'I think it is more than possible. I have come to know Mr Beck a little better: I see his nature is a forgiving one—warm—I was going to say perhaps too warm, but then how can one have *too* warm a nature? No, he has—he has as great a regard for you as ever. And if you find that this is a pleasing thought to you, then all the better. Let us see what happens. There is no need for haste. After all, a great deal has—has happened: and so perhaps the best thing is to begin your relation again, without undue expectations on either side: enjoying each other's company, and . . .' All at once Lydia caught sight of herself in the looking-glass, talking away: her mouth making dull pruny shapes: propriety. She twitched away from it, and caught Phoebe's hands tightly in her own. 'Oh, be damned to that. Phoebe, do you love Mr Beck?'

'Yes!' she half sobbed.

'Well, by God, he loves you. And there's an end! Or a beginning. A splendid beginning. Oh, my dear Phoebe, don't weep for it! Well, weep if you like—I feel a little like it myself.' Lydia knelt down beside her. 'What with tiredness—and relief—and horticultural curtains—and knowing that you are going to be happy . . .'

Sniffing, searching for a handkerchief, and tearfully laughing, Phoebe said: 'I have loved him all along. How simple it sounds. But the simplest things can be the most difficult to apprehend. It was when he proposed to me—and I saw his love, and I saw my own love—I was frightened of it. I wanted to say yes, but I was afraid of the—the *leap* of saying yes: though so much that I longed for in

454

life lay there, just on the other side, if only the leap could be made . . .' She wiped her eyes, and suddenly the old Phoebe smile was restored. 'Dear me—am I being metaphorical? And is that the word? I do believe I am going to use them all at last.'

'It is a very good word,' Lydia said, 'and a very good metaphor. And I would add that I can think of no one who better understands that leap than Mr Beck.' She patted her hand, with a strange brief plunge of sadness. 'Now, have you breakfasted? Surely not, unless you were helping yourself to those onions. Go down, and join the gentlemen. The ham is good. I don't advise the eggs.'

Phoebe rose, and with a little shy dart kissed her cheek. 'Aren't you coming?'

'By and by. I need to—to do something with this unfortunate hair.'

In truth she did feel like weeping—the relief, perhaps: she couldn't tell: she only felt that she must be alone for a space. She bathed her eyes with cold water, and ventured near the looking-glass again. Where was that tedious woman she had caught sight of? Was that her? She gazed at herself until her head began to swim. It was perturbing to look long at your reflection: to realise that all the time you were there in the world, visible, undeniable.

There was a knock at the door. She had only taken the room for the night, and no doubt the chambermaid would be waiting to turn her out and make up the bed . . . But it was Mr Durrant who came in.

'I hope you don't mind. I wanted to see how you are. You must have had a fatiguing time of it—

455

travelling through the night like that. Yes, I know, no feminine frailty. Also I wanted to scold you for disobeying me and not staying in Bath. Also—well, there is a lot of soulful gazing and blushing going on down there and, feeling rather *de trop*, I thought I had better leave them to it. Is that—I mean, will they do, do you suppose?'

'Yes,' she said decisively, with a glance at herself in the looking-glass: better. 'Yes, they will.'

'Hum! Well, I also wanted to know . . .' He began prowling, hands in pockets, and then caught sight of her nightgown folded on a chair. 'You—you are sure you don't mind me being here?'

'There is *impropriety* in it,' Lydia said, 'but it may be overlooked.'

He repressed a smile. 'The thing is this—I hope you don't think ill of me for what I did to Hugh. I have never done anything—ruffianly before, and now my blood has cooled I don't like it.'

'Mr Durrant, I assure you, if I had been there I would have assisted you by taking hold of his boots. And I know you are no ruffian. But tell me, you did not disabuse him? You did not tell him that there is no—no engagement after all? That his fears were groundless?'

'No . . . No, and not because I wanted him to go on suffering, though of course I do. It was simply a subject that I would not care to touch on with someone like him.' He pondered silently a moment. 'Lord above, look at those curtains.'

'What do you think he will do now?'

'Oh, join his regiment, as he must eventually; and then, I don't doubt, he will seek out another heiress. Hugh will soon bounce back, and though this didn't work, I am sure he will keep hold of the

456

idea, and try it again.'

'Well, if he does, so be it: you cannot hold yourself responsible for that. You had every right to decide to marry, after all.'

'Had I?' He stood gaunt and irresolute at the window. 'I don't know. This sorry business has had, thankfully, one happy result—downstairs. And also another, in a curious way. It has made me realise that I was wrong—wrong to do it—to come to Bath, and . . . everything.' He dug into his pockets. 'No . . . I thought not. Miss Templeton, I don't have fifty pounds about me: but as soon as I can make a draft on the bank, it is yours. The wager is lost, and I am glad of it.'

She shook her head. 'I do not have the sum either—for I was going to give it to you. I did not succeed. Perhaps, after all, one should not make wagers on matters of the heart. That sounds very portentous . . . But you know what I mean.'

'I do,' he said, his face dark.

'I am sorry for what happened,' she said as levelly as she could: this stupid urge to weep was upon her again. 'I do not really blame Juliet—of course she had to keep her engagement secret, because of Mrs Allardyce, as you said—but it was rather hard on you, finding out so late.'

He was so still and silent that she thought she had offended. Then he stirred and cleared his throat. 'Well, I'll tell you how it was.' He did not look at her. 'First, it was simply a matter of Hugh. Yes—here was a sensible sympathetic woman: I got along very well with her: let Hugh hear of it, and gnash his teeth: excellent. Then it became something more. I found I was drawn to her—that courtship was not a mere mechanical business—

457

that I did have, if you like, a heart, even if it was not entirely captured.'

'Not entirely . . . ?' She could not look at him either: she tried the looking-glass, but there was a very odd, stricken creature in there.

'She is an uncommonly perceptive woman, Juliet Allardyce,' he said, with a brief rasp of a laugh. 'At the Dress Ball—that mother of hers was making much of our being together, and other people were noticing, and I asked her if she minded. As I didn't: I was all rather pleased with myself, and said I had come to Bath with the very purpose of forming an attachment, and so on. And she took me aside, in the cloakroom: and that's when she told me that she was already engaged. And yes, I felt it rather a blow. To my pride, most of all.' He offered a twinge of a smile. 'You would know about that. But anyhow, I thanked her for her frankness, and said there could now be no possibility of a misunderstanding, and whatnot— but she stopped me, and insisted that we should remain on as friendly terms as ever; and that's when she suggested that if I wanted my rascally nephew to think there *was* an attachment, she would be quite happy to play along. I said I hoped she didn't think I had paid her attentions merely for that; and she smiled and said no, but there was another person in the case. You.'

'Me?' Lydia sat down: legs weak: fatigue of travel.

'There was another person I wanted to impress, she said—very gently, kindly: someone to whom I wanted to demonstrate that I was heart-free, that I could marry a girl any time if I chose. Lydia Templeton, said she. Uncommonly perceptive . . .'

He ran his hand along the windowsill, looked in surprise at the dust on his long fingers. 'Of course I spluttered and retorted like any pig-headed fellow—but she wasn't having it. It was not only that she was already engaged, she said: much as she esteemed me, she could never have felt there could be anything between us, when it was so plain that my heart was not mine to give. However I tried to deceive myself, I could not be in love with her—because I was plainly still in love with—with Lydia Templeton.' He turned, braced like a soldier facing the enemy. 'With you.'

'I . . .' All at once the room seemed very small, and yet somehow very large too: she could not place herself in the world any more. 'Phoebe saw you. In the cloakroom. She thought—*I* thought . . . What did you say to this—this peculiar speculation of Juliet's?'

'Oh, I thanked her. I thanked her from the bottom of my heart. She had told me the truth, and there must always be a value in that: even if it is a truth that can—that can lead to nothing, no alteration, no action . . . Indeed it was as if a weight fell from me—or rather—I don't know—like some jagged splinter drawn from your flesh, and you realise how much it has been hurting and nagging away all this time . . .'

'A splinter,' she repeated, hardly knowing what she was saying.

'Yes—or any damn thing you please—a nail—something that hurts, that can fester and poison. That's what it did to me: denying that I was still in love with you.'

Lydia bit her lip: this damnable weeping. 'I'm sorry you were hurt, Mr Durrant.'

He sighed. 'You don't understand. I inflicted that pain on myself. After you turned me down—well, I should have been like Beck. I should have beaten my breast—written poetry—cursed the heavens—and still have been ready to show you, at a moment's notice, that you were the love of my life, and nothing could change that. Well, at least now I have learned better, and that is why I thanked Juliet, and remain grateful to her. It is difficult to know yourself, to be at peace with yourself, when you are actually two people. One was the man who didn't care—content to be a bachelor—thankful, aye, thankful for his lucky escape: and the other was the man whose heart still skipped a beat when he drew near to Heystead—who lived only to see you, to hear your voice, even to quarrel with you. Now I am only one: the true one; and so, you see, I had to tell you.'

She broke from her seat, but there was nowhere to go. The window—he was there. The looking-glass—she was afraid of what it might show her. 'Mr Durrant, I—I don't know what to say. Upon my word, you do choose your moments—I have felt the world turn inside out so many times this last day or two that really I am giddy with it, and could almost wish for a little dullness . . .'

'Ah, the right moment. That's another thing I have learned: there is no such thing. Miss Templeton, I ask nothing of you—'

'Don't you?' she said, surprising herself: facing the looking-glass after all, and seeming also to ask the question of the woman she saw there. Not a bad-looking woman at all, in some ways; and with something—well, something radiant about her.

'No—because I have asked enough. I have

asked you to accept something that cannot conduce to your peace of mind—that must, to however slight a degree, be a trouble and embarrassment to you in our future relation. Yet I cannot regret saying it. I have done with regrets.'

'Regrets are indeed unpleasant things. They dig in—and poison—as you say. But speaking of right moments . . . is this not the right moment for you to call me Lydia?'

He started: seemed forcefully to gather himself in. 'Gladly. But does this mean—Lydia, does this mean—'

'I don't know what it means, Mr Durrant—I don't know anything any more, except—yes, I do: I was afraid to leap. And I am still afraid to leap. Isn't that absurd? When everything you want is on the other side. My dear Mr Durrant, you are assuredly no charmer like your nephew—you with your nails and your festering—and yet when I think of you all these years—feeling so . . .' She fought down the urge to weep, though it seemed to be half transformed into an urge to laugh. 'And yet did you—did you not take heart from the fact that all that time I never married—that I never looked at another man with the slightest interest?'

He took a soft step towards her, then paused. 'I wondered at it. I greatly wondered at it.'

'I always maintained that I was content as I was, and had no intention of marrying. But that, I began to see—or pretended not to see—was only because I could not marry you: because I had lost you. For ever.'

'For ever?' he queried gently.

'You are a proud man—insufferably proud, sometimes,' she said, wiping irritably at her eyes,

461

'and I did not think you would ask again. Oh.'

The 'oh' was because he was kissing her, or she was kissing him: it did not seem important to allocate responsibility. For some time speech was both unnecessary and impossible.

'Lydia,' he breathed, 'I'm going to ask again.'

'Oh, are you?' she said vaguely. 'Dear me, now we *are* being improper. Lewis, you haven't shaved, or brushed your hair. Neither have I, mind. Not shaved, I don't mean that. Lord, one wonders whether it is right to feel so happy. And there goes my splinter—you were right, it is just like that. Lewis, am I talking too much?'

'Yes.'

Her smile grazed his. 'You had better put a stop to it, then.'

Presently breath was required, and her trembling legs demanded a seat: his knee did very well. For a silent moment they gazed at each other with profound interest. He looked tremendously young.

'About our wager,' she said. 'However are we going to work it out? I failed on my side—and yet looking at Phoebe and Mr Beck, I think I may have succeeded after all. And on your side, you were to find a bride in Bath, and you didn't. But you *have* found a bride. Here, in a coaching-inn in Tewkesbury, to be exact.' She traced the shape of his lips with her finger. She didn't mind the world turning inside out now: she had found her place in it. 'So how are we to decide it?'

'I am content to be called the loser,' he said, drawing her close. 'For I have won everything else.'